MW01258394

SEVERANCE

www.apexbookcompany.com

SEVERANCE

Chris Bucholz

An Apex Publications Book
Lexington, Kentucky

Copyright © 2014 by Chris Bucholz
All rights reserved. No portion of this book may be copied or trans-
mitted in any form, electronic or otherwise, without express written
consent of the publisher or author.

This novel is a work of fiction. All the characters and events portrayed
in these stories are either fictitious or are used fictitiously.

ISBN: 978-1-937009-27-4
Cover Art © 2014 by Kimmo Lemetti
Title Design © 2014 by Mekenzie Larsen and Chris Bucholz
Typography © 2014 by Maggie Slater

Published by Apex Publications, LLC
PO Box 24323
Lexington, K.Y. 40524
www.apexbookcompany.com

Printed in the United States of America

First Edition

A Distinct Odor

Laura Stein rolled onto her side, taking care to not crush the bag of urine strapped to her thigh. Through the vanes of the air damper, she could see the upper side of a suspended ceiling facing her. An art studio lay underneath that, assuming the occupancy database was accurate, which it occasionally was. She waited a few seconds, listening for any sign that art was currently happening, and after hearing nothing, pried open one of the damper vanes, creating a gap wide enough to drop through. Feet first, she passed through the damper and set herself down on the suspended ceiling, confident the frame would support her weight. She repositioned the damper vane in place, then rolled to her side and opened a tile in the ceiling, peering into the space below. Empty.

She lowered herself out of the ceiling and dropped to the floor. Standing on a chair, she repositioned the tile above her, then made her way to the closet at the back of the studio. From the webbing strapped around her waist, she withdrew a tool to remove an embedded floor panel, exposing a dark cavity. She descended feet first into the hole, again mindful of the flexible package of urine, then awkwardly positioned herself face up and dragged the access panel into place above her. In darkness again, she tapped a luminescent patch on her shoulder, shedding a dim light in front of her. Rolling over onto her stomach, she began dragging her way down the crawlspace, scraping her hands, chin, and every other part of her body as she went.

Designed for maintenance robots, utility crawlspaces could theoretically accommodate human-sized travelers—the theory essentially being: "but they *really* have to want to be there." The number of scrapes, abrasions and calluses on Stein's hands and knees attested to the number of times she'd really wanted to be in such places. Typically for work-related reasons, but she wasn't working tonight. Stein was one of the enviable few Argosians whose profession—ship's maintenance—overlapped significantly with her hobby—light burglary.

Reaching a junction, she checked the identification tag on the wall. L3 -UC-3401. The odds of her being in the wrong place were slim, but the next section would be a dead end, and she didn't want to back in and out of any more side passages than she had to. She patted the satchel of urine strapped to her hip for the tenth time since entering the crawlspace, reassured that it was still dry to the touch.

She shimmied a few meters down the side passage, counting the number of panel seams above her as she went. When she reached the sixth seam, she stopped. Reaching behind her, she fished a cutter from her tool webbing, then began to roll over. She stopped abruptly, perilously close to wetting herself, shivered, then rolled over the other way, maneuvering her body until she was lying on her back. Exhaling, she tapped the terminal on her other hip and spoke softly, "How we doing?"

"Still clear," Bruce replied. "I told you, this guy's definitely befouling someone's party right now. Take as long as you want."

"Well, just keep watching. I've got a shy bladder," Stein whispered.

"Just relax and it will come. Imagine you're in a really crowded room and everyone's watching—that's what I do when I need to go."

Stein laughed.

"Or maybe imagine my mom. That sometimes works for me too."

She grinned and adjusted the controls of the cutter. "Okay, here we go," she whispered. Positioning the tool, she drilled a tiny hole in the panel above her. Applying light pressure to the cutter, she listened to the torch as it cut through the sandwiched materials into the room above. A change in pitch announced the end of the cut, at which point she turned off the tool and tucked it back in her webbing. Her hand returned with a micro-lube gun. Positioning it in the hole she'd just made, she began threading the sturdy tube up until she was confident it had breached the threshold of the floor above. Pausing, she rolled her shoulders, releasing the tension that had crept into her neck. After a deep breath, she reached down to her right hip and delicately detached the sack of urine from the webbing. Carefully, she twisted off the cap of the sack and slid the lube gun's feed tube into it. She exhaled. Slowly, she depressed the trigger of the lube gun.

"Ahhhhhhhhhhhhh."

The contents of the satchel traveled up the tube at high velocity, ejecting over a small patch of floor in the room above. The donor of the urine was not Stein herself, but a gentleman by the name of Gerald Lehman, a

Marker. Lehman had not known he was donating the urine at the time, and indeed would have been impressively paranoid if he had. A small device attached to the trap underneath his toilet had been collecting his urine for days, a trap implanted during a similar subterranean raid a week earlier. But however upset Mr. Lehman might be after discovering the theft of his urine, it would pale beside how he'd feel if he knew its ultimate destination: the living room of Sebastian Krol, leader of the Markers, and his nominal boss.

Throughout the course of human history, peeing on your boss's living room floor has always been regarded as a pretty bad move, but in an organization like the Markers, it was particularly ill-advised. The Markers were a club/society/street-gang—one of many on the Argos—that distinguished themselves from their peers by pissing on things and off people. Markers, when queried about this behavior, would usually expound on the importance of keeping in tune with humanity's ancient mammalian roots, or recite a prepared speech about the tyranny of indoor plumbing. Everyone else, when queried about this behavior, would suggest that they just liked being dicks. Markers were a particular annoyance for those whose work involved crawling around in poorly drained and ventilated areas, people such as Laura Stein and Bruce Redenbach.

Stein and Bruce's scheme involved placing an ambitious junior's Mark within the leader's home, which they hoped would incite an internecine conflict within the Marker organization and possibly some mild bloodshed. "And if it does lead to some murders," Bruce had noted, "then so be it. Horrible smelling murders that security doesn't try very hard to solve."

The satchel empty, Stein withdrew the tube and stowed everything in her webbing. As gracefully as possible, she scuttled her way back down the corridor. "All done," she whispered.

"Bet that feels better," Bruce said. "Coast is still clear. Do you smell? I bet you smell."

Stein ignored him, concentrating on her awkward backpedaling retreat. Five minutes later she was back in the closet, sealing the access panel shut. Standing, she peeled off her coveralls covered in the dirt and grime of the crawlspace, and stuffed them into an expandable bag she extracted from her webbing. Now somewhat presentable looking, she exited the closet back into the art studio. Her hand fluttered to the terminal to call Bruce and check if it was safe to leave by the front door, before she stopped.

A strange buzzing noise was emanating from somewhere, and she turned, looking for the source. A half-dozen canvases lay in a stack by a set of shelves. Beside them, a pair of easels toiled, holding up a wall. The shelves themselves contained art supplies, a selection of horrible clay pots, and a thin layer of dust. She frowned. She wasn't surprised to find the studio abandoned—there were a lot of similarly disused rooms scattered across the ship. But she hadn't thought this was one of them. When they were planning out her route for the evening's excursion, the occupancy database—admittedly not always reliable—said this room was still in use, owned by an M. Melson.

The strange noise was still there, growing louder. Out of a sense of professional curiosity she continued searching the room, thinking it might be a short circuit arcing behind a wall panel. She stooped to peer behind a bookshelf in the corner, nudging it slightly.

Bright blue light obliterated everything. She jumped back, falling on her ass, scrambling backwards like a crab, one hand clamped over her eyes. A piercing noise filled the air around her. Stein opened her eyes a fraction. The blue light was still there, still blinding. Blinking, she could see the negative afterimage, a bright slash of orange imprinted on her retinas. Strange black images danced in her vision. Keeping her eyes shut, she clamped her hands over them, squeezing. The images floating on the bright sea of orange coalesced into distinct shapes. They almost looked like letters.

VLAD

The letters started to fade. Stein opened her eyes, to again be blinded by the blue light. Again, the weird, misshapen letters appeared, VLAD, dancing in a sea of orange. She rolled over, facing away from the light, trying to blink away the image. Finally, after a half minute, the blue light disappeared. Silence.

"You having trouble getting your smelly ass out of there?" Bruce asked over the terminal.

Stein ignored him, blinking in the corner. After a few frantic seconds, her vision began to return, a circle of clarity spreading outwards in a sea of black. A minute passed without any further noises or horrible ocular attacks, and she stood up, wobbling. Deciding that that room was no longer a place she wanted to be, she made her way to the front door of the studio and whispered into her terminal, "Okay, I'm ready to go."

"Hang on, someone's just...okay. You're clear."

Stein exited the front door of the art studio, letting the door lock behind her, and began walking away. A half block later, Bruce appeared at her side, matching pace with her. When they'd gotten another couple blocks away, Bruce made a point of sniffing her.

"You smell like a bar toilet."

Stein blinked, recent blinding events having overshadowed her earlier work. "Thanks." Feeling sluggish, she parried with, "Hey, maybe next time you get to handle the urine while I stand around hurling insults and disparaging your mother."

"Oh, you couldn't possibly disparage her. Such a poor reputation, that girl," he said. "All those sailors," he added after a moment's thought. She chuckled, forcing it slightly, then pretended not to notice his eyes narrow. They continued for another block, the silence between them growing in import. Eventually, he asked, "You okay?"

"Yeah," she said. She blinked again, still seeing traces of VLAD. "Saw something weird is all."

"How weird?"

"Dunno. All the way weird. Will tell you later."

Bruce looked at her curiously, but she held her ground, knowing he wouldn't dig too much. "Okay," he said, relenting. "Want to do something then?" He cocked his hand up to his mouth and tilted it backwards, inhaling an imaginary beer.

"Smelling like this?" Stein said, smiling genuinely this time. She checked the time on her terminal. "Was supposed to meet Sergei in the bow for the countdown. But I'm not really feeling it."

"You'll be in trouble."

"Ehh. I'm always a little in trouble. This will be no worse than the background levels of trouble."

Bruce snorted. They reached an intersection. "See you tomorrow then, piss-girl?"

"Yeah."

With a nod, Bruce turned and headed off towards the rest of his evening. Stein silently thanked him for not badgering her more. For a burglar, the big man had an excellent sense of when not to pry.

She turned the opposite direction and began walking home, passing a crew working on one of the ladders mounted to the ceiling. Up and down the length of the ladder, scorch marks dotted rungs that had recently been repaired or replaced. She stopped at America Street; her eyes followed the ladder north towards the bow. She'd brushed Sergei off the last time he'd tried making plans with her. And the time before that, actually. The static pressure of guilt was building up to the point where it could no longer safely be ignored. She smelled her hands. "Clean enough," she declared. She set out towards the front of the ship.

Stopping on the lower tier, Stein saw she had made a mistake. The observation lounge was packed, every bench and table occupied with families, couples, and friends. People had started stretching out on the floor itself, daring their shipmates to tread on them, perhaps unwisely given the number of alcoholic beverages being consumed. A steady series of minor catastrophes unfolded in every direction she could see.

Turning her back to the huge curving expanse of the lounge window, she looked back at the entry of the lounge. Still filling up. She scanned the crowd. There. Sergei in his uniform, waving her over. Stein started picking her way through the crowd, moving parallel to the great window. The stars slowly spun past as she walked.

The great window was built up in square panels, three meters a side. The inner surface, the one with thousands of handprints, was a thin, transparent plastic sheet, put there exclusively to collect thousands of handprints. Next lay the pressure panels, twin layers of a thick polymer, there to support the pressure of the ship's atmosphere. Beyond that, the exterior shielding was a two-meter-thick chunk of some exotic polycarbonate. The curvature of the intervening pressure layers kept this shield out of focus, but a careful eye could detect its presence from the pockmarks it wore, marking the graves of objects small and fast.

In the next few seconds, Stein stepped on a woman's hand, hopped away, apologized, nearly crushed a small child, hopped away, and stepped on the woman's other hand. Several more apologies and hurried escapes later, she arrived at Sergei's bench. He slid over to make room for her, casting a meaningful look at the man on the other side of him, whom he had probably been arguing with about the space he was saving for his errant lady-friend. Stein offered a weak smile to the man, earning a sneer for her troubles.

Sergei leaned over and kissed her on the cheek. "Hey. I didn't know if you'd come."

"I'd hate to miss absolutely nothing," she said, somewhat cruelly. "Sorry," she said, squeezing his hand.

He smiled, always so frustratingly pleasant. "Seeing nothing happen seems to be a popular choice tonight." Which was a rarity—people on the Argos were rarely interested in the same thing at the same time. Nor were they normally this sedate; even the alcohol-fueled collisions seemed somehow subdued.

Like she did every time she came to the bow lounge—like most of the people were already doing—Stein looked up to the single stationary star in the sky. Not quite stationary anymore, but it was hard to see it moving. Where every other star in their field of vision was in motion, a single star stood almost in the center of it all, rotating imperceptibly.

"Maybe they're hoping that nothing won't happen?" she offered.

"If nothing didn't happen that would mean..." Sergei trailed off. "What would that mean?"

"Something."

"Oh."

Slowly, the individual conversations died off. "What's that smell?" Sergei asked, looking at his feet. Stein simply stared out the window. She wondered if anyone would count down.

"I wonder if anyone's going to count down?" Sergei said. The man on his other side shushed him. No one did count down, though almost everyone had their eye on their terminals as the seconds slowly ticked down. Three. Two. One. Midnight.

A consummate showman, nothing happened right on schedule. The stars continued to rotate slowly by, oblivious to the gathered crowd and the sound of hundreds of people all drawing breath at the exact same time. Collectively a hundred different conversations started again, punctuated by clinking glasses and laughter.

"I'm surprised. I thought people would be more excited," Sergei said. "Though I guess it was just a practice run."

Stein wasn't surprised at all. "You don't seem excited."

Sergei licked his lips. "Doesn't feel real I guess. What? Only seven months away. Don't know how to feel about it."

"Kind of scared?"

"Me?" His cheekbones rose, halfway through a smile before he reconsidered. "Not scared exactly."

"If you say so." She turned back towards the window, people-watching as the crowd started to thin out. Someone at the front of the lounge caught her eye, a man right up against the window, his hand on the glass. He had something on his head, some kind of homemade helmet. She tilted her head and squinted. It looked like a pair of glass bowls taped together to form a transparent sphere.

Beside her, she felt Sergei tense. Stein looked at her sometime-lover's face, saw his eyes fix on something. She followed his gaze to see the helmeted man, who had produced a hatchet from somewhere. He screamed something, the words muffled by his helmet, and raised the hatchet above his head.

"Oh, shit," Stein said. Beside her, Sergei sprang forward.

The hatchet came down, cracking the inner plastic surface of the window. The blade twisted and jammed itself into the plastic, and as the man struggled to free it, Sergei plowed into the side of him, smashing him into the window, shattering the plastic barrier. Chunks of plastic rained down on the pair.

Pandemonium, bodies upon bodies pushing for the exits, desperate to escape. Another security officer arrived, helping Sergei free the hatchet from the man's grasp and subdue him as gently as they knew how. Stein got to her feet but otherwise stayed put, out of the crush of people pushing for the exits. She relaxed a bit, seeing Sergei and the other officer get the maniac under control. More security officers arrived to help subdue the man more thoroughly.

As they dragged the fellow away, Sergei left his colleagues and returned to Stein, his face flushed, a single scratch along his forehead. He smiled, and she hesitated a moment before hugging him, sensing it was the appropriate reaction. She couldn't have been completely wrong; he hugged back. Chin resting on his shoulder, she watched the stars, suddenly clearer with the plastic safety barrier gone. Instinctively, she looked up again to the nearly-fixed north star, getting her first clear look at the sun their ancestors had left behind.

Two hundred and forty years had passed since then, as the ISMV Argos slowly plowed its way to the star called Tau Prius and its third planet. The bulk of that long voyage had been spent coasting, the engines sitting idle as generations of passengers lived and died within the confines of the vast ship. Six months of acceleration had gotten the Argos up to its cruising speed, and once set in rotation to provide a semblance of gravity for its inhabitants, the Argos was again little different than the inert rock it had been carved from. Though it now moved at five percent the speed of light—an admittedly glamorous life for a rock.

Thanks to the hard work of Isaac Newton, the end of the trip would look much like the beginning, with the ship, now flipped around, decelerating for six months. According to the original itinerary, April 3rd, 239 A.L. —the date currently displayed on the front of every terminal—was the day that the brakes were to be hit. But plans had changed.

The Argos was running late.

Stein let the door to her apartment close behind her and leaned back on it, exhaling. After leaving the observation lounge, the arch in Sergei's eyebrow gave away his hope for what the rest of the evening had in store. But the near suicide and lingering smell of urine had left Stein feeling distinctly unsexy, and when she'd firmly told him she was going home, he hadn't forced the issue.

"Smart guy," she said to herself as she lurched across the apartment to the bathroom. Sergei was sweet. She performed some mental gymnastics, imagining more weeks and months, maybe even years, in his company. She probably would be pretty happy with him, based on what she understood the word 'happy' to mean. But for a variety of reasons—none of them very clear, even to her—she still didn't seem terribly interested in letting that happen.

After a quick shower, she returned to the living room and slumped on the couch. Her eyes drifted up to the lamp embedded in the ceiling. She blinked. No secret messages. *What the hell was that all about?* It was definitely something. Unless it wasn't. The shapes were muddled, but definitely looked like letters. VLAD. Probably Vlad. *Who the hell is Vlad?*

She had been to doctors before. They had never said a thing about anything unusual in her eyes. Not that they had been looking for VLAD. But those guys had no problem telling her about her other faults; if they had known her eyes belonged to someone called Vlad, they would have said so.

They hadn't exposed her to a blinding blue light though. She hadn't seen anything like that before either, during any of her aboveground or subterranean wanderings. She was confident none of the regular electrical or mechanical systems could make that kind of light, having seen most of those systems violently malfunction at one point or another in her life. Besides which, there was nothing terribly exotic in or around that room, equipment-wise. She tried to piece together the sequence of events that had led up to the light. She had bumped something in the corner. Some kind of booby trap? What kind of self-important maniac thought art that crappy was worth booby trapping? And what kind of booby trap blinded someone with strange messages about eastern Europeans?

Bruce would know. She decided she would tell him the next morning. It had been smart not to tell him immediately—he would probably have gone back there that night with welding goggles and a sledgehammer to plunder the room like some kind of contemporary Viking . No, she would let him get his beauty sleep.

Stein got up from the couch and crossed the room to Mr. Beefy, the potted meat plant in the corner of the room, and the sole other living creature in the apartment. Mr. Beefy was a steak plant, a smaller version of the monsters in the meat farms downstairs. A metal armature of braces and feeding tubes supported several dangling 'fruits' swaying slightly under her touch. She poked thoughtfully at a couple of them, then adjusted the nutrient settings on the panel mounted into the plant base. "You're all right, Mr. Beefy. Steady, not too lippy. And you never want to know where 'this' is going." She patted the tree gently, then went to bed.

Previously

Harold approached the first level of the hospital, coming to a stop just outside, dismayed by what he saw. The front doors were obstructed by a cleaning crew, a man and woman haphazardly swabbing the ground. The man was resting a large portion of his body weight on his mop, pushing it forward in straight lines before stopping and turning around, moving back and forth in a grid. The woman was using more of a slapping motion, bringing the mop head a short distance off the ground before slamming it back down, spraying water around. None of this appeared to be having any effect on the street, which didn't even look that dirty in the first place. It never looked dirty, being made from that grey composite purposely designed to have that effect. A stack of plastic 'Wet Floor' signs lay to one side of them, unused.

"Hey, come on, guys. You should put those up when you're doing that," Harold complained as he approached them. He gestured at the signs. "There are people coming in and out of here on crutches."

The slapper looked Harold up and down slowly, eyes lingering on the hem of his lab coat. "Fuck you, doc," she said finally.

"Yeah. Right." Harold shook his head and sidestepped the woman, entering the hospital basement behind her. *They should be happy they even have a job.* There were a lot of people on board who'd jump at the chance to mop perfectly clean floors. Seventy years into its voyage, the population of the Argos was going through its latest malaise. A 'Crisis of Purpose' was what the news feeds called it, usually when captioning a picture of someone fiddling with himself on a park bench.

Harold walked past the emergency room waiting area, down the hall, and into the elevator, riding it up to the fifth floor. Here, he walked past the nurse's station to his office.

"Dr. Stein?"

Harold stopped and turned back to Cliff at the nurse's desk. "Hey, Cliff. What's up?"

"Dr. Kinison was looking for you. You just missed him."

"Ahh, okay. Thanks." Harold tried to think of a way to avoid the ship's senior naval doctor for a bit longer. A soft vibration came from his pocket as his terminal received an incoming message. He looked at it. A message from Kevin.

"How was your weekend?" Cliff asked.

"Hmm? Oh, good." Harold looked up, distracted. "I went to see the new orchestra that's just formed up."

"Were they any good?"

Harold blinked, remembering the experience. "Wow. No. Still, nice to have a new way to kill time."

"Isn't that the truth."

Harold smiled and backed away from the small talk as gracefully as he could. Some days he had more patience for it than others.

In his office, he tapped at the desktop display to bring up the latest genetic variance survey. The Argos had passed through a wave of extremely high-energy radiation a year earlier, and the damage, thought minor at first, had since gotten much, much worse. A host of growths, cysts, and other odd-looking complaints had swamped their front-line medical staff. A stalagmite erupting on the graph of cancer rates wasn't even their greatest concern; with the tools available, cancer was easily treated and even more easily found. It was the subtler damage that was more worrying, and far harder to find.

He had closed the survey and opened up the code for one of his automatons when he remembered the message from Kevin and looked at his terminal. Nothing there. Frowning, he poked around the archive, looking for the message, not finding any trace of it. Kevin must have recalled it. Odd, but not a terribly big deal—if it was important, the boy would certainly send it again.

Setting his terminal down, Harold began wrapping his head around the problem he'd been working on. He pulled up one of the trial genomes he'd been working on, sighed, then started the debugger. One at a time, he stepped through the changes his automaton would make once let loose. Pausing at the error he'd been stuck on for the past week, he growled, then leaned back in his chair, tugging at his beard.

With the long-term viability of the ship's population at risk, the captain and mayor had stumbled into one of their rare agreements and ordered mandatory rounds of genetic screening to take place. Over 2000 nano-biopsies per individual, analyzed for statistical variations and compared against baseline samples stored in each individual's file. What would be done with the problems found was as-yet undecided; the gene-tinkerers were able to repair the damage, but only on a small scale.

But that wasn't Harold's problem. The ship's senior naval medical officer, Dr. Kinison, would be the one planning the triage. Harold just had to figure out a semi-automated procedure for making a single repair. Gene tinkering had always been done on a case-by-case basis, with multiple levels of human oversight for every change to the patient's genome. They simply didn't have enough time to do that for the entire population, a surprising problem on a ship where spare time was never in short supply.

"Which is why you need to smarten up," Harold told the automaton, pointing at the screen accusingly, "and stop turning this guy into a flipper baby."

Sniffing

Plastic letters held in place by chipped brackets on the front of the locker announced that its contents belonged to L. Stein. Cast in green-gray plastic, its edges rounded off by decades of human erosion, the locker was equal parts ugly and homely. But it opened and closed and kept stuff inside of it, making it one of the few things on board the ship that could still claim to perform all of its assigned tasks well.

The Argos's second-greatest burglar and assistant ship's engineer yawned and yanked the door open past the point where it jammed. Inside hung a maintenance uniform, which she quickly changed into. The uniform itself had no distinguishing marks, notwithstanding the very distinguishing solid orange hue of the fabric. Every engineer and technician wore a similar one, though none were identical, depending on how well each owner took care of it. Other technicians began streaming in and changing. With nods and thin smiles, Stein acknowledged her colleagues as she put on her tool webbing. She closed the locker door, leaning into it, and left for the main office.

The maintenance office was wider and taller than most rooms on the Argos, thanks to its location on the unfashionable but roomy first level. Tool benches lined the back and side walls, bracketing the large table in the center of the room. The Big Board—essentially a wall-sized terminal—dominated one side of the room, displaying a list of the recent maintenance problems around the ship. Below that it displayed issues lingering from the previous day that had proven particularly troublesome to fix or that required repairs on a larger scale than a day or two. At the bottom of the list were months- and years-long projects and repairs. The Board displayed only a fraction of the known maintenance issues on board the Argos; many others, though very real, simply weren't going to get fixed. If the Big Board were to display all the known faults on the ship, the wall would have had to be a half kilometer taller, which would necessitate a substantially larger ship to accommodate it, and the larger list of problems which would go with that, and so on.

Stein sat down in a battered chair, propped her feet up on the table, and examined the list of issues. As the team lead, she was responsible for allocating staff and resources to all newly identified problems, normally the chief engineer's job, but Curts had been busy with other work over the past year. A few months earlier he'd offloaded the responsibility to her, an honor that she'd accepted with mixed feelings. She had the technical aptitude for it, just didn't enjoy the demands the role placed on her soft skills.

All of the older and medium-term issues already had resources allocated to them, leaving all the problems identified in the past few hours for Stein to handle. Anything that couldn't be fixed within that time would be communicated to Curts and the swing shift supervisor during the next shift change. Of the new issues, there were just under thirty heating and cooling problems that morning, making it fairly similar to the last several thousand mornings. Her eyes scanned the complaints, picking out the usual patterns. Two more residences around Europe-3-midships complaining about the chill. The floatarium was too hot. A whole slew of shops along Australia-2 complaining of stagnant air. Some bureaucrat says it's too hot in America-3, right near the aft. Another one, next door, says it's too cold. And finally, just as a bonus, someone in the garden well complaining. Probably a Whiner, but Stein didn't recognize the name.

Keeping a ship the size of the Argos at a livable temperature wasn't a terribly difficult task from a theoretical point of view. They had a reliable power source, in the form of two massive matter/antimatter reactors. And little heat had to be added in the first place—the Argos's multi layered insulation was in excellent shape. It was mostly a matter of circulating air from the hot parts of the ship to the cold ones. This was no small task. Massive circulation fans, venting, and ductwork —having been installed for the job—were all constantly in the process of breaking down. Consequently, the maintenance team on board the Argos had been well occupied for the past two hundred and forty years. And even with the ship stopping soon, their role was still an important one—the Argos would stay at least partially populated for years to come.

"Who the fuck is complaining in the garden well?" Bruce said from behind Stein's back. Stein turned, not showing any surprise at the stealthy arrival of her friend. Despite his bulk, Bruce had a natural affinity for moving quietly. "Like a fat whisper," he had once bragged. She considered mentioning the strange light she'd observed the previous night, but seeing other technicians streaming into the room behind him, held her tongue.

She returned her gaze to the board and looked at the complaint he was referring to. "Janice Carow? No idea. Never seen the name before."

"I'll give her something to complain about," Bruce said. He stroked his chin.

"Of course, Bruce. It'd be irresponsible of me if I *didn't* let you rough up an old lady."

Bruce then pantomimed grabbing a small woman and breaking her back over his knee. She laughed, then caught herself. She wasn't worried for Ms. Carow's safety—in all the years that they had been friends, she had never known Bruce to do anything more than threaten to break an old woman's back. But she knew she shouldn't encourage this too much further, not in front of the rest of the team. She moved to the front of the room, ignoring Bruce as he stood flexing over his imaginary victim's shattered corpse. She took a deep breath. *Being in charge sucked.*

The rest of the maintenance team clustered around the Big Board, chatting. Stein cleared her throat. "Okay, everyone. Work." She rubbed her face and looked at the Big Board. "Jean and Forth, you're still working on the damper calibrations on L3. Rob, have a look at the Europe-3 problems—probably just air balancing again. After that, go help out Jean and Forth. Bruce, I want you to check out these stagnant air problems on Australia-2. After that, you can go see Ms. Carow in the well and find out what her beef is."

"Oh, she'll have some beef when I'm done with her."

"Bruce," Stein said firmly, shaking her head. "Be good." She assigned the rest of the team their roles. Finally, she turned her attention to the last technician in the room.

"Gabelman, go check out the pencil pushers." She gestured at the conflicting complaints from the government workers in the aft. "Remember these guys don't want to hear what the problem is, or why they're morons, or why no one will ever truly love them—even if it's all true. Just tell them it will get fixed. They will give you shit, which you will accept, gladly. Do not, under any circumstances take any advice from Bruce on how to handle them." The young technician had joined her team only a couple of weeks earlier, and after a couple mishaps, Stein had grudgingly started supplementing her instructions to him with tips on customer relations. It was all common sense, stuff he already should have known, and she was disdainful of having to mention it explicitly. But Curts had told her to, and open insubordination wasn't her style; she preferred the casual, indifferent variety. Longer lasting, less likely to get her fired.

And none of them wanted to get fired. Challenging work though it was, roles in the maintenance department had long waiting lists and strict term limits. When the Argos was originally conceived and built, no one really knew how fifty thousand people were going to manage themselves in a confined space for over two hundred years; initially, most behaved like they were just on an extremely long vacation. But after a decade of tropical drinks, people began getting restless, and after a few highly festive riots, the ship's leaders cobbled together an economic plan for the ship. A currency and limited free market was created, allowing enterprising sorts to busy themselves in the grand human tradition of gathering filthy lucre. On top of that, a system of job rotation was implemented for the meaningful—and thus highly desirable—positions in the public sector.

As everyone got up to leave, Stein lingered behind, pretending to work on something on her terminal. Finally alone, she crossed the big meeting room and entered the supervisor's office, where Curts normally presided, and sat down in the big chair. Another little ritual of hers. They all liked their jobs, but she liked hers more, and definitely more than she let on. Not the ability to order people around so much, though she knew that's what most of them probably thought. No, she just liked being in charge of *stuff*. Every morning she allowed herself the momentary self-delusion that she hadn't sent them off to fix *the* ship. They were fixing *her* ship. And this battered maintenance office was the drafty and damp seat of her power.

Her moment over, she levered herself out of her chair and walked out of the office. The heating complaint from the floatarium—a simple task that she could have easily assigned to someone else—had caught her eye. There was someone up there she wanted to talk to.

Outside, Stein turned north and began walking down the street, picking her way past the thicker slicks of grime and puke and a hundred years of neglect. *Fifty thousand people on this god damned ship, and no one wants to swing around a mop.* She caught the escalator upstairs. "What the hell happened to you people?" she wondered aloud, not for the first time.

From the outside, the Argos looked like an imperfectly rolled cigar, three kilometers long and three hundred meters wide, its outer surface lumpy, bulging in a variety of places. In cross section, the ship looked like an onion, the majority of livable space concentrated in the four outermost layers, where the pseudo-gravity caused by the ship's slow rotation was most comfortable. Aside from some low-rise apartment complexes within the garden well, few people ever had cause to go higher than the fourth level, other than the handful of maintenance and naval personnel who worked in those areas. This was the domain of ship systems, and storage space, and bare rock. In the aft, the ship's main engines and control systems occupied this central space, partially jutting out behind the ship.

In the bow, the lone civilian use of the vast, floaty space was the floatarium, a multipurpose area near the central axis, where Argosians could amuse themselves in the micro-G environment. Stein tugged her way down the access corridor using the hand holds mounted on the walls, beads of sweat quickly forming on her brow. It was always warm up here, though Stein conceded it was probably a little warmer than normal. Not that Griese was the sort to complain unnecessarily. As she neared the end of the access corridor, she palmed herself to a stop and looked down into the floatarium.

Griese Otomo stood on one of the twenty different surfaces in the room that laid claim to the designation "floor." Above him floated a half-dozen other people, scripts clasped in sweaty hands, rehearsing a scene from what appeared to be *Taming of the Shrew*. Stein watched quietly as Petruchio, gesticulating wildly in the course of a monologue, accidentally struck his assistant, sending the boy backwards and into the gathered crowd of players, scattering the group like billiard balls. Everyone broke down laughing.

"Having some problems with your blocking?" Stein asked from the entrance.

Griese looked up, recognizing his old friend. "That was intentional." Which was entirely possible. No one attended a low-G play to see it go right. "So, you finally got around to us?" he asked, though Stein could tell the annoyance in his voice wasn't genuine.

"It's nine thirty!" Stein replied. "You're my first call of the day." She kicked off the floor of the entrance and sailed across the room to Griese. "I'm amazed you're even awake. I thought you artsy types didn't roll out of bed until noon."

Griese watched her approach, offering up an arm for her to catch. She caught him by the wrist and planted another hand on the back of a chair, spinning her body around to land roughly on this new floor. "That's my wife you're thinking of," he said. "As for us, would you believe we were trying to beat the heat?" He poked a finger at a bead of sweat on Stein's brow. "You see our problem then?"

"Yeah, it's pretty steamy. Are you guys growing drugs up here?" Stein looked at the gaggle of actors, which had retreated to the far side of the space, still giggling. "Or just consuming?" Griese laughed, though not with his eyes. Stein decided not to prod him anymore. "Let me see if I can do something about that."

She pulled her terminal out of her webbing, and called up a display of the bow's ventilation systems. She immediately spotted the error, two thermostats reading the temperature in the room at 15 degrees Celsius. The system had thus concluded it should stop supplying cold air to the room. It was even trying to supply hot air in its place, though she knew that that wasn't going to work, thanks to a damper that had been deliberately bent shut eighty years previous. She tapped a couple of commands on the terminal to enable an override, pumping chilled air into the room temporarily while she replaced the sensors.

Looking up from the terminal, she scanned the many floors of the room, trying to figure out where the thermostat was hiding. Spotting it, she bounced across the room, landing neatly on the wall where it was hidden, and with a practiced twist, disconnected it. The designers of the ship had been acutely aware that every element of it would be replaced at least a dozen times over the length of the journey. Every system on board the ship was based on nearly antique designs, all with decades-long track records of reliability. And they were all designed to use parts that could be easily recycled and re-fabricated onboard the ship. Almost everything was made of soft metal or thermoplastics, capable of being scavenged, melted down, and recycled. A routine piece of trivia delivered to school field trips in the vessel's fab shops was that these shops were just as critical a part of the ship's life support systems as the hydroponics or carbon dioxide scrubbers. As with most pieces of trivia delivered during field trips, it failed to impress.

Stein turned the old thermostat over, quickly diagnosed it as a worthless piece of junk, and reached into her tool webbing for a new sensor. With it popped in place, she checked her terminal to see if it was registering on the ship's internal systems. Satisfied that it was, she pushed off back to the entrance of the floatarium.

For all the efforts made to make the ship maintainable during the design phase, some mistakes were inevitable. And these thermostats, at least amongst those who had the task of replacing them, were considered the biggest of those mistakes. Every decade or so someone attempted to redesign them, invariably someone who had to work with the fucking things every day. None had succeeded, and replacing wonky thermostats remained the most common chore for the maintenance team. At any given moment, Stein had two or three replacements on her person, more during working hours.

Stein backtracked a short distance down the entrance corridor. An air duct ran under one of the surfaces, supplying cooled air to the observatory. Her terminal had indicated that the second broken thermostat was within this air duct, so she pried open a panel, earning a blast of cold air in the face. Inside, she quickly found and replaced the sensor. That done, she looked down the duct towards the floatarium, blinking in surprise at a lumpy obstruction. Opening another panel in the corridor revealed a dead robot wedged into the ducting.

"Hey, little guy," she said, reaching inside and yanking it out.

A huge gash had nearly ripped the maintenance robot in half. Somewhere upstream the thing had lost a fight with a supply fan. She frowned. If left to their own devices the robots were normally smart enough to avoid that kind of damage. Stein guessed that if she downloaded its memory, she'd see a custom program another technician had entered, sending the robot to go un-jam a fan. The proper way to do that—shutting off the fan, isolating the area, physically securing the blades—was time consuming. Reprogramming a robot wasn't. And if the fan started up again and sliced the fucker in half, well, they were replaceable. A technician's free time wasn't. Stein didn't have a problem with that reasoning; she liked free time. But she didn't approve of the stupidity of leaving the shattered robot in the ducting. They were lucky it hadn't jammed another fan. She tucked the husk of the robot into her webbing and closed up both hatches.

Returning to the floatarium, she launched herself back down to where Griese sat. Stein examined her terminal again, and disabled the override to check that the system would continue cooling the room on its own initiative.

"All done," she announced, satisfied.

"Thanks," Griese replied. "Sorry I was pissy with you. Just frustrated with the sweat running down my ass for two days."

Stein smiled. "No worries. That's why I thought I'd deal with you myself. Don't need you ripping the head off any of my doofuses." She flicked her eyes at the actors floating above them. "Can we talk for a second?"

Griese raised an eyebrow. "Sure." He waved away his troupe. "Go towel off, guys. We'll meet back here in ten." After they had dispersed he turned back to Stein. "What's up?"

"This is going to sound kind of weird."

"Only kind of weird? That's a big improvement for you."

Stein snorted. "Thanks. Okay. I'll just ask. What does a blinder look like?"

Griese narrowed his eyes. "A blinder? As in a stun grenade?"

"Yeah."

"And you think I'd know because..."

"I know we don't talk about it."

Griese cocked his head. "Fair enough. I guess I could know." He held up his hands. "But I don't. Never had that misfortune." He looked at

Stein. "Ellen will have." Griese studied her face for a moment. "Do I want to know why you're asking?"

Stein smiled. "It's nothing bad. Not too bad at least. Not yet. I just thought I might have stumbled upon one."

"I guess we all need our hobbies." Stein hadn't told him everything about her nocturnal activities, but he was smart enough to guess, if Bruce hadn't drunkenly told him everything. Griese waved his arm at the room. "For me, it's low-gravity prose. More classy."

"Oh, highly classy. I like the way Kate's skirt keeps billowing up. You know, I think they did have undergarments back in Shakespeare's time."

"We can't completely defy the audience's expectations, Laura. This is still the Argos."

Stein smiled. "All right." She looked at the door, then the time on her terminal. "I think Ellen and I are meeting at the Prairie tonight. You coming?"

"To chaperone you two? Sounds dangerous. I'll see."

"It won't be any fun without you."

"I've been told by several reliable sources that Ellen is much more fun without me around," Griese said, smiling. "But your kind words are appreciated."

Sergeant Sinclair Hogg walked down the street at a measured pace, scanning back and forth. Tall, wide, and solid, Hogg looked like a cop; even in plain clothes, his size and bearing marked his profession as clearly as if he had a little rotating blue light on his head. He had exited the trolley a block earlier than necessary so he could arrive on foot. Good for seeing what he was walking into, but more importantly, it allowed people to see him coming. He could tell a lot about someone by how they reacted to a security officer approaching. That was something his partner, Steve Ganty, had told him on his first rotation. That Ganty had been stabbed in the stomach by someone who saw him coming, did temper the value of the advice a bit, but in situations where stomach stabbings were unlikely, Hogg still regularly followed it.

Hogg was currently on his fifth rotation in the corps, not an uncommonly high figure. Unofficially, the rotation policy had been intended to reduce the risk of corruption and complacency amongst the security corps by repeatedly introducing new blood into their mix. Whether this was effective or not was open to debate; it took a certain type of person to want to be a cop in the first place, and given the variety of perverts and recreational substance abusers on board the ship there was a limited pool of suitable volunteers. Consequently, security officer jobs tended to rotate amongst a fairly small group of regulars, and in practice, the only difference between a security officer and an off-rotation officer was that one got to wear kind of a neat hat.

Hogg rounded the corner and set off down the side street, moving away from the main shopping traffic along Asia. Ahead he could see the rest of his team along with Sergeant Koller, clustered outside the door of a modest apartment. Standing in front of the door was a balding middle-aged man, wearing stained, fraying clothes. He was yelling obscenities at the gathered security men. Not very original ones, Hogg was disappointed to hear.

As he approached, the distressed man noticed Hogg and immediately shifted the focus of his anger, having correctly pegged Hogg as someone in charge. "You can't do this! You bastards can't do this!"

Hogg waited until he was close enough to the man to not have to shout. "Sir, you were informed months ago that you'd have to relocate. You have no one to blame for this but yourself."

"You don't have the right to make me move, you fascist fucker!"

Hogg arched an eyebrow. "Sir, the ship's government has the right to reallocate space and personnel as it sees fit, if it's in the interest of ship-wide operations. I'd suggest you look it up; it might make you feel better."

"You can't just take away our home! My family has lived here for a hundred and fifty years!"

Hogg inhaled deeply. "And you were given multiple opportunities to sell it at a fair price. Now you'll sell it at an unfair price." Hogg wagged his finger at the man. "Not too bright, was that?"

He extended his big paw to push the man out of the way, the poor dummy nearly falling over at his touch. With a flick of his head, Hogg directed one of his officers to open the door of the apartment. The young officer slapped the back of his hand against the door controls, overriding the lock, then stepped aside, making room for Hogg.

The apartment was woefully decorated, the walls covered in amateur art that Hogg immediately despised, the type sold by idiots to other idiots in parks every weekend. The back of the suite was dominated by a pair of paper walls dividing the space into separate rooms. In the main living room stood a woman, arms clasped around a young boy in front of her.

"You can't do this," the woman whimpered. Behind him, Hogg could hear the father pushing to get past Sergeant Koller, who had moved to block the door.

"Yes, I can," Hogg said. "It's really quite easy." With three big steps he covered the distance between them and plucked the boy from his mother's surprised grasp. Holding the shocked child out in front of him like a bomb, he spun around and walked out the front door of the apartment. The mother's tiny little fists played percussion on his back, not slowing his movements in the slightest.

Outside, he set the child down abruptly. Hogg estimated that the boy was about four years old, and either too scared or stupid to cry. The mother darted past him and threw her arms around the child, before hurling some language at Hogg of the type generally not recommended for use around children. Hogg observed the boy's father staring at him, his hands balled into fists; a couple seconds of eye contact was enough to prompt them to unclench. The father cautiously circled Hogg and came up behind his wife and child.

The man whispered something to his wife and child, who withdrew a few steps away. Turning around to face Hogg, the man approached within a couple of steps and stopped. Teeth clenched, he said, "I didn't know I was working for them. They didn't tell me. How could I know? *How could I have known?*"

"What?" Hogg asked, genuinely baffled.

The man's eyes watered. "The Breeders. I didn't know it was them. They didn't tell me. *They didn't tell me.*"

Oh. He had worked for the Breeders? Hogg hadn't known that. He didn't actually know why they were removing the man from his home, hadn't even considered that he should care. It seemed a little late to be beating on Breeders; that had been settled years earlier. But orders were orders. He took one step towards the man, digging something out of his pocket. He thrust a terminal onto the man's chest.

"A map to your new home. Your possessions will be delivered shortly."

The man clutched at the terminal as Hogg released it, bobbling it slightly. Hogg pivoted and walked back towards the apartment, knowing he would have to keep an eye on the security men lest too much of the family's possessions go missing in transit. But before he reached the door, he stopped, an amusing idea having revealed itself to him.

"Stop!" he said, turning around to face the family again. They hadn't actually moved anywhere, but upon hearing his command, somehow moved even less. Hogg walked slowly towards them, eyeing the young boy standing at his mother's side. Hogg opened one of the cargo pockets on his trouser leg, fishing around for something. Finding it, he bent down in front of the boy and offered him what he had withdrawn. A plastic security badge.

"Here you go, son. Maybe you'd like to be a security officer some day?" He waggled it gently in front of the boy, who hesitated a second before snatching it from him. Hogg nodded curtly at the parents, before turning away from their gaping faces. He returned to the apartment, a grin spreading across his face.

The rest of Stein's day had not gone smoothly. After dropping off the robot at the recyclers, her terminal informed her of an urgent request in a hydroponics pond, and she'd spent the rest of her shift ankle deep in water and cucumbers.

After changing, she left the maintenance office and walked down Asia to the nearest escalator, her feet squishing as she went. The streets on the Argos were laid out in a grid, those running the length of the ship named after continents, historical leaders, and interesting plants, with the cross-avenues assigned more mundane numbers. All four of the inhabited levels of the ship had identical layouts, with escalators running up and down at major intersections. Stein caught one of these escalators up to the third level.

Here, she crossed the street and waited for the Argos' dully competent mass transit system to arrive. Trolleys ran down tracks mounted in the center of the major streets and avenues of the third level, allowing people to move about the ship with some semblance of rapidity. The trolleys themselves were autonomous, and didn't actually require the tracks to operate. They had managed just fine without them until a hundred years earlier, when a lunatic managed to hijack one, crash it into every damned thing on the third level, and only *just* fail a spectacular attempt to move it down to the second level. In response, the government of that era decided to mount the cars securely to tracks running the length of their dedicated routes. It was the greatest public works project Argosians had ever initiated themselves, a feat which had inadvertently made that lunatic the most influential person in the ship's history. There had been some talk of putting up a small statue of him. Stein was relieved—and a little surprised— that it had yet to happen.

One of the leashed and humbled trolleys arrived in front of Stein, which she boarded by the rear doors, glad to see it was mostly empty for the trip around the ship. She was going to the Prairie to meet Ellen, or— she glanced at the time on her terminal—to try and catch up on the head start Ellen had established.

Stein sat, observing the world as it passed by. Another ladder crew busied themselves repairing the ceiling handholds that had served as monkey bars for generations of daring children. It had been easy to ignore for a while, but that certainly drove the point home: the ship was stopping, and soon. The ladders would be a necessary element of navigation once deceleration began. When the engines fired up again in a little over six months, the concept of down was going to get a little confusing. And dangerous. She hadn't seen them install any net riggings yet, harnesses that would string across the massive north-south streets that would become well shafts when the ship started decelerating. She decided that the nets probably wouldn't come until the last minute. The ladders at least were vandal resistant. Once strung, a net was likely to get shredded and turned into some sort of distressing male lingerie within minutes.

She loathed them, her fellow travelers, and had long since given up feeling guilty about it. The majority of people who shared this space with her were colossally, flagrantly, mouths-hanging-open-while-they-read stupid. Worse, stupid with nothing to do. A variety of different ways to close the gap between the amount of work that actually had to be done and the number of man-hours available to do it had been invented over the past centuries, each one championed by a different species of moron. Video game addicts, body modifiers, roaming dance troupes, anarchists, bearded anarchists (they did not get along), and a panoply of sexual fetishists were amongst the most visible, but there were hundreds of other overlapping groups and clubs and sects active at any given time.

On a street corner, a crowd of people surrounded two grown men dressed as babies, who had evidently agreed to meet there to wrestle. The crowd surged and pulsed, exchanging wagers and hurling advice at their chosen champion. The trolley crept past before the fight began, but judging by the roar that went up a few seconds later, Stein could tell that something stupid had happened.

She set her jaw and turned away from the window. She used to be worse. She'd hated everybody when she was younger, though had granted a half-dozen or so exceptions as she mellowed with age. Perhaps by the time she died she might genuinely like someone.

"Would you like me to tell you about the cutting?" a voice above her asked, jolting her out of her thoughts. Standing over her, a man with wild hair and strained eyes peered at her, smacking his wet and chafed lips. Scars lined his hands and arms, and were it not for the blessed presence of his clothes, she knew she'd see scars on every other part of his body as well. A Cutter. Worse, a proselytizing Cutter.

"Please, don't," she said through gritted teeth. She had heard the Truth of Pain before, even dated one of its prophets briefly. Once he had gotten his hooks sunk in, he'd been impossible to get rid of. Anything she did to get him to go away caused him pain, which only delighted him. Reverse psychology worked, but only until he realized what she was doing. She had needed Bruce's help to finally get rid of him, and even he had to set the guy on fire a little bit.

"But you look like you know something of the Pain yourself, young lady. You deserve to know the truth of it," the Cutter rasped, leering down over her.

Stein glanced to her side, looking out the window. "Perhaps," she said. "Perhaps, indeeeeeeeeeeeed..." she held the last syllable, stalling, while the trolley pulled to a stop. Leaning back in her seat, she raised a leg, and planted her foot in the Cutter's chest. She pushed, sending the man backwards out the just-opened trolley door. Seeing the shocked looks on the other passengers, she growled. "What? I waited till we stopped."

The trolley continued on its way, though by now Stein wished she had simply just gone up to the garden well and walked. The trolley seemed to bring out the worst in people, a symptom of mass transit systems which had survived the trip to the stars. A mass transit system within a mass transit system: Russian nesting dolls stuffed with awful, awful people. She shook her head and looked out the window as they pulled into another stop with another confrontation, this one more one-sided.

A man pushed down to the street was being kicked by three others, one of whom she recognized as Sebastian Krol, the alpha-Marker whose living room carpet she had befouled. Which would make the sorry figure having the piss kicked out of him poor Gerald. As the trolley pulled away, her smile faded as the attackers began urinating on the defenseless man on the ground, streams of piss trailing away into cracks on the grated floor. She flinched and looked away. "Well, of course that's what they were going to do. And I guarantee there's something underneath there that I'm going to have to fix." She shuddered. "You dummy."

The Argos sunset entered its most attractive stage, the banks of lights in the enormous light towers dimming, the yellow light fading to orange, bathing the entire garden well in a warm glow. In the park, everyone's skin took on an orangish hue as they laughed and chatted in the evening breeze. Stein sat on the grassy area outside the back deck of the Prairie, her preferred watering hole. Of all the places on board the ship with other people in it, this was by far the most tolerable. Here, the edge to everyone's manic behavior felt duller, and Stein's general loathing of humanity waned.

The Prairie was located in the garden well, the large open-air cylinder in the center of the Argos. The well's outer surface, covered in parks and boulevards, took up most of the fourth level, aside from a few blocks near the bow and aft of the ship. A handful of apartments, stores, and other low-rise buildings lined the streets within the well, forming the ship's high-rent neighborhood. Stein had mixed feelings for the people who lived amongst the tree-lined streets here. They were substantially more sane than the bulk of the population, due to some ancient instinct for wanting to appear more proper than one's lessers, but this in itself irritated Stein. She found it awkward, feeling better than someone who in turn was clearly confident that they were better than her.

"Hey, buddy." Ellen appeared behind her, interrupting her thoughts. Short and loud, Ellen Katsushiro wore her adjectives proudly. To her side and a little behind her stood a young man. "I want you to meet a friend of mine. Kasey, this is Laura. Laura, Kasey."

"Hello, Kasey." Stein stared blankly at the young man. Seeing Ellen's pained expression, she forced a thin smile on her face.

"Hi," he replied.

"Kasey here is thinking of applying for a job with the navy." Ellen sat down in the grass beside Stein, gesturing for Kasey to do the same. "I told him you had done a bit of that yourself."

Stein half opened her mouth, managing to fight off an urge to moan. "Not quite." She stared at Ellen. "You know that."

"It's all the same to me," Ellen said. "Plasma and robots and such."

"So, uh, what do you do?" Kasey asked.

"I'm an assistant engineer in the maintenance department." Seeing Kasey's expression, she added. "I fix the heat."

Stein watched the drive train in Kasey's brain slipping gears. "So, like a plumber?"

"Sure."

"Huh. I was thinking of applying to be a naval engineer."

Stein looked at the ground, suddenly fascinated with the grass. In anticipation of their arrival at Tau Prius, for the last two decades kids had been encouraged to take up skills that would be useful on the ground. And, as was their custom, the kids had done anything but.

"So, you don't want to land either?" Ellen asked.

"I dunno. What's the rush, right? The planet's not going anywhere."

Stein plucked some of the grass, twisting it in her fingers. The whole ship had a case of separation anxiety. The psychologists on the feeds all had excellent explanations for this. Agoraphobia. Santiago Syndrome. Big Scared Baby Condition. Whatever it was called, with less than a year to go until the most fundamental change of address possible, every person on the ship still went serenely about their lives, pretending that nothing was about to change.

And she couldn't admit to feeling much different herself. She too had had a hard time wrapping her head around the idea of living on a spinning ball. Topography, for example, was pretty fucking crazy. And the sky? She could never visualize the geometry of it. When she closed her eyes to try, more than once she felt an enormous sense of panic, eyes opening wide, heart pounding at the vision of the ground curving *away* from her. Easier to just not think about it.

Kasey continued, "Besides, they'll need people to keep the ship running. I think it'd be cool to work with the engines. You know. Vroooooooom."

Stein continued fidgeting with the grass, not looking at him. "You should definitely do that."

"I heard it's tough, though."

"Oh, it is."

"I heard they only take the best. I wouldn't want to waste my time."

Stein examined the little braided loop of grass she'd made, before crushing it into a ball. "I wouldn't worry about that. That kind of consideration hinges heavily on how valuable your time is."

An exasperated look descended on Ellen's face. Kasey smiled tightly, his eyes casting around the rest of the park. Seeing something behind Stein, or maybe just pretending to, he stood up. "I'm going to go get a drink. I'll catch up with you later, Ellen. Nice meeting you," he said to Stein, doing a passable job of faking it. He walked back into the crowd.

The two women sat there in silence for a while. Finally, Ellen said, "I think he's in love with you."

"Ha." Stein shook her head. "Where did you find him? You wearing those short shorts around playgrounds again?"

Ellen scoffed. "I'll have you know I'm a happily married woman, Laura. And as a happily married woman, I'm perfectly entitled to let a young man buy me a drink, provided I have no intention of doing anything other than drink that drink and make polite chit chat and maybe make him buy me another drink. Thanks for your help with the polite chit chat, by the way. I think you're really starting to get the hang of it."

Stein snorted. Ellen leaned back, staring up at the far side of the well hanging overhead. "So, what's your beef, anyways?" she finally asked.

Stein tilted her head. "No beef."

"You're acting beefy. I can see the beef on your face."

Stein smiled but offered no reply.

After a few seconds of waiting, Ellen finally asked, "So, how's what's-his-face? Does he still want to make you incredibly happy?"

Stein knew it was coming but groaned anyways. "I don't want to talk about it." A pause, before she ignored her own protest, saying, "And I didn't think you approved of Sergei."

"Based on his clothes, yeah, I think he's a son of a bitch," Ellen agreed. Most of Stein's friends had well-founded reasons for disliking the ship's security department. Stein held no great love for them either, but she and they had managed to stay out of each other's hair for quite some time. "But, if he likes you, that makes him a rare breed, an improbable genetic mutation, a gift not to be turned away casually. And besides, if you're willing to date a guy in uniform, he must be well armed," Ellen concluded, patting her crotch. Stein grinned. Ellen cackled.

Across the lawn, Griese appeared through the crowd, spotted the pair, and crossed over to meet them. Griese was about the same height as Ellen, and possessing a similar haircut and fashion sense, it was sometimes difficult to tell the pair apart from a distance. Jokes about narcissism had dogged the pair their whole married lives.

"My old lady hassling you again?" Griese asked after sitting down.

"Yes, but she also appears to be employing some sort of outsourcing agency now, judging by the young man she brought by earlier."

"Oh, yeah?" Griese asked, nodding. He turned to Ellen. "You get a drink out of him?"

She held her glass up like a trophy.

"Atta girl."

Stein had been introduced to the pair a dozen years earlier by Bruce, and had slotted them in as numbers two and three on the slowly growing list of people she didn't hate. Where some people on board the Argos itched at the boredom of ship life, inventing disgusting hobbies to keep themselves busy, both Ellen and Griese had been born with some specific combination of genes that made extended bouts of directionless leisure time perfectly tolerable to them. 'French genes,' Ellen had suggested. Griese, with his five-week-a-year commitment to the dramatic arts, was by far the more industrious of the pair. The rest of the time, they drank and told jokes to each other.

Stein spotted the final member of their foursome, making his way across the patio, the crowds parting around him like the bow wave of a ship. "Where the hell have you been?" she asked as he drew within talking distance.

Bruce stopped, eyes widening. "Work, jerk. A whole bunch of membranes clammed up around the hospital this afternoon, and we were short staffed."

"Why didn't you call me?"

"Didn't need you. Also, you work too much anyways. I'll take any chance I can get to keep you out of the office. Also, you smell like piss."

Stein sniffed the air. "How about that." Something clicked. "What do you mean, short staffed?"

"Clay dropped a vent cover on his foot. It was awesome; his toe looked like a fucking eggplant. And Gabelman fucked off somewhere. No one's seen him since this morning, and he wasn't answering any calls."

Stein frowned. For all the complaints she had with Curts, he did fairly well at keeping the complete morons out of the maintenance team. Stein herself had a pretty good handle on which of her team members were responsible or not, and although Gabelman was new, he hadn't given her the impression he would just wander off like that. She groaned, knowing she would have to have a talk with him. "Well, glad you finally made it," she said, pushing herself off the grass. "Let's get a drink."

"Yes, let's," Bruce replied. "I seem to have finished this one on the walk here from the bar."

"So, what I'm hearing is that at least some of that piss smell was your own," Bruce surmised, hunched over his beer.

Stein tipped her chair back, leaning against the wood-like wall behind her. The two sat at one of the tables in the back of the Prairie. On the wall above her, a horned replica of an animal's head loomed over their conversation. Griese had wheeled Ellen home for the evening, leaving the pair alone to recount the events of the previous night's expedition. Stein had retold the story from her point of view, explaining everything up through the blinding blue light. She omitted the part about Vlad though, not knowing where to begin with it.

"So, I'm thinking this M. Melson has something in there that he wanted to keep hidden," she said.

Bruce spun his glass in his hands. "And has—or had—a booby trap installed to do just that. Yeah, could be."

"That's what I was thinking. It sounds like some kind of blinder, right?"

Stein had managed to corner Ellen earlier to ask her what blinder grenades looked like. "Fucking blinding, innit?" was the slurred response. "A pure faschist ray of bullshit photons that violatsh your fucking shkull through the ocular cavity," Ellen had added. "Why?" Stein had answered her by ordering her another beer, which had gone over well.

Stein watched over Bruce's shoulder as a group of revelers filled the dance floor. A complicated, synchronized dance started up, people lurching and weaving in unison while the sound system blared a song about a truck. "I guess you could jury-rig one up to be a booby trap," Bruce finally said. "Any idea what set it off? You said you were swinging your huge ass around like a wrecking ball?"

"I don't think I phrased it like that, but yes, I think I bumped into something. I can't recall seeing anything there that looked the slightest bit interesting, but a lot of it was wrapped up, or in boxes."

"Didn't even have to be something visible. Your massive and terrifying hindquarters might have jostled a secret compartment behind the shelves or something."

"Indeed. I could have disturbed M. Melson's secret collection of..." Stein paused, searching.

"Body grooming products."

"Locks of hair."

"Holograms of shirtless nuns boxing." Bruce leaned back, contemplative. "Hmmmmmmmmmmmmm."

Stein saw the next bit coming. "You want to go back."

Bruce waggled his head back and forth. "Maybe. Not tonight. I'm just curious, is all. Might do a bit of research on who exactly this M. Melson is."

"Caution? Research? Reading and quiet contemplation? Bruce, what have you been drinking?"

"Professional-level recklessness requires a surprising amount of planning and forethought," he said, wagging his finger at her. "Hours of work for every pratfall. I just make it look easy."

A few hours later Bruce lurched over to the desk in the corner of his apartment, and sat down heavily. "Who you at, M. Melson?" he asked the desk. Not receiving a reply, he smacked a meaty paw on the display, beginning his investigation.

The name M. Melson itself was unusual. Bruce had never seen a property record registered using an initial before. After pounding his fists on the desk display for awhile, then slightly softer with his slightly smaller fingers, he was able to bring up the census database, where he found out the second unusual thing about the name: it didn't exist. Thanks to the ancient custom still practiced on the Argos of a child taking one of their parents' names, there was a strict upper limit of surnames on board. And Melson wasn't one of them.

Bruce got up from his chair and looped his way across the living room to the liquor cabinet, where he picked out a bottle of Berry. Unscrewing it with his teeth, he returned to the desk and sat down. The property transfer process was pretty straightforward: two parties came to an agreement, transferred whatever funds or sexual favors they had agreed on, co-signed an electronic form, and sent it all to the central records department. The signatures were the tricky bit; the transaction system had a variety of biometric and anti-coercion scanners in place that made those hard to forge. Which meant that whoever this M. Melson was, he had somehow fooled the signature system to accept his false identity. Or, that there actually was an M. Melson who later deleted himself from the census. Neither of these possibilities seemed very likely, but they did both seem interesting.

Curious, he checked the property transfer database itself, something he had access to thanks to a highly successful bit of blackmail he had once pulled off. The studio had apparently been sold to Maurice Melson by a Charlotte Redelso nine years earlier. No indication why the name was truncated in the public listings, but at least he had another clue to work with. Further back into the studio's history, it had been in the Redelso family for sixty years.

He turned his attention back to M-for-Maurice Melson. Despite the close confines of the Argos, its citizens still had a reasonable expectation of privacy with regard to their personal records. The security forces could do detailed traces, background checks, and off-duty stalking, but Bruce was limited to searches of publicly visible news sites and records. Which turned up absolutely nothing when queried for "Maurice Melson." "Melson" returned substantially more results, but nothing from the past thirty years; it was a dead name. With breeding sharply limited by government edict, the number of named descendants was similarly restricted, and thanks to disease and accidental deaths, a few family names inevitably died off. A bit more searching showed that the last living Melson was a Greg Melson, who died in a well-wall climbing accident thirty years earlier. News feeds at the time all made note of the fact that Greg had no children, and that—notwithstanding the fact that 'we were all cousins'—the Melson family's journey on board the Argos had come to a close.

So where did Maurice come from? And how did he go from not being a person to being a person who bought properties and booby-trapped them? Bruce's bladder interrupted his investigation, and after tending to it, he decided he wasn't likely to make further progress on the problem until he rampaged through the studio itself. And now the hour was too late, and the drink too heavy in him, for proper rampaging. But he had other things to do anyway. He checked the time. *Probably safe now.*

On his terminal, he opened the control panel to remotely monitor a maintenance robot. Over the past week he had slowly maneuvered it across the ship until it reached the roof of Curts' garden well apartment. It was painstaking, tedious work of the sort he would normally shun were it not in support of such a good cause. Curts, his boss, was an *enormous* wiener, and fully worth the time and effort Bruce dedicated to aggravating him.

He maneuvered the robot out of its hiding spot and over the edge of the building to a perch directly above Curts' bedroom window. When it pressed its manipulator against the windowpane, Bruce triggered a subroutine that rapidly vibrated it against the windowpane, creating a makeshift but surprisingly effective speaker playing a loop of a low, almost sub-vocal voice, slowly whispering to Curts as he slept, *"Curts. Currrrrrts. I am Curts. I love Curts. I love you. I love me. Love. Love. LOOOOOVE. Now peeeeeeeeeeeeeee. Peeeeeeeeeeeeee. PEEEEEEEEEEEEEE."*

Satisfied, Bruce activated a second subroutine that instructed the robot to return to its hiding spot if it heard any disturbance from within the room. He shut off his terminal and left the robot to its work. If everything went according to plan, Curts would wake up feeling ashamed and damp, and need a couple of personal days to straighten himself out. Rolling into bed himself, Bruce conceded there was at least some possibility Curts would react by stepping off a light tower instead. "I'd feel bad if that happened," Bruce said aloud, turning off the lights. "Though I'd probably feel worse if I knew that I hadn't tried."

Stein opened the double-wide doors and stepped through into the reactor room. "And this is the bow auxiliary power room," she announced to the group of kids trailing behind her. A couple of technicians looked up at the crowd of tiny wriggling projectiles that two beleaguered teachers struggled to ride herd on.

The room was large for this part of the ship, the curvature of the floor readily visible. Only a few decks away from the core, the pseudo gravity was about a tenth of normal. The room was dominated by the reactor, or more precisely, the reactor shielding, a large cylinder oriented parallel to the ship's axis, half embedded in the floor. On the far side of the space, a figure in a naval uniform jumped up and landed on top of the engine shielding with practiced grace. Stein nodded to Max, the bow auxiliary engineer.

"This is what fires the rockets?" one of the kids asked.

"Not quite," Max replied with practiced patience. Aside from having to explain that to every school group that went through here, Max was used to fielding this question from grown-ups as well. Most of the adults on board the Argos didn't know where their heat and electricity came from. "This engine powers the electrical and heating systems for the bulk of the ship. The propulsion engine is in the aft." He gestured to the far end of the room. "But otherwise, the reactors are basically identical. Does anyone here know what antimatter is?" Max launched into his spiel, leading the group deeper into the room.

Stein held back at the door, eager for the break. Not for the first time, she wondered about the intent of these field trips. The kids didn't want to see any of this, far preferring the simple joys of mucking around in low-gravity. The cooling plant, network relay, and heat recyclers had similarly held little interest for them. She didn't blame them—most of this stuff wasn't that exciting, and she didn't recall enjoying it that much when she was a child. But the teachers felt it important, and every few months or so another group of children would crawl all over the vital organs of the ship and grow immediately bored of them.

One of the children held back from the group, looking at his terminal with a bored expression. He had been asking lots of questions earlier in the tour, but appeared to have lost interest. This was a seventh year class, which would make him about eleven. Stein thought his name was Bert, based on some exasperated shushing from one of the teachers.

"You're going to miss learning how antimatter reactors work," Stein said, deciding to try her luck with the child's name. "Bert, was it?"

Bert didn't correct her. "I already know how they work," he said, with the air of a practiced know-it-all. "Deuterium molecules go into anti-deuterium molecules and it goes BANG and then we get energy."

"Pretty good," Stein said. "You've read all about that in school?"

"Laugh!" Bert replied, saying the word instead of laughing. "They don't teach us any of that stuff in seventh year. I had to teach myself all about it. Like the 8-D magnets they use to control it."

Stein's eyes widened. "You're a smart kid."

"*Obviously*. Did you know that it takes a hundred times more energy to make antimatter than we can get out of it?"

Stein nodded. "I think I knew that, yes."

"That's why we can't make any more of it," Bert said. He bounced up and down. "But we can make more matter!"

"I don't know if that's right."

"Well, we can't 'make it,' make it. But we didn't bring enough of it. That's what the terminal says. We were burning it wrong. So, we've had to start mixing it with ground rock! Isn't that crazy?"

"That is crazy." It sounded familiar though, the sort of factoid she'd heard before in school, but evidently not something that had stuck.

"Do you know where they get the rock from?"

"I don't know. You'd have to ask Max."

"Okay! Can he show us the rockets?" Bert sniffed. "'Cause this is all boring." He glared at the reactor, which was the beating heart of the ship.

"There's no tours of the aft engines any more, Bert. They're busy working on them—getting them back into shape." Stein held up her hands in a what-can-you-do gesture.

"For the Big Push," Bert said.

"That's right." The Big Push was the braking sequence the Argos would have to make if it didn't want to smoke into its new home at several thousand kilometers per second. It was supposed to have begun the previous day, but thanks to a navigational error and massive course correction a hundred and seventy years previous, the schedule had been pushed back. "That's pretty advanced stuff for a kid your age."

"I think it's neat is all."

Stein smiled. "It is neat. I can see why you'd want to see what the drives look like." Bert nodded earnestly, as though he hoped that Stein, impressed with his moxie, would magically pull some strings and get him an all-access pass to the ship. Stein continued, "But, boring as it is, this guy here is what's kept us alive for the last couple hundred years."

"Laugh," Burt said. "You sound like my dad."

Stein felt enormous sympathy for Bert's dad, and all the other adults in his life. As the tour group made its way back from the far end of the engine room, she exchanged a glance with one of the teachers, who let out a short bark of a laugh after recognizing the look on Stein's face.

Bert crossed the room to bother the naval technicians who had moved off to the side when the kids arrived. A twisted black box lay at their feet, some component of the reactor that Stein couldn't readily identify. That wasn't surprising—she was well out of her element in this room. She guessed they were in the middle of a repair when the tour group interrupted them.

She wouldn't normally have chaperoned one of these, but she was short staffed again that day—Gabelman still hadn't shown up for work. Bruce was great with stuff like this, but that morning the big man had strongly hinted that he'd found out something interesting about M. Melson and was going to dig up more that day. With Bruce, this 'digging' process could entail almost anything, and although Stein knew enough not to ask any questions, she couldn't not worry about it. Visions of Bruce putting small children in armlocks danced in her head. Best to leave him to his own devices when he was in such a mood, as far away as from the distressing 11-year-olds as possible.

It was the best place on the ship to see why the garden well had been so named, a floor-to-ceiling window offering a panoramic view of the entire well. Although any observer in the well could see it was a massive hollow cylinder, only here at the end, four stories above the surface, was it possible to look down the entire length of the ship. The illusion of looking down a well was dizzyingly strong.

The rest of the office was well appointed. A massive desk sat in the center of the room, lightly scuffed, but very precisely curved to match the curve in the floor. The carpet on the floor was aggressively purple, plush on the sides, worn in the middle. In truth, everything in the room was worn, maybe a bit less so than other parts of the ship, but still noticeable. That was a never-ending source of annoyance to the room's current resident, who wanted, even *needed* everything in this room to impress.

Nothing here impressed the captain, and Mayor Eric Kinsella hated him for it. Every other person on the Argos who held any real power owed their position to Kinsella in some way, whether they knew it or not. Nominally, Captain Helot did, as well. The ship's constitution was very clear about the relative authority between the civilian government and the commander of the vessel itself. But there was a certain lack of deference in Helot's behavior that suggested to Kinsella that his counterpart thought otherwise.

"Diagnostics on all the rotational thrusters have been completed. We should have eighty-five percent of them working before deceleration begins," Helot read without looking up from the terminal in his hand.

Helot had been made Captain almost twenty years earlier by one of Kinsella's predecessors. Kinsella didn't know the whole story, but got the impression that Helot had been given the job ahead of older and more experienced personnel as part of some multi-layered political stratagem being played by the mayor at the time. He couldn't recall if the stratagem worked or not, and indeed it didn't really matter—that mayor was long gone.

The next mayor had chosen to leave Helot in place, seeing no need to rock the boat as it were. A mistake as far as Kinsella was concerned. By being made Captain at such a young age, Helot had spent a third of his life in office, plenty of time to become a familiar and comfortable presence to the ship's citizens. This left Kinsella handcuffed by a captain who was—though no one would come out and say it—significantly more popular than he was.

Bored, Kinsella drummed his fingers on his desk. Realizing he was being rude, he stopped, then just as quickly wished he hadn't. He didn't have to care if he was rude. He was tired of dealing with Helot. He smiled involuntarily, then caught himself when he realized he never smiled during cabinet briefings. Concentrating, he focused his energies on not fidgeting with the terminal sitting on his desk, recently delivered to him by Thorias, the security chief.

Helot had given every appearance of a man dedicated to his career. His list of dependents was short: no wife, no children, one ship. In a society where the privilege of breeding was a precious commodity, the lack of a family marked him as unusual. Kinsella tried to hide a smile. How would people react if they knew their captain's brave solitude wasn't a reflection of his commitment to public service? Just a side effect of a secret and dark perversion? The information on the terminal in front of him was toe-curlingly detailed.

Kinsella allowed himself a thin smile as the captain continued to drone through his briefing. Yes, Helot was going to be out of his hair soon. And Kinsella had big plans for his going away party.

One day, this will all be yours. Bruce strolled down one of the leafy tree-lined streets in the garden well, looking up at the low-rise apartment buildings around him. *Gonna move on up. Get me some windows. Live like a pope.*

While Stein burgled merely for her own amusement, Bruce had actual goals in mind when he worked the nights. Although many dwellings below decks did have windows, when they fronted out to a hallway, this wasn't a lot to get excited about. Not like the expensive and hard-to-come-by windows in the garden well, with their breezes and laughter and classy women leaning out of them. It was a nice goal, stealing for windows. It certainly felt more romantic than stealing for money, which is what it looked like he was doing most of the time.

Bruce spotted the address, 2835 Begonia, and walked in the front door. Taking the stairs up to the third floor he examined the interior halls thoughtfully. Dust and grime, but much, much less than in his place. Ms. Redelso had done quite well for herself since selling the old family studio in the aft. Finding the right apartment, Bruce rang the buzzer and waited.

He had to hurry, window-wise. There was no point getting a window after the ship had stopped and they were all living in caves or whatever. Then everyone would have windows. They would be worthless. Worse than worthless—they would be liabilities. Letting in cold and dirt and leopards. He had no use for those windows.

The door opened, revealing a modestly attractive middle-aged woman. Bruce recognized her from his research: she was the semi-famous, artistically-middling painter, Charlotte Redelso.

"Maintenance," Bruce said, by way of introduction. "You have a problem with your heat?"

Confused, Charlotte shook her head. "No. I don't think so." She looked behind her. "Nope, we never have problems here."

Of course not, woman, you live in a tropical paradise. "Hmmmmmmmmm," Bruce said, checking his terminal. "Looks like we've got a problem, then. Do you mind if I come in and take a look?"

"Well, actually..."

"Thanks," Bruce said, "my boss will kill me if this doesn't get looked at. I'm not kidding. She has these knives, and is just constantly looking for an excuse to use them. It's a real bad scene. Thank you for your understanding." As predicted, this barrage of information overwhelmed Redelso, who retreated inside the apartment, wide-eyed.

Bruce followed her inside, putting his terminal carefully into his webbing. At the center of the room, he stopped and looked around slowly, turning a complete circle. Spotting the membrane above the door he had just entered with a look of surprise, he reached up and prodded it with a temperature probe. After examining the probe with the most thoughtful expression he could muster, he made a noise that he hoped sounded like something a man who was solving a complicated problem would make.

He turned again, passing a quick smile at Redelso as he did so. "Looks okay so far." He moved across the apartment to one of the two—two!—windows and peered outside.

"You open these windows very often?"

"Sometimes. How often is often?"

Bruce furrowed his brow. "I honestly don't know. Eighty?" He turned back to the window, opened it, and stuck his head out.

"Eighty what?" she asked.

"That's an excellent question," he responded, closing the window. "I'll have to look it up. Anyways, our sensors might be getting confused when you open or close the window. I'll make a note of it, so we don't bother you anymore."

"Thanks," she said, exasperation showing. "I guess?"

"You're very welcome," he said with a big smile. "Have a nice day."

From the roof of the building directly across from Charlotte Redelso's window, Bruce aimed the piton gun and fired. As the piton sailed away, the thought occurred to him that he probably should have aimed above the window rather than directly at it. The nano-piton smacked into the window, bouncing off it with a crack before clattering to the ground below. Wide-eyed, Bruce quickly recoiled the piton and cable before ducking down behind the short wall at the edge of the roof. After a couple of minutes had passed without any cries of alarm, he cautiously peeked over the edge. No lights on. *Let's try that again.*

Another thought lurched into view, this time thankfully before he fired. Redelso had two windows in her apartment, and he had only tampered with one of them. Moving a short distance down the edge of the roof, he took aim at what he was sure was the correct window, caught himself, shifted his aim upwards, and fired again. The piton sailed across the gap and impacted the wall of the building, embedding itself easily in the surface. Bruce glanced at the piton gun's display: a solid hold.

Designed for rock climbers who mucked about and occasionally died on the exposed faces at either end of the garden well, a nano-piton's holding capacity was highly variable, dependent upon how squarely it had hit whatever it was fired at. Their average loading capacity was supposedly three hundred and fifty pounds, but the standard deviation on that figure was wide enough that Bruce, and the two hundred and fifty pounds he carried with him at all times, was always reluctant to use it. Bruce attached the piton gun and cable to a second gun using a jury-rigged binding. He fired the second piton at the wall of the roof access staircase he had climbed up, then reeled in the gun until the whole apparatus—cables, guns, and ramshackle binding—was taut.

The next part of the plan was where things got stupid. To describe it to any right-thinking man was a guaranteed way to see him wince and inhale sharply. It gave even Bruce, no stranger to ill-advised schemes, some pause. Grabbing one of the piton guns in each hand, he flipped the setting of one to reverse, then triggered them both simultaneously. The apparatus of madness whirred forward slowly. Bruce sat up on the roof's edge and spun his legs out over the edge. He grabbed both piton guns firmly. "This will not seem like a better idea the longer you wait," he said, then lowered himself off the roof, putting his weight on the apparatus. The pitons, cables, guns, and makeshift binding all held. He swallowed, adjusted his balance slightly, then pulled both triggers. With a faint whir, the large man sailed through the night sky.

Ten seconds later, Bruce had crossed the street and gently set some of his weight down on Charlotte Redelso's windowsill. After a few frantic moments fumbling with the window's edge, he finally felt it slide up. Quietly, Bruce lowered himself into the apartment and its blessedly solid ground.

The plan entered its marginally less crazy second phase. Bruce trusted that like most people, Ms. Redelso kept some information about herself offline. Every device on board the ship was networked, sharing a common, instantly accessible storage space. All totally private—every desk and terminal was capable of identifying immediately who was using it, rendering private information inaccessible to a malicious third party. Yet, few people trusted this security with their most personal information, and almost everyone stored some information offline on dumb, non-networked terminals, even paper in a few cases. This desire for enhanced privacy ironically made the information much less secure, at least for someone with a knack for prowling around the physical world.

Bruce pulled out his own terminal and flipped the camera to scan in infrared, a useful utility familiar to few people other than maintenance workers. A light glow from the bedroom was Charlotte, still evidently asleep. He surveyed the apartment, picking out the few locations he had already spotted as potential hiding places, then switched from the infrared scanner to another, far more interesting application. He placed the terminal in his chest webbing and proceeded to search the apartment, checking all the drawers, cupboards, and other nooks and crannies.

Ten minutes later he had found it: a dumb-terminal stuffed in a desk drawer. Although the main interface of the terminal was password protected, this security feature had been broken two hundred years earlier. No one capable of fixing the problem had ever been willing to do so, leaving all such terminals highly vulnerable to people like Bruce. Using his own terminal, Bruce made a copy of the contents of Redelso's before returning it to its hiding place.

That done, and satisfied he'd seen everything interesting in the apartment—at least everything not in a room occupied by a sleeping woman—he examined the application he'd set running earlier. It was an image-recognition and logging program that scanned the apartment as he searched it, identifying and cataloguing all the objects within. Then, using a database created from publicly listed recycling values and estimated uniqueness, it calculated an estimated value/weight ratio for each object and presented a ranked list to him. An efficient way of deciding what to steal, though it had a hard time determining the value of items it had no record of. Which wasn't that big of a problem; those were typically the items rare enough to be worth stealing. Bruce scrolled through the list, then retraced his steps, picking out the fifteen pounds he felt confident would make it back across his sideshow of an escape route.

Ill deeds done, Bruce carefully stepped outside the window and closed it behind him to do the second-stupidest thing he'd done that day: return across the street. With an exhalation of relief far more audible than was appropriate to the current level of subterfuge, he alit onto the neighboring roof for a minute or so of shaking before he detached and reeled in his apparatus, and retreated into the shadows.

Stein stayed up late that night, hoping that Bruce might spring up with some fantastic news about what M. Melson was all about, solving the mystery without her having to get off the couch. But her terminal stayed resolutely silent. She kept an eye on the news feeds in case the headline "Fat Man Arrested for Horrible Activities" cropped up, but that also didn't happen.

Crawling into bed, but not yet tired, she began hurling general searches at the network, looking for clues about what she'd seen in the bright blue light. "Bright Light + messages" mostly returned tips about advertising, mixed in with a handful of stories about near-death experiences. Stein was pretty sure that wasn't what happened to her, as to date, no theologians had identified any greater powers claiming the handle 'Vlad.'

A search for 'eyeball messages' uncovered a lot about corneal tattoos, which had gone in and out of fashion at various points in Argosian history, usually by people whose idea of a message worthy of being permanently branded on their eyeballs was "Fuck the Police." That was decidedly not what Stein had, but she amused herself for a few minutes with images of people who had gone down this road. This search led to the history of tattoos, from the painful early methods with burning charcoal, through the ink and needle glory years, and up to the genetic tattoos of skin cells manipulated to form what were essentially artificial birthmarks. That article came with some pretty upsetting pictures of lab mice and other test animals, and she turned off her terminal before she saw too much.

Had she imagined it? It all seemed a lot blurrier now. She closed her eyes and rubbed her knuckles into the sockets, sending flashes of lights up her optic nerve. There. That was kind of a shape. A shoe-shaped shape. Was that then a secret message about shoes? That seemed just as plausible as a message about Vlad, which was to say, not plausible at all. She checked the time, decided that it was past even Bruce's bedtime, and reached the lights.

As she was drifting off, another image appeared, this one deliberately, as she imagined a mouse with "Fuck the Police" emblazoned on its back. She laughed herself to sleep.

Previously

"There's no way you're getting 850 babies a year out of your bakery."

Harold exhaled and looked at the curved ceiling of Kinison's office. He couldn't stand Kinison when he was lecturing. "I know that, Lewis. But if the radiation starts coming in again, the poor things are getting zapped in the womb. At least the cans can shield them from that. I get it; we don't need to match the whole replacement rate. But we can get at least a fraction of that surely? Maybe a hundred?"

"A hundred a year? Never happen. And you know it," Kinison said. That wasn't a lie; Harold did know it. First impressions count, especially when they're impressively violent, and the first few can-born souls had certainly been that. Even when the kinks had been worked out of the process, the stigma around canned babies still stuck. It was kind of a weird hobby for him to have taken up. Not that the ship was lacking for those.

"Look, Harold," Kinison said. "You'll get some. It's a good safety net if nothing else." He smiled, with only the slightest hint of condescension detectable. Dr. Kinison was one of only two or three people on the ship capable of speaking with Harold intelligibly about his work. But where Harold had stumbled upon his career by accident, Kinison had been groomed for the role of senior naval medical officer for decades, the one man responsible for the long-term health of the ship's current and future generations. "We can't ignore your research," Kinison continued, "or the results you've had thus far. But we can't do what you're proposing. Not at that scale. We'll stick with the conventional methods. End of discussion."

Harold bit his tongue. It was the end of this phase of the discussion, but he wasn't prepared to concede any future phases just yet. "All right."

Outside Kinison's office in the aft core of the ship, Harold tried to get his bearings in the curving hall. He hated this part of the ship. So obviously a space ship up here, it made him claustrophobic. Picking a likely direction for an elevator, he set off.

He guessed right and shortly thereafter spotted Chief Hatchens, the head of ship's security, standing in front of the elevator doors. The chief looked up at him, eyes flickering in recognition. A small lump of fear pinballed through Harold. He hadn't had many dealings with the famously heavy-handed security department and preferred to steer clear of them when he could, but an abrupt U-turn would only bring more attention to himself.

"Dr. Stein. How are you?"

Harold swallowed and hesitated, concerned that Hatchens knew him by name. Then he worried that his hesitation made him look suspicious, and hesitated some more. Finally, in a hurried voice, he said, "All right." *Because taking five seconds to come up with 'All right' doesn't sound suspicious at all.*

Hatchens looked at him intently. Harold wondered if the man ever blinked. "That's good."

Harold swallowed again. *This is going well.* They stood quietly for a while, Harold passing the time with silent curses about the elevator's speed.

"I was sorry to hear about your friend," Hatchens said. "Kevin Delise? You two were fairly close, right?"

Harold blinked. "Pardon?"

Kevin, the first canned baby on the ship since it launched, was not his son, just the next closest thing: one of his success stories. They were not in any way genetically related—Harold wasn't that mad of a scientist—but he was still the closest thing the boy had to a father.

Hatchens' eyes widened, but Harold got the impression that his surprise wasn't genuine. "I'm sorry. You don't know." His mouth twisted into a knot. "I'm sorry to tell you, but Mr. Delise has been murdered. I thought someone would have contacted you about it by now."

Harold's mouth went dry. He leaned against the wall. The colors around the edge of his vision started to fade.

"When was the last time you heard from Kevin?" Hatchens asked.

"What? I don't know. A week ago?" Harold looked down , then up at Hatchens. "Yeah, a week or so ago. We talked about work. My work. My god, are you sure it was Kevin? What happened?"

Hatchens studied him for a second before turning his attention to the elevator door. "It was a knife. The neck, you see?" Hatchens' hand moved up towards his own neck as if to demonstrate, before he seemed to think better of it. "First deck," he said instead. "No idea who might have done it, but we're checking the feeds now."

The elevator finally arrived. Harold blinked, lurched into the car, and turned. Hatchens remained outside, looking at something on his terminal. "Oops, looks like I have to go. I'll be in touch. Sorry again." The doors closed, obscuring Hatchens' face and an expression that didn't look very sorry at all.

As the elevator accelerated downwards, Harold's legs gave out. Finding himself sitting on the floor, he looked at his shaking hands. *Oh, Kevin, my boy. Oh, Kevin, Kevin, Kevin....*

3

Brash

Ron Gabelman had an excellent excuse for missing work; his head had been nearly lopped off. Stein found this out when she arrived at the maintenance office to find a red-eyed Curts already there in the company of a bulky security officer, Sergeant Hogg.

Hogg asked Stein what she knew about Gabelman's activities over the past few days. She explained the task she had assigned to Gabelman the last time she had seen him, when she sent him to investigate the hot and cold complaints in the aft government offices. She pulled up the complaints on the Big Board for them to observe, although from the dismissive glance Hogg gave them, she got the impression that Curts had already walked him through this. The two complaints were both flagged as 'Resolved.' One had a brief note attached to it: "Adjusted air balancing." The other simply said, "No Issue. Complaint was mistaken." A couple of taps on the screen indicated Gabelman had made these notes shortly after ten in the morning the day he disappeared, at which point he should have reported back to the maintenance office.

"So, he should have returned here at, what, 10:30?" Hogg asked.

"Sure. But it isn't unusual for techs to take their time walking back," Stein replied. She exchanged a glance with Curts, who nodded.

Hogg eyed Stein carefully for a few seconds. Finally he said, "His body was found this morning on the first deck, off 45th and Fir Street. Do you know of any reason why Gabelman would be in that part of the ship?"

She shook her head—she really had no idea what the kid did for kicks.

Hogg nodded, and continued, "We also found a couple tabs of guru on him. Did you ever know Mr. Gabelman to use narcotics? Did he ever arrive at work intoxicated? Tardy or absent often?"

"He was new, so I can't be completely sure. Not necessarily a model employee, but I never saw him doing anything like that."

"How was he not a model employee?"

Stein waved her hands back and forth defensively. "I don't mean anything bad. He was just a little slow. Sometimes took longer, needed more help with tasks than I'd prefer. That's all."

Hogg stared at her for a few seconds more, waiting to see if she would elaborate further. She recognized the ploy and stayed silent. Hogg frowned, looked down at his terminal, then the door. "Okay. If I have any further questions, I'll be in touch." With a nod, he turned and left.

Curts slumped forward on the table, head resting on one hand. He yawned, then repeated all of Hogg's questions, apparently checking to see if Stein had decided to withhold information from the security man that she would for some reason share with him. She answered his questions, not bothering to hide her annoyance. Eventually, satisfied that Stein wasn't omitting anything, Curts stood up and straightened his ridiculously clean orange jumpsuit. Whatever he'd been doing the past few months, it clearly hadn't been very dirty work. As he tucked away his terminal and adjusted his webbing, Stein detected a hint of indecision in his movements.

"Let me know if we have any more w-w-weird calls like this," he finally said. He gestured at the board. "Hot and c-c-old complaints right on top of each other. That's weird. I don't like seeing that."

"Yeah, I noticed that at the time. Thought it was just people being bitchy. Guess that's why Ron flagged one of them as a mistake." She frowned. "You want me to go follow up on it?"

Curts shook his head and waved her back. "Don't bother. I might go check it out myself, actually. If I need you I'll c-c-call, but for now don't worry about it. Just let me know if something like that shows up again."

"No problem, boss."

Curts nodded, his eyes unfocused, head slumping forward. He blinked, looked around, seemed startled to find out where he was, then smiled weakly and left the maintenance office. Stein squinted at the retreating orange buffoon. *Strange service calls?* Curts didn't seem the slightest bit concerned by the news that one of his technicians had been decapitated.

She was looking up at the Big Board and the day ahead of her, when she realized she wasn't that concerned about it either.

"Do you know if your son had any enemies?" Hogg asked, straining to sound gentle. A blubbering stream of nonsense greeted him in response. The sympathy he had forced himself to muster for Gabelman's mother was beginning to subside. He was growing annoyed, though not with the poor woman crying in front of him. Just his colleagues. The whole security apparatus in fact. It had been hours; someone really should have told her that her son had been found dead before Hogg got there. He watched the woman sobbing and felt the annoyance grow. Because, however unfortunate this whole murder business apparently was for Gableman's mother, it was really quite a lucky break for him, and one that couldn't have come at a better time, career-wise.

At some point Hogg had pissed someone off, though he still wasn't sure how, or where, or even who. He had suspected it for a while, had seen evidence of his career sputtering for the last couple of rotations. The most recent such hint had occurred only two days earlier, when he had been transferred to command the community policing center in the northern end of the ship. Remote, under-equipped, staffed with incompetents, it was, on paper, a promotion. And, in reality, an extended middle finger.

"Do you know who Ron's friends were? Who he spent time with?" Hogg asked, trying a different tack. Mrs. Gabelman became somewhat more intelligible, and he dutifully recorded everything she said, though none of it sounded very useful. He was still pretty confident this was a murder of opportunity. Big nasty knife wound, drugs, scuzzy part of the ship. 45th and Fir was certainly a rough neighborhood on the first level, a likely enough place for a drug deal to go bad. On the other hand, Gabelman simply didn't have the look of a user. Hogg definitely knew what those looked like, having swept them in and out of the drunk tank for much of his career. He supposed it was possible Gabelman was simply a high-functioning user who happened to mouth off to the wrong person.

The search of his apartment had turned up exactly nothing. Gabelman had apparently been a single, slightly messy, slightly dorky guy, with an interest in electro funk and pornographic images. No cache of suicide letters or severed doll heads or, interestingly, drug paraphernalia. Not that there would be much for a guru user.

And there was certainly nothing anywhere to indicate the guy had any enemies who wished him harm. Although his work colleagues were interesting people—Hogg had run background checks on them while riding the trolley over to Mrs. Gabelman's. His supervisor, the Stein woman, had an extremely interesting past. A canned baby—those were rare enough, especially one that hadn't self-imploded—she had then managed the even more impressive feat of getting a job. It had been a close thing though—during her youth she'd run afoul of the law more than once. But she had managed to settle down by the time she'd finished her schooling, and landed a spot in the engineering department. She still seemed to roll with a pretty shifty crowd, many of them connected to the Breeder groups that were cropping up around that time. Nothing had ever been tied directly back to her though. The author of the background summary seemed surprised by that.

Still, it was nothing to link Ron Gabelman directly with anyone shady. If there was anything in Gabelman's life to suggest he had stab-happy enemies, it would be on his terminal. Hogg had already sent that to IT to unlock. An easy job for them, Hogg was confident it would still probably take them several days to get around to it. But he wasn't the type to complain, and he still had a few other avenues, however unfruitful they appeared.

He looked at the current unfruitful avenue blubbering in front of him and suppressed a sigh. Time to stop badgering this poor woman. Stowing his terminal, Hogg began the process of extricating himself from Mrs. Gabelman's tedious sadness, giving himself a couple of minutes before he'd stop even pretending to be nice. He wondered if a plastic security badge would speed the healing process any.

"Wouldn't be the first young guy to get mixed up with drugs," Bruce said. "They are, after all, incredible." He had his feet up on the desk in the supervisor's office while he worked on his sandwich.

"If so, he kept it pretty quiet. I certainly never saw him high. You?" Stein asked.

Bruce shrugged. "I never paid a lot of attention. You know me and people." He munched on his sandwich for a bit. "Did the cop say who they think did it?"

"Nope. And I didn't think to ask. Kind of a rough part of the ship though. Were I to guess, I'd say he was rolled for the guru. That seemed to be the vibe the cop was putting out."

They sat in silence for a few seconds. "Pretty shitty," Bruce finally said.

"Pretty shitty," Stein echoed. More silence. "It's weird though. I mean, I feel bad that the kid died, but I also don't feel too bad. You know? Like I'm almost more concerned with how this will impact my workload. Does that sound sick?"

"I wouldn't worry about it. It probably just means you're a monster."

Stein snorted. "Thanks." She poked lamely at her lunch with a spork. "Actually, check this: Curts might be even more of a monster than me." Stein related Curts' request after the security officers had left.

Bruce chewed on a thumbnail as he listened. "Well, it sounds like he had a little more time to react than you. And he didn't really know the kid, did he? I can see why he'd be more worried about the ship. Not like you, you fucking monstrosity."

Stein considered that for a moment while working on her salad. "Okay, sure. I can see a chief caring more for the ship than his staff.

That's almost a requirement of the job. And I can see him not caring about drug users on staff because, I kid you not, he looked like he was coming down off something himself."

Bruce started chuckling to himself. She narrowed her gaze, wondering what he was so amused about, before deciding she would probably prefer not knowing.

"But asking about conflicting complaints? What the hell? We get a couple of those a day. They're no big deal."

"Simple diagnosis: he's getting anal retentive."

"I guess."

Bruce burped. "Oof. That felt good." He shifted in his chair. "Wanna hear what I was up to last night?"

"Is this that thing where you watch women go to the bathroom? Because, no, I don't want to hear about that."

Bruce shook his head. "Better than that."

"I am at a loss to think of what you could think is better than that. Surely something pretty foul. A violation of deep, universal principles."

"Ha." Bruce recounted the story of his aerial work at Charlotte Redelso's apartment. Stein listened, wincing and inhaling sharply when Bruce got to the stupid parts. She had known about Bruce's insane climbing apparatus, and even seen it in use once, but the thought of the contraption still terrified her.

"Hang on just a second," Stein said when the story had concluded. "To dig up information on what could potentially be in a room that is quite easy to break into, you performed a ridiculously daring stunt to raid the apartment of someone tangentially related to what you're actually interested in?"

"At first, I was just going to ask her. But then I saw all the nice stuff she had and revised my plans."

Stein shook her head. "And did you find anything interesting?"

Bruce tapped something on his terminal. "Dear Charlotte has been keeping copies of personnel correspondence on a dummy. Love letters mostly, shockingly tame ones I'm sorry to report. But alongside those I found several pieces of communication from one Mr. Maurice Melson."

"Which said?"

"It looks like this Melson had been pressuring Charlotte to sell that studio for several years. The first messages I saw refer to earlier correspondence. By the time Charlotte began recording their talks offline it looked like Melson was getting creative."

"How so?"

"She's an artist. Melson evidently had contacts in the mayor's office. He promised he could get some of her work placed visibly in public are-as—even in the Bridge, apparently."

"If she agreed to sell the studio to him?" Seeing Bruce nod, she frowned. "So, a guy with a dead man's name has access to some big-shit mandarins, and uses that leverage to buy a shitty little apartment, and then hide something in it."

"That appears to be what happened, yes. I couldn't find anything else about the guy on there—no pictures or anything like that."

The two occasional thieves sat alone with their thoughts.

"So, what next?" Bruce asked. "Can I go set off some more booby-traps now?"

"Have you ever asked my permission to do that before?"

Bruce's jaw jutted out, eyes to the ceiling, making a big show of think-ing about that. "Good point. I retract my request, and will proceed as per normal, i.e. recklessly. I'll let you know what I find later tonight."

Stein stared at her friend. "Are you kidding? Weren't you up all night hanging from lampposts? You stopped sleeping again?"

Bruce grinned. "Gabelman's not the only one who knew how to party."

Stein sagged in her chair. No one seemed to take the kid's death seri-ously, but Bruce's ability to brush it off grated at her for some reason. The multiple layers of irony he wore at all times was a familiar act, and usually a welcome one. He'd been that way ever since she first met him in school, and she'd learned from his example. Kids were jerks, and the walls he had helped her raise had proven very useful. Though she was never as good at it as he was, and sometimes wondered if that was a good thing. Maybe his walls were just a bit too thick.

Seeming to sense the shift in mood—*see, he was more sensitive than he let on, dammit!*—Bruce clammed up and resumed work on his lunch. Eventu-ally he asked between bites, "This Curts thing with the conflicting jobs. What were they again?"

Stein blinked a couple of times, shifting gears. "One hot, one cold, right next door to each other," she replied. "The cold one Ron apparently fixed. Air balancing thing. The hot one was a non-issue. Ron said it was a mistaken call." Out of curiosity, Stein tapped on her terminal, pulling up a schematic of that part of the ship. Numbers appeared on the map, indicat-ing the current temperature and humidity in various areas. "Looks fine now," she said, tapping on the two rooms as she shoved the terminal over to Bruce.

Bruce looked at it. "All snug as a bug," he agreed. He dragged his fin-ger around the screen. "What's that?"

Stein looked at what Bruce was pointing at. Another room, a series of rooms in fact, registering temperatures well below normal. The terminal indicated it was occupied office space.

"Says it's occupied. Should be a complaint logged I'd imagine," Stein said. She tapped at her desk display. "Nothing," she said after scanning through the list of active complaints.

"The occupancy database is never right," Bruce pointed out. "That's probably a storage area now. No one but boxes to complain."

"Yeah, probably," Stein said, nodding. She looked at the map, trying to identify the occupant of the space. Part of the Logistics branch. More government workers, and boring ones at that. She frowned. This part of the ship was often called 'The Annex,' being the former storage space that had been reallocated for government use a few years into the ship's flight. The speed with which the civilian government had outgrown its original space was the basis for some of the oldest, creakiest jokes on the Argos, the punch line to most being "More People Doing Less Work."

Bruce was a couple steps ahead of Stein, frowning at a map on his terminal. "Nah, that room's occupied. I was by there a couple weeks ago. Definitely not storage."

"Well, then, what the fuck? They all wearing sweaters or something?" Stein's gaze flipped back and forth between her terminal and desk. "Oh," she said, figuring it out. "Dummy."

"Busted t-stat," Bruce finished her thought for her. "Well, add it to the list. I'll get to it sometime in the next six years."

Stein leaned back in her chair, staring up at the box of spare thermostats she kept on the shelf. A room with a perfectly acceptable temperature that was indicating it was too cold was about as far down the priority list of re-pairs as was possible. There were literally dozens of better things she could do with her time. But something about figuring a problem out like that would eat away at her if it wasn't fixed. And there was still something weird about it which bothered her. She hated weird things on her ship.

"I think I'll go handle this one now," she said, standing up. The only weird thing she did tolerate, now happily munching away on his second sandwich, looked up at her. She scooped up her terminal and strapped on the tool webbing she had hung on the back of her chair. "Even us man-agement types can get our hands dirty sometimes."

Bruce rolled his eyes. "Yeah, boss. You go replace your busted 'stat. Let me know if you get in over your head."

When Stein arrived, she found that the thermostat was perfectly fine. The office in question was freezing.

"Where the hell have you been?" a woman demanded when Stein and her bright orange uniform entered the Logistics office. "We called you hours ago!"

Stein blinked, surprised, half ready to pick a fight with the woman with her fur on end. But after a deep breath, she slid into customer relations mode and deployed a thin smile. She had handled angry customers before—many days had handled nothing but. After the first few months on the job and the near-fistfights from just such encounters, she'd learned to play these a little more softly. In particular, people who had made a mistake when filling in their service requests were always the touchiest. After long practice, Stein had learned it was easiest to fix the problem first, and then give them the tutorial on how to use the service request system. Starting a conversation with "Here's why you're an idiot," was Bruce's manner.

"Sorry," she said, feigning an exasperated expression. "It's been a hectic day. Let's see if I can't get it a bit warmer in here."

Although still clearly annoyed, the woman didn't say anything else, which Stein took to be a good omen. Digging out her terminal, she set to work.

In fairly short order, Stein found the problem. This office was downstream of the air distribution network in one of the rooms Gabelman had visited. Gabelman had messed up the settings on the dampers, directing the majority of the hot air into a single office. A stupid mistake, and proof enough that he was on drugs as far as Stein was concerned. "Rest in peace, buddy," she added quietly. After retrieving a ladder from a tool closet a half block away, she opened the panel outside that gave her access to physically manipulate the damper's actuators and adjust the air balancing, carefully setting it to correct the current problem without interfering with anyone else's comfort.

After replacing the panel, Stein returned the ladder to its closet. As she was hanging the ladder up, an idea popped into her head. "While I'm in the neighborhood...."

"Hi, is, uh..." Stein hesitated as she read the name from her terminal, "Greg Watson here?"

The receptionist left the front desk, retreating into the back of the office to fetch Greg. While she was gone, Stein looked at the terminal again. Something about the name on this service request was funny. This was the office that Gabelman had visited, with the mistaken too-hot service request. If anyone asked, she would say this was to ensure Gabelman's adjustment of the air balancing hadn't thrown anything else out of whack. The office was occupied by the ship's licensing department. "Licensing," she said aloud, feeling a headache coming on, unable to think of a single activity on the Argos which required a license.

Greg Watson appeared from a smaller office at the back and walked towards the reception desk with a gait that suggested he thought he was important, and a look of dismay at the sight of Stein's orange uniform. "Can I help you?"

"Yes, I'm just following up on a service request that was submitted the other day. You complained that it was too hot in here?"

Watson's gaze narrowed. "I don't know what you're talking about. It's perfectly fine here."

Stein frowned, biting the inside of her cheek. "Two days ago we got a service request saying it was too hot here. We sent a technician around to check on it."

"Don't know what to tell you. But I didn't see any technician." He looked her up and down, his nose elevating fractionally. "It's actually been a little chilly around here lately to be honest. Better today, though."

"Huh," Stein said. "Okay. Glad to hear it." Smiling, she backed out the door and returned down the hall to the Logistics office, to see if things had improved there.

"Getting warmer in here?" she asked when she entered, not needing a response. The sensors on her webbing told her as much, as did those on the surface of her skin.

"Yes, thank you," the woman replied, a lingering note of annoyance still in her voice.

"How long was it cold like that?" Stein asked.

"It was bad yesterday, and worse this morning," she replied. "That's when I put in the service request."

Stein swallowed, as she prepared to gently explain to the woman how she was mistaken. There was a simple approach to take when handling cases like these. She forced a frown on her face. "Hmmm. Can you show me the service request on your screen?"

"Sure." The woman tapped at the screen on her desk. "Right here. See? *It's too cold! Please help!* That's me. Oh. That can't be right." She pointed at the timestamp on the request, which said 5:15 p.m.

Stein frowned, genuinely this time. That was two hours in the future. Which was probably why the request hadn't shown up on the Big Board. She checked her own terminal, looking at the queue of active service requests. Not there either. "That's weird," she said to the woman. *You're not an idiot at all. Or you may be, but not because of this. At minimum we're lacking enough information to make a determination one way or another.* Stein carefully noted down the ID number of the request on her terminal, offered another apology, and quickly left the office, her mind racing.

Hogg trudged down 8th Avenue, avoiding eye contact with everyone who crossed his path. He was chasing up the third and last of Gabelman's friends from the list Mrs. Gabelman had provided. The first two interviews each followed an entirely predictable arc. No, they didn't know Gabelman used drugs. No, that didn't sound like him at all. No, they didn't know if he had any enemies. They offered helpful suggestions for how the investigation should proceed. The general thrust of these suggestions—"Stop looking for dirt on the poor boy"—Hogg was beginning to agree with.

Hogg turned on to another side street, little more than a hallway. He used to live near here himself, in a tiny little apartment on 7th. The south of the ship had long been the unfashionable end, populated by low-rent, artistic types, as well as more than a few security officers, being close to their headquarters. Some government workers, too—their offices were predominantly in this part of the ship, on the second and third levels, clustered around the Bridge.

Gabelman's friend, a Tyson Enlopo, wasn't any of those. He was a Loafer, though that wasn't very remarkable; close to a quarter of the ship's population avoided work for extended periods. The government had tried mightily to curb this attitude for the last few years, in anticipation of landing several thousand people on Tau Prius III only to watch them starve to death. But the lessons hadn't stuck, at least not yet. Might take a few practice starvations first.

Hogg hit the buzzer of Enlopo's apartment. From outside, it looked like one of the doublewide units that were so coveted in this neighborhood. There was no immediate answer, so he buzzed again. Finally, the door opened to reveal a middle-aged man in a naval uniform. "Can I help you?" he asked, confused.

"I'm looking for Tyson Enlopo."

The man's brow furrowed. "No one by that name here."

Hogg blinked. "Well, I have him down as living at this address."

"Oh!" A flicker of comprehension crossed the man's face. "No, no. He moved. A couple weeks ago, I think. I don't know where, I'm afraid. Guess they haven't updated his address in the system?"

Hogg exhaled heavily. "I guess not. Do you know why he moved?"

The man swallowed. "No idea. This is a great apartment."

Hogg thanked the officer and left him in the doorway. He had a couple of different avenues for tracking down Enlopo, but couldn't see much point. He fully expected to get absolutely nothing out of an interview with the man. He checked the time. Another half hour left in his shift, easily killable with a meandering walk back to the office.

"Fuck it," he said. Something bothered him about this Enlopo and his sudden change of address. He opened up his terminal, and tapped out some commands.

DEPARTMENT OF JUSTICE

WARRANT REQUEST—COMMUNICATION DEVICE TRACE

SUBJECT: Tyson Enlopo
REQUESTING OFFICER: Sergeant Sinclair Hogg
REASON FOR REQUEST: Subject has incorrect address listed in both the ship's public database and security database. Contact with subject needed for investigation into murder of Ron Gabelman, deceased April 3rd, 239 A.L. Subject was known to be an acquaintance of Gabelman's.

DEPARTMENT OF JUSTICE

WARRANT REQUEST—COMMUNICATION DEVICE TRACE 903783343

SUBJECT: Tyson Enlopo
STATUS: APPROVED
JUSTICE OF PEACE NOTES: Attending officer is authorized to seek communication device trace for subject TYSON EN-LOPO. When contact with subject is made, officer is permitted to collect current address for ship records. Access to search private residences occupied by subject is explicitly NOT granted by this warrant.

Turnaround for the warrant was less than five minutes, but the terminal trace itself took almost half an hour. *Fucking IT.* He knew very well it was a 10-second chore for them.

Consequently, it was well past the end of his shift when Hogg finally tracked Enlopo down in his new and distinctly shabbier apartment. As Hogg suspected, Enlopo didn't know anything relevant to Gabelman's death, although the young man did have several impolite things to say about Hogg, security officers in general, and the sexual proclivities of recent members of his maternal lineage. Tired at the end of a long day, Hogg didn't spend long listening to the shrieking asshole, only vaguely gathering that Mr. Enlopo hadn't moved voluntarily. "Couldn't happen to a nicer guy, dick," Hogg said under his breath as he walked away.

Stein sat, hands clasped behind her head, staring at the wall. She had just confirmed that the surly woman's service request was actually in the system. Unusually, she could only access it by directly referencing the request ID. The service request refused to show up using the system's search and filtering features, or on the Big Board.

There was only one place she could think of where the system could be making this error. A pseudo-AI scanned each service request as it was submitted, correcting mis-categorizations and deleting duplicates as necessary. This pseudo-AI was pretty good—Stein hadn't known it to make mistakes before. Which wasn't to say that it wasn't *blamed* for making mistakes—blaming the computer was a healthy part of being human. But in Stein's opinion, most of that was unwarranted.

But she couldn't think of any other explanation here. Users couldn't edit the timestamp on their service requests, which meant this one was getting mangled somewhere else. She drummed her fingers on her desk, then pulled up the IT service request page on her terminal. *Filing a service request for a problem with the service requests.* This alone might cause the system to explode. She began filling in the form, looking down at her desk display, as she decided how to paraphrase this problem. "No Service Requests Found!" her desk reported in a friendly orange font. Her eyes widened.

She had filtered the desk to search for heating and cooling service requests reported from that specific room over the last week. She expanded the location to include most of the Annex. Some service requests popped up, including the two Gabelman had recently worked on. She expanded it to include everything south of 14th Street, which included the Annex and the entire aft—over a quarter of the ship in fact. Almost a hundred requests. She narrowed the search to the last day, which shortened the list to seventeen.

Looking over the list, Stein was surprised to see that she didn't recognize most of them. She had by no means an encyclopedic knowledge of the ship's heating and cooling complaint registry, but as the nominal day shift supervisor, she did see most of them. Most people on the ship worked from nine to three, and consequently most service requests were submitted during those hours. There were always a few submitted at night, which the skeleton and swing shifts handled when they could. But looking at this list, Stein was surprised to see the majority of these service requests were submitted in the evening, after she had clocked off for the day. Which was why she didn't recognize them. Her team hadn't handled them.

Thinking back, Stein realized she had seen very little work in the aft in the last week, or even in the last month. There were the calls Gabelman got sent on, but those were in the Annex, not the aft proper. She adjusted the location range to include only locations aft of 10th Street. The list of requests narrowed to thirteen. All of them submitted in the evening or overnight. She checked over the last week. The same pattern. And again over a month. Going back two months, the pattern returned to normal, with the majority of service requests again being filed during the daylight hours.

"That is fucking strange." She catalogued all the facts at hand, rotating them around in her mind, trying to piece them together. For the last month, it appeared that someone was manipulating service requests to keep her shift away from the aft of the ship.

She cancelled her IT service request, feeling unsettled. Something else was going on here, bigger than she understood. If someone had tampered with the service request pseudo-AI, they'd have to have IT support for that. Which meant the navy. A wave of paranoia washed over her; she suddenly got the distinct impression that she should have been a lot more subtle over the past few hours.

"Hang on. Fuck that," she said aloud. "I'm just doing my job." Stein looked at the time displayed on her desk. Quitting time. Actual quitting time even, not even a half hour late. And she wasn't going to let this stupid mystery eat into her time. "Unacceptable," she said, standing up quickly, knocking over the chair behind her, but not caring. Tired of mysteries, she left the office, wanting only to go home and do something simple and obvious.

"I don't know if I've ever heard you sound so enthusiastic," Sergei said. "I'd almost say you were glad to see me."

"Oh?" Stein said, smiling. She watched the young security man rotate his beer on the surface of the bar. They were sitting on stools pulled up to the bar in the Peregrine, a watering hole on the 3rd level. "The Ship's Oldest Pub," a sign above the bar proudly claimed, although Stein had heard that it held that record by only a couple of hours. She had called Sergei as soon as she left the office. "Long day at work, I guess."

"I'll bet. I heard your name mentioned today."

Stein's eyes widened. "About what?"

"You might be an emotionless monster," Sergei said, "but when a person is murdered around here, it's kind of a big deal."

Stein's shoulders sank. "Oh. That." She hoped her body language would communicate how little she wanted to talk about it.

Sergei didn't pick up what she was putting down. "I shared a trolley with Hogg this afternoon." He took a drink. "Do you think he was using? The kid I mean. Ron."

Stein chose her words carefully. "Nope. And if he did, he wasn't using a lot. I never noticed a thing. Not that he was a terribly social person."

Sergei took a long pull from his beer. "Hogg says the same thing. Wonders if the drugs were planted on him. I think he's a little detective-happy to be honest. Don't know why they haven't sent someone competent to take the case off his hands." Sergei flagged down the bartender and ordered another beer, Stein matching his pace. "He was on quite the rant. Apparently had to crawl across half the ship because someone's address was wrong in the database."

Stein considered relating the similar odd behavior she had seen in the service call database, but decided against it. Not the right topic for small talk. Not with a cop anyways.

It had been a dirty trick, approaching her out of uniform. A smile, and a pair of big friendly eyes. A damned dirty trick. If she had known he was a security officer, she wouldn't have looked twice at him. But with his charming earnestness, and her fluctuating loneliness waxing on that particular night, she did look twice, and then several times more. She hadn't bothered asking what he did. Didn't care. Too often the answer to that question was "Nothing," which always made her feel awkward. One encounter became four, and by the time she ran into him on the street, smiling his big goofy smile in his big ugly security uniform, it was too late. The hook had been set.

Her childhood antics had caused her to run afoul of security, but not enough to create any lasting ill-will. She thought they were jerks, but truthfully, she had thought everyone was a jerk at that stage of her life. It was later, during the Breeder thing, that it became harder. Peaceful protesters, wanting child allowances, beaten down by uniforms with clubs. Stein hadn't been hurt, but friends had. Things got bad after that, though Stein had mostly excused herself from that part of the fight, a decision which probably saved her life. Ever since then, she'd found it damned hard to look at a security officer without imagining a set of crosshairs superimposed on them.

Until she met one with dopey, puppy dog eyes.

Problems on the horizon though, just like always. He wanted more. More of her time, more of her thoughts, more of everything. She didn't. It would come to something bad and painful, eventually. Always did. But for now he was fun to share a beer with, and, occasionally, a bed.

But not someone to trust with crazy hypotheses about AI systems tampering with the maintenance database to inconvenience government workers. Instead she asked, "So, even the Security database is incorrect sometimes? Sergei, Sergei. Letting slip these chinks in your armor. People will stop fearing you soon."

Sergei snorted. "It happens. Not that I've ever seen it happen, but it must. People move. Addresses change. I don't even know how it updates, but it does. Any system built by man will break sometimes."

Stein silently assented, her day job a result of it. A sudden punch in the back of her shoulder announced the arrival of Bruce, and shortly thereafter, many more drinks.

"And that's why everything you believe in is wrong," Bruce concluded, three hours later.

Sergei nodded, his face composed. It wasn't the first time he had met Bruce, but he had been on his best behavior on that occasion. Less so tonight—Stein had been stifling laughter all evening watching Sergei's reactions to Bruce's antics.

"Fair enough. I guess I'll have to make some immediate changes in my life," Sergei said. He held up his glass, allowing Bruce to lustily collide his own with it. Stein smiled. *Maybe I'll keep him around a bit longer.*

Sergei's eyes drifted over the bar, to the mirrored wall with the stacks of bottles and glassware on it. He focused on something. Stein followed his gaze, but couldn't see what he was looking at.

"That prick can't even drink properly," he said.

"Who?"

He blinked in surprised, seeming to have forgotten where he was. "No one. Koller. Some asshole I work with." He jerked his head backwards. Stein looked behind them, seeing a burly looking man sitting against the back wall, staring at the table, a nearly full glass in front of him. "Real son of a bitch," Sergei continued. "Wouldn't know a good time if it sat on his face."

That sounded like most cops to her, but she kept that thought to herself. On her other side, Bruce, who rarely kept things to himself, was busy noisily licking the inside of his glass, trying to get the attention of the bartender.

Sergei tugged at the sleeve of Stein's shirt. "We have to go now," he said.

"What, why?" Stein asked, alarmed. She searched his face for clues, finding only a pair of twinkling eyes. She smiled. "Oh. That. Yeah, all right." She turned to Bruce. "We have to go now," she repeated loudly.

"What's all this I hear about you having to go?" Bruce asked, squinting at the pair.

"We have to go," they replied in unison. Stein giggled, her eyes widening, surprised at herself.

Bruce nodded, looking down at the new drink which had just arrived. "Well, it's a school night for me, too." He finished the drink in one swallow, then flagged down the bartender again. "So, I'll be here for awhile. You two have fun."

They stood up and began walking from the bar, Sergei casting another glance at his mopey friend in the back while Stein eyeballed her own. She felt a flicker of guilt leaving Bruce there. He had certainly left her alone many times, pursuing one of the many lady friends he'd had. He could very well have another one tonight. Still, that flicker of guilt lingered as she walked out, catching a final glance of him. Every now and then the massive walls that he carried around seemed to get a lot heavier.

"VAV 341-E15 is...at sixty-four percent. Hooray," Bruce called out over the terminal.

"Sixty-four percent," Stein confirmed, noting that down on her screen. "Delta of seventeen percent," she relayed to Curts, who was sitting at the other desk in the room.

"What eq-qu-qu-quipment number again?" Curts asked.

"Uhhhhhhhh. VAV 341-E15."

"Got it."

Stein looked up and stretched her arms out. She had arrived to work that morning to find Curts and a controls diagnostic waiting. Apparently Curts wanted to identify every busted sensor on board the ship, by yesterday. It was completely unnecessary, considering that of the thousands of problems they would identify, exactly zero would be fixed. Make-work of the very worst kind—work that someone made *her* do.

A controls diagnostic involved a technician physically inspecting every control sensor and actuator on every piece of heating and ventilation equipment on board the ship. They then communicated its current status back to Stein and Curts, who compared it to what the ship's central system was reading. A simple matter done once, a hair-tearing experience when multiplied by fourteen thousand sensors and five thousand actuators. A full month's worth of work, if they worked around the clock. Which she most assuredly would not.

The strangest thing about it was that Curts had stayed in the office assisting her for every minute of it, despite how fantastically dull the work was. Stein resented the implication of this—that she would potentially shirk the chore if he wasn't there. Curts had suggested that this diagnostic was particularly important, potentially relating to the ship's upcoming deceleration. Stein mentally called bullshit, knowing the laws of momentum didn't care one whit about how comfortably ventilated its projectiles were.

Curts had an awkward position, nominally reporting to a mayor who had no interest in what he did, spending most of his time around the navy guys who looked down on what he did. Responsible for every system on the ship that wasn't related to the naval operation of the vessel, which encompassed quite a bit, this had kept most of Curts' predecessors pretty busy. But Curts had lately spent most of his time liaising with the naval engineers, serving as the bridge between the two worlds, conducting joint work in anticipation of the Push. Stein had seen little evidence of what exactly Curts' work entailed, though if it meant he was generally around less, that was good enough for her.

Three in the afternoon finally rolled around, and the technicians began filtering back into the office. Those that did return were in a uniformly foul mood—many didn't even bother coming back, opting to head straight home or places less reputable. Curts loitered in Stein's office—really his office, she glumly conceded—double-checking something on his terminal. Stein left him there and went to change back into her non-orange clothes. In that sense, she was one of the fortunate ones, having not gotten dirty that day.

Bruce entered the locker room, facial muscles twitching. She knew he was putting it on but let him be. Truthfully, she was in no mood to talk either, about work or anything else. She had lost all interest in whatever M. Melson was hiding, and the strange booby traps he had planted there. The issue with the service requests still bothered her, but she wasn't in the mood for puzzle solving anymore. The only thing she was in the mood for, being away from here, was all she was hoping the evening provided. She exchanged a perfunctory greeting with Bruce, swapped some half-hearted insults directed at their stuttering ass of a boss, then left the maintenance office and went home.

Outside, she began walking in the direction of her apartment, wishing she could be there faster than her feet were capable of moving. As she rounded the corner onto 38th, she heard a voice calling, "Hey! Hey, uh, ma'am!"

She turned to see a girl walking over to her, all teeth and knees. Stein recognized her as the receptionist from the licensing office she had visited the previous day. "Oh, it's you, uh..." Stein began. "Miss...?"

"I'm Carrie," she said, coming to a stop in front of her.

"Nice to meet you. I'm Laura."

"Hi."

"Hi," Stein replied. Silence. Stein braced herself as the conversation swerved violently towards the ditch.

"So," Carrie began after a few more awkward seconds. "The reason I came to find you is I heard about Ron. That's awful."

Stein blinked. She'd only paid a passing glance at the news feeds that morning, and was mildly surprised to see that the news of Gabelman's death had only just broken that day. She'd assumed everyone else had found out about it when she did. "Yeah. Awful," she agreed. The conversation lurched and shuddered along.

Carrie bravely continued on. "So, when I read about what happened this morning, it got me to thinking. You know how yesterday you were asking about that request? The one Ron was working on?"

"What about it?"

"Well, it's weird. Greg didn't make that request. My boss. At least I don't think so. Because when Ron came to check it out, he asked for a different name."

Stein's eyes widened fractionally. *Oh, lord. No more puzzles, dammit. Not today.* "What name?"

"I think it was Arlo Samson?" Carrie said. "I don't know how it's spelled."

Stein recognized the name. Arlo Samson was the original caller for the service request. She remembered it from the Big Board when she'd dispatched Ron to deal with it. That was why she had done a double take when she saw Greg Watson's name appear on the service request yesterday; it had been changed.

"I had no idea who that was," Carrie continued. "I'm pretty new. But I asked one of the other girls there, and they said he had been promoted six months ago and is working in the Bridge now."

"And you told that to Ron?"

"Yeah. When he left, he said he'd go ask around the Bridge." She blushed. "He looked like a nice guy, you know?"

The corner of Stein's mouth twitched up. The girl thought Ron was cute. *Wow. Way to go Ron.*

"So, I thought if you were his friend maybe you should know what I saw him doing that day. Maybe it'd help you somehow."

"Did you tell security about this?"

"I didn't think to. Do you think I should?"

"Maybe," Stein drummed her fingers on her pant leg. She was feeling considerably more awake now. "Wait. Did anyone from security talk to you at all yesterday? Like come by and interview you or anyone at your office?"

Carrie shook her head. "Nope. That's kind of weird, isn't it?"

Stein frowned. "Not necessarily," she said, lying.

"Do you think I should go talk to them now?"

"I don't think so. I'm sure they'll come talk to you when they're ready," Stein said. The important part of the conversation had ended at that point, with Stein not really paying attention as they exchanged banalities for another few seconds before making their goodbyes.

She walked away, her mind racing. That was a lot of mistakes to crop up all of a sudden in the service request system. Was someone trying to conceal what happened on Ron Gabelman's last day? And why wasn't security investigating his murder? Retracing a victim's steps before they were murdered seemed like pretty basic police work to her.

She looked up to realize she had been wandering in the wrong direction and stopped to reorient herself. She was no longer dealing with a puzzle, a broken widget to diagnose and repair. Definitely much bigger than that. She was reluctant to believe in conspiracies, having never observed anything that couldn't be explained by small-scale human selfishness and stupidity. She looked back in the direction she had come. There was a person who had no problem believing in crazy far-reaching conspiracies. She picked up her terminal to send a message to Bruce, then hesitated, looking at the terminal with mistrust. *Now that was definitely being paranoid.*

She tucked the terminal back in her webbing, setting off for home again. Maybe a little paranoia would be healthy for the time being. Besides, it felt more appropriate to conduct this sort of conversation in the dead of night.

There was a reason they had sent Stein and not him this way on their first time through, Bruce realized as he came crashing through the ceiling of Maurice Melson's mystery studio. As the dust settled, he rolled over on his back and took an inventory of his various parts and organs, eventually deciding that they were all in place and in working order. Also noteworthy, his sudden and wildly unorthodox entrance into the room hadn't triggered any booby traps. He sat up. He had scanned the room before opening the damper, firing every type of useful electromagnetic radiation he could from the safety of the ducting, looking for anything dangerous. Finding nothing, he created his own danger via his rapid room penetration technique and the sudden stop at the end it necessitated.

He hadn't told Stein he was coming back here—it was apparent his colleague had lost most of her interest in these sorts of hijinks in the wake of Gabelman's death. She had her responsibilities. She never said it, but she liked being the boss. And he was proud of her. It was a tough job, and she did it well.

It wasn't for him though; it required a certain amount of effort that he didn't like to apply in public settings. Effort attracted attention. He had once snapped a kid's arm in half during a wrestling match, thanks to effort. That was awkward, but less so than when he did it again, three months later, to the same kid. Very embarrassing. The kid's dad was furious; he had come running out onto the floor, yelling at the coach, yelling at the referee, yelling at Bruce. Raising his fists. Everyone agreed that when Bruce broke the dad's arm, it was justifiably self-defense, but that it was probably a good idea to quit wrestling for a while. He quit a lot of other things not long after.

So, he let Stein do the trying, while he assisted with the much safer chore of making clever observations from the sidelines. He saved his real effort for when everyone else went to bed. Stein tagged along with that sometimes, but she had always been a bit of a fair-weather burglar. She was in it for the fun.

Although perhaps not containing a lot of fun, Bruce was still convinced there was *something* interesting going on in this particular room. He had been considering what he knew about Maurice Melson over the last couple of days and decided that it was an alias used by someone in the navy. Someone fairly senior, possibly within the IT group, capable of creating false records in the ship's database. And this person owned this room to keep something hidden in it—something he couldn't keep in a place linked to his real identity. Bruce concluded that it was something embarrassing, probably illegal, and if so, very valuable, if only as blackmail material. And assuming he hadn't crushed it when he had entered the room, Bruce desperately wanted to find out what it was.

Moving gingerly now, Bruce stood up and slowly looked around the room. It was bigger than he had imagined it, or at least bigger than Stein had described it. There were shelving units along three of the four walls, and a doorway that led to the closet that Stein must have used to access the service tunnels. He frowned. Which shelving unit did Stein think she had jostled to set off the booby trap? Where was the booby trap for that matter? Above the ceiling space seemed likely. Retrieving a chair from the far end of the room, Bruce positioned it under the hole he had just made and peered up above the false ceiling, using his terminal as a light. Nothing interesting up there.

What would a blinder booby trap be used for anyways? It would only be useful for momentarily stunning someone, or maybe scaring them away. But he didn't see what use it would have in an unguarded room against a dedicated thief. If Stein had been so inclined, she could have set it off, blinded herself, waited for her vision to recover, and then kept stealing whatever she wanted. Unless the room was monitored, there would have been no way to prevent her from doing just that, or, for that matter, him doing that right now. Of course, if the room was being monitored, he was already caught. But Stein would have been caught, as well. "So, probably not monitored," Bruce said aloud, daring the room to prove him wrong.

He began his search, unwrapping the cases and dust covers off of the various items on the shelves. Nothing that remarkable—he didn't even bother with his value scanner. Just old art supplies and several pieces of fairly mediocre, or fairly fantastic, art—he freely admitted he didn't have an eye for the stuff. What he did have an eye for was blinding booby traps, and he noted a complete lack of them. Having checked everything on or under the shelves and around the room, he began systematically shaking and rattling every piece of furniture. Nothing. Not even any signs of a booby trap mechanism—no lines or springs or sensors or pits in the ground with foliage over them.

"What the fucking fuck?" he asked the room, spinning around. Frustrated, he began pacing back and forth in a grid, inspecting the grayish ceiling tiles, looking for anything out of order. He had decided that whatever Stein had seen was much smaller than the blinders he was familiar with. Maybe something embedded in the support grid of the suspended ceiling itself. Something small like a button, or a crevice, or...that enormous meter long gash.

Running almost atop a member of the support grid, and mostly camouflaged by it, lay a thin black gash in the ceiling. Standing on his toes, Bruce could see that both the ceiling tiles and support grid were completely cut through. He retrieved the chair, moved it over to the spot with the gash, and stepped up, cautiously moving the slashed ceiling tile out of the way. Above him, he could see the rough rock surface of the ship's frame, with a matching black gash.

Bruce scratched his ear. This mystery had become a completely different one, and one which had considerably less likelihood of producing valuable loot. Instead of loot, he had a mysterious gash in the ceiling—and a fresh one. Something had cut through here from the floor above. But, what? There was nothing on board the ship that he knew of that could cut through that much rock in one sweep. Back when the ship was constructed, the crews hollowing out the asteroid had used fusion torches to cut chunks out of the ship—those would clearly do the job, but none had been left on board the Argos when it pushed off. Indeed, a tool which could casually punch a hole through the hull of a spaceship was a real fucking liability for the people who had to live on that spaceship. Which meant someone would had to have built it.

"What the fucking fuck?" Bruce asked again. The room continued to offer no answers.

Stein knocked on the door as quietly as she could.

"What?" a voice yelled, muffled by the closed door. She knocked again, this time louder. The door slid open, revealing Bruce, naked. "Who the hell knocks?" he asked.

Stein blinked, and directed her gaze upwards at Bruce's less objectionable upper half. "Just let me in," she said, walking past the man before he could answer.

Bruce allowed the door to close, then turned to look at her, and the bulky brown coat she was wearing. "Why are you dressed like a bag of meat?"

Stein ignored him and took off the formless jacket she had slipped on earlier, hoping to disguise herself from any watching sensors. She considered asking Bruce to wear it himself, but she knew from long experience that if she called attention to his nakedness, he would just do something to make her more uncomfortable. Tumbling probably. Instead, she asked, "Do you know who Arlo Samson is?"

Bruce placed his index fingers on his temples and rubbed them around. "Can't say as I do."

"Wanna do me a favor?"

"Without hearing what it is first? Absolutely."

Stein smiled. Forcing her eyes to look at his face, she told Bruce everything she had learned about the altered service requests, the strange timestamps, and finally, the critical meeting with Carrie the receptionist. "I'm getting the distinct impression that someone is trying to keep people, or at least me and my team, out of the aft of the ship."

"The timestamps on the service requests..." Bruce began.

"For maintenance in the aft of the ship," Stein finished his sentence. "The timestamps have been altered so that they won't come up during the day shift. They get delayed until the swing or skeleton shift, at which point those crews handle them."

"Why would anyone want to keep us out of the aft, but let those maniacs back there?" Bruce asked.

"No idea. But I think that it's been happening for at least the last month. Then yesterday, the same thing started happening for service requests in the annex."

"And you think that's why Gabelman got murdered? Because some bureaucrat observed him doing his job? I know those lazy bastards don't like being made to look bad, but that sounds a bit farfetched."

Stein shook her head. "No, listen. He got assigned to a pair of service requests in the Annex. When he got there, he found out one of them was called in by someone called Arlo Samson. Arlo Samson used to work in the Annex until he changed offices a few months ago. The service request system had filled in his old address automatically, and he never noticed when he submitted it."

"So what?"

"So, Ron attends the call and figures out the address was incorrect. He finds Arlo Samson has moved to the Bridge somewhere."

"In the middle of the aft." Bruce turned away from Stein and began pacing back and forth, making a show of thinking. "Okay, let me get this straight. You think that if the system had got his address correct, the timestamp would have been manipulated to steer the request away from us?"

"That's right."

Bruce sat down. "And you think security is in on this?"

"Do you have to sit like that?" Stein said, looking at the ceiling. A quick glance showed the man had crossed his legs at the knee, one leg swinging jauntily. Looking back up, she continued, "Yeah, I do think security is up to something. They don't appear to be investigating Ron's death too thoroughly."

Bruce crossed and uncrossed his legs as he thought. Eventually, he leaned back and said, "Okay. Let's think this through a bit. Say that there is someone on board this ship that wants to keep people from snooping around the aft. This person—or persons, I guess—would have to be a fairly senior security or government or IT guy. So, question number one is, why would they do this?"

Stein held up a hand in front of her, angled to block specific parts of Bruce. "No idea. The engines and fuel pods are the most sensitive things in that part of the ship, but we wouldn't go near those anyways. Most of the aft is City Hall, government offices, and crappy apartments. Can you think of anything?"

"Oh, holy shit, yes." Bruce said. "M. Melson's studio? With the mystery blinder? Guess who was there again tonight?"

"You, pantsless."

"Partial credit," Bruce confirmed. "And you didn't see a blinder. You saw a fusion torch." Bruce explained the scar in the ceiling that he saw.

That explained at least part of the mystery, the part that didn't have a fusion torch tell her about Vlad. "Of course," she said. "I am so stupid. That was in the aft too. How did I forget that?"

Bruce nodded. "On 6th."

Stein drummed her fingers on the desk. "Okay. So, someone—hell, let's not kid ourselves, this must be a lot of people—is doing something weird in the south of the ship. Cutting through rock. Why?"

Bruce shrugged. "Because fuck that rock, that's why."

Stein laughed, then stared at the floor, slowly shaking her head. "Yeah. I can't think of anything either."

"Which I guess brings us to our next question: so what?" Bruce said. "I mean, do we even do anything about this? Aside from the insatiable sense of vengeance you must feel for what happened to a valued team member, why exactly do we care about this? Because it kind of looks like something people are willing to kill for. I think that makes this interesting as hell, but I've got well-known problems. So, using you as a better barometer of sense, why do you care?"

Stein frowned. It wasn't because of some deep-felt connection to Gabelman—she was already struggling to remember what the kid looked like. But someone was doing something on her ship and wasn't telling her about it. She couldn't believe she felt tired earlier this day. Until this was solved, it was going to drive her up the wall. She hated secrets, despised locked doors.

Stein eventually reached a conclusion. "Because I don't like being jerked around, and I can feel my leash getting tighter and tighter. That's why I want to do something."

Bruce seemed to weigh that statement carefully. "Like a couple of private detectives?"

"Yes. Don't you think that'd be fun? Solving murders? Running around with magnifying glasses and solving crimes, just like we always talked about?"

"Fuck, yes!" Bruce said, genuine excitement in his voice. He uncrossed his legs and sat up, flopping about excitedly. "We are so doing this! Okay, what do you want me to do?"

Stein swallowed. "You'll have noticed that our respected and farsighted chief engineer has just assigned us several weeks of tedious work?"

"Yes, sir. I will notice that, sir," Bruce replied.

"It might be nothing, but I wonder now if Curts isn't in on this as well." She looked at the ceiling, collecting her thoughts. "I mean, he was acting strangely about the service requests. Told me not to look into them. And when I did, the next day he springs this little chore on us. And babysat me all day."

"He's also kind of a wiener," Bruce observed. "That's enough reason right there to rough him up a little to see what he knows."

"Heh. Or we could not do that, and do something smart." She paused, as Bruce held up his nose and pouted. "Here's my thinking. If Curts is assigning me make-work to keep me from investigating this any further, I'm probably going to have him all over me for the next little while. Which means I need you to look up this Arlo Samson and retrace what Gabelman was looking at that day."

"You want me to recreate the same series of events which led to a man's death," Bruce stated.

Stein grimaced. "I'm aware this plan has some flaws."

"Oh, good. It'd be rude of me if I had to point them out to you."

"I was hoping you could do everything Gabelman did that day, and then at the end, omit the 'dying gruesomely' part."

"I see." Bruce sat back on his couch. "Okay. It's done."

"Are you sure?"

"Totally done. I've already got a couple ideas."

"Yeah, this is Bruce. Damper 2X-333-uh-3 is at, uh, three percent," Bruce called into his terminal.

"You mean Damper 4H-993-L, right, Bruce?" Stein's voice queried through the terminal.

"Uh, yes. That's what I said."

"Copy."

Bruce was nowhere near either of those dampers. He was instead in the garden well, walking down the center of America, amongst a crowd of revelers dressed in horse costumes in the opening stages of what would become a lengthy orgy. For better or worse, Bruce would be long gone before anything interesting broke out, but for now it provided excellent camouflage. Should anyone be watching, being surrounded by a hundred or so people in costumes rubbing up on each other was a great way to appear uninteresting.

The ship-wide diagnostic had remained waiting for them when they arrived at the office that morning, Curts still there, hovering over Stein's every move. This time, Stein had steered Bruce to a rarely visited corner of the ship to trudge through the diagnostic process there. And as they had discussed, he was doing nothing of the sort, radioing back completely fictional results while he made his way through this slow-burning pool of phony equine delight on his way towards the Bridge.

Located just beyond the aft edge of the garden well, the Bridge was home to the seat of the civilian government, and in the levels above it, much of the control apparatus for the actual operations of the ship. Back when cavemen were sailing their ocean liners around the Earth, there was an obvious purpose in putting the men in charge someplace up high, where the visibility was best. But as there wasn't a great deal to see in space, there was little purpose in putting the ship's brains on its outer surface, and, consequently, the control apparatus of the Argos was buried right in its heart. As anticipated, over time the decks underneath the proper control room had become a type of city hall and was where the elected officials rummaged around in the shit and mud of Argosian politics. Although the civilian government had no direct control over ship systems, the whole general area still retained the name 'Bridge.'

As he approached the Bridge, Bruce reached into his pocket and pulled out a little bottle. Gently opening it so as not to spill the contents, he reached in and fumbled around, trying to grab one of the brightly multicolored pills from within. After a couple of tries, he eventually fished out a bright red pill and carefully recapped the bottle. The color of the pill would reveal its function to anyone who saw it: Brash. Bruce looked at it sitting in his palm, considering it for a second, before he reopened the bottle and pulled out another red pill. He tossed the pair down his throat and swallowed quickly.

"Whooo. Yeah. Everything is a gooooood idea!" he said to himself as quietly as he could. His plan was to figure out where Arlo Samson was and then look at the heating and cooling systems in that area. The fact that this wasn't much of a plan at all had started to bother him on the walk over, which was what necessitated the chemical backbone infusion.

Reaching the main entrance of the Bridge, Bruce marched in the front door and approached the reception desk. "I'm looking for Arlo Samson's office," he said, choosing the direct approach.

"Sure," the receptionist replied. "I'll just call him now."

"No, no, don't do that. I need to go to his office. There's a problem with his heat." Bruce looked at the young man, and realized he hadn't blinked in a long time. He blinked. And then once more, just to set the fellow at ease. "I'd have gone straight to see him, but his address got messed up. Was wondering if you knew where he sat?"

"Oh, I see," the receptionist said. "Okay, he's on the second floor, office 238. You can take the stairs just back there."

Bruce blinked again, then launched himself across the room. *This is going great.* He noticed a bulky guy standing in an office doorway on the other side of the reception foyer, studying him closely. Bruce gave him a friendly nod, and then a blink for good measure.

The Bridge was one of the few places on board the ship where civilians could access areas above the fourth level. The mayor's office itself was all the way up on the eighth level, although within the Bridge complex itself, this was confusingly called the fifth floor.

Bruce climbed the stairs to the second floor. Walking down the hall, he peered into offices, seeing various mid-level mandarins busy doing absolutely nothing. Some of them looked up from their desks as he walked past, startled to see him in his bright maintenance coveralls. He distributed some cheerful blinks and kept walking. *This was a really good idea.* He congratulated himself on the foresight he displayed in agreeing to it.

Bruce found office 238 with its door open and entered to see a man at work over his desk. Arlo Samson was in his forties, slender, balding prematurely. He looked profoundly unhappy, like a man who never understood jokes. "Can I help you?" Arlo asked.

"Arlo Samson?" Bruce asked. The man didn't make any indication that this was incorrect, so Bruce continued. "You had a problem with the heat?"

Arlo swallowed, his eyes widening. He stayed frozen for a few more seconds before he quickly shook his head. "Nope, no problem here. I think you must be mistaken." He looked around the room, as if checking the temperature of the room by sight. "See, perfectly fine."

"Oh, I didn't mean now," Bruce said. "I meant a couple days ago. You had a problem with the heat a couple days ago."

Arlo tried to maintain a blank face, though he did a poor job of it. "Nope. I haven't had any problems with the heat in here that I remember." He paused, studying Bruce's face. "Now, if you'll excuse me, I've got a lot of work to do."

Bruce shot Arlo in the chest. Stunned at his own rapid movement, Bruce froze, his eyes flickering from the unconscious form of Arlo Samson to the stun pistol that had emerged in his right hand. "That was...brash." He reslotted the pistol under his arm, where it had been concealed in a pocket underneath his tool webbing. He turned around to see the door yawning wide open. Startled, he hurried over and closed it, leaning against it heavily. "Boy, I sure hope stunners are as quiet as I think they are."

After a few seconds passed without anyone inquiring why he had shot a man, Bruce crossed the room again and grabbed Arlo under the shoulders. He laid him on the floor behind his desk and looked up. Realizing the desk had no front panel, that the top surface was partially transparent, and that Arlo was still completely visible to anyone entering the room or even walking by casually, Bruce grabbed and hauled him over to the wall the door was on, rolling the unconscious bureaucrat into a nook, out of sight.

Things were still going great, but maybe, Bruce decided, a bit less great than before. As he recalled, stun shots left people unconscious for twenty minutes or so. They also had a nasty habit of causing heart attacks, but he was glad to see that that had not appeared to happen here. He'd only had to use a pistol once before in his life, eleven years earlier. He didn't recall it being so much fun, though he didn't believe he was as incredibly high at the time.

What would Gabelman have done now? Excepting the fact that Ron probably hadn't shot Mr. Samson in the chest, Bruce was now in roughly the same situation Gabelman would have been in three days earlier—in a client's office investigating a complaint of too much heat. Well, one obvious place to check was the thermostat in the room. Bruce checked it against his own sensor on his webbing. No problem there. He looked at the main diffuser, then pried that off and looked at the damper in the vent beyond. No problems there either.

Bruce then realized he wasn't specifically looking for a heating problem. He was supposed to be looking for whatever it was that Gabelman saw, something that he wasn't supposed to see, while he was investigating a heating problem. Bruce looked around Arlo's office. He poked and prodded at various surfaces on and around Arlo's desk, not finding anything of interest. Arlo Samson appeared to be a government worker of middling importance, whose sole job was managing slightly less important government workers. Bruce couldn't even tell what department the man worked in. A few minutes of poking around convinced Bruce that nothing Arlo Samson did was of interest to anyone. Nothing worth killing over.

A knock on the door. A second later, it slid open to reveal a middle aged woman, who looked at Bruce in surprise. "Oh! Is Arlo here?"

"He had to step out," Bruce replied.

"Oh." The woman looked unsure about that for a bit, before saying. "Okay. I'll just drop this on his desk then." She entered the room, terminal in hand and walked over to Arlo's desk.

Bruce sighed, and walked around behind her, closing the door as she reached the desk. She turned around, an annoyed and self-important look on her face as she saw Bruce blocking the exit. Her eyes drifted to the corner where Arlo's body was heaped. "Oh!" she said before being stunned to the floor.

Bruce surveyed the room, and finding nowhere better, hauled the woman over and deposited her on top of Arlo. He stood up, wiping his sleeve across his brow. *Detective work is hard.*

The next place Gabelman would go if he couldn't find a problem here would be the air balancer servicing this area. Bruce checked his terminal and found the air balancer down the hall from Samson's office. It looked like it was set correctly. Bruce left the office and walked down the hall a short way, where he stopped, looked up at the ceiling, and popped out the access panel. There was the air balancer. It looked completely normal. As he was stretching up to replace the panel, he saw an older gentleman come down the hall and stop in front of Arlo Samson's door. "Oh, for fuck's sake," Bruce said under his breath. He hurriedly set the panel down and jogged down the hall as the man entered the office.

A minute later, Bruce re-emerged from the office, locking the door behind him this time. For a wienery little guy, Arlo Samson certainly was popular. Bruce reset the access panel into place. So, he had committed three assaults, and found absolutely nothing. A half hour ago, he had felt on the cusp of uncovering an enormous ship-wide conspiracy, but now it dawned on him that he might in fact be a psychopath. This troubled him.

"Well, in light of the fact that I can't go backwards," he said, steeling himself, and looked up. Onwards and upwards. If Gabelman had retraced all these steps and still had not tracked down the heating problem, he would visit the fan room for this section of the ship, which was on the third floor. Bruce found the staircase and made his way upstairs, managing not to incapacitate anyone along the way. Following his terminal's directions, he found the fan room and entered it.

The fan room was tight and cramped, an awkwardly shaped space dominated by a series of enormous fans enclosed in a mass of twisting ductwork. Within these ducts, huge coils heated or chilled the air as it was distributed to the surrounding rooms.

Bruce crawled into, over, and around the fans and ductwork, looking for anything out of the ordinary. The fans looked fine. No dead bodies or ancient secrets or anything. He did find a multi-tool on the floor underneath a duct, identical to the one secured in his own tool webbing. There was nothing to indicate that it was Gabelman's, but there was nothing to *not* indicate that it was either. He checked the time on his terminal. He had zapped Samson and the woman again when he had knocked out the old man. That meant he had another ten minutes or so until they woke up, unless it had killed them, in which case he had quite a bit longer.

In the back of the room, set on the floor, was an enormous wall panel off its mounts. Bruce walked over to examine it, leaning it away from the wall it concealed. Behind it lay a massive hinged access hatch, much bigger than anything he had ever seen before, set into a steel bulkhead wall. Normally held in place by large fasteners, Bruce could see most of them hanging loose. He loosened the rest of the fasteners and swung the hatch open.

Behind the hatch, a dark cavern. Turning on his terminal light, he directed the beam into the darkened space. It was room-sized, a bit smaller than the room he was in now, and cramped by an enormous piece of heavy machinery sitting right in the center. He stepped into the cavity and looked closer at the equipment, still not recognizing it.

The room smelled, oil and metal and something acrid. Moving around, he could see the machinery looked like someone had carved an enormous S out of incredibly thick metal. After circling it once, he decided it was actually two interlocking C's. Each half of the machine—each C— was braced by enormous pistons. Flecks of corrosion covered the surface, but after looking closer, Bruce could see scratch marks, as well. It looked like it had been scrubbed clean recently. Each half of the mechanism was supported by massive metal pillars extending out through either side of the cavity. Bruce recognized those as the ship's main structural members, laid out along the length of the vessel like ribs.

For all the mysteries the room did contain, notably absent was the secret hiding spot of a cabal of assassins who possessed the answer to Gabelman's death. Disappointed, Bruce snapped a couple of pictures of the mechanism with his terminal, then stepped outside to cover his tracks.

"Thanks, Forth," Stein said, noting down another set of figures on the desk display in front of her. Her eyes lingered on the clock. It had been almost twenty minutes since she had checked in with Bruce. He would be in the midst of doing something pretty stupid right about then. Hopefully, Curts hadn't noticed she had stopped using Bruce, and he hadn't seemed to—he had been busy tapping out messages on his own terminal for the last few minutes.

He looked up at her just then, seemingly startled by her staring back at him. He smiled thinly and asked, "S-s-sorry about that. How's it going?"

"Okay," she said. "Been making good pace." Seeing a chance to stall and buy Bruce some more time, she tapped the clock on the desk display. "Might use a break though. Could go for a quick walk to work out the kinks."

Curts nodded slowly, then stood up and moved behind her, looking down at the data she had been gathering. "Sounds like a plan. But how about we finish this next batch of p-points first, okay? That'll t-take...what? Another ten minutes?"

Stein suppressed a low growl. "Yeah, about that. Okay. No problem." Curts patted her on the shoulder and returned to his chair as she began ordering her troops around to the next batch of control points. They were at a perfectly good stopping point as near as she could tell. But if Curts wanted to micromanage, she wasn't going to rock the boat. Not today.

The two security men who found him in the fan room evidently hadn't found the pile of unconscious bureaucrats first, or they would have had their weapons drawn when they entered. Bruce would later conclude that this meant they were guarding the fan room specifically, or at least had sensors nearby that were. It was probably how they had found Gabelman.

Bruce didn't have his weapon drawn either, but he did have the enormous plastic wall panel in his hands, which served first as a useful method of concealment while he did arm himself, and then as a shield during the brief and haphazard firefight which followed. Emerging victorious from the gunplay, Bruce spun his pistol around on his finger. *That was exciting.* He hadn't had anyone shoot back at him for a long time. This was probably a good sign that his welcome was worn out, and along with the slight twinge of fear which signified the wearing off of his Brash, he decided that was enough reason to go ahead and make his escape. Stepping over the unconscious security officers, he exited the fan room and jogged down the hall towards the main staircase.

At the bottom of the stairs, Bruce saw another security officer waiting, and cheerfully shot him in the face. He then ran down the stairs two at a time, waved to the young man at the reception desk as he sprinted by, and gave him one last blink for old time's sake.

"Hey, Bruce? You got that reading on VAV-4H-340-20 yet?" Stein's voice, sounding distant over the terminal. Bruce snatched it from his pocket as he ran towards the escalators half a block away.

"Yes, I got it right here. It's fuck all percent, sir."

"Ahhhhhh, gotcha. Forty-five percent."

"Can't talk for long, chief," Bruce said as he reached the escalator bank. He pushed a couple of people out of his way as he descended. "Fan room on Bridge third floor. Behind the south wall panel," he gasped into the terminal as he reached the bottom of the escalator. He ran around the bank of escalators to go down another floor, trying to think of how to describe the mechanism he had seen in the cavity beyond. Suddenly, it hit him, the device and its purpose rendered clearly in his mind. He blurted a single word into the terminal before the sizzling sound of gunfire cut him off.

A cloud of dust erupted in the wall beside him as a cluster of charged particles smacked into it. Two more sizzling sounds and clouds of dust bracketed him before he dove forward, rolling onto the escalator.

He gracelessly descended to the second level in a series of bumps and tumbles. The terminal fumbled out of his hands and bounced across the street. He regained his feet and scrambled after it, more gunshots impacting the ground beside him. The terminal danced and skittered away from him, evading his clutching hands, before he finally was able to scoop it up and turned again, running to the other side of the escalator bank. Here, he stopped and waited.

The security officer on his heels rounded the corner of the escalator bank and gaped like a fish for a second before he caught a blast right in the chest. Bruce mentally applauded his cool hand as he ran down the final escalator to the first level. From here, he picked his way down familiar side streets and corridors in a roughly northeasterly direction, heading to the dankest part of the ship he knew. This area had had its security sensors obliterated long ago, so that by the time the next security officer cautiously set foot on the first level, the big man had effectively disappeared.

"Bruce? Bruce?" Stein said, staring at her terminal accusingly, blaming it for the dropped connection. It was therapeutic, but a frivolous act. She knew it was Bruce who had stopped talking.

She ran Bruce's words over again in her mind. It sounded like he was asking to shut the power off for some piece of equipment in the Bridge fan room. But Stein couldn't tell what specifically. He was pretty excited about it, whatever it was, but whether that was about Gabelman or his own easily excitable nature, she couldn't figure. What she did know was that he was probably in trouble.

Stein looked up at Curts, who was staring back at her, wide-eyed. "What was that about?" he finally asked, a forced edge to his casual tone.

Stein looked down at the desk, trying to mask her expression. "Bruce being weird," she said, which was normally a fairly conclusive explanation.

She wasn't sure there was much she could do to help Bruce at the moment. And she wasn't in any danger herself—she hadn't actually done anything. But as Curts continued staring at her, her eyes drifted over to the terminal clutched in his hands, the terminal he had been rapidly tapping out messages on over the last few minutes. It hit her. *He knew.* He had been dragging out the diagnostic process, stalling for time. But stalling for what?

Not wanting to find out, she stood up and walked past Curts towards the door. "Where are you going?" Curts asked, standing suddenly as she passed him. She ignored him and broke into a jog. This was going to look suspicious as hell if it turned out she was wrong. And even if Bruce had been caught, she could simply plead she knew nothing about his antics. *I simply thought my team member was assisting with the sensor diagnostics, Officer. Now that you mention it, he has been acting unstable lately, yes.*

When she reached the door her ruminations on cowardly betrayals were cut short when she spotted the security van, a block away and moving towards her. Free of rails, and only allowed on the first level, they were permitted to be used by few people, usually for cargo. The smaller, faster vehicles were used exclusively by security, one of which was rapidly heading in Stein's direction now. A bit too much of a coincidence for Stein, she turned the other direction and broke into a sprint, no longer mindful of looking suspicious.

Behind her, she heard shouts as the security van accelerated, plowing its way through a population unaccustomed to avoiding traffic. A loud thump behind her announced that someone hadn't gotten out of the way fast enough. Stein looked back to see a pair of security officers exiting the van, one yelling at the person he had just struck, the other chasing Stein. As she ducked around the corner, Stein silently thanked the man who had bounced off the front of the security van, and in doing so, bought her that valuable time. And himself some broken ribs, judging by the way he was bleating.

Two blocks down the street, Stein ducked inside a pressurization-fan room, where she knew there would be an access point for a utility pipe-chase. Hurling herself to hands and knees, she scrambled into the tiny crawlway. These spaces were completely unnavigable to anyone who didn't regularly work in them and only marginally less confusing to someone who did. By the time she heard the security officer enter the room behind her, she was already out of sight behind the first turn.

A few minutes of frantic crawling passed before she remembered to turn off her terminal to prevent security from using it to trace her. Several more minutes of more labored crawling passed before she stopped for the second and final time, this time over a metal panel set into the floor. Popping it up revealed a space not much larger than herself. She rolled into this, then carefully reset the cover in its spot above her, sealing herself off in a secret coffin, alone in the dark.

Whether he had been preoccupied or simply lying, Security Chief Hatchens had yet to contact Harold since their first meeting, when he had breezily passed on the news of Kevin's death. What little Harold had learned since then was thanks to the news feeds, though judging from the lack of useful information they had, it seemed Hatchens wasn't talking to them much either. Most of their content consisted of artistic reinterpretations of the murder, none of which Harold found terribly helpful. Or tasteful.

After a day of waiting, Harold finally decided to go to Kevin's apartment himself. Kevin didn't have any relatives to bestow his belongings to, and Harold supposed he should go there to safeguard anything of value before the government packed it all off to the recyclers. He might be obligated to in fact; he realized there was a good chance he may actually be the boy's next of kin himself.

A block away from Kevin's apartment Harold stopped, a thick security officer blocking the door. Harold hesitated and considering turning back for a moment, until the officer swiveled his meaty neck around and looked straight at him, at which point Harold gritted his teeth and continued on his way. As he approached, the officer leaned inside the open door and said something to an unseen figure inside. A moment later, Chief Hatchens stepped out and moved to intercept Harold before he could reach the door. "I'm afraid you can't come in right now, Doc," Hatchens said, placing his own bulky frame between Harold and the apartment. "This is a crime scene."

Harold looked over the security chief's shoulder to Kevin's front door. It was open, but from this angle he couldn't see very far inside. "I thought his body was found on the first deck?" he asked. "Why's this a crime scene?"

"Because I said so," Hatchens said in a tone meant to end conversations. An uneasy moment passed between the two men. Hatchens cracked a thin smile. "Come on. I don't tell you how to do your job, Doc."

Harold stared back at Hatchens' face and its display of false mirth. "I'm the next of kin," he said, guessing. "I've got a right to go in there."

Nothing changed on the man's face, but Harold could feel the security officer working through the implications of that. "You're right," Hatchens said finally. "I'll personally ensure that nothing is disturbed beyond what needs to be for the sake of our investigation. I don't think it'll be much longer. I'll let you know when we're done."

Harold grunted something which he hoped would be interpreted as sounding appreciative and left the security man. Although he had always kept his distance, he had never held any specific ill will for the security department, and had always been suspicious of those who did. *Students and assholes, with student and asshole theories.* Even here, he knew Hatchens was well within his rights; it was entirely legitimate for them to secure Kevin's apartment to conduct their investigation. But he was starting to get a sense of what the students and assholes were on about.

The next day he awoke to find a message informing him that security had cleared out of the apartment and Harold could attend to Kevin's belongings as he saw fit. When he arrived at the apartment a half hour later, Harold found the front door closed, the area completely vacated of thick people.

As he'd guessed, the door unlocked for him without incident. He watched it slide open, revealing the simple two room apartment within. He stepped inside and allowed the door to close behind him. It was quiet. Harold felt like an intruder—he had never been there without Kevin.

After he was hatched, Kevin had been placed in the care of the ship's social services department, legally an orphan. Which wasn't a huge problem for Harold's work, as he had essentially unlimited access to Kevin throughout his childhood so that he could continue his work.

And that work ended up going very well. Kevin was a remarkable boy, smart as hell, good in school, sociable, and well adjusted as could be. He had even made it into the navy. The antithesis of every stereotype of canned babies, Kevin was the perfect poster child for Harold's work, even if he hadn't wanted to be.

There was more to it than work of course. Harold's involvement with the boy may have fallen short of what an ordinary father would provide, but it was more than just a professional obligation. Whether as a mentor, or just an older, gray-haired brother, Harold was always there, ready to listen, or help steer the boy through the trials of adolescence. It wasn't a textbook kind of relationship, nor a textbook kind of love. But it was still love.

And now he was gone.

Harold blinked away some of the moisture building up in his eyes and pushed himself into his clinical, data-gathering frame of mind. He started picking through the apartment, finding it full of the standard artifacts and detritus that tended to wash up in young men's apartments. Sporting equipment in the closet. A picture of an unpopular musician on the wall, placed there for ironic purposes. Beside the desk, a framed image of Harold and Kevin on skates, taken when Kevin was about eight. Harold's throat grew thick.

But there were no pools of blood, or stained knives, or threats carved in ancient runes on the wall. Whatever Hatchens and his men were looking for, it probably wasn't forensic evidence. But they had been in there for hours at least and could have searched it top to bottom several times over. It wasn't torn apart—as promised, Hatchens' men had reassembled everything in the same state as they had found it. Harold couldn't figure out what any of this meant. Short of forensic evidence, what else could they be searching for? Some other sort of clue to the identity of Kevin's killer, perhaps. Which would mean that it wasn't a stranger—someone Kevin had known had done this.

Harold mentally tried to assemble a list of Kevin's acquaintances. He had given Kevin more space during recent years—young men didn't need bearded geneticists cluttering up their social lives. It was Kevin who initiated most of the contact between the two, in fact; Harold never let on just how much he appreciated this. But their conversations had mostly been about work, trading grievances about that particular day's labors. Nothing about the interactions with Kevin's friends and—presumably—lovers. Harold simply didn't know much about Kevin's personal life. And he certainly didn't know why someone would want to murder the boy.

Weary, Harold sat down on the bed. There was nothing here for him. He'd assumed that when he got here he would spot some trinket or belonging of Kevin's that he would immediately recognize as a perfect memento or keepsake. But there was nothing like that. He wasn't even the sentimental type, he realized. The memories were good enough for him.

Harold tensed, remembering the message that Kevin sent and recalled before he could read it. That must have been just before Kevin's death. His mind raced, spitting out wild theories. Was it a plea for help? A warning? This time Harold refused to chide himself for his paranoia. An erased message just before Kevin's death was too much to be a coincidence. There must have been something in that message. Something important.

And Hatchens knew it, too.

That explained Hatchens' oddly casual behavior around Harold. Hatchens would know all about Kevin's communications on the day of his death; it was probably standard procedure for such an investigation. So, it was reasonable to assume he knew of the message Kevin had sent and then recalled. Maybe he had read it himself. Would he know that Harold hadn't read it, or simply assumed he had? Harold didn't know enough about the messaging system to be sure.

He wondered if the message explained the lengthy search Hatchens had been doing of Kevin's apartment. Maybe the message referred to something he had hidden in the apartment? But, what? That, Harold couldn't say. He looked over the room again.

The picture was wrong.

Harold tilted his head to look at the framed picture beside the desk of him and Kevin at the skating arena. Harold hadn't been in Kevin's apartment in over six months, but he knew that picture had changed since the last time he had been there. The flimsy digital frame normally displayed an image of Kevin's graduation from the naval academy—Kevin in his uniform and an embarrassed grin, Harold beside him, eyes obviously watering. The only time Kevin had ever seen Harold uncomposed. That was why he had liked the picture so much; it had been in that frame for years.

Harold swallowed, working through the permutations of what that meant. For him, the picture on the wall was a huge glaring clue; he knew exactly what it was pointing at. For anyone else—like a searching security officer—it would be meaningless. If Kevin had left a message only he could read, he had done it for a reason.

Harold felt various muscles tighten, suddenly sure he was being watched, remembering his confrontation with Hatchens just outside. The security chief had calculated a little too obviously when he agreed to clear out of the apartment. He had wanted to see what Harold would find in this place, what the security officers missed. Harold looked around the room, trying to figure out where they would hide a sensor if they wanted to watch him. He then realized he had no idea what a sensor looked like or even how large one was. He turned his terminal over in his hands. That had a massively powerful sensor in it *somewhere*. A security sensor would probably be even smaller. He had read that during the war, the Hungry had rigged up special programs on their terminals to spot the things, which is how they'd been able to destroy them. But Harold, mild-mannered genetic engineer, certainly didn't have anything like that with him now. He flexed his fingers, and took several deep breaths. *Slow down, Harold.* He reminded himself that the ratio of

Actual Massive Shadowy Conspiracies to Predicted Massive Shadowy Conspiracies was vanishingly small.

That said, *some precautions probably couldn't hurt.*

In a stack of boxes beside the desk, he found a paper book he had given to Kevin as a birthday present. It was from Earth and was decidedly worthless—everyone on board the ship had been hoarding natty Earth objects, convinced they would fetch them vast sums one day. He walked out the door, clutching the book tightly in his hand. As good a token as any to remind him of Kevin. And if his paranoid musings were correct, it would serve as one hell of a red herring for his watchers.

4

Stuck

The first hour of every morning was Kinsella's time, which he spent alone in his office, often doing nothing more productive than breathing. Sometimes he stared out the window, an enjoyable compliment to, but no substitute for the breathing. Mostly, he daydreamed. Winning fistfights. Laying multiple women at once. Replaying recent conversations in his head, with wittier lines for himself. Winning fistfights with multiple women at once.

He wouldn't have much more time to spend like this. Probably wouldn't have much free time at all for the next several months. He tried to enjoy the moment while it lasted. By himself, away from all those troublesome people.

At 9:01 a.m., his assistant Bletmann opened the door to the office and stood quietly at the threshold. "Chief Thorias is on his way, sir. Should be another ten minutes." Kinsella dismissed him with a wave, then watched the door close, before exhaling slowly. *It was really happening.*

He spun around again in his chair to face the window, then allowed himself another couple of rotations, just for fun. He would make sure to have this chair brought up to his new office. Or, get a second one made. Couldn't hurt to have two. He couldn't recall what Helot normally sat on. Something dull and utilitarian he imagined, just like the ass it supported. Kinsella extended his feet to the carpeted floor, allowing them to drag himself to a stop. He looked out the window at the garden well in front of him.

He was doing it for them, not that they would appreciate it. Not that they would even understand it. Not that they really *needed* to understand it. He didn't need to understand them to do his job. Kinsella had watched from his window the previous day, as the horse-orgy wound through the streets below, progressing to its inevitably distressing conclusion. "Morons," he said, shaking his head. And yet, it was ultimately the morons' ship. They had a right to be heard, to have a voice. And he was the morons' choice to be the morons' voice.

The morons' voice spun around in his chair at the sound of the door opening, seeing Chief Thorias standing at the threshold. "You asked to see me?" the security chief said, his voice barely audible. Kinsella knew he did that deliberately, the big man that spoke softly; a trick he had read somewhere to appear more intimidating. Kinsella wished he had thought of it first. Awkward to copy it now.

"Yes, Chief. It's time," Kinsella said, pausing for effect. "Will you accompany me to the command center?" A thin smile crossed Thorias' face. He had been relishing this nearly as long as Kinsella had. Maybe longer.

The pair left the mayor's office and walked out to the upper-levels of the Bridge, passing several extra security officers stationed throughout the halls. Another one of his morons, bless his little voting heart, had run through the place shooting people in the face yesterday. Kinsella had thought it pretty funny, more so when he had found out that no one had gotten seriously hurt. Still, a pretty shocking lapse in security. Thorias had taken the matter very seriously, resulting in a city hall swimming with thick-necked security officers. Their presence comforted the mayor. Although he doubted anything drastic would need to be done, it was nice to know when heading into a meeting like this that the men with guns were on his side.

From her stomach, Stein peered down the length of the crawlspace to the room at the far end. It was hard to be sure without checking her terminal, but if that was a pump room, she would definitely be able to get water there. She listened carefully for any noises that a group of heavily armed men might make.

She had heard someone speaking a few minutes after she'd found her hiding spot. Not close enough to make out any words, but it was a safe bet the voice belonged to one of the two security officers who had been chasing her. The voice never came back, but if she heard them speaking once, that meant they'd been bold enough to come into the crawlways after her.

So, she stayed put, worried they might be waiting nearby for her to come out. There was also the small matter that she didn't have anywhere to go. Minutes passed, then hours, while she shivered and quaked and, with no one else around to see, cried. Sleep may have come, possibly multiple times—she wasn't sure. There was little difference between consciousness and unconsciousness anyways; if she dreamed, it was about hiding in awful little spaces.

During her periods of probable wakefulness, she mostly thought about Bruce. She never should have asked him to do something so stupid. It was a pointlessly risky plan she'd come up with, and she should have known he was incapable of turning those down. Pointless risk was in his blood, might very well be there *in place* of his blood, shuttling around oxygen and bold dares to his organs as necessary.

"Check this out," he had said, surprising her in the back row of the classroom. She'd looked up from her terminal, annoyed at his sudden interest in her. This was usually the first step in a chain of events which ended with her punching someone in the groin, or more rarely, sleeping with them and then punching them in the groin.

She squinted at him, trying to dredge up the name attached to the big doofus. It was her second and final crack at this school thing, and she didn't know anyone in her class. But, eventually it clicked; Bruce was the kid's name. She turned away from him. *Definitely one of the situations that ends with a punch to the groin.*

Oblivious, he gave her a big thumb's up and turned to face Ms. Sallans at the front of the room, who was stressing something extremely important about the Zhang neo-dynasty. Ms. Sallans turned her back to the class for a moment, zooming in on something on the front display. Suddenly, Bruce sprang out of his chair, moving swiftly to the front of the room, almost completely silent. He snatched Ms. Sallans' terminal from her desk and retreated to his desk just as quietly. A faint trill of laughter rose from the room, but no sudden outbursts. The class was familiar with Bruce's antics.

Stein watched from the corner of her eye as Bruce messed around with the terminal. As soon as he picked it up, it would have locked out all of Ms. Sallans' content, so she wasn't sure what he could do. He finished whatever it was he was doing and flashed another grin at Stein. The teacher had turned back to face the class but hadn't noticed her terminal had gone wandering. Masking his smile, Bruce raised his hand. "Ms. Sallans? Was that where the March of the Thousand Equals happened?"

Ms. Sallans shook her head. "No, that was in Chengdu and wasn't until much later. I'm surprised you know about that, Bruce."

Bruce frowned and furrowed his brow. "Oh. I thought it was right there. Can you show us?"

"Sure," Ms. Sallans said, turning around again, zooming out on the map. Like a ghost, Bruce slid to the front of the room again, replacing the terminal on her desk. "So, we'll talk about this more tomorrow, but the March of the Thousand Equals was down here. That was organized by Yao-sen—Zhang's right hand man—and it was basically these thousand guys demanding the right to larger data caps and then getting lased from orbit."

Having retaken his seat, Bruce nodded energetically. "Ahhhhh," he said, clearly pleased with himself.

Stein couldn't keep the silent treatment going any longer. "Okay, what was the point of that?" she whispered. He held up a finger to silence her, a gesture which would normally have infuriated her. But she obliged him, if only because she was so curious to see what he had done. She wasn't the only one, and could feel the tension in the room rising as the class simmered, waiting for something to happen. Ms. Sallans had never had such an attentive class before and enthusiastically continued her lecture. Fifteen entire minutes passed before she sat down at her desk and picked up the terminal to assign their homework. Looking at it, she furrowed her brow for a second and then tapped a command into it.

"FAAAAAAARRRRRRRRRRTS," the terminal bellowed in a robotic voice. The entire class erupted in laughter.

After that, if he had actually tried to make a move on Stein, she probably would have relented. But he never did. Which she found a bit confusing, though she never forced the issue—she had hated every guy she had ever slept with and wasn't sure the two events, fucking and hating, were unrelated. The pair simply became friends.

More than that, she would realize years later. Bruce became her ballast. Slowed her down, steadied her rocking. She probably wouldn't have finished school without his voice over her shoulder, and although he was no stranger to intoxicated mayhem himself, it was all quite tame in comparison with her life before she had met him. When she landed the maintenance job a few years later, her case workers assumed it was that opportunity which caused her to calm down. But Stein's calming process was already well under way by that point, with the help of her fool of a friend.

And now she might have gotten him killed.

Only might have though. Not definitely. She nodded, trying to convince herself. Even if he had stumbled upon a room full of assassins, that would just be rough luck for the poor assassins.

And if he had escaped, he would be hiding out somewhere, probably someplace similar to where Stein was now. *Maybe a bit bigger.* They did have an agreed upon meeting spot in the event of a "fan hitting the shit"— Bruce's phrasing—but it was a long way from where she was hiding. Getting there by completely subterranean means was probably possible, but not without her terminal and the maps it contained. And several days' worth of crawling.

Eventually, her own body forced her from her hiding spot. She found a grate several meters away that looked like it would drain in the other direction and used it as a makeshift washroom. "My territory now," she muttered. But after the pressure in her bladder subsided, other complaints surfaced.

Hunger was there, though not bad yet—she knew intellectually that she could go without food for a long time, and during her chemical-fueled youth, had on multiple occasions gone more than a day without eating. But the thirst was a more pressing matter, which was how she found herself on her stomach, listening to the sounds of an empty pump room.

A minute later she exited the crawlspace, and on shaky legs, stood on her own two feet for the first time in almost a day. She was glad to see that it was indeed a pump room, and that it was, indeed, not full of armed men. After a short search, she was able to locate a sampling fixture on the potable water line and drank from it sloppily as the cold water poured forth. Finally, she turned off the tap and sat down on the floor, exhausted by the effort.

"This is bullshit," she said, wiping her face on her sleeve and then immediately regretting it, hours spent in the bowels of the ship having not left it suitable for facial application. She didn't know what she was doing. Running was a bad idea. She hadn't done anything wrong. She had gotten paranoid, had spent too much time listening to Ellen's rants about security officers lurking underneath children's beds. Security goons weren't all bad. Hell, she should know. She was almost dating one. She considered for the first time whether Sergei might be able to help her, but quickly decided against it. Let him ruin his own career.

She stared at the room around her. She couldn't keep doing this, living and pissing in ditches. No, it was time to get up, go outside, and get on with her life. If they arrested her, she would at least get a shower out of the deal. She swallowed, proud of the mature decision she had made, then pushed herself to her feet. She wobbled over to the door and opened it.

From the hue of the street lights, she could tell it was morning. Almost a full day had gone by. She looked around to get her bearings and eventually realized she had traveled nearly seven blocks underground. She looked down at the badly stained knees of her jumpsuit, which told the same story. "Well, let's see if I can manage a shower and change of clothes without getting arrested," she said. Turning south, she set out for her apartment, walking as nonchalantly as she could manage. The ship was quiet at this hour, most people sleeping off the effects of whatever they had done the night before.

A few minutes later, she reached an intersection, and hearing running footsteps, peered around the corner cautiously. Three security officers jogging down the street, coming right at her. Time to put her very sensible and mature plan to the test. She stepped out into the intersection, smiled weakly, and held her hands out at her sides, giving herself up. "Hey, guys," she began to say, before she stopped, watching in amazement as all three of them jogged past her. She looked in the direction they were going, watching them move quickly to the south.

"Where's the fire?" she asked. Annoyed at the possibility that she had just spent a day living in a coffin for no reason, and worried that they might be off to subdue a large man she knew, she turned to follow them.

Kinsella stopped in the doorway of the command center. Naval officers at their stations, chattering away in that strange manner of theirs. Numbers and acronyms and pale skin. They were busier than he had seen them before, preparing for the Push. That was something he knew too little about, he ruefully acknowledged. That would soon change, but until now he'd had his own maneuvering to worry about.

Buried in the aft of the ship, several decks above and a bit behind the Bridge, the control center held all the navigational, propulsion, and engineering controls necessary for classifying the Argos as a spaceship and not just an extremely fast rock. As the mayor, Kinsella had every right to be here, but it had never felt welcoming. This was the domain of the Captain of the Argos.

There were a lot of very good reasons why the ship's naval operations had been kept separate from the civilian government's direct authority. Sense of tradition. A need for specialized expertise. Speed in decision-making. Kinsella understood all of that and agreed with it completely. Besides, there were extensive provisions for civilian oversight—the captain did ultimately serve at the mayor's pleasure. What was happening now was really just aggressive oversight.

Most of the naval officers looked up at their mayor, curious expressions on their faces. Kinsella was amused by this, their eyes wavering back and forth between him and the imposing figure of Thorias behind him. "Helot, can we speak for a moment?" Kinsella asked the captain from across the room, speaking in his well-practiced, very serious voice. "Privately."

From his position on the raised portion in the back half of the command room, Helot's only reaction was a set of slightly raised eyebrows as he carefully returned the mayor's gaze. Kinsella's deliberate omission of the man's title had failed to provoke him; if anything, the bastard actually looked amused.

"Everyone, please carry on," Helot ordered his staff. After a moment's hesitation, most of the command crew put their heads back down to their consoles and continued their work, albeit in a manner Kinsella thought was more subdued. "In my cabin?" he asked Kinsella, gesturing to a door at the back.

Kinsella suppressed a laugh. He had seen the captain's 'cabin' before. Barely more than a closet. *These navy cretins did like to cling to their ancient vocabulary. Like it was...something boaty.* A life-preserver, he decided after a moment's consideration. He followed Helot into his 'cabin' and sat down in the chair across from the captain's desk without waiting for an invitation. He got a good look at the Captain's chair, glad to see that it was dumpier-looking than he imagined.

"What's this about, Eric?" Helot asked, seating himself in the utilitarian chair.

Kinsella set his jaw and composed himself—he had practiced this next bit a dozen times in the mirror. "Captain James Edward Helot, it has come to my attention that you may be morally compromised to the point that you should no longer hold a position of authority on board the Argos."

Helot's expression, still one of modest amusement, didn't waver. "How so, Mayor?"

Kinsella sneered. *Fine, let the fool play one.* "Images and movies depicting sexual activities with minors have been found in your possession during a routine network scan."

"A network scan of my belongings? That doesn't sound very routine." Helot asked, barely suppressing a grin.

Kinsella ignored him and continued his rehearsed speech. "The evidence tying you to this *filth* is incontrovertible and damning. I have not seen the images myself, but I'm told that they do not appear to be historical in nature – and that several appear to have been taken on board the Argos itself. Which, if true, suggests not just a moral lapse, but a far fouler and more serious crime."

Helot looked up at the ceiling thoughtfully. "If true. Images can be doctored fairly convincingly."

Kinsella's nostrils flared. He couldn't believe this. "Forensic teams have already confirmed they're authentic, Helot," he lied. He looked up at Thorias for some sign of support, but the big lummox only stared back at him dumbly. "Look, you're not going to get out of this on a technicality or charm your way past a jury," Kinsella said, turning back to Helot. "If these pictures get out, you *will* go down. Your only alternative is to submit your immediate resignation. In exchange, these pictures need never see the light of day." Kinsella swallowed, the hard part over. "I will give you a few seconds to think about it." He sat back in his chair, crossed his legs, and laced his fingers over his knee.

Helot sat behind his desk looking at the mayor curiously. Kinsella realized now just how much he hated the man. Even as he worked to push him out of office, he had never thought of him as anything more than a hurdle. But now, looking at the captain, with his infuriatingly calm gaze, Kinsella realized he actually hated the man. He hated his arrogance. He hated his calm self-righteousness. And his face. Kinsella sat and stewed, hating the man's fucking face.

Finally, Helot spoke. "I was wondering if you were going to spring this little plot of yours in time. I'd honestly have felt more than a little guilty if you hadn't. Thank you, Mayor. You've done my conscience a great service here."

Kinsella sat up in his chair, leaning forward, blood rushing to his face. "That doesn't sound like a resignation to me, Captain! You can save your false displays of bravado for someone more easily impressed. If you don't resign, *immediately*, this evidence will be sent to every person on board the ship. If I don't instruct my assistant otherwise in...," Kinsella checked the time on his terminal to illustrate the point, "...four minutes, this *will* happen."

"By assistant, you mean Bletmann, correct?" Helot's eyes flicked up to Thorias.

Thorias cleared his throat behind Kinsella and spoke, his voice louder and clearer than normal. "He will have been relocated by this point, sir. The entire Bridge should be by now. The mayor would have been as well, but then he asked me to come here with him," Thorias said with a hint of mirth. "I thought this might be more amusing."

Helot's brow furrowed, and he leaned forward, resting his chin in his hands. "Tough call. We do have some pretty tight time constraints today, Chief. But I will grant that this is pretty amusing. And things have been running ahead of schedule. I think I'll let you get away with it." He sat back and smiled.

Kinsella leapt from his chair, back arched, fur on end. "What the hell are you two talking about?" He was furious at Helot, and at Thorias, and at himself for losing control of the situation. He withdrew his terminal and attempted to call Bletmann. These efforts were interrupted by Thorias' meaty paw smacking the terminal to the ground. Kinsella jumped back, aghast.

"Mayor," Helot began calmly, "you don't have any evidence. It was all fabricated. I should know. I'm the one who ordered it."

Kinsella's brow creased. He had received the photos from Thorias himself. The security man had come to him months ago with the evidence, and the idea for how to best stick it in Helot's back. Kinsella had thought—had been sure—the security chief loathed the captain as much as he did. Kinsella looked up at Thorias now and the bemused expression he wore on his face. It had all been an act. "Why?" he asked Helot. "Why would you do that?"

Helot smiled. "To keep you out of our hair, mainly. If we gave you this, we hoped that you wouldn't do any actual digging of your own." Helot smirked. "Seems to have worked."

"Oh? So, you've got more important secrets to hide?" Kinsella snapped. "What are you, fucking meat plants instead?"

Helot laughed. "Wow. No." He looked over Kinsella's shoulder to Thorias, then down at the desk display. His head wavered back and forth as he appeared to weigh a pair of alternatives. "It's a long story...."

Stein had to hurry to keep pace with the three security officers, moving rapidly south along Europe. She lost sight of them at 10th when they ascended the escalators there, but by the time she reached the escalator bank herself, something else had caught her eye.

Another block south of her, a crowd had gathered in front of a massive wall that wasn't supposed to be there. Stein cautiously approached them, coughing, the air unusually dusty. She moved carefully through the crowd until she could get a better look. It was a bulkhead door, having slid out from concealed pockets on either side of the street to meet in the middle, sealing the street off. "When did that happen?" she asked a young woman.

"Couple minutes ago. Just came out of the wall, all rumble bumble rumble, you know?"

"It was more of a gnsssssssh gnsssssh gnsssssssh sound," someone else offered.

"You've got too much shit in your ears," the young woman said.

A heated disagreement broke out amongst the people gathered there about what noise the doors had made, which Stein escaped, confident she had acquired the total of useful information available from the group. Retreating back to the intersection at 9th, she could see more people a block east, also gaping at something to the south. She hurried over to see for herself. There, a small crowd was watching a security officer, his pistol drawn and aimed at the floor, guarding a maintenance worker, whom she recognized from the skeleton shift. He didn't see Stein, instead intent on something behind a recently removed wall panel. A small cloud of dust emerged from the wall, serving as the honor guard for another bulkhead door, which slid into the street accompanied by an unpleasant grinding sound. Only a single door on this smaller street, it slid across dirt encrusted tracks in the floor and embedded itself into a thin gap on the far wall. The security man, the technician, and everything else south of the door disappeared from Stein's view.

She continued like this for a while, walking along 9th, following the gentle curve of the ship uphill as she did so, looking at closed and closing bulkhead doors. Arriving at Asia Street, she found the same situation, only with a larger, angrier crowd. One of the men gathered here, an anarchy-dancer to judge from the facial hair and stench, accosted Stein.

"What the fuck, man?" the filthy man yelled, his hands flailing in the air. "You can't just kick us out of our homes like that, you fucking fascists!"

Stein realized that, still in her orange uniform, she looked like someone in charge of things like doors. "Sorry, buddy, I just got here," she said. "I haven't done anything to anyone. Where'd they kick you out of?"

He explained, using language filthier than his appearance, that he had been dragged out of his home—an illegal squat it sounded like—by a half-dozen security officers and hauled to this side of the bulkhead doors. More people gathered around, shouting similar tales of woe at Stein. Offering brief and completely false promises to fix things, she managed to extract herself from this group and continued down 9th.

Stein didn't know anything about bulkhead doors, having never seen one closed in her entire life. Curious, she continued to the next side street, and finding this one deserted, walked south towards the obstruction. On one side of the street, she spotted a likely wall panel and opened it. Sure enough, there were the bulkhead door controls. Examining it for a few seconds, she found she could see the current status of the door and environment. Atmospheric pressure on both sides. She hit the button marked "Open." Evidently, whoever was shutting these things had already thought of such a countermove, and an error message flashed across the screen, reading "Access Denied." She saw a couple of potential ways to override that if she had had her tools with her, but she had left those behind during her flight from the law. She dropped the panel cover on the floor and returned back to 9th Avenue.

Everywhere she looked on the first level, bulkhead doors were shut between 9th and 8th Avenues. Curious, she walked back up to the escalators on 10th and ascended to the second level. Stepping into the middle of the street, she looked south. The bulkhead doors were closed here at the same latitude as below. Taking another escalator up, she saw the pattern repeated. She stopped and tried to figure out what this looked like. They were sealing the entire aft of the ship, kicking people out from the other side. She immediately assumed that it was related to what she and Bruce had uncovered, and although she didn't know who precisely 'they' were, it was clearly not a small group. The entirety of the security department at least. And, probably, her goddamned boss.

Whatever was going on, it seemed no one was paying much attention to her. She turned on her terminal again, hoping to get in touch with Bruce. As soon as she started it, a dozen different messages came in, which she paged through. Most were work related, notes from her team asking why she had stopped the diagnostic process so early. One message jumped out at her from an 'Abdolo Poland,' a name she didn't recognize. She opened it, realizing immediately that it was from Bruce, who had somehow managed to doctor up a terminal to send from a false identity.

"I'm OK. Playing Hide and Seek and kicking ass at it. You?"

The message had been sent hours earlier. She sent him a quick note indicating that she was fine, asking if he knew what was going on. She set off exploring once again, this time picking her way back west. It was more of the same everywhere she went. Closed doors and confused people coughing in the dusty air. Children asking their parents what was going on. Parents wishing they had someone to ask themselves.

At Europe, she found another crowd, this one in an angry mood. Here, Stein could see that the bulkhead door hadn't closed yet; in its place was a massive group of security officers in riot gear, standing in a line. Periodically, the line would part, and a civilian would be shoved across. None of these evictees appeared terribly happy about the situation, but the security men were being very liberal in the application of their clubs, and no individual protest lasted very long.

Stein looked around. This was the biggest crowd she had seen yet, composed of a slightly rougher representation of the Argos' population. Aft dwellers. Recently evicted ones. Word seemed to have spread that the doors hadn't shut on this street, and people were filtering in from the escalators and side streets. Stein sensed an ugly mood in the air. Even without knowing exactly what was going on, the mere presence of cops in riot gear was enough to aggravate many people. Stein had seen situations like this before and moved sideways through the throng, backing into a doorway.

There was no obvious signal, no leader shouting a call to arms or firing a gun in the air. Suddenly, some sort of critical mass of anger had been broached, and the crowd surged forward. They advanced on the line of security guards, a storm of filthy language filling the air. Stein kept her back pressed into the doorway, confident about what was going to happen next.

But before things could reach a head, a deep rumbling sound announced the closing of the bulkhead doors. Stein could see over the heads in the crowd as the doors slowly slid out of the walls, presumably just in front of the battle lines the security officers had formed.

Her terminal buzzed, and she looked down to see another message from Abdolo.

"I've got no idea. What do you think of the disconnect?"

Stein frowned. That was the word Bruce had squawked at her just before they'd got cut off. To a maintenance worker, a disconnect was a switch used to isolate a piece of equipment from its power source. Disconnects were completely innocuous—there were literally thousands of them scattered around the ship. And that's what Stein had first thought Bruce was talking about.

She wasn't thinking that any more, as she looked at the picture Bruce had sent of a massive set of clamps hidden in a cavity of the ship. She looked up at the just closed set of bulkhead doors as the cloud of dust washed over her.

They were now dealing with an entirely different type of disconnect.

"You're going to do what?" Kinsella asked, his mouth suddenly dry.

Helot had stopped smiling. The corners of his eyes sank, and his throat clenched. "We're going to split the ship in two," he repeated.

Kinsella closed his eyes. He frantically shook his head, rubbing his hands over his face, trying to hide from Helot's words. "No way. Not possible."

"Very much possible," Helot said. "The ship was designed to do it. It's a backup measure. Obviously. The ship was always intended to arrive in one piece, just as you learned in school. But if you look at the complete plans for the ship—and you couldn't, because they've been very well hidden—you'll see the entire aft core of the ship can pop out like a cork. Engines, fuel tanks, and a modest amount of living space. Life support, hydroponics, water treatment. All inclusive. A smaller ship hidden within the larger one."

Kinsella struggled to assemble a picture of the ship in his mind. He knew that above the fourth level the aft portions of the ship were substantially more spacecraft-like. But there was never anything to indicate that the whole apparatus was designed to separate. "I don't buy it. You're talking about a cork that's a hundred meters wide. And I've never seen any seams."

"The seams are artfully hidden, most between decks. But they're there."

"Let's say for the sake of argument that you're not insane..."

"For the sake of argument, I'll allow it..."

Kinsella ignored the interruption. "And you take your cork-ship to Tau Prius."

"Right..."

Kinsella started to quake with rage. "Leaving the rest..."

Helot swallowed. "Leaving the rest to go past Tau Prius without stopping." He stared down at his shoes for a moment. "I'm sorry, Eric," Helot mumbled before looking Kinsella in the eye. "I really am. I'd have told you sooner, but...well. You know. You'd just have gotten upset."

Kinsella lashed out at Helot's desk with his foot, knocking it back against the captain. Behind him, Thorias threw his massive arms around Kinsella, clutching and squeezing. Kinsella didn't struggle, just screamed, "Upset? You think I'd have gotten fucking upset? Upset that you're about to murder us? Why would that fucking upset me?"

"We're not murdering you, Eric. Just letting you go on without us."

"To die alone in space!"

"We've been dying in space for centuries, Eric. It's no big deal. You'll have a hundred years worth of energy to get your affairs in order. More if you ration it carefully."

"But we can't fucking stop," Kinsella screamed.

"There is that," Helot allowed. "But this is the best chance for at least some part of the ship to form a viable colony." He blinked, his eyes glistening.

Kinsella twisted in Thorias' grip, which only caused it to tighten further. "Why can't we all stop?"

Helot breathed deeply, obviously fighting to control his emotions. He shook his head, once, twice. Another swallow. He continued to stare at the wall above Kinsella's head, avoiding the mayor's gaze. "It's a fuel thing."

"What?"

"We don't have enough fuel left to stop the whole ship. We made a mistake, okay? We used some during the course correction. And we've had annihilation efficiency problems. We don't have enough fuel left to decelerate. Not the whole ship." Helot took another deep breath, growing more comfortable while describing the nuts and bolts of his plan. "But if we detach the aft core of the ship, we'll only have a fraction of the mass to decelerate. Plenty of fuel to spare."

Kinsella stared at him. He started to laugh. "That's insane."

"It's the truth," Helot replied, his voice trembling.

"You're going to murder thousands of people because we ran out of gas?"

"I'm not murdering them," Helot whispered, barely audible. "I have to save at least some of the ship. I can't save them all." He looked away from Kinsella, staring at the wall in front of him. "I'm not murdering them," he repeated.

Every muscle in Kinsella's body tensed. He could feel Thorias squeeze tighter, but he didn't care, full of hate for the pathetic figure in front of him. Through clenched teeth he said, "Chief, would you please bring me close enough to the captain to pull his throat out with my teeth?"

Helot snorted, blinking rapidly. He sneaked a quick look at Kinsella. "Brave, Eric. But it's over."

"You fucking murderer!"

"I'm not murdering anyone. Security's been closing bulkheads for the last half hour, shepherding people to safety." Helot looked at something on his desk and nodded. "We've already quietly relocated a lot of them over the past few years. It's just a safety measure—the aft of the ship has an excess of bulkhead doors, so with luck you'll lose almost no space to vacuum. But we're evacuating a much larger area just to be safe. You'll be taken back to the other side of the doors in a few minutes' time."

Kinsella's mouth hung open, wanting only to scream obscenities at the man, but unable to think of anything foul enough. "Look, Eric," Helot said, getting up from his chair. "I know you. You're an adaptable guy. Look at what you were planning to pull on me today. That showed real gumption! This ship is going to need that part of you now. You'll still get to be mayor of the Argos. I'm not taking that away from you." He paused, smiling weakly. "Just part of your mandate." He walked around his desk towards Kinsella, then stopped, seeming to think better of it. "I know we've never been friends, but I always admired you. You're a pragmatist. Not one to fight the hopeless fight. You'll get on with your life, and you'll die an old and happy man," Helot said. He returned to his desk and shoved it back into its original position. He looked down at something on the display. "Now, I have a bit of work to do here, so if you'll go quietly with the Chief...."

Kinsella did not wish to go quietly and explained as much using the strongest language available. A brief and lopsided struggle followed, which inevitably left the mayor of the Argos unconscious on the floor.

The entertainment value of seeing their mayor's body dragged from the captain's cabin and out of the command center was appreciated by the naval personnel present, whose morale had been suffering of late due to the implications of recent job-related duties.

In the fan room on the third floor of the Bridge, the heavy access hatch had been resealed a few hours earlier by a couple of harried naval technicians. The lighter wall panel remained on the floor, where it had sat since Bruce had removed it. The technicians had long since left the room, as it was located on the wrong side of the gap that would soon form.

The mechanism located within the cavity came to life. With an audible clunk, the disconnect sprang open, both halves of the enormous clamp releasing the handshake they had begun two hundred and forty years previous. At the same time, at a hundred and seven similar spots throughout the aft, a hundred and seven identical clamps did the same.

Pistons mounted within the cavities began to push off against each other. Six months of accelerating at a tenth of a G, followed by two hundred and forty years of waiting, had caused the two halves of the Argos to bond tightly together. A shove would be needed to knock them apart.

As the pistons began pushing off, the cavities began to be exposed to vacuum, beginning with the ones closest to the exterior of the ship. The thin insulating foam began to crumble away as the two halves of the ship struggled to free themselves from each other.

But after so many years, not all of the pistons operated properly, even with the secret maintenance that they had received over the past half-decade. Knowing this could happen, a contingency plan for such a failure was in place. The pistons that were operational began pushing and relaxing in concert, trying to rock the aft end of the ship back and forth, working to pry it off like a champagne cork. Terrifying, otherworldly groaning noises permeated the ship as forgotten joints and bonds began flexing.

After minutes of this, the aft of the ship finally broke free, but critically, along one side only. The other side held fast, metal screaming in protest. The pistons continued their frantic rocking action, as the separation on the other side of the ship increased, growing to almost half a meter. The creaking and groaning noises increased, as the whole ship started to vibrate.

Suddenly, the pistons in the disconnect cavities ceased their fruitless shoving match. The aft of the ship, still partially attached, hung motionless for a second. Then, the massive forces stored in the bent metal on the stuck side, began to slowly tug the ship back into alignment, like a spring returning to its original shape. The ship slammed shut, unimaginable forces smashing the separated sides back into each other.

Some of the pistons leapt into action again, this time much more feebly. Many had been destroyed in the impact, and a significant chunk of the disconnects, having tasted freedom ever so briefly, slammed shut around their opposing members in the sudden impact. The ship was together again.

"All sections report they're intact. No penetration of core compartments reported."

"Disconnect 6-3-2 reports full connection. 5-3-1 does as well...fuck. Okay, let's just say that *a lot* of them are reconnected. Most are still offline though, no reading."

"I've lost readouts on the rest of the Argos. Have we lost the hardline?"

The control center was a flurry of activity, men and women hunched over their control screens, shouting status reports to the room, all assuming that someone was listening.

"Everyone, shut up!" barked Helot from his perch on the upper-level of the command center. "I want everyone to calm down. Nobody say a thing unless I ask for it." Helot scanned the room slowly, locking eyes with every officer in turn, reassuring them that he was still in charge. That done, he stood up straighter. "Okay, first things first: how's the core envelope?"

"Okay, sir," replied the officer sitting at the engineering panel. Curts, hovering right behind him, nodded at Helot. "There is no sign of vacuum in the core, sir. All bulkhead doors are online and appear to be intact."

"How about the rest of the ship?"

"I can't tell, sir. I think the hardline must have been disconnected."

"Can we fix that?" Helot asked.

"Maybe. That will take awhile. In the meantime, we should be able to patch back in over the wireless. We're working on that now."

"Good, let me know when you do that."

"Sir?" the officer at the engineering panel interrupted him.

"What is it?"

"Our bulkhead doors along the Africa and America side elevators are showing a loss of pressure on the other side."

"Vacuum? Is it just in the space between the doors, or is there a breach on the other side? At street level? Don't answer, I know you can't tell yet." Helot exhaled. "Okay, Smith, give me a status report on all the disconnects. A *summary* status report."

"About a third of them are offline right now. During the detachment, a bunch of them failed to release—mainly in the two and three series. Then, after the detachment, a bunch of them slammed shut again. It's hard to tell how many."

Curts had crossed over to look at the officer's screen and turned to Helot. "We're going to need to inspect these all visually before we try that again."

"*I know*," Helot said, annoyed at Curts' obviousness. He turned to the officers perched in front of him on the upper-level of the command center. "Engines? Navigation?"

"Engines and positioning thrusters are fully operational. We're rotating well off axis though. 0.12 degrees per second."

"Hardly our biggest problem right now," Helot muttered. "Okay, keep an eye on it."

"Sir? We're patched back in to the main Argos network via wireless. Everyone should be seeing that on their screens now."

Helot turned to the officer at the engineering panel. "How's the rest of the ship?"

"The bulkhead doors along 9th Avenue are all intact. No signs of vacuum at street level."

Helot nodded, repeatedly clenched and unclenched his hands, mentally working through his options. "Okay, everyone. I don't want to see anyone panicking. We've got a year long window here. Lots of time to try again. But, let's not waste any of it. Curts, get your people and start inspecting those disconnects right away."

He looked at the images of the crowds gathered on the other side of the bulkheads, knowing they weren't likely to give him a year.

A clang rang up from the darkened hole in the floor, followed by a thud. Helot and Thorias looked at each other with concern. "You okay, Curtsy?" Thorias asked.

"Yeah," Curts' voice echoed up from the hole. "Hang on."

They were standing in a dormitory on the fifth floor, just above the threshold along which the ship was to have split. Bunk beds had been shoved aside, along with the confused civilians in them, family members of security and naval officers. This had uncovered the massive access hatch which opened up onto one of the jammed disconnects. Curts' head appeared in the access hatch and looked around, blinking. He hauled himself out of the hole and flopped down on the ground, covered in sweat and grime following six hours of uncomfortable work.

"It's going to t-t-take at least a couple months," he reported, getting to his feet. "We've only inspected a fraction of them, but I think I can fairly safely say that we're going to have to physically c-c-cut through almost a quarter of the disconnects with fuse torches. There's a problem though."

"They're in vacuum?" Helot asked.

Curts bit his lip. "Probably some, yes. But most evidently aren't." Eyes closed, he shook his head. "No, wait. That's not what I'm, err...that's not the p-p-problem. I'm thinking...I mean. The issue is—a lot of them have resealed. Or there's not enough separation to blow the seals completely. That's part of it. The other part is that...it's hard to explain. I mean, most of the disconnects can only be accessed from the other side of the ship."

Helot's knuckles whitened. *Spit it out you fucking idiot.* "It means your men will need access to the other side of those cavities," Helot said, seeing Curts' mouth open, wanting to pre-empt him. He had already guessed that would be necessary. Curts nodded.

Helot turned to Thorias. "So? This is what you were worried about, yes?"

Thorias turned his head to the side, cracking his neck. "If the people on the other side of those bulkhead doors don't know what happened, they will soon." He looked at Helot meaningfully.

Helot grimaced and twisted his fingers together. It had been stupid telling everything to Kinsella. But it had been irresistible—to have kept a secret like that for so long and be home free. Telling that oily bastard where he could stick his kiddy-diddling pics was fantastic, the best part of what had admittedly been a pretty shitty day. "Can we maybe find him and make him be quiet?" he asked softly.

"We can try."

"Okay. Quietly, if possible. And alive, please," Helot said, wishing he didn't have to specify that, not wanting to take the chance. "Now, what else? We'll still need to keep people out of the aft. So, we'll keep the bulkhead doors down. But people will ask questions."

"Call it a terrorist attack," Thorias said. "Everyone will have felt the shaking. That will give us an excuse for sending officers out hunting for the mayor. We'll keep most of them back here. Open a few bulkhead doors to serve as gates. Set up barricades. Call it a security perimeter. A few squads will roam the bow, looking for the terrorists who did this. And we already have a couple readymade terrorists to pin this on."

Helot rubbed his fingers together. "Okay. Do all that immediately." Thorias turned away and began making calls. Helot directed his attention back at the filthy chief engineer. "Curts? Get started with those fuse torches. *Quickly, please.*" He left the engineer by his hole, and left the room, waiting for the door to close behind him before rubbing his face. What was supposed to be a clean cut, surgical procedure now felt an awful lot like picking at an open sore.

Sergei swallowed again. He had had to do that a lot lately. He had too much damned saliva in his mouth. He guessed it was just nerves. No one had ever told him of all the saliva that came with the nerves.

Four in the afternoon and he was standing guard at a hastily erected barricade on Africa-1. Another eight security guards were there, working through their own symptoms of the nerves, casting nervous looks down the street to the north.

It had been an interesting day. He had slept uneasily the night after leaving the bar with Laura. Sergeant Koller had been at the bar, staring right at them both. For a while, Sergei had thought it was just a coincidence Koller was there, and that he had been staring at them like a pervert simply because he was one. But a part of him couldn't shake the idea that Koller was there specifically to watch them. Sergei had sleepwalked through the next day, constantly checking over his shoulder to look for any familiar faces, finding none. They weren't watching him. Which meant they were watching Laura. He had decided that he should probably warn her about that, but he hadn't decided on the safest way to do so when he had gone to bed, hopeful he would think of a solution by the morning.

No solution was waiting when he awoke, but a message was, one accompanied by the distinctive chirp indicating it was a priority message. Still a couple of hours before Sergei was scheduled to come on-shift, he knew it was almost certainly a "Get the fuck in to work right now" chirp. The chirp, unwelcome though it was, was at least familiar. The message that accompanied it was not:

COMMENCE DRILL 1A. ARRIVE AT SECURITY HQ IN 30 MINUTES WITH 1 STANDARD BAG OF PERSONAL BELONGINGS.

Sergei read the message twice before reluctantly getting out of bed. He knew what the drill was—they had done this once a year since he had joined the security ranks. It was intended to prepare the security corp for the possibility of a long term deployment in a fortified aft, on the chance that a massive civil war would break out in exactly the same way as the first one. Sergei remembered his first such drill clearly. "They'll know who you are and where you live," his commanding officer had told him. "And will have no hesitation about destroying everything you own. Take everything that's valuable to you." Sergei had thought that a particularly overdramatic touch. They had been doing these drills regularly since the Breeder conflict, though they had always been announced in advance and never via a message. That was odd. Sergei couldn't recall any drills announced via a terminal message before.

Sergei lived close to the headquarters and was able to get to the office quickly. Shortly after he arrived, another message told him to report to a room on the sixth level where he was to wait for further instructions. Now very confused, Sergei made his way to the elevator bank within the headquarters and took it to the sixth floor. He rarely had cause to go above street level, and it took him awhile to find the right room. The whole level was far busier than he would have imagined, with a lot of similarly confused people wandering around. Once he found the room, he entered to find a dozen sets of bunk beds laid out in dormitory fashion in long rows. Sitting down on a bunk at random, he waited and watched as for the next forty minutes security men streamed in, all carrying bags full of whatever they considered valuable. Sergei noticed with some interest that both current and off-rotation security officers were amongst those arriving. Retired and off-duty officers could always potentially be called into service again, but he had never known them to be included in a drill before.

Around this point, the ship began the violent lurching which marked the death of any notions that they were still involved in a drill.

The next few hours were filled with increasingly confused speculation in the dormitory, not tempered in the slightest by the terse messages from command telling them to hold their position. Eventually, Chief Thorias himself arrived and ordered them back down to street level to muster in the security headquarters. There Sergei got his first glimpse of the sealed bulkhead doors.

After another few minutes had passed, by which point it appeared that the entire security contingent was gathered in the streets surrounding the headquarters, Thorias announced that terrorists had just attempted to destroy the ship. All security officers were now on permanent around-the-clock duty, their numbers supplemented by recalled off-duty officers. All would be assigned to barricades securing the aft of the vessel or to roving patrols to calm the public and hunt for the terrorists. Pistols and commlinks—earpieces with integrated microphone, linked to the terminals—were also distributed.

On Africa-1, the construction of the barricade had proceeded remarkably smoothly. When the bulkhead doors had opened, only a handful of curious civilians were on the other side. They were instructed to return to their homes, and none put up any fuss. Over his commlink, he could hear that things were not progressing as easily for the other units. There was a near riot occurring on Europe. Shots fired.

Within a few minutes, Koller and some others had arrived with temporary barricades of the flimsy plastic variety used for managing parades. After directing where to set these up, Koller left, explaining that more instructions would be forthcoming. Sergei snorted at that—a clear euphemism for "we don't really know what to do yet, so don't do anything." Rumors quickly began circulating, based on overheard conversations, stray commlink chatter, and, no doubt by now, amphetamines. The Mayor had been killed. No, just injured. Thrown overboard. But he was definitely not in power anymore. Unless he was faking all this to gain more power.

Sergei watched the small cluster of people that had gathered a few blocks down Africa. They milled about without any clear purpose, but the focus of their attention was clearly the security officers gathered behind their flimsy plastic barricade. Thankfully, none of them approached. Maybe news had spread that there had been shootings at Europe. The terminal chatter had settled down a bit by this point, and it was clear that only a single civilian had been stunned in the earlier fracas and not hurt badly. Still, Sergei kept a nervous eye on the crowd. Even when keeping a distance, their presence was worrisome. The crowd slowly increased in size.

A high-pitched noise pierced the air. Sergei looked around, confused. A rumbling noise followed soon after, then silence. The sound of voices murmuring in the background. Sergei reeled. He had no idea the ship even had a public address system. Every terminal on the ship, and presumably every desk and wall display, began playing the same message.

"Good morning. This is Captain James Edward Helot. This morning, criminals attempted to destroy critical parts of the ship's propulsion system. This violent and senseless attack was the cause of the tremors felt throughout the ship. Thankfully, these villains were unsuccessful in their goal—the damage, though serious, could have been far worse.

"However, until these criminals are brought to justice, for the protection of the public, enhanced security measures will be put in place throughout the ship. No doubt some of you have already observed these measures. I'll explain them here clearly now and explain why there is no cause for panic.

"A security perimeter has been established along 9th Avenue. No traffic will be allowed south of this perimeter except when authorized by the ship's security forces. Applications to cross this security perimeter can be obtained from the security officers operating on Level 4 at Europe and 9th. They will begin accepting said applications at noon today. Priority will be given to those separated from family members and those separated from their homes. Please be patient with this process.

"The lawful government of this ship is still in power. Government officials will experience some difficulty crossing the perimeter, and we apologize for their displacement. However, I want to make perfectly clear that these security measures are temporary. When the culprits behind this attack are brought to justice, and the critical areas of the ship are repaired and secured, the security perimeter will cease to exist. In the meantime, I would ask everyone to please cooperate with all security officers you interact with.

"Security forces are currently seeking two specific people we believe to be responsible for this attack. Arrest warrants are currently issued for Bruce Redenbach and Laura Stein, members of the ship's maintenance department. If you've had any contact with these individuals, please report it to security at once. Additionally, please report any other unusual activity that you think may be a threat to the ship's security.

"With your help and support, I am confident that we will be able to get through this, and I sincerely thank you for your patience."

A soft click announced the end of the message. A few seconds later, every data terminal on the ship beeped to indicate that the full text of the captain's statement had arrived in their inbox, along with still images of Laura and her friend Bruce and a recording of Bruce sprinting through the Bridge, gun in hand.

Sergei fought to control his reactions. He'd had contact with the two most wanted criminals on board the Argos. In one case, quite a bit of contact. He couldn't imagine Laura getting involved in this. Well, he could imagine it, but it took some flexibility. As for her friend Bruce—that seemed...really, extremely plausible.

But what did this mean to him? He had never advertised it, but his relationship—was that the word?—with Laura was no secret. And Koller certainly knew about it. If they were looking for Laura, they would be looking for him, as well.

Unsure of what to do, Sergei did nothing, fighting with the saliva in his mouth. Even aside from the part about Laura, there were other parts of this that weren't making sense. Like the fact that the security officers had been recalled before the attack occurred. And that dorm room they were in beforehand—what did that have to do with a terrorist attack? It was like Thorias had known this was coming. Despite Helot's assurance that the civilian government was still in power, Sergei saw precious little evidence to suggest that that was the case. If it was, why hadn't the mayor delivered the message himself? That guy loved an excuse to talk.

In the control room, Helot looked at the gathered crowds on the monitor screens.

"You think that worked?" Curts asked from behind him.

Helot didn't spare a look for the tiresome man. "I don't know, Curts. Maybe we should look at these glowing rectangles and find out?" To his credit, Curts chose to ignore the insult, a skill most cowards had. The mousey engineer stayed mute, avoiding eye contact and watching the screens with his head bowed. The crowds in the garden well and on the streets around the bulkhead doors weren't dissipating. But they weren't growing, either. Close-ups showed confused people, milling about without any real purpose. If they were angry, they weren't outwardly angry.

"Looks like you bought us some time," Curts finally said.

Helot knew that was never in doubt. The question was, *How much time?* Someone amongst the cattle would be able to figure out that the bulkhead doors had closed *before* the 'terrorist attack.' And about the two thousand naval and security personnel who had all migrated south at the same time. Finally, there was the mayor, the oily wonder. Thorias had men searching for him, but in the confusion, Kinsella had managed to disappear. Helot wasn't optimistic they would find him. The mayor had probably scuttled somewhere well out of sight.

"Shouldn't you be working on something?" he snapped at Curts. That was unfair—the engineer could do much of his coordination from this room—but Curts scurried away regardless. Helot watched the little bastard's retreat with disdain. It had been ten years since Curts had approached him with the schematics to the ship and its disconnects, revealing in a casual way that he knew what it was capable of. Shrewdly, he had come with no threat of blackmail. Only an offer to help, to assist with the preparations that Helot wouldn't even confirm were taking place. The help was needed; it would have been difficult for the naval personnel to complete their work unnoticed without Curts running interference. But it was the cowardice the man displayed that grated at Helot. He wasn't doing it because he believed in what Helot was doing. He hadn't even asked why. He was just doing it to save himself. Willing to betray and abandon his friends and coworkers and shipmates. That wasn't the kind of person Helot needed on Tau Prius. That wasn't the kind of person Helot wanted anywhere near him.

Curts' two team members, the man and woman who had come so close to stumbling upon the plan, were different. Helot was glad they were around. They had fallen perfectly into his lap—the footage of the fat one shooting his way out of the Bridge was almost too good to believe. He knew now that he should have been planning something similar all along, had contingency plans with fake scapegoats ready to go, so that he wouldn't be scrambling now. Even with the painstaking years of preparation, it was amateurish to think that everything would have worked perfectly on the first try.

And now they had to try again. He felt his frustration start to mount and ducked into his cabin, closing the door behind him, preparing for a frustrated bellow.

The bellow never came, but swallowing it didn't feel much better. Dragging the process out like this was going to be awful. He would have to keep thinking about *it*, thinking about his choice. A multitude of opportunities to change his mind would present themselves, and each one would require a new gut check. He sat down heavily behind his desk and pulled up the math, the interlinked series of files and tables he had dwelled in for the past twenty years.

He knew that separation was the right decision. He had run the calculations a thousand times, tweaked every variable, agonized over every probability and weighted value. More people would survive this way; he knew it. They had left the decision to him, those old, dead bastards, not wanting to play the villain in the story they had written. Well, he had made the decision. And taken it seriously. Years spent alone in his office with his awful spreadsheet.

He had stopped crying about it at least, after spending the first year of his captaincy hiding red, swollen eyes. And he would have to keep holding it together, especially in front of his crew. *And doubly especially in front of Thorias.* Helot didn't want to show any blemishes in front of the man, even if he knew the chief would ultimately follow orders. That was one perk the old, dead bastards had left behind: a loyal staff.

He closed his calculations and brought up the navigational display, scrolling it over to center on Tau Prius. 11.8 light-years from Earth, one of almost two dozen habitable candidates within twenty light years of home. Not the closest, nor the most attractive, but somehow the consensus favorite of the various members of the Argos Development Consortium. None of them would admit to it being their first choice, but because it wasn't anyone's adversary's first choice either, well, there you go. The system, working.

Helot zoomed in on Tau Prius III, his booby prize, a cold and soggy orb on its best day, less pleasant in the winter. If anything, he was doing these people a favor by not landing them on that dump. They'd hate it there.

This was a good lie, and he told it to himself often.

They were watching him. When Harold returned home from work the day after he had visited Kevin's apartment, a misplaced hair told him the book had been moved. They had seen him take it, wanted to know what was so special about it, broken into his place, and stepped over his dirty laundry to find out. He was surprised to find that he was comforted by this. Paranoia was a lot easier to live with when it was justified.

Knowing he was being watched made everything that followed proceed much slower. Harold spent the next few weeks going through the most mundane routine possible, trying to bore even himself. Work, home, sleep. Work, home, sleep. Work, sleep, home, sleep. By the time he found himself in the skating rink, almost a month after Kevin's death, he hoped that anyone watching him had long since died of understimulation.

The skating rink was the largest of the many broken and forgotten toys on the Argos. Wildly popular when the ship first launched, there had been problems maintaining it, something to do with the artificial surface not regenerating as expected, or that it was more bother to manufacture than it was worth, or that it was really hard work, or something. As the surface grew grittier and stickier, skating had grown less popular. The rink was all but abandoned now, the ship's elected officials having spent the last decade farting about deciding what to do with the space.

But as a kid, Kevin had loved the rink, his eight year old brain not knowing or caring that it had gone out of style. Harold had taken him here a couple of times a week, marveling at the pace at which the boy's skating skills outgrew his own, while hoping that wasn't a metaphor for something.

And when Kevin ran away a few months later, Harold wasn't surprised that he would run here. Harold couldn't even recall the reason he had run—some childish fit with one of his case workers. Security hadn't paid much attention. Their thinking, that runaways couldn't run very far on the Argos, was solid. But Harold had paid attention, more father than not at that point in Kevin's life.

Harold finished strapping up his awful, smelly skates—they were reason enough for the sport to go out of fashion—and stepped out onto the surface. Not ice, but a special self lubricating polymer, it had supposedly worked fantastically for the first forty years of their voyage before running into its life expectancy like it had hit a wall. Harold lurched and stumbled about the rink, plowing through the areas of inconsistent friction. He was the only one skating—the attendant had been sleeping when he had arrived. So, anyone watching him would look suspicious as hell. But now that he was a full month into 'Operation: Bore Big Brother,' he didn't anticipate anyone else showing up. He was safe, though perhaps not from his skating skills he realized while halfway to the ground, one of his skates having stopped dead in a divot.

After another five minutes of lurch-filled, chancy skating, with no suspicious-looking goons arriving to watch, Harold decided that he was probably alone. He picked his way to the edge of the surface and hobbled along the side of the rink to the locker rooms.

This was where he had found the boy when he had run away. Kevin had already been gone for a day by the time anyone bothered to inform Harold. Harold had come to the rink almost immediately, guessing the boy's thinking. One of the rink attendants mentioned that he had seen a kid that looked like Kevin hanging around, and Harold had spent the afternoon searching the place. The lockers were an obvious choice, as Kevin himself later attested. His first night away he had tried to sleep in one of them, learning the hard way about the human body's preference for consciousness when upright.

Harold checked the lockers now, just for the sake of completeness. No lost little boys. He backed up, returning to the entrance to the locker room, where, partially blocked behind the swinging doors of the entrance, was a smaller door. He opened this, the janitor's closet. It didn't look much different than the first and last time he saw it eighteen years earlier. The only difference was the shelf full of cleaning pads, which was now a little further away. During his time here, Kevin had moved the shelving unit back off the wall, creating a gap behind it, wide enough to build a little nest. It was artfully done; Harold didn't know that there were any janitors actually using the closet, much less any janitors capable of caring about a shelving unit that had moved.

Harold moved some of the cleaning pads out of the way, setting them down on the floor beside him. Leaning into the shelving unit, he peered along the edge of the wall. A terminal. He had to rearrange a few more stacks of cleaning supplies before he could get at it, but once he did, he turned it over in his hands, examining it. Someone had vandalized it somehow. With a flash of recognition, he realized it was a dummy terminal, the network interface crudely deactivated with something sharp.

He turned the terminal on. Front and center was a video message, sitting in a directory full of confusingly labeled files. Harold opened the video. It was a tight shot of Kevin, sitting on the floor of the same closet, speaking quietly at the camera. His face was shiny—oily or sweaty, Harold couldn't tell—and he seemed to be blinking too much.

Hey. I don't know what I'm doing. I don't know who's watching this. I hope it's you, uh...you know who you are. But if it's not, then oh well.

I really don't know what I'm doing.

Okay. The basics. The captain of the ship has a plan to split the ship in two. Yeah. Just look at the attached files. It's all in there.

I know this because I'm a lieutenant in the navy. Three months ago, I discovered we were off course. Not badly, but we're definitely off course. We can correct it, but it will cost us a lot of reaction mass. Fuel. I don't know the complete details, but that means we might not have enough fuel to stop. Not stop the whole ship, anyways. A smaller ship could arrive at Tau Prius. And this ship can do that. Split in two, I mean. But the thing of it is, there's stuff that doesn't make sense about the fuel. But then I'm told to shut up, and.... Listen, like I said, it's complicated. Look at the attached files. It's way clearer there.

Anyways, whether I'm wrong or not, the ship needs to know about this. The public. These kinds of decisions can't be made behind closed doors. You should hear the way they talk. So, I took copies of everything. For weeks, I've been copying everything I've seen. It proves everything. You're holding this right now.

Actually, what you're really holding is my backup plan. I'm going to try sending this into the feeds. That won't be easy. I think IT is scanning for this. And they've got programs to wipe material off of the network. But I think I've got a way around that. I've taken some precautions.

And if it doesn't work, well, I guess that's my career over, then. It's worth it, though, I think. Gotta try.

But that's why I've hidden this here. The backup, the last copy. The proof. If you find this, be careful with it. Maybe just pretend you didn't see it? It hasn't done me much good. But I couldn't let it disappear. This has to get out sooner or later.

I better go now. Good luck confused janitor, or whoever you are.

Harold realized he was leaning heavily against the wall. *Oh, Kevin. You brave, foolish boy.* Ignoring Kevin's warnings, Harold tucked the terminal into the waistband of his pants, rearranging his clothes atop it. Then, he returned to the locker room. As he was leaving, he caught a glimpse of himself in the mirrors and stopped, suddenly light-headed. There, looking back at him, was the same bleached and hunted look that he had just seen on Kevin's face.

5

The Lam

"This is bullshit," Bruce wheezed as they jogged along the first level.

"Bullshit," Stein agreed, measuring her pace so he could keep up with her.

"We haven't done anything!" Beside her, Bruce came to a stop, hands on his knees. She stopped to watch him vomit noisily on the ground.

"No, not that part," Bruce said when he was done. "That part's okay. I have done things." Extending his finger like a gun, he shot Stein several times. "No, the bullshit is how they waited for us to get drunk first. They coulda...they coulda...waited for tomorrow. Issss bullshit."

Stein didn't remember much after the violent shaking had rattled the ship. Dust everywhere. People rushing into the streets. People rushing off the streets. She saw at least two people literally running in circles. She might have herself for all she knew. Mostly, she had wandered in a daze, replaying what she knew. They had split the ship in two. She could see it, a model of the ship spinning around in her head, as the aft of the ship detached like a cork and rocketed away. They had been working on disconnects and cutting the ones that were jammed. They had been evacuating and evicting people from the aft. And when Gabelman had stumbled upon this, a week too early, they had killed him for it.

And now, it was over. She was on half a ship.

She didn't know why they had done it. She still didn't even know *who* had done it. Kinsella and his trolls? The navy, alone? She didn't care. She eventually washed up at a table in the Prairie with a bottle of Orange in her hand. She was mildly surprised to find the bar mostly empty; apparently, everyone else had gone south to gape at the bulkhead doors. A few messages had convinced Abdolo Poland to leave his nest—the promise of booze worked well. And there was no need to hide any longer. Their hunters were thousands of miles away by that point and weren't coming back.

Reunited, the pair quickly got obliterated. Ellen arrived not long after they did, easily lured to midday bar missions, and protested that she had trouble keeping up with their self-medicating—"No small statement, coming from me." Bruce and Stein told her what had happened, Bruce pantomiming maybe a few more karate chops into his part of the story than were probably accurate. Ellen didn't believe a word of the plot, it all being too big for her to swallow. "Also, no small statement, coming from me."

And then the news feeds announced that the doors had opened back up, revealing the security troops and all the rest of the ship still there. Ellen had fallen out of her chair laughing. The drinking didn't abate, taking on a lighter but more confusing tone.

Stein had been *so sure*. Everything had made sense. But there were the security officers, coming back through the just opened doors. Her mind lurched through explanations, trying to shoehorn this new information into her theory.

Helot's announcement an hour later, informing Stein and Bruce that they had nearly destroyed the ship, had not clarified matters. It did get Ellen's attention however, their friend leaping into action, immediately hustling them out of the bar. She whispered instructions to Bruce as they swerved down to the first level, then parted ways with the pair. Together, Stein and Bruce moved as quickly as their equilibrium allowed to a safe house, one Ellen and Bruce had used in a previous life.

"Are you hurt?" Stein asked Bruce, who had been walking for the past half block with his hands over his face.

"No. I'm hiding."

"You're a bit bigger than your hands there, buddy."

"Your *face* is bigger than your hands."

Stein checked. "Nope. I'm good."

"You should disguise yourself, too. We're fugitives now." Stein had noted a few curious glances as they retreated. All people who could point them out to security later.

"You don't think that a couple people walking down the street with their faces hidden in their hands won't attract more attention?"

"Yeah, because that's the weirdest thing anyone's ever done in public." That argument seemed airtight to Stein and the two bottles of Orange she'd had. The pair covered the rest of the distance clutching their faces.

The neighborhood around their hideout on the first level was almost completely abandoned. The lights and heating didn't work as reliably in that part of the ship, and aside from people who didn't like other people, it was mostly deserted. Most importantly, none of the security sensors in the area were working—something Ellen evidently checked as a hobby.

"In here," Bruce whispered, flicking his eyes at the non-descript door of what looked to be a disused fabrication plant. The pair huddled around the door while he did something funny with the locking mechanism. Stein looked at his hands; they seemed to be tapping a hidden sensor underneath the lip of the door panel. It slid open, and they entered into what Stein now understood to be a Breeder safe house.

"What's that smell?" she asked. "Did someone die in here?"

Bruce looked at her, his face suddenly tight. "Yeah." The door slid shut behind them.

Hogg slowly panned the terminal back and forth, looking for heat signatures in the room across the street. Scattered up and down the block, his team was doing the same, half of them with their sidearms ready. They had all seen the footage of the terrorist rampaging through the Bridge—it was one of the most popular clips of the day—and Thorias had reported that two officers were killed in the explosions last night. Enough to put an itch in any cop's trigger finger. Especially if the cops in question didn't get to use guns very often. No one had shot themselves accidentally yet, but Hogg sensed it was coming.

They were searching a nearly abandoned section of the first level in the northern end of the ship. The streets were more unkempt than usual for the bottom deck, littered with broken furniture and disused machinery. These rooms and buildings were mostly warehouses and machine shops, clustered in one of the ship's original and long unneeded fabrication centers. At different times in the ship's history, this area had been repurposed into various forms of residential and commercial space, but in the current epoch, living in chilly caverns wasn't that popular, leaving many of the spaces vacant. A good place to hide, and when sensors had spotted Stein and Redenbach descending to this area a few hours earlier, Hogg and his team had been ordered after them.

Stein had completely fooled him. During their first meeting, he had only had the vaguest sense that she was concealing something, but as he got that feeling from most people, he hadn't thought much of it. Not a very useful skill, really, thrown off by the simple truth that most people *were* concealing something.

He hoped they weren't *all* concealing murder.

He supposed it might not have been her specifically, more likely that Redenbach character with the blood on his hands. But it was clear that one of them murdered Gabelman after he had stumbled upon their plot. The background check on Stein had changed within the past few hours, now heavily stressing her connections to the Breeders. He wondered what other surprises Stein had that he would find out about too late.

This was a logical place for them to run. Along with half the criminal groups in the ship's history, the Breeders were known to have used some of the buildings in this area. All the sensors were scrapped, and few people were around to see something they shouldn't.

Though not completely abandoned, Hogg's team had already scared up a half-dozen false positives. In one room, a couple of teenagers had been interrupted practicing basic population growth techniques. He had also kicked in the door on a group of fake homeless squatting in an old hydroponics bay, gathered around a cooking fire. Hogg hated the Fauxmless. No one on board the Argos *could* be homeless—there was just too much damned space. Indeed, the minimum standard of living had always been very high by most human standards. Compared to the slums of the big inland cities of Earth, it was a utopia. Which inevitably meant that after a couple of generations, homelessness had turned into an exotic hobby for certain types of Argosians. Hogg was not among that type—he thought they were idiots, an opinion that wasn't changed by this particular group. They weren't even cooking, just singeing meal bars over a fire. He'd had to fight off an urge to launch one of the idiots into the flames himself.

They rounded a corner and resumed their search on the next street over. Hogg was frustrated at the stupidity of their hunt. It was way too much ground to search with only a dozen bodies. If these terrorists were as dangerous as Thorias said, why hadn't he released more security officers to help with the search? Keeping hundreds of officers on guard duty in the aft didn't make any sense at all. Hogg had long been smart enough to spot and suppress the instinct to suggest better solutions to his superiors, but this one was particularly challenging. *What could they be thinking?*

Sergei watched the man a few blocks away, standing perfectly still in the center of the street. Sergei's hands flexed, fingers rolling and unrolling around his pistol. The guy had walked into the street a few minutes earlier and was now facing the barricade, perfectly still, his hands at his sides like a gunslinger. Sergei didn't have to look to know that every other officer on the barricade was watching the same man.

They had spent twelve hours on the barricade before being shifted off for a too brief rest. Now, midday on the day after the attacks, they were back on guard duty, an uneventful shift until now. The few people that had approached the barricade were different shades of annoyed, frustrated by the bizarrely complicated approval process for getting access to the aft. But all had been civil. At least until this maniac stepped into the center of the road. People with that kind of haircut tended to lack a bit in the civility department.

"What do you think he's doing?" one of the other officers asked.

"Hard to say," Sergei said. "Being incredibly crazy, I'd guess."

As if to underscore Sergei's point, the man broke into a run, charging straight at the barricade, screaming like an animal. For thirty seconds they watched him run, his scream uninterrupted but for short gasps to catch his breath.

"What the fuck is he doing?"

"Whatever it is, I think he's lost the element of surprise."

"What should we do?"

"I don't know. Sergei?"

Sergei didn't respond, only readying his pistol. When the man got within five meters of the barricade, Sergei fired. The man slumped to the ground, his scream finally silenced.

"Nice shot."

"Yeah, nice shot, Sergei."

"Did you have to lead him much?"

Lacking any better ideas, they left the man lying there, offering helpful comments on how he should best regain consciousness. Sergei finally got a good look at him, bare-chested, apparently completely unarmed, and, as suspected, wearing a haircut that was not a sane man's. Finally, Sergei reported the incident to command, who sounded more bemused than concerned.

Twenty minutes later the man stirred, moaning into the ground. Over the next few minutes, he rearranged his limbs under himself before eventually sitting up. He stared at the security officers watching him from the other side of their plastic fortifications, squinted, then put a hand over one eye. His head bobbed around unsteadily, and he blinked several times before finally saying a single word—"Rad." Getting to his feet, he rocked back and forth on his heels a few times before retreating to the north. Collectively, all the officers at the barricade exhaled.

Five minutes later, he pulled the same stunt again, charging at the baffled security officers as before, achieving an identical result. But before he could stir, he was joined by another lunatic, who charged behind him a few seconds later. As Sergei explained what was happening to an extremely confused dispatch, a group of three more men and a woman tried the same stunt, the last one screaming "Wheee!" as she was brought down.

A crowd of onlookers had gathered down the street. Laughter and large gestures. They were egging each other on, and every few minutes another one joined the lunatic pigpile forming at the base of the barricade. Sergei's frantic calls for reinforcements eventually yielded fruit, and more security officers streamed to the barricade to witness—and participate—in the spectacle.

Within an hour, the Argos' latest sport had established a codified set of rules, with points based on speed, distance, and style. Not long after that, someone elbowed Sergei, showing him a terminal and the current leader board. He turned away, wondering if the stunned expression he surely had on his face would become permanent.

"Well, what the fuck do you make of that?" Helot asked. One hand was pressed to his face, massaging his cheek, eye, and temple, and everything else exposed to the stupid he had just seen on the screens. Across the table, Thorias watched the scene unfold, arms crossed.

"I think there are two ways to look at it," Thorias finally said. "One, they're not angry at us. It's a game to them. That's good news. They wouldn't be assing around like that if they suspected what we were doing." Helot nodded, seeing the logic in that. "The second interpretation," Thorias continued, "is that this means they're not scared of us."

"And that's also a good thing."

Thorias' head waggled back and forth. "I guess it is for now."

"Ohhhhhh, I don't like the sound of that. I don't like it at all when you get contemplative."

Thorias flicked his head at the image in front of them. "This is just games so far. And we'll let them play. In a controlled fashion. Install extra padding, get some medics there, that kind of thing. Have a lot more officers on hand. For safety's sake." He smiled.

"For safety's sake," Helot echoed.

"But we have to plan for something a lot worse than this happening. We still haven't found Kinsella," Thorias said, giving Helot a knowing look. Helot's toes curled, regretting his master villain moment yet again. "It's only a matter of time before he starts telling people what we're up to. And when he does, these little games will become a lot more serious. We should be ready for that."

"Ready for what, exactly?"

Thorias reached down to clear the display, bringing up a map of the aft of the Argos in its place. "The worst case scenario I can see is a group of several hundred of them, armed with pistols." Helot's eyes widened. "Now, we don't think they're armed yet. But it won't take long once they decide they want to. The schematics for the pistols will be floating around somewhere— I'm all but certain Kinsella has a set—and they certainly have the fabrication capacity. We could try to station guards around all the fabrication areas, but there are a lot of them, and that would leave us spread very thin in the aft. Hard to defend the core and Curts and his cutting teams then. So, yeah, I think they could put together pistols. And rounding up a few hundred maniacs is something I can imagine our mayor doing." Thorias reached down on to the map and pulled up a custom layer. Colored lines and arrows appeared, thrusting and parrying back and forth across the 9th Avenue threshold.

Helot held up a finger to interrupt Thorias while he composed his next words carefully. *"Are you out of your fucking mind?"* he finally asked, struggling to keep his voice steady. The words hung in the air as the rest of the control room went quiet.

"Sir?"

"You're planning a ground war?" Helot's hands shook as he gestured at the map. "You have, readily available, incredibly detailed plans on how to fight a ground war on this ship. Is this a hobby of yours?"

Thorias stood up straighter. "I think it's prudent to consider all the possibilities."

"All the possibilities? Really? All of them?" Helot's voice started shaking. "This arrow here," he said, pointing at the map. "What's this arrow represent?"

Thorias examined the map. "Twenty enemy troops circling behind one of our positions."

"Enemy troops! They're not our enemy! They're not even troops! What the fuck?"

"Sir..."

"No. No! Not gonna happen." Helot pointed a finger at the security chief, the closest he had come to a threat in years. He was *livid.* His careful calculations had accounted for no loss of life during the separation itself. Certainly not for an extended ground war. "You're going to find Kinsella, we're going to keep him quiet, and there's not going to be any fucking arrows on any fucking maps. We'll keep the doors closed and politely ask everyone to stay out of the aft."

Thorias exhaled through his nose. "Sir, those doors will not stay closed for long—the locks aren't foolproof, and there are people over there capable of bypassing them. If that happens..."

"If that happens, then you'll have to deal with the couple drunk idiots who figured it out. Not twenty enemy troops. Shit." He shook his head, still unable to believe the madman he had working for him. "Shit," he added.

Thorias stared at him for a few agonizingly slow-moving seconds. "Yes, sir," he finally said and reached out to turn off the map. It was a gesture which should have caused Helot to relax, but he had a hard time doing that. He knew the map wasn't going anywhere, that Thorias would simply keep his plans to himself from now on. A worrying thought. But there was no way he could replace the security chief now.

"There is one other thing, Captain," Thorias said, interrupting Helot's train of thought. "When are we going to tell my officers about what we're doing here? And their families?"

Helot swallowed. They had plans for that, pamphlets and other reading material that would have been a lot easier to digest when read in the detached engine core, several thousand miles away from the rest of the ship, several thousand miles away from any chance of turning back. "They won't need to know for now, will they?" he asked.

Thorias stared back at him, not committing to anything. "No, I don't see the advantage of telling them. Not yet." He panned the map back towards the bow.

"You were leaving officers behind, correct? Have they contacted you? How have you handled that?"

"Hogg's unit. I put them on to Stein and Redenbach. I figure if they find them, hey, great, and if they don't, then at least it keeps them out of our hair for the next few days."

"How is he? This Hogg?" Helot asked. He was glad for anything to change the subject.

Thorias stared back at him, expressionless. "Well, he's not great." Over the past few years, Thorias had been altering security officer assignments, moving the least desirable men off rotation where he could, and when he couldn't, to the lone security outpost in the north of the ship, the Community Outreach and Policing Center. "Most of the ones we're leaving are low achievers, as discussed. And everyone with weak Sheeping. Hogg's one of those. We'd actually tried to get him off-rotation for this month, but there was an injury, and he got pulled back in."

Helot nodded. The "Sheep gene" was a useful misnomer, a label for a complicated set of genetic tweaks designed to make someone more docile. Not precisely mind control, it only twisted the personality to embed a sense of deference towards authority. A useful trait, at least from the perspective of authority. It was also, obviously, wildly illegal and had been secretly introduced into the population a couple of centuries earlier by one of Helot's predecessors, slipped in during routine prenatal genetic screening. There was some unknown complication with the technique, however, and it had only been partially effective, even leading to a few surprising side effects. By the time Helot found out all of this, only a fraction of the population retained anything approaching full Sheeping. Unsurprisingly, a large fraction of that number found themselves serving in naval and security roles.

"Otherwise, Hogg's not that bad," Thorias said. "I almost wish we could have kept him."

Of course you did, always handy to have another arrow for your map. Helot ran his hand through his hair, just a little surprised when no clumps came out with it.

Clicks and bumps and satisfied noises drifted over to Stein from somewhere to her left, the sounds of Bruce playing with his new toys. He had a lot to choose from; their hiding spot was well salted with firearms. And unlike nearly every other thing on the Argos, pistols were simple in design and incredibly durable. Whatever Bruce was cooing over was evidently still in working order, despite its advanced age.

The first Argos-wide conflict had also been the nastiest. Whatever experience the participants of that conflict lacked in space-bound guerrilla warfare, they made up for in exuberance. What would later be called Argos War I occurred a little more than thirty years after the ship had departed. The cause of this conflict was predictable to the point of being droll: people were being jerks and not sharing. Specifically, a group of vocal media figures and protestors began shrieking that the government was hoarding higher quality food, resources, and living quarters for themselves and their families. The protesters even began calling themselves 'The Hungry'—although later historians would agree that label was a wild exaggeration. The government shared a similarly low opinion of the merit of these complaints and did little to address them. A famous political cartoon from the era depicted a large pig in a top hat—labeled Mayor Bradley—perched atop a balcony, depositing a large bowel movement on a group of peasants below. "Eat my shit!" the pig-mayor says.

Eventually, a group of peasants, tired of eating shit, tried something a little more direct. The ship had a smaller security force at the time, with security officers and small security substations scattered throughout the ship. When a sizable group of civilians attacked these isolated stations simultaneously, the officers stationed there were quickly overwhelmed. And once armed with the security weapons available at the time—dual-setting and very lethal—the protestors weren't shy about using them. By the time the remaining security forces could mobilize, the protestors had seized nearly three quarters of the ship. At that point, the rebelling faction nearly equaled the remaining security forces in numbers, and over the next few weeks the Argos saw a number of extraordinarily bloody, yet ultimately indecisive, engagements between the two sides.

Thanks to either a brilliantly executed military maneuver or a piece of blind luck, the government forces defeated the Hungry and vigorously scrubbed the Argos' gene-pool of their genetic legacy. Based on lessons learned during the war, the government soon adopted some considerably different security procedures. Almost all of the security substations throughout the ship were shuttered, with only a single community policing center left active in the bow, along with the main Security HQ in the aft. All officers were equipped with stun-capable weapons only, with the bulk of the lethal weapons destroyed, aside from a small cache kept on hand inside the main Security base.

Similar disputes about resource distribution would flare up a couple more times in the history of the Argos, but never with the same ferocity. Using undercover agents and a network of informants, security kept a very tight lid on any vocally aggrieved groups that did form, and the few times violence did break out, it was met with immediate, overwhelming force. Any willing combatants fighting the security forces soon found that they weren't willing for very long.

The only other time the government of the Argos had been seriously threatened was when Stein was a young woman. Since the ship had launched, people had always chafed at the external approval needed before having a child—a necessary but uncomfortable fact of life on a generation ship. Two hundred years of bureaucratic growth has caused those restrictions to grow bloated, cumbersome, and blatantly unfair. When Stein was just finishing school, the fight against these restrictions was quietly taken up by a group calling themselves the Breeders. Their cause was a popular one, at least amongst the people who cared about things. More critically, the Breeders also had the support of two or three high ranking people within the ship's government, who helped steer attention away from the fledgling group, aware of the efforts the security forces would use to disrupt them.

Over time, the Breeders worked up the nerve to attack the government directly, using a stockpile of homemade weaponry they had been quietly fabricating. A group of the bravest, possibly dumbest, and certainly angriest of the Breeders staged a ridiculously daring raid on the security headquarters, going after the weapons cache. They were able to penetrate right to the heart of the base without meeting any serious resistance, aided by the use of a secret maintenance tunnel discovered by a certain Breeder sympathizer called Laura Stein, working in her brand-new position in the maintenance department. There, the Breeder team secured a portion of the weapons cache, only to find themselves trapped by the security forces as they tried to retreat.

Both sides had stories about what happened next, but only one side's became accepted history. The way that story goes, the Breeder fighters began using some of their newly acquired lethal weaponry to fight their way out, killing several security officers, and thanks to their unfamiliarity with the properties of the weapons they were handling, at least some of themselves in the process.

That revelation pretty much killed whatever public support there was left for the Breeders, and the handful who weren't involved in the violence, along with those who had escaped from the battle at the security base, went into hiding. The witch-hunt that security enthusiastically conducted afterwards caught some of them, but at least a few managed to escape detection, including three of Stein's best friends. But with their organization in pieces, the code words and safe houses and weapon caches they had used were mothballed and left dormant.

Until now. Stretching out, Stein rolled over on the floor of the safe house, careful to keep her cloak over her as she repositioned her cramped limbs. "You're sure these things will work?" she asked the shimmering lump beside her.

"Try it and see," the lump responded with Bruce's voice.

Stein pulled out her terminal and instructed it to scan in the infrared, panning it back and forth over Bruce, hidden beneath his own shimmering infrared cloak. A bright spot appeared on the screen, glowing orange-red. "I can see your leg."

"Oops." The cloak shifted. "How about now?"

"Now, I can see the top of your head. Your cloak a bit small, champ?"

"Was that a fat joke?"

Stein laughed.

And so they waited, waiting to be hunted down, waiting to be declared innocent, waiting for the universe to decide what to do with them. While Bruce busied himself with the pistol and stun grenades he had dug out of the weapons cache, Stein sat and fumed.

She had already sent a message to Sergei from a false identity using Bruce's rigged terminal. He hadn't responded. She wasn't surprised by that. Even if he didn't think she was a bomb-throwing anarchist, there was little chance he would be seen talking publicly with her now. For a few seconds, she entertained the idea that he had known about the plot the whole time. She dismissed that idea quickly; Sergei had trusting, kind-of-dumb eyes. If he had any secrets, they weren't that big.

"Are you thinking what I'm thinking?" Bruce asked.

"I'm never thinking what you're thinking, buddy. Woe be the day that it happens."

"Well, I'll tell you then, since you didn't ask. I'm thinking maybe we should do something. About this, I mean. The...the everything." Stein peeked under the edge of her cloak, seeing Bruce's eyes peering back beneath the hem of his. "We should do something about everything."

"Assuming we're right about the...everything," she said. "I don't even know what to call it."

"Split Plot."

"I'm not calling it that."

"Yeah, you will. And we are right. They are doing it."

"Yeah," she agreed. "They are." She thought about it for a moment and added, "You think they'll try again?"

"You think they won't?" Bruce asked.

She sighed. "I guess if it was worth trying once, it's probably worth trying twice."

"Okay, then," Bruce said, satisfied. "So, they'll try again. Which brings me to my original question: Do we want to try and do something about it?"

"Not much we can do under these cloaks."

"Lots we can do under here." Bruce punctuated the thought with a fart.

"How do you do that on command?"

"Does it show up through the cloak?"

"Gross."

Bruce waved his cloak around for a bit, clearing the air. "I mean, let's be realistic," he said. "Doing something about it is unlikely to be very tidy. Or conducive to living. At least knowing the methods we prefer."

"The methods *you* prefer. And what, are you trying to talk me out of something? Because I'm not proposing doing something about this."

"Neither am I. I'm just trying to fill time with a rhetorical dialog."

"Rhetorical dialog? Where do you come up with this shit?" she asked.

"My brain," Bruce said. After a few moments, he continued, "So, let's look at the flip side. Do we want to do nothing about the Split Plot?" Another pause, then, "You know what type of question that was?" She groaned. "Maybe when I answer it myself you'll figure it out." Underneath her cloak she made a rude gesture at him. "I mean, is it so bad that we end up on half a spaceship, flying uncontrollably through space?" he continued.

"That's assuming we could even survive on half a spaceship."

"Why not? We've got a reactor. Fuel. Scrubbers. Recyclers. Plenty of sexy dames and virile studs. We could keep going for centuries."

Stein had come to the same conclusion, but still didn't want to admit it. "I'll think of some reason it won't work."

"There's that *can't do* spirit I love."

She smiled under her cloak. "Okay, how's this: we wouldn't be able to stop at that planet. You know? The big one we've been going to this whole time?"

She could hear Bruce exhale and roll over. "Do we even want to stop at Tau Prius? We don't exactly live bad lives here. You seem pretty happy."

Stein shook her head. "Oh, I'm happy as hell. Living and breathing in a crappy cramped ship. Every god damned surface with a hundred layers of human filth on it. It's lovely."

"I guess when you put it that way."

"You don't want to land?"

Bruce looked away. "No. I do. I guess."

"You guess?"

"I mean, it's not so bad living here. We'd die old and happy."

"Our descendents would freeze to death."

"They'd be cool with that."

Stein laughed despite herself.

She could practically hear Bruce grinning. "Okay," he finally said. "So, we'll stop them, then. Fuck the bad guys, whoever they are."

Stein laughed. "Yeah. We'll just punch our way through a massive, deadly conspiracy."

"Let's do it. Let's kick this ship's ass to save its ass."

Stein smiled, enjoying their brave talk. But she could tell that Bruce was treading dangerously close to convincing himself to do something stupid. Madness, knowing what they were up against, Captain Helot—the announcement of her 'terrorist attack' confirmed he was behind this—and presumably the entire naval and security departments. And her goddamned boss, that little wiener Curts. So, just the major pillars of power on the ship. *And that little wiener Curts.* She shook her head, knowing she would have to talk Bruce out of this before too long.

She was spared the need to pull her friend back from the abyss by the quiet beeping noise of one of their proximity sensors. Two right hands moved to two pistols, both she and Bruce fumbling with their weapons and terminals, checking to see who was coming.

"I got a hit," Croutl said over the commlink. "A machine shop at...4825 Slate."

"What's the IR say?" Hogg called back.

"One person, I think. It's weak though. I think he's pretty far back in there."

"Or she. Okay. Set up across the street. Cover the front door." He looked at the map on the terminal. "Linze, take your team to the entrance in the hall around back." Linze acknowledged his order, while Hogg signaled his own unit to follow.

Only one of them. He wasn't sure whether Stein and Redenbach would split up or not. Maybe. But it was also just as likely they were dealing with another Fauxmless.

Hogg led his team down the block, setting up a short distance away from where the machine shop was. Croutl, Petronus, and Deek had taken up position behind two packing crates across the street. He approached the main door, a double-wide, checking his own IR sensor. There. A strange figure in the back of the warehouse, prone. It was human, but something was obstructing part of it. Only a pair of legs was clearly visible. Just as he was about to shut his IR off, he spotted something else, a patch of blue, unnaturally darker than everything else. It was hard to make out, backgrounded by another wall, almost as cool. But it was definitely there. The patch seemed to shift and shimmer as he looked at it.

"I count one man in there, with a possible camouflaged second," he whispered into the radio. "Okay. Full breach, everyone. Linze, take position." He gestured his team members to positions on either side of the entry door. "Croutl, keep your team outside to cover us. Linze, ready?"

"Ready."

"Five, four, three, two, one, now."

Hogg tapped the access pad with his ungloved hand. Recognizing him as a security officer, the door slid open.

"Security!" someone shouted. "Security! Put your hands up!"

Behind her, gunfire, Bruce shooting wildly. That was the plan—he would cover one door, she would cover the other. But she couldn't move, all muscles locked in place out of terror. Security officers streamed in the door she was supposed to be covering, shooting, stun shots sailing over her head in the direction of Bruce. A bright flash of light and a thud behind her. The officers in front of her ducked, blinded, having missed the brunt of what she guessed was a stun grenade. They were less fortunate when the second grenade exploded on her left, scattering them like leaves.

"Come on, Stein! Back way's clear!" Bruce yelled from somewhere behind her. But she was still stuck, arms and legs refusing to respond, bound tight by fear. More officers streamed in the door in front of her, a vicious volume of fire erupting from their guns. They still hadn't seen her, or hadn't cared, too busy fighting her brave and useful friend.

Finally, one of the officers saw her, a look of recognition splashed across his face. He raised his pistol.

A bright flash of light and then darkness.

Outside the back of the hideout, Bruce stopped, gun pointed at the door he had just exited from. A security goon appeared in the door, Bruce pegging him neatly in the face with a stun shot, blood spurting from the goon's nose. Bruce backpedaled, gun still trained on the door. Another flicker of movement, Bruce scaring it back inside with two more stun shots that thudded into the door frame. He reached the corner of the street and sidestepped, taking cover behind the edge of a building.

"Dammit, Stein!" he hissed, though he was more angry with himself than her. He should have known she would freeze, should have come up with another plan. At minimum, he should have gone down fighting with her. But there had been no time for thinking, barely time for manic reactions. Just shooting and ducking and hurling grenades like a monkey.

Footsteps. Bruce steadied himself, waiting. A security officer appeared around the corner in front of him, Bruce firing a shot in his chest. As the officer fell to the ground, Bruce fired another pair of shots into his groin. *That felt good.* More footsteps. "Crap!" Bruce said, steadying himself.

By the third iteration of rounding a corner only to be dropped by a shot to the face or groin, the security officers had learned their lesson, and he heard no more advancing footsteps. But he knew they would be circling around him or calling for support. Still too many of them left, too many to charge, too many to fight off and rescue Stein. He wished he had some Brash with him, wished he wasn't so useless. Bruce turned and ran, hating himself more with every step he took.

The officers sprawled across the briefing room, making a mockery of the furniture's ergonomic design. The tables and floors were littered with helmets, pistols, intimidation knives, thumping sticks. The men looked tired and angry, Helot thought, realizing with a start that at least some of that anger may have been directed at him.

Thorias stood at the head of the room, not sprawled in the slightest. Helot had invited himself along with Thorias, curious to see the ship's security forces up close. As they had traveled to the briefing room on one of the upper-levels of the security base, he had been surprised at how empty it was. Considering the amount of activity that must be going on, he had assumed the place would be swarming with security men. Which meant that hundreds of security officers were elsewhere. Helot realized that his security chief had been furtively moving his officers about, setting up the lines and arrows on his map without telling him. He wasn't going to dress the chief down in front of his men, but this was something he would have to keep an eye on.

Sergeant Koller entered the room and sprawled amongst the rest of the officers, his position towards the front of the room the only sign of his seniority. He directed a long, disdainful look at Helot before turning his attention to Thorias.

"Well?" Thorias finally asked.

Koller shook his head. "Nothing." Koller and his team were the ones Thorias had sent out mayor-hunting. Unsuccessfully, it seemed.

"Care to expand on that?" Thorias asked.

"It was empty," Koller said. They had found footage of Kinsella entering his home shortly after the failed attempt to split the ship. "He had a hidden back door in his bedroom. The hooker door, I guess. Staircase there, went all the way down to level two. No footage of him coming out, but he could have been in disguise. He had a ton of wigs in that bedroom.

Like, a ton." Koller extended his arms to indicate how many wigs the mayor had. Helot raised his eyebrows. It was a lot.

"How about his associates?"

"Bletmann's place was empty too. No wigs though, thank fuck. Tried a couple other of his friend's places, too. All blanks."

Thorias turned to look at Helot for instructions. Helot just stared back at him blankly. *What else can we do?*

Thorias turned back to his officers. "Well then, keep trying," he said. "Friends of friends. Acquaintances of acquaintances. Find out who the hell is making all these wigs and break some of his fingers."

Helot stepped outside and rubbed his face in his hands. *Why was every-thing so hard?* A moment later, Thorias joined him outside. Wordlessly, they began walking down the nearly deserted corridors of the security base.

"He doesn't wear wigs in public, does he?" Helot asked after a while.

"No, not that I'm aware of."

"Which means he's wearing them in private."

"That stands to reason."

"Why am I thinking about that?" Helot shouted. "Why can't I stop think-ing about the mayor's sexy wig time? What a fucking disaster!"

"I'd try not to think..."

"What if there aren't even any hookers? *What if it's just him and the wigs?"*

Helot's despair was interrupted by a beep from Thorias' terminal and Thorias' abrupt and grateful grab for the device. The pair of them stopped in the entrance lobby for the security base. The chief clucked his tongue a couple times. "Well, there's some good news," he finally said. "We've tak-en Laura Stein into custody."

"Who?"

"The terrorist. The lady one."

"Oh, right. The Argos' most wanted criminal. I guess the danger's over then." Helot chuckled.

"She's being held in the bow detachment. Looks like she and her bud-dy tore up Hogg's team pretty bad. They lost the fat one entirely."

"I thought Hogg wasn't that bad?"

"So did I." The pair resumed their journey, stepping out of the securi-ty base into the street. A couple blocks north of them, the massive bulk-head door loomed. "What do you want to do with her?" Thorias asked. "Throw away the key?"

Helot stared at the bulkhead door and all the bad decisions its pres-ence reminded him of. He closed his lips and exhaled, inflating his cheeks. "How close did she come to figuring it all out?"

"Close. Her and her buddy were snooping after the other dead technician. We know they saw one of the disconnects."

Helot's eyes narrowed. The other dead technician. The other *murdered* technician. Yet another reason to reign in Thorias and his goons. "Think she'll start squawking about it?" He shook his head, knowing the answer. "Of course she will. I would." He exhaled. "Can we bring her down here? Away from anyone who might be willing to listen?"

Thorias nodded. "I'll have her moved to the main holding cells right now." He tapped something into his terminal. "How long we going to keep her for?"

Helot turned away from the door. "I guess we can probably just hang on to her until we're ready to try again," he said. "Then cut her loose."

"Or just leave her there in the cells. The security base should remain intact when we detach."

Helot snorted. *Should.* Another life tossed around pretty casually. "Fine," he said and walked away from the bulkhead door, wanting to get away from the security man. From all the security men.

Stein opened her eyes. She was looking at something large and flat. Something that looked pretty floorish. *I know this. I know this thing. This is a floor.*

She closed her eyes again, the strain of piecing this together having exhausted her. Her head throbbed. Her legs throbbed. Her stomach throbbed. The volume of half-digested food rocketing up her throat may also have throbbed, but given its rapid movement, it was hard to tell. The probable floor in front of her was soon coated by a definite layer of vomit.

She opened her eyes again. Everything outside the center of her vision was blurry, as was everything inside the center of her vision. She could tell she was in a room, empty save for a couple of large, blurry objects and a puddle of blurry vomit. Rushing things, she tried to sit up, failing completely. Her hands seemed to be bound together behind her. A couple of minutes passed, as she let her brain reacquaint itself with her body. Eventually, she tried sitting up again, this time more or less succeeding.

"Look who's awake." A man's voice, behind her. She dragged herself around to face him, her vision finally starting to clear up. She was in a jail cell, a small room with a bunk on one side, toilet in the corner. One end of the room was sealed with heavy plastic bars, behind which stood a security officer, looking at her sternly. She squinted, recognizing him. The officer who'd been investigating Gabelman's death. Hogg.

"Where am I?" she tried to ask, though her ears told her that what she said sounded more like "Hurk." Her mouth filled with saliva, the act of speaking spreading the bile taste in her mouth.

"Where?" Hogg said. "In trouble. More specifically, a holding cell in the Detachment on 40th. So, Big Trouble. And don't move around too much. It just makes things worse."

"Gotcha," she replied, her ears informing her that she had gotten that sound basically right. She twisted her body around to face the rear wall, and waggled her arms, still bound behind her back. "So, you're not going to take these off, then?"

"No."

"Okay," Stein said, after a moment's consideration. "Is that even legal? Isn't that, like, abuse?"

"I think the laws prohibiting abusing you would be rapidly redefined if this ever went to court," Hogg said. "You have pissed a lot of people off."

"Oh." Any despair she might have felt at her situation quickly turned to annoyance, that familiar feeling of self-righteousness coursing through her. "So, you're just here to mock me, then?"

Hogg looked at her carefully for a moment before responding. "I'm here because I want to know where your friend went."

Stein laughed. "Slippery, isn't he? I've honestly got no idea. Someplace stupid I imagine. Good luck bringing him down. Better men than you have tried."

Hogg smiled, his lips tight on his teeth. "You weren't that hard to find once. I think we'll manage."

Her shoulders sagged fractionally; he had a point. She tried to stand up, nailing it on her first try. She celebrated by sitting down heavily on the bunk. "We aren't terrorists," she said.

"Okay. Don't care."

Ah. She'd forgotten what it was like dealing with a security officer she wasn't fucking on the side. "Why not?" she finally asked. "Seems the kind of thing you should care about." She banged her head against the wall behind her. She'd had a speech prepared for this, her innocence speech. But the words were all scrambled now. "Everything that Captain Helot said about us was a lie." She looked at Hogg, who was wearing an expression that implied he was daring her to make him care. "You probably don't believe me right now," she continued. "That's okay. I wouldn't either."

"You and your friend incapacitated a half-dozen security officers in front of my eyes," Hogg replied.

"I guess there's that," she allowed. "Wasn't really me that did that though."

"And then there's the two men you killed last night."

"We didn't kill anyone last night." She shook her head. "That's part of the lie. What were their names? The people we killed?"

Hogg's eyebrows furrowed. "And there's Ron Gabelman."

Stein shivered. She'd forgotten about Ron. "That wasn't us, either." She looked Hogg in the eyes. "Do you really believe I killed Ron?"

"I do now." Stein looked away from him and his smug face. Then she realized something: he didn't seem to be lying. Which meant he honestly wasn't aware of the plot. Helot had kept it from him, too.

Twisting around, she struggled to prop herself up on the hard pillow, trying to face Hogg from a sitting position. "Okay, I get it. Time to lay all the cards on the table." She hesitated, and looked at her feet for a while, ordering her words. "The captain is trying to divide this ship in two. I mean literally, physically, run it through a saw, divide the ship in two. The entire aft section of the ship, above the fourth level, the part with the engines and main fuel tanks—it's designed to pop off like a cork. The massive shaking we felt wasn't a terrorist attack. It was a botched attempt to *split. The. God. Damned. Ship. In two.*"

Hogg had been pretty stationary during this whole process but somehow became even more still, his only movement being a gradual widening of the eyes. Seconds passed. A smile thawed his face, and he began to chuckle softly. "I get to hear a great deal of bullshit in this job, but that? That's the best one yet. That bullshit is *classy.*"

She continued, ignoring his sleight. "Everything since then has been an effort by the captain to conceal what he did. The announcement about the fake terrorist attack. The bulkhead doors and the barricades. The entire aft has been locked down while he tries again."

"To saw the ship in half?"

"Yes!"

Hogg let out a short bark, the opening fraction of a laugh. "You people can always tie every damned thing into your conspiracies. Everything's proof if you squint at it long enough."

Stein swallowed, working to control her frustration. "So, you honestly didn't know?"

"Know what?" Hogg asked, enunciating each word carefully. "Did I know the captain was slicing the ship in two? No. I didn't know that."

She stared at the ceiling, knowing it was hopeless, but feeling her old familiar stubbornness rearing its head. Slowly, she eased herself back to lean against the wall. "Okay, think about this. Yesterday morning, you remember being ordered to report to the aft? All the security officers rushing to the rear core? Why do you think that happened *before* the bulkhead doors closed? Which happened *before* this terrorist attack?"

Hogg snorted. "I wasn't ordered anywhere."

Stein blinked. "I saw it happen. I saw security officers running south just before those bulkhead doors closed. You must have been."

"I don't know what to tell you, crazy lady," Hogg said, smiling. "I was in bed. Went to the office around nine. This office. *In the bow*. Rest of my unit was here, too."

She shook her head. "That doesn't make sense. They would take all the security with them. Unless..." She looked at Hogg and started laughing. "Heh. Okay. Wow. You're not going to like this."

Hogg cocked an eyebrow. "What's that?"

"If you weren't recalled to the aft before they tried to separate, that means they were going to leave you behind, too."

Hogg laughed. "Oh, that's cute. I love you guys. Everything's always a neat little package."

It did sound a little neat and tidy, Stein had to admit. *But didn't the truth always tend to do that?* "Okay, fine," she said. "I get that you don't believe a word. I don't care that you don't care. I just thought you should know." She looked him in the eye. "If you don't believe me..."

"I don't."

"Fuck, I get it, okay? Look, try doing your own research. See if you can find out why every security officer except for you was ordered to the aft of the ship yesterday morning. At the very least, it might let you know where you stand."

Hogg's lip curled a bit, as if he was about to say something, before it slid back down. Then, without a word, he walked away, the sound of his footsteps retreating down the hall. A door closed.

"Hit a nerve, did I?"

She rolled over onto her stomach, her arms sore behind her. She didn't know why she had told him all that. A pointless endeavor. He obviously wouldn't believe a word she had said. But lying there on her scratchy gray blanket, she had felt a burning need for him to believe her. She buried her face in the hard pillow.

Stein had spent a large chunk of her youth on the outside, looking in. With a bit of work, she had managed to convince herself that she liked it, that the life of a loner suited her. But lying to yourself was a kid's game. She had grown up, gotten friends, a good job, a veneer of social respectability. For a decade, she had been on the inside, and *it was awesome*. People talked to her. Sought out her opinions. She mattered.

And Helot had taken all that away from her, condemning Bruce and her to a life as fugitives. That's what really annoyed her. The scope of what he was really doing—the stupid goddamned Split Plot—that was too big. Too much to comprehend. But taking away her life? Her reputation?

That was small enough to just piss her off. That's why she had tried to convince Hogg. She wanted him to believe her. She remembered Ellen's laughter upon hearing the same story. *That bitch.* Stein rolled over to her other side, trying to find a comfortable position to orient her constrained limbs. Hell, she would settle for *anyone* believing her.

For the fifth time, Kinsella read the news bulletin. He drummed his fingers on the desk, then checked it once more to see if it had changed.

UNDER INTERROGATION, TERRORIST LAURA STEIN CONFIRMS SHE WAS ACTING UNDER ORDERS OF MAYOR ERIC KINSELLA. ERIC KINSELLA IS CURRENTLY BEING SOUGHT FOR QUESTIONING. CURRENT LEVELS OF SECURITY WILL REMAIN AT ELEVATED LEVELS UNTIL THE THREAT OF MORE TERROR ATTACKS SUBSIDES.—SECURITY CHIEF THORIAS.

"Well, that was only a matter of time." He leaned back, the filthy chair beneath him creaking and groaning in protest. He hated that chair and lashed out at it, kicking wildly with his heels. "Arrrrrrrgh!" he yelled, connecting with it solidly with one of his bruised heels, bruised from a similar tantrum an hour earlier. "Stupid damned traitor chair!"

He stopped kicking and slumped down in the awful chair, his chin coming to rest on his chest. When he was thinking calmly, Kinsella knew he had done about as well as he could, given the circumstances. Unfortunately, calm thinking was a bit of a challenge. He worked on that now, impeded somewhat by his throbbing heel.

He didn't recall how he had left the Captain's office, he only had the headache to tell him it wasn't a gentle trip. The shaking that had rattled the ship had roused him to consciousness, coming to in the middle of a small side street on the fourth level. He had spent the next hour wandering the crowded streets in a rage, hurling obscenities at closed bulkhead doors and any members of the electorate who dared look at him. Bletmann had eventually tracked him down, politely shepherding him back to his spacious home in the garden well where he could vent without further damaging his approval rating.

Then the bulkhead doors had opened. *The bastard messed it up.* The images on the feeds of security officers setting up barricades made that clear enough. And when the feeds showed small groups of officers moving through angry crowds, Kinsella immediately realized where they were going. Helot would be scrambling to salvage his plot, and as perhaps the only other person who knew what had actually happened, the mayor was now a hunted man. Within a minute, Kinsella had abandoned his home, traveling belowdecks to this regrettable little hovel belonging to

Bletmann's cousin's friend's drug dealer. The place was appallingly ugly, stains upon stains upon green paint. Perfect for his purposes; no one would ever think he would spend a moment in such a place. He was uncomfortable even knowing it existed.

There, he tried not to sit on anything, and to think. Helot was going to try again. If what he had said was true, he had no choice but to leave half the ship to die. And Kinsella had to stop him.

Or more precisely, Kinsella had to swap places with him. If half the ship had to die, who was he to argue with that? He just wanted to pick the teams himself.

But if swapping places with Helot was the endgame, then he was currently still stuck setting up his pieces. Hell, he didn't even really have any pieces yet. Right now Helot's pawns and knights and queens were standing across the board from Kinsella's forces, which consisted of two buttons and a grape. So, that would be his first order of business: find more buttons and grapes.

The sickly green door of the hovel opened, and Bletmann entered, closing and locking the door behind him. "Everything's set, sir."

"Good," Kinsella replied. A big public speech, that's what the situation called for. Like something from an old movie. Screaming crowds. A huge picture of his face in the background. Women fainting. He had directed Bletmann to make all the necessary arrangements. It evidently hadn't proven too much of a challenge for him—a wide assortment of people owed his lackey a variety of favors, earned over a long and successful career of politicking and the light blackmail that that entailed.

"Tomorrow afternoon," Bletmann continued. "I know you wanted it sooner, but the fainting club has a thing tonight they couldn't cancel. I tried," he added, shrinking from the withering glare Kinsella was directing at him. He slunk across the room to a chair and sat down, carefully moving a wig out of the way. "Do you know what you're going to say?" he said, trying to change the subject.

Kinsella blinked. He always knew what he was going to say. *How else would I say it?* That said, a big speech on a stage was a new thing for him; he usually did his speaking on feeds. But the concept was the same, surely. Nouns, verbs, slurs. Pounding his fist into his hand. More slurs. He even had the facts on his side this time. Helot's plot was the most offensive crime the Argos had ever seen. As soon as the crowd heard it, they would be clamoring for their captain's head. Kinsella would just tell them about that, then finish it off with more slurring. Simple.

"Yes, idiot," Kinsella finally said. *See? I knew I was going to slur him, and then it happened. Don't overcomplicate things, son.* His eyes flickered down to the announcement on the desk display. "How far in advance are you announcing it? I'm a wanted man, you know." He tapped the display.

Bletmann rubbed his fingers against his pants leg. "I talked to some guys about that. People are bored, sir. The whole ship's primed to show up for anything. I figure if we give them five minutes, we'll fill the square easy." He jerked his head at the door. "Your bodyguards will provide cover to spot for security, and the place I picked out has a couple escape routes. It should work fine."

"Should work fine," Kinsella echoed. *Of course, if it didn't work fine; unlike the mayor, Bletmann would only be out a job, not his life.* Kinsella briefly considered making a threat to bind their fates together a little more tightly. "You know I can still kill people from beyond the grave, right, Bletmann?" Kinsella said. "You specifically, if necessary."

Bletmann seemed almost bored by the threat. "Yes, sir. I remember my job interview quite well, sir."

Hogg sat at his desk in the back of the Community Outreach and Policing Center, wishing it didn't feel so quiet. Although large enough for fifty full-time security officers, less than a dozen now occupied the space. Outside Hogg's office, he could see his team of high achievers moping around in the bullpen. A depressed—and depressing—group at the best of times, getting their asses handed to them by a pair of civilians had had a predictable effect on their morale. The officers he had sent out searching for Redenbach had returned empty handed, although all still thankfully conscious. Tired of looking at the sorry bunch, a sizable minority of which were massaging their bruised groins, Hogg stalked to his office door and pounded the control to close it.

He returned to his desk, sat down, and re-read the terse message from Thorias. *Deliver prisoner to barricade at Africa-1 and 9th Ave.* He stared at the words, willing them to say something more. He had captured the most wanted person on the Argos. The chief should have been ecstatic. And yet, he hadn't given Hogg so much as a scratch behind the ear. He didn't even ask about the one that got away.

The news bulletins only added to his confusion. Every word of them was a lie. There had been no interrogation of Stein—he wouldn't even call what they had a conversation. Her talking and him ducking her slippery words. The woman made him uncomfortable. Too many things were happening that he didn't understand, and she had an eerie ability to pick at the doubts already fermenting in his mind. The central premise of her story, that the captain had gone insane and was going to destroy half the ship, was nonsense, but like all good conspiracy theories, there was enough genuine facts lingering at the fringes to lend the mess an air of plausibility.

A beep on his desk. Linze, letting him know the van was ready. Hogg stood up, picked the pistol from his desk, and slotted it into his pocket. He would handle the transfer himself, not wanting to expose his men to Stein's lies. They probably weren't stupid enough to buy her story, but there was just a bit too much wiggle room in that 'probably' for him to feel totally comfortable with the idea.

Bruce licked his lips, took a deep breath, then rounded the corner across the street from the Community Outreach and Policing Centre. On 40th Avenue, flush with the northern end of the garden well, the northern security outpost had a smaller and friendlier public facade than the monolithic security base in the aft. This was where security's "Say Later to Drugs" campaign and other soft programs were organized. But it housed regular police operations as well, including holding cells. It was also the closest security base to their hideout, and according to a couple of Fauxmless who had seen her get moved inside, where Stein was apparently being held.

With his shoulder-length blonde wig, Bruce was disguised as either an extremely unattractive woman or an unremarkably unattractive man. Just a reconnaissance trip; otherwise, he wouldn't have bothered with the subterfuge. It was really a role for Ellen or Griese, but he hadn't told them what had happened yet. They would just warn him to stay hidden. And, fabulous new disguise aside, he had no interest in remaining hidden.

At a measured pace, he walked along the street, across from the front door of the security office. He held his terminal in front of him, tilted slightly towards the door of the security office with his head firmly fixed forward, pointedly not looking across the street. He rotated the terminal around as he walked, keeping the sensor pointed at the front door. Rounding the corner at the end of the street, he continued a few more steps until he was out of sight, then stopped and replayed the recording he had just made.

The doors were transparent, and he paused the playback at the point where he was directly across the street from them. Here, he had gotten a clear shot inside the office and could see a short entry hallway and a large central room just beyond. Inside, two or three officers could be seen. From the ship's drawings, he knew the holding cells would be on the far side of that room. The layout was problematic—with only one way in, they would see him coming. A frontal assault would be both ballsy and stupid, though Bruce was reasonably well-stocked with both of those commodities.

He resumed the playback, watching as the image panned past the entryway to less useful angles. Just as he was about to stop the replay, the front doors opened, three officers stepping outside. Bruce nearly choked when he saw they were leading Stein out the door, her hands behind her back. He dashed back around the corner, catching a glimpse of them entering the escalator at the other end of the block. He walked as quickly as he dared towards the escalator, not wanting to prematurely draw any attention to himself. When he reached the escalator, he took the steps two at a time, stopping on the third floor, dashing into the street, spinning around. Not seeing them, he circled around to the escalator down to the second floor, panicking slightly as he finally guessed at their destination. They were taking her to the first floor. Where a security van would be waiting. He withdrew his pistol and sprinted down the escalator.

He caught a glimpse of the gray wall of the security van driving away as he leapt off the end of the escalator, nearly colliding with a pair of security officers as he did so. "Easy, lady," one of them said, his smile fading as he recognized Bruce and the object in Bruce's hand. Bruce faintly recognized him too, and, for the second time that day, knocked him unconscious with a shot to the face. The other officer reacted, but not quickly enough. Bruce stepped over their bodies and stared down the street, watching the back of the security van retreat to the south.

"Assey shit!" he yelled, knowing it was going to the main security headquarters. Behind the barricades and bulkhead doors, completely out of reach. Furious, he shot both officers in the crotch. "It'll be more of the same if you don't let her go!" he yelled at their comatose bodies before tossing his wig to the ground.

Hogg pulled the van to a halt in front of the plastic barricade. Through the windshield, he waved at the helmeted officers on the other side. "Come on, guys," he said to himself, knowing they couldn't hear him. "Move that thing." He waved again. One of the officers waved back. "What are they doing?" he asked.

"Dunno," Linze said from the passenger seat. She opened the door and stepped out of the van. One of the less regrettable officers under Hogg's command, he had let Linze stick around for the delivery. Linze walked up to the barricade where she proceeded to get in an animated discussion with one of the officers standing there. Hogg turned to look through the interior door to the passenger compartment, checking that Stein was still there. She was, head bowed, looking defeated. Satisfied, Hogg opened his door and stepped out of the van.

"What's up, guys?" he said, approaching the barricade. "Move that piece of junk. Thorias is expecting us." He stopped beside Linze, facing off from the morons on the other side of said piece of junk. The head moron turned to him, looking him up and down carefully. Hogg didn't recognize the man's face. Which was unusual, doubly so in this case. He thought he had met all the on-duty officers, or at least seen their faces around. And this particular face was ugly enough to remember.

The moron held his terminal up to his ear, a finger raised to silence Hogg. That was a gesture Hogg let few people get away with, and he started to consider simply driving over the buffoon. Finally, the pig-faced officer lowered his terminal. "You've been ordered to hand over the prisoner and the van to us and to continue hunting for the remaining terrorists."

"Have I?" Hogg asked. "You'd think that if I'd been ordered that, someone other than you would be telling me about it." The smile that was spreading across his face stopped, interrupted by a beep from his own terminal, no doubt telling him exactly that. He ignored the message and set his jaw. "Get out of my way. This is my damned prisoner, which my damned team got shot in their damned faces for. I'm handing her over to Thorias myself."

The ugly officer sneered at him. "No, you're not, Sergeant. Turn around."

"No."

Suddenly the ugly, stupid officer withdrew his pistol. "Sergeant, I am under orders to let no one cross this barricade. That includes you. Don't make me use this."

Hogg took one large step forward and punched the officer in the jaw, sending him to the ground. "Then don't use it," he told the squealing ass-hole. He stared down two of the other officers on the barricade, daring them to say something. No one moved, so Hogg stepped back and grabbed the barricade, Linze moving to the far end of it. Together they started shifting the flimsy barrier out of the way of the van. They were interrupted by the sound of a gunshot, Hogg feeling the back end of the barricade hitting the ground behind him, a second before the sound of Linze doing the same. He turned to find himself staring down the gun of the pig-faced asshole.

"I told you you're not crossing this thing, Sergeant," the asshole said. "You're not going to get any more warnings."

"Warnings?" Hogg yelled. He bent down to check the warning that had thudded into Linze. "Are you fucking crazy?" he yelled. "WE'RE ON YOUR SIDE!"

"You're on that side right now, Sergeant," the officer shouted back. "And until that changes, stay the fuck away from this barricade." He twitched the pistol back down the street. "If you doubt me, read your fucking terminal."

Hogg's hand slid down to his terminal, calculating how much farther it had to travel to reach his pistol. A bit too far. Frustrated, he opened his terminal and read the message. It was from Thorias, and it confirmed everything pig-face had just said.

"Fuck you," Hogg said, but the words felt perfunctory. The fight had gone out of him. He looked down at Linze, then up at the van, then down at Linze again and growled with frustration. Finally, he bent down and hoisted Linze up onto her knees, then up and over his shoulder. Without saying another word to pig-face, he slowly returned back in the direction he had come.

Sergei watched in dismay as Hogg retreated around the corner. Hogg hadn't noticed him on the line, distracted by his confrontation with Chester. Sergei wondered if he should have interjected himself in that confrontation, talked Hogg down somehow. Chester was one of the recently recalled officers and had been put in charge of the barricade only an hour previous, apparently rewarded for some favor he had earned a decade earlier.

After Hogg disappeared from view, Chester moved around to the back of the van, opened the door, peered inside, then slammed it shut. Sergei felt his muscles stiffen; he knew who was in there. As Chester strutted back to the front of the van, Sergei imagined himself the star of a big romantic scene, professing his undying love for the terrorist mastermind, making a daring bid for her freedom.

But he only imagined it.

The message he had received from Kay Sampson had been pretty confusing, until he finally realized it was a pseudonym Laura was using. Which was a neat trick; he would have to ask how she did that sometime. The message was coded, referring to completely fictional friends, and encounters, and plans the pair of them supposedly had. But between the lines, he figured out what she was saying. She had said she didn't do it. And he believed that.

But there wasn't much he could do about it. Certainly not with a dozen other cops watching him.

Chester stepped inside the van and prodded it forward, the van slowly inching past the barricades. Sergei watched it pass, feeling a little guilty. But just a little. It certainly wasn't his fault she had gotten into this mess. And it would be sorted out soon enough. He would talk to her then. If he squinted, he could sort of imagine her understanding that. Apologies after the fact were cheaper than career-limiting stunts up front. *That was exactly the kind of thing she liked to say.*

Done lying to himself for the moment, Sergei helped the officers shift the plastic barricade back into place, turning his back on the van carrying away his sometime lover.

Previously

Over the rim of his glass, Harold surveyed the room of happy little people having happy little conversations. It looked like fun. He missed fun.

It had been six months since he had found Kevin's message, months spent with his back in knots, waiting for a hammer blow that never came. They didn't know he knew. He still barely knew himself—most of the evidence that Kevin had compiled was impenetrable, miles outside of Harold's expertise. He had spent weeks trying to figure out the navigational and fuel consumption data before giving up, his vision swimming with important looking tangents intersecting important looking hyperboles. There were also instructions on how he could verify all these fuel consumption calculations himself, but they looked useless to anyone who wasn't standing right beside the reactor, a location he would have a hard time explaining his presence in. "It's all right; I'm a doctor," could only get away with so much.

But the memos and recorded conversations were far more clear-cut, and as Kevin had suggested, at times terrifying. The captain and his staff, casually discussing mass-murder. By the time Kevin had gotten around to recording their conversations, they had even started joking about it. Harold felt proud of Kevin for trying to stop these monsters. He hoped he could live up to the young man's example.

Except for maybe the last part of that example.

A month earlier, Captain Barston, the monster-in-chief, had announced that the ship was off-course, though assured the ship that it was 'Nothing To Worry About.' A course correction—the Turn—was coming and would fix everything. The news had not gone over well, the ship more than a little nervous to hear tell of this little mishap, so close on the heels of their inadvertent basting with cosmic radiation. The news feeds had been hounding everyone in a naval uniform relentlessly since then, looking for someone to hang. The only responses they got mirrored the official explanation: they were off course not because of malice, but simple stupidity. An unsatisfying explanation, though a convincing one.

Harold had struggled to feign surprise when the news broke—he had been neck-deep in navigational calculations for months and had forgotten that their cross-eyed way-finding wasn't common knowledge. The planned course correction was accounted for in Kevin's evidence. Kevin thought it was small, and would have a negligible effect on the fuel load, but this was the part of the evidence Harold was least sure of. He was hopeful someone else could do better with it.

To that end, he had been loitering in the bar for the past week, a copy of Kevin's data, less the video message, on a dummy terminal tucked in his waistband. All three of the main news feeds had offices in this neighborhood, the hacks and pretty boys who worked there regularly spending their free time in the bar. Any one of whom would potentially be very interested in what he had stuffed in his pants.

For much of the past week he had been weighing the pros and cons of simply handing the evidence over to a reporter. But the months of fear and paranoia, and the memory of Chief Hatchens' mirthless smile, had convinced him of the folly of that plan. He had instead decided he would find some way to dump this information off anonymously.

His eyes settled on three of the carefree bastards standing on the far side of the bar, easily picking them out by their teeth, white to the point of fluorescence. One of them in particular caught his eye, a reporter from *NewsFantastic!* Chet Something. Big, broad-shouldered, constantly grinning. He had been more aggressive than most of his colleagues while harassing his sources about the Turn, even managing to use his big toothy grin to bed a junior naval officer, apparently getting the poor girl thrown into the brig. It had been the talk of the bar a couple of nights earlier. For Harold's purposes, he would be perfect. Not only would he be interested in the story, but to an outside observer it would be plausible that he had dug it up on his own.

How to actually get the terminal in his hands was trickier, though a number of feeble ideas had been battling it out in Harold's mind for the past hour. As he watched the three reporters, Chet Something got up from his chair and crossed the bar, heading to the men's washroom. Harold sat up straight, watching this with interest. Sensing an opportunity, he made a snap decision and followed the big reporter.

Inside the washroom, Harold saw his quarry at the far end of the bank of urinals, his back turned to the door. Harold went to the sink and washed his hands, looking over his shoulder. The rest of the washroom appeared to be empty. Harold tugged the terminal out of his pants and set it down beside the sink, setting it to display "READ ME" in bright green letters. Drying his hands, he turned and went for the door, casting a glance at Chet, just shaking himself off.

Outside the washroom, Harold picked his way back across the bar floor to his table. As he sat down, he looked up to see Chet Something's big empty smile as he was already sitting back down with his friends. Harold realized Chet must have left seconds after, right on Harold's heels. He wasn't in possession of the terminal, nor had the expression of a man who had just uncovered a diabolical conspiracy. "You filthy bastard," Harold said, shaking his head, the doctor in him dismayed by the man's hygiene.

While he berated himself for the short-sightedness of his plan, he watched another sap enter the washroom. Assuming he wasn't a filthy degenerate himself, he would be in for a surprise. For the next two minutes, Harold sat extremely still, only his hands moving, but those not stopping. Finally, the man walked out of the washroom, terminal in hand, a wary expression on his face. Harold looked down at his own glass, eyes locked on the rim, not daring to look directly at the man. He watched through the corner of his eye as the man sat down with his friends, not far from where Harold was sitting himself. His ears strained to pick out their conversation over the music and clamor of the crowd. Nothing about a mysterious terminal or murderous plot to sunder the ship. They were talking about work—it sounded like they worked for one of the feeds. Harold realized he had been holding his breath and inhaled deeply, then rewarded himself with a hefty pull from his now warm drink. Ass-backwards, he had managed to get the terminal to someone who might do something with it. Harold finished his drink, stood up, and left the bar, feeling a long-forgotten lightness return to his step.

The next morning, Harold woke up and immediately flipped on his terminal, hoping to see if the captain had resigned in disgrace thanks to a heroic anonymous tipster.

That had not happened. Instead, the front page was dominated by a headline:

ARGOS EXTREME NEWS ASSISTANT EDITOR FOUND DEAD.

He had been found strangled, killed in a suspected drug deal. Harold slumped back in his bed, knees curling up to his chest. *How can washing your hands after using the bathroom be a bad move? What kind of a moral is that?*

6

Everything is Ruined

Bruce made his way down the middle of the road, warily eyeing the cluster of children ahead of him. There hadn't been any school for the past two days, which was about two days longer that it took Argosian children to devolve. These particular children appeared to be playing a game which combined many aspects of soccer and gang shoplifting, with a scoring system based on who could swear the loudest. The massive meat fruit they were using as a ball squirted away from them, rolling down the street to stop at his feet. Bruce stopped, considered his options for a moment, then punted the orb of meat back at the children as hard as he could, knocking two of them off their feet. Although intellectually he understood that this was a pretty horrible thing to do to children, he found himself unable to take any joy from it.

After watching Stein get taken away to the aft and placed out of reach, he had retired to one of his own hiding spots. Two days of running and gunning had left him exhausted, and even racked as he was with guilt, it hadn't taken him long to drift off to sleep, curled into a nest made of wadded lumps of insulation.

He awoke some time later in a sweat, shaken awake from a dream filled with swarms of codpiece-clad security officers chasing him through endless halls. Unable to get back to sleep, his mind wandered, adventured, even gallivanted, as he ran the situation over in his head.

Rescuing Stein wasn't impossible. *It was just really unlikely.* "Eat my shit, probability," he had said, fluffing the insulation under him, trying desperately to ignore the fact that probability was probably right in this case: rescuing Stein was not a terribly likely thing to happen. She would be in the main security base by that point, behind the closed bulkhead doors, behind hundreds of armed men who hated him.

There were ways past them of course, secret, hidden ways through the stinkier parts of the ship. But Stein was always better at that stuff than he was; he had only been in a fraction of the ship's bowels himself and couldn't think of any useful passages that would help here.

This thought led to an attempt to consult the ship's drawings and the discovery that he wasn't the first to think of that. Perhaps anticipating assholes like him doing asshole stuff like what he was considering, the conspirators had put a lock on the ship's schematics. And Bruce had never bothered to put those drawings on a dummy, had never even considered that they would be unavailable to him.

Which was why he was attacking children on the way to the maintenance office. From what little Bruce knew about the network, there was a chance one of the desks in the maintenance office would have a copy of the drawings stored in its local cache. It was only a faint chance; if IT had thought to lock down the network copies, they would surely have some way of dealing with the cached sets.

He found the maintenance office empty, no one from the swing shift apparently bothering to work anymore. He entered the small back office, and sat down at Stein's desk. Sure enough, its cache had been blanked. Any attempt to gather information on the ship's systems refused to work. The Big Board was a cascade of red error messages, all complaints about access levels. He cast a baleful look at the floater desk shared by himself and the other technicians for their work, confident it had been wiped too. Looking at it for a long couple of seconds, something twitched in his head. He decided he should probably still check it.

"Stupid asshole desk!" he yelled, finding that it too had been wiped. He wondered how they were expected to maintain the ship without any drawings of it. He wondered if they even cared. *Helot. That ship splitting fucker.* He kicked the desk, which unsurprisingly, made his foot hurt. He checked the desk for damage. Not a scratch. "Bullshit durable asshole desk." Another brain twitch.

The floater desk had been replaced a couple months earlier. One of the overnight idiots had managed to crack the screen with his enormous ass. The whole unit had been sent to recycling, where it might very well still be in one piece. He knew they didn't recycle things straightaway—they just picked and chose from the scraps at hand as they needed them. Which meant there was still a chance it was intact, but unpowered, its cache intact. "Thank you, bullshit durable asshole desk," Bruce said, kicking it again affectionately before heading for the door.

"So, when you get a desk like one of these sent to you, what do you do with it?" Bruce asked.

"A desk like one of these? We put it right here," the recycling plant supervisor replied. "Beside all these desks." He pointed at the massive stack of desks, just one stack in the room full of shattered furniture. He winked at Bruce with one of his heavily wrinkled eyes. On board the climate controlled Argos, it was hard for any person to look weathered, but this man managed it somehow. Bruce wondered what effect the recycling process had on the local atmosphere.

"You don't do anything else with it? Like wipe its memory?"

"Oh, sure. We're definitely supposed to do that."

"Supposed to? You mean you don't?"

The recycling wizard licked his lips. "You know how many people care about the recycling department? How many people come here and ask questions?" He studied Bruce's face.

"A lot?" Bruce guessed. "Because people find you and your work enthralling, and love to hear your stories?"

"Hah!" the recycler said. "No one gives a good goddamn about recycling."

Bruce's heart raced. "Okay. I'm looking for a specific desk. Which hopefully still has some data in its memory cache."

"A specific desk, you say? Well, what does it look like?" The recycler waved his hand at the stack of cracked and broken desks, all identical, save for the damage and disfiguring marks that presaged their visit to the room.

"You don't keep an inventory?" Bruce asked.

The recycling wizard's eyes narrowed. "Do you know how many people care about..."

"No one cares. Got it. Okay, I'll look around."

It only took forty minutes before Bruce found the right desk. The crack across the screen wasn't terribly distinctive—it was a common problem with desks and asses on board the ship—but the corners and edges of the desk's surface were badly chipped and scuffed from its life in the maintenance office. He stared at it, a mixture of excitement and worry washing over him. He had no idea how he would find out if there was any information on there, much less how to get it off. By powering on the desk, it would probably connect to the network and be immediately wiped.

"If I wanted to get the data off here, do you know how I could do that?" Bruce asked.

"You mean without anyone finding out about it?" the recycler asked, grinning. "I might be able to help you out with something like that."

Bruce gritted his teeth. "And will you?"

"Why should I?"

"Because I'm the first person to have spoken to you in months?"

The recycler considered that for a moment. "Fair 'nuff." He retreated to his little office, returning in a minute with a modified terminal with its rear cover removed, a long strap protruding from the circuits within. The recycler crawled under the old maintenance desk, and after some prodding around, popped off a panel. Some more fiddling attached the thin strap to something inside the desk. He set the terminal down on the floor gently and crawled back out. "Takes a few seconds," he explained.

"Done this before, then?" Bruce asked.

The recycler scratched his cheek, then made a vague gesture with his hand. "Sometimes find some pretty interesting things on these units. Usually not. Usually not worth my time." He looked up at Bruce and winked. "Sometimes is."

Bruce desperately wanted to avoid learning what was worth the man's time, so he stopped talking to him. They waited in silence for the next few seconds until the terminal beeped. The recycler undid his handiwork with the cables then tapped a few commands into the terminal. "I'm wrapping all the information within a generic document with no access restrictions," he explained. "Makes it a little cumbersome to read, but it won't look the same if anyone on the network is scanning for it. Your terminal?"

Bruce held up his terminal, thumbing the confirmation to accept a terminal to terminal file transfer.

"Though if this is real important, I'd put a copy on a dummy. Got a spare one right here I can sell you."

"Maybe another time," Bruce offered. The file downloaded, he tucked his terminal away. "Can you keep a copy yourself, though? Just in case?"

"Was going to anyways."

"Thought so," Bruce said, backing away from the strange little man.

Thumping and groaning sounds heralded the arrival of Griese, the man himself arriving a minute later, crawling headfirst out of the crawlspace. He stood up in the pump room, clothes spotted with grime, offered a wan smile to his wife, turned to Bruce, and shook his head. "I checked three. Two of them had doors down and locked."

"And the third?" Bruce asked.

"That was the vent. Same deal, different door. Kind of a slatty kind of door."

"Damper," Bruce corrected him.

"Well, it was also locked."

"Ffffffuuuuuuuuuuuuck," Bruce said, exhaling heavily. He kicked over a chair. "Fuck you, chair."

Using the drawings that he had recovered, Bruce had been trying to find a way into the aft of the ship that didn't involve strolling past a dozen security officers. But there were only a handful of between-deck passageways large enough to fit a person, all of which were apparently shut with the same kind of bulkhead doors blocking the main streets. Griese had offered to investigate those on his behalf—the underground stuff had always been Stein's specialty due to Bruce's diameter issues.

"I did only check three," Griese said. "Maybe one of the others will still be open?"

Bruce shook his head. "Don't bother."

"So, what now?" Ellen asked. "Can't you bypass that somehow? Isn't that part of your job?" she asked. "What is your job, anyways?"

Bruce righted the chair he had just kicked over, then kicked it over again. "Probably. No, definitely. It just won't stay secret for long. They'll have a big screen which will start flashing red, saying some asshole is opening doors."

Griese sat down at the crate that was serving as their workbench. He gave his wife a grimy hug, which she squirmed away from. He then turned to the plans open on the terminal in front of her. Neither of them had actually admitted yet that they believed the theory about the ship splitting in two. But given the goodwill they generally felt for Stein, and the ill-will they generally felt for security officers, it hadn't taken much convincing on Bruce's part to get them involved.

"Have you come up with any brilliant scheme we would employ if we could actually get past these doors?" Griese asked.

Bruce jabbed the terminal, dragging the image on the screen, his heavy touch spinning the terminal around as he did so. "Sort of. If she's anywhere, she'll be in the security base. Not that we've really got a good way of getting in there anymore. Not one that doesn't require shooting a bunch of dudes in the face, anyways."

"I still don't see what's wrong with that plan," Ellen said.

"Too many dudes. Too many faces." Bruce tapped idly on the terminal, the map shifting in a jerky manner. "If she is here," he said, pointing at the holding cells, "she's completely on her own."

Ellen snatched the terminal from Bruce's hand and concentrated on it. Suddenly, a startled look appeared on her face. "I've got it! Okay, here's what we do. Bruce, you put on a skirt. I'll bake a cake with a file in it. Then you go to the security chief, seduce him, eat the cake, and stab him in the neck with the file. Ok? Good, because next the plan gets *weird*."

Bruce snorted, not especially amused, and not game enough to return a volley. He nodded absentmindedly, eyes moving up, drifting across the pipes running across the ceiling, continuing to nod, the nod starting to make him look a bit unhinged. He stopped mid-nod. "Oh, shit. Cake. Of course."

"Shit cake?" Griese asked.

Bruce looked at Griese solemnly. "That's right, friend. Shit cake."

A lengthy pause, accompanied by more crazy nodding from Bruce. Griese and Ellen shared a glance. "I sure hope he's using that as a figure of speech," Griese said.

"Bad news for them if he isn't."

"Bad news for *everyone* if he isn't, I think."

Leroy Oliver made his way to the front of the crowd, his best friend Rick close behind, helping him through the mass of people with judiciously timed shoves. The plaza in the northern end of the garden well was already full, crowds spilling over into the surrounding streets. Even with the short notice, a lot of folks had shown up to see their mayor speak. Or get arrested. Or shot. Anything interesting, really.

Leroy collided with a bulky blond man, who pushed Leroy back harder than Rick could push forward. They had reached the front of the crowd, on the southern edge of the plaza. There wasn't much to see—a desk had been dragged out of an apartment building and placed against the wall. A loose semicircle of stupid-looking guys was arrayed around it. On top of the desk, Leroy could see men adjusting some sort of device on a stand, the sound equipment that would be used to broadcast the mayor's voice and make it sound more regal. The whole operation looked laughably makeshift.

Eventually, the men on the desk stepped down, satisfied with whatever they had done. The crowd began to simmer, bubbles of anxious whispering percolating to the surface. Another five minutes passed before Mayor Kinsella stepped out of the apartment door, where he was hoisted gracelessly onto the stage by one of his large men. A handful of people began clapping, but this failed to catch on, the applause lamely petering out a few seconds later.

A growl deep in Kinsella's throat, which he struggled to tamp down. Normally, Bletmann would have salted the crowd with more clappers, but he evidently hadn't had the time for this occasion. No applause would have been better than that feeble exhibition; it would have lent the event a somber, sober effect. Now, he just looked unpopular, some asshole with a microphone.

"Good evening, citizens," the asshole said into the microphone. "I am here to speak to you about the events of the past week—the events that have caused so much confusion and mayhem. I apologize, deeply and sincerely, for the lack of communication from myself and your government. I can only state that this disruption has affected me just as much as it has you. Perhaps more." He frowned, looking down at the text Bletmann had insisted on preparing for him. *That idiot.* Eyes back up at the crowd. "No, not more. You have suffered more than me."

"Although a victim myself, I have not been idle. Your government has been working tirelessly to uncover the truth about what has happened over the past few days." Kinsella took a deep breath and put his 'very serious and extremely concerned' face on. "But I'm sorry to say that the truth is far different from the story we've been told by our captain.

"First, the parts that you already know. Captain Helot has seized control of the aft of the Argos. In doing so, he has deposed the Argos' rightfully elected government from power and forced several hundred innocent civilians from their homes. He has slandered and falsely accused me and other innocent people. These acts alone rank amongst the most outrageous crimes ever perpetrated in our history. But they pale when compared to what Helot tried to do first."

A chorus of chirrups interrupted Kinsella, erupting from every terminal in the audience. A small cough, then the diffuse sound of Helot's voice speaking via the ship's public address. "The only thing I've tried to do is protect the ship from your plot, Mayor. Everything you've said is a lie. Everything you'll ever say is a lie."

Kinsella swallowed and remained calm. He looked down at Bletmann on the floor below him. Kinsella said nothing, letting his eyes talk for him. "*Blind rage,*" the eyes politely informed Bletmann.

Bletmann swallowed. "*Keep talking,*" he mouthed, pointing at the audio system they had set up. Kinsella got it: the system was a hack job, completely independent from the ship's main PA system. Helot could interrupt, but not silence him.

"Everything I've said is the truth!" Kinsella shouted back. "Asshole!" he added. A few hurrahs from the crowd.

"Ladies and gentlemen, I hope I'm not spoiling your innocence when I point out that the mayor does occasionally lie to us," Helot said. "We all know this. We expect it from him. That's why we voted for him. Because he was the *best* liar."

"I am not a liar!"

"Hands up if you suspect the mayor might lie sometimes," Helot asked the ship.

Hundreds of outstretched hands appeared almost instantly, their numbers swelling as the crowd exchanged reminders with each other of his past over-promises.

"The reason the mayor is lying right now is to cover up what he's done," Helot continued. "He was planning to destroy the engines of this ship so that we couldn't stop at Tau Prius."

Gasps filled the crowd, most still standing with their hands up.

"That's the biggest lie of all!" Kinsella shouted. "You were trying to split the ship in two!"

Helot laughed, a fake, forced, utterly unbelievable stretch of a laugh. But the audience laughed alongside him. "Kinsella," Helot began, his exasperation clearly feigned, at least to Kinsella's ear. "Do you have any proof of this at all? Of these wild accusations you're throwing around?"

"You told me all of this yourself!"

"Do you even know what evidence means?" The audience laughed again. A woman in the front row fainted. *Not now, you idiot.* Kinsella glared at Bletmann, who waved frantically at someone in the crowd, which only seemed to prompt more women to faint.

"Allow me to show you what evidence means," Helot continued. "You'll recall our conversation right before you tried to blackmail me into silence?"

"What?"

"Security Chief Thorias is shortly going to be transmitting proof to the ship that you ordered the creation of falsified images of child pornography, which you intended to plant in my personal effects. To blackmail me to stand aside as you attempted your plot."

"That's not why I was trying to blackmail you!" Kinsella shouted. He groaned at the exact same time that everyone else in the crowd groaned. "That was a joke," he shouted. "I was joking." At the edges of the crowd, people began filtering away. "Come on! I'm not the bad guy here."

Helot went in for the kill. "Kinsella's been on the run ever since his plot failed. That's why you haven't seen him; he's been hiding from our security teams. And now he's trying to orchestrate a coup. Or more of a reverse coup." Clearly seeing the same looks of confusion on the crowd's faces that Kinsella was looking at, Helot hesitated. "A coup is when the army...never mind. A coup is a bad thing. Kinsella is doing a bad thing."

The crowd had no problem accepting that. A discontented murmur started to build, punctuated by a few angry shouts and at least two more faints. "Stop doing coups!" someone close to the stage yelled, pointing at Kinsella. "Stop couping us, Mayor!"

"Are you fucking serious?" Kinsella shouted, quivering. "You fucking imbeciles."

"I would ask the citizens of the Argos to please restrain the mayor until security can arrive to take him into custody," Helot said, the punch line echoing off the buildings lining the plaza.

Kinsella knew when cowardly running was the better part of valor, and had already leapt off the stage by the time Helot had finished his request, retreating into the building from which he had emerged, his bodyguards forming a vanguard behind him. They, at least, had understood who was really couping who, or perhaps more likely, hadn't followed the conversation at all.

A click interrupted the daydream Stein had been having about punching her boss in the face. In an alcove on the side of the room, a meal bar rattled down a chute, bounced once in the dispensing alcove, then fell to the floor below, marking the arrival of lunch time.

Getting up from her bunk, Stein crossed the room and picked up the meal bar, her bruised body complaining with every movement. It turned out that Hogg was amongst the gentlest of the security goons; every other one that Stein had met since her capture had taken a vigorous interest in foiling the many attempts at resisting arrest they imagined she was making. Although not an expert on the matter, she suspected she was earning a little more attention than most criminals in custody. *So, they actually think I set off a bomb.*

The cell was nicer than the one in the bow, not much different from the basic ultra-low-end studio apartment she'd had in school but for the door that never opened. A solid platform mounted to one of the walls held a pair of mattress approximations, one above the other. In the opposite corner sat a toilet, beside that a sink. Further down the wall was the alcove where food regularly crashed into view. An armored security sensor in the upper corner of the room watched over everything dispassionately. Opposite the bunk was a desk, outwardly identical to every other desk on board the ship. Inwardly, it had a sharply limited interface and was unable to send messages or access many parts of the network, only allowing the cell's occupant to read filtered selections from the public news feeds and library. Stein had done little but read this for the past two days, at least when not fantasizing about making her boss wet his pants in front of his new peers. She slumped down in the chair, and began picking at her meal bar, paging through the news feeds.

Kinsella's impromptu debate with the captain was all anyone was talking about. Even knowing that he was telling the truth, she still thought he had come off poorly. That said, it appeared there were still a few people taking his side; being labeled a criminal had actually improved his reputation somewhat. Argosians loved an underdog.

She turned off the desk and painfully flopped into bed, rolling onto her back, her eyes sliding up the wall towards the ceiling and the membrane housed just over the door. The membrane regulated the carbon dioxide differential between the room and the corridor and could seal shut in the event of a vacuum on either side. The only opening in what would otherwise be an airtight room, this particular membrane, unlike most, was secured behind thick metal bars. She had already identified it as the only potential route of escape. But two days of staring at it—and she couldn't have been the first of the room's residents to do that—had yet to reveal a way through those bars.

Another click and a rattle from the food chute. Stein sat up in bed, brow furrowed. It was far too early for another meal. She watched as a small maintenance robot crashed out of the chute, landing with a thump on the floor. Righting itself, it scurried around the floor, banging into the cell door. "Beep," the robot said, then crashed into the door again.

Stein darted out of bed and scooped the robot up, finding the unit's power switch and deactivating it. Flipping it over again, Stein could see that it had a terminal strapped to its back, the phrase "Shit Cake" written on it in large letters. An inside joke she wasn't in on, but at least it was clear where it had come from. "You big, beautiful bastard," she whispered to the comatose robot. She hurried back to her bunk, shoulders spread wide to hide the robot, then dove into the lower bunk, where she would mostly be out of sight of the security sensor.

Now, what to do with this? With the terminal she could start communicating with the outside world again. A message to Bruce thanking him for his care package might be in order. On the other hand, she had no idea how closely she was being watched. Terminals could be tracked—security would probably notice the second she turned it on. And a message to Bruce—or Abdolo Poland or whatever the fuck he was calling himself now—might similarly get him in trouble. He was still a fugitive, too.

The fact that the robot came with the terminal rather than just dropping it off was important. Bruce wanted her to use it. He wanted her to rescue herself. *The lazy fuck.* She turned the robot over in her hands, inspecting its manipulators and built-in tools, and started mentally applying them to various surfaces in her cell.

Hogg stomped down the center of the street, ignoring the wave of insults and curses that followed in his wake. His particular uniform hadn't been very popular since Kinsella's big speech. Although most people seemed to think their mayor was rehearsing some kind of hilarious new comedy routine at the time, at least a few people had believed his story. And now that openly hating security was a thing to do, it was a thing they did.

Hogg couldn't say for sure that he believed everything the oily man had said, but damned if it didn't make just a bit of oily sense. The similarities between the mayor's story and Stein's were too close not to notice. Though that would make sense, if they were working together. *But...*there wasn't much actual evidence they were working together. Just a press release from Thorias about a fake interrogation that hadn't occurred. Why would Thorias lie about that? The permutations spun around in Hogg's head. It was all very complicated.

And then he had received a message instructing him to go arrest Kinsella and felt instant relief. This, at least, was simple. Something he could do. Something he had to do.

Even if he kind of didn't want to.

The mayor had probably traveled in disguise to the square on the first level where most of the sensors were broken. But he had left the event in a bit of a hurry, too much of a hurry to change disguise, and also hadn't shed the four large, highly visible men traveling with him. The sensors had tracked the group until they entered the abandoned arena on the first level, the arena Hogg was standing in front of now.

At one time, this had been the ship's skating rink, although it had long since been repurposed to provide a big empty room where people could slide around on wheeled desk chairs and crash into each other. Whether the mayor and his pals were doing that or not, Hogg wouldn't guess. The odds were low, certainly. But not zero.

As a base of operations, though, it was a legitimately smart choice. Multiple entrances and exits, located on wide streets that were hard to sneak up on. It would take a lot of officers to lock down completely. And Hogg only had himself.

He approached the two highly visible men at the front door. They weren't taking any particular pride in their work, seemingly distracted by a group of prostitutes down the street, and didn't notice Hogg until he was within a few meters of them, at which point they did notice him, hard. "Relax," Hogg said, coming to a stop a nice, non-threatening distance away. He held his hands up in a calming gesture. "I'm not here to arrest anyone."

Looks of relief, mistrust, and confusion played across each guard's face, colliding into each other in often hilarious combinations. "You're not?" one of them finally asked, the smart one, presumably. His hand nevertheless slid around to rest on the weapon he clearly had concealed behind his back.

"Nope," Hogg said. "I just wanted to talk."

"About what?"

"Not here." Hogg jerked his head inside. "You know. Given the circumstances." Not waiting for a response, he stepped past the guards and into the arena.

It was empty, or at least mostly so. The room was dominated by the massive curved floor of the old rink, lined with low walls. A drift of wheeled chairs had washed up against one of the walls on the side of the arena. To the other side, he saw a group of bulky men just outside of the main rink, standing around the mayor. Hogg began walking across the arena towards his prey, one of the door guards in tow, feebly protesting.

"Mayor Kinsella?" Hogg said as he drew within conversing distance. "I'm here to place you under arrest."

"Hey!" The guard behind him shouted. "You lied to me!" He stepped in front of Hogg and put his hand on his chest before turning to the mayor. "He lied to me!"

Kinsella looked profoundly unimpressed. This was the first time Hogg had actually seen the man without all of his teeth showing in a massive smile. The rest of Kinsella's friends spread out around Hogg, puffing up their chests, playing with their weapons. Hogg watched them click the safeties of their pistols on and off, trying to make menacing noises.

"You're here to arrest me?" Kinsella finally asked. Not frightened, but wary.

Hogg nodded.

"By yourself?"

Hogg looked around. "It seems that way."

"Is that true?" Kinsella asked, turning his head to look at his assembly of highly visible men. A lot of vacant expressions looked back at him. Eventually, one of them began messing with his terminal and reported back that Hogg indeed appeared to be alone.

Kinsella squinted at Hogg, shaking his head slightly. "Whhhhhhhy.....no...that's not...nooooo," he said quietly. "There's something not right here." He turned away from Hogg, took a step, then immediately turned back to face him, still obviously unsettled. "Could someone shoot him, please?" he asked politely.

So someone shot him.

Tiny signs of movement on the barricade two blocks away, anxious security dorks shifting around. Bruce crossed his legs, his back against the bench armrest, and watched them carefully. He was in the southern end of the garden well, watching one of the barricades. He couldn't make any of them out individually but knew they would be watching him. For the third time since he arrived, he gave them a cheery wave.

Here he was, the ship's most wanted criminal, sitting in plain sight of a dozen or more security officers, none of whom dared come get him. It was shocking really, his tax dollars at work, not catching him. Bruce opened his terminal and examined the locations of all the other known security personnel, double-checking that none of the roving patrols were sneaking up on him. Not a new tool, just one that had recently grown in popularity, his terminal was currently set to identify security officers and report their locations to a shared database. The database's accuracy improved with the number of people using it, and it had been *very* accurate lately.

He shut off the terminal and looked back up at the barricades guarding the aft. Obviously, they were there to do a lot more than just guard Stein, but they were inadvertently doing a pretty good job of that, as well. A shame, because it was looking more and more like she needed some help.

He had watched the robot come crashing down into the cell and shut itself off almost immediately. He didn't get a look at who shut it off, but it had to have been Stein. It was the only occupied cell, and she was the only one on the ship who would see a maintenance robot appear out of nowhere and know instinctively what to do with it.

And then she hadn't even said thank you.

The robot must have been taken from her. Those cells were monitored, something he knew from the jail time that was an occasional side effect of the rich life he had led. He felt stupid, should have found something more subtle than programming the robot to chuck itself down the feeding chute. The cell's sensor had probably flagged it on the second bounce.

Bruce leaned back on the bench, looking up the nearly vertical wall of the garden well that stretched above him. Looking up the length of the wall from this vantage point gave most people vertigo, and it wasn't an uncommon sight to see puddles of vomit around these benches. But he had a strong stomach for heights, or depths, or whatever this view was, and even found it relaxing.

With Operation Robot Surprise a seeming failure, he had been considering brasher ways of retrieving his friend. He had found a bulkhead door on the other end of the ship and spent most of an afternoon fiddling with its various controls, eventually figuring out how to open, close, and then jam it open. The latter proved almost comically easy, the communication chip clearly visible and vulnerable to stabbing. Which solved at least part of his dilemma—he could now at least get closer to Stein. Where several hundred security officers would be waiting, possibly mad about all of their colleagues that he had shot.

Shadows passed over him. He tilted his head to see a group of teenagers walking past, coming to a halt a short distance away. They stared straight up, peering up the same length of garden well wall Bruce was.

"I don't feel anything," one of them said.

"You will."

"Yeah, just give it time."

"Try spinning," another suggested.

Bruce watched the teenagers staring straight up, spinning around slowly. Before too long one of them abruptly stopped, squatted down, and tried to brace himself with his hand, not quite succeeding, toppling to the ground on his side.

"Ahh, you flinched!"

"I'm going to be sick," the one on the ground said.

"That's the point."

"Oh, shit," another said, lowering her head, her eyes swimming. Her neck curled back then propelled her head forward, a voluminous stream of vomit spewing from her mouth, spraying her friends. This set off a chain reaction, three others barfing in quick succession, spraying the ground in bile, causing the sole survivor to slip and fall, laughing.

Bruce hadn't seen a vomit club in a while. It was a hobby which hadn't been in fashion for at least a couple of years. A reminder that even though the ship was in desperate peril, most people didn't know or care enough to be anything other than bored. With no government jobs to go to, and no school to sleep through, the amount of time being wasted on the ship was reaching a generational peak. Even the mayor had been able to get nearly a thousand people to show for his 'Old Tyme Politic Rap Session' at a moment's notice, simply by the promise that something interesting might happen.

Bruce watched one of the teens attempt to stand up, putting his foot in a slick of vomit and slipping, legs jackknifing in the air as he came down in a thud. Just a bunch of stupid kids, looking for stupid to do. *Sitting at the feet of the Argos' biggest stupid-dealer.* A plan was forming in Bruce's head. It wasn't, happily, a smart one.

"He's waking up, boss."

"Then shoot him again."

So, someone shot him.

"Coming around again."

Hogg raised his hands in protection. At least, he tried to. He knew that he probably wasn't moving much, having seen more than a few people recover from stun shots before. He was probably curled up in the fetal position, pawing at his own face.

"Shoot him again?"

No answer. So no one shot him.

Slowly, the remainder of Hogg's senses reported in. He was still in the arena, apparently right where he had been shot. Feet, all around him, belonging to Kinsella's posse. Hogg looked up, spotting the mayor himself walking over.

"Why'd you come alone?" Kinsella asked.

Hogg ignored him, knowing from experience that it would take another minute or two before he would be able to say anything intelligible. He instead maneuvered himself into a sitting position, wrapping his arms around his legs and squeezing. He held up one finger to Kinsella, indicating he hadn't forgotten him, and began the unpleasant process of clearing his throat.

"Hrrrk. Haaap. IIIIch. K. Okay. Okay."

"Okay, what?" Kinsella said. "Why did you come alone?" he asked again.

It was a good question, and Hogg wasn't sure he had an answer. Finally, he said, "Orders. Gotta do 'em." A pause. "Don't have to do 'em well."

Kinsella's nostrils flared. "I will shoot you again. I will do it and like it. You guys say I'm a terrorist? Well, maybe I'll terrorize your unconscious ass. Now, stop speaking in riddles. Why are you here alone?"

Hogg looked down at his feet. "Because I'm not even supposed to be working right now."

"What the fuck did I just say about riddles?"

Hogg smiled and looked up at the mayor. He swallowed and collected his thoughts, wondering if he could explain it even to himself. "I was supposed to be off-rotation right now. It'd been scheduled for months. It'd been *deliberately* scheduled for months. About a year ago someone made a real fuss about messing with my rotation schedule, which ended up with me being off-rotation this quarter."

"What the fuck does this have to do with anything?"

"Depends." Hogg studied the mayor's expression. "Are you lying about this whole thing? About the captain?" Kinsella closed his eyes, rubbing his face. With a flick of his hand, he gestured at one of his goons, who obediently raised his pistol. "Whoa!" Hogg said. "It was just a question. I believe you." He stopped speaking, suddenly tired. "I believe you," he repeated, trying the words on for size.

Kinsella's gaze narrowed. "Why wouldn't you?"

Hogg snorted. "Don't you get it yet? I was supposed to be on a freaking staycation right now. On this side of the ship. Not that side," he jerked his head to the south. "I was getting left behind, too."

"Bullshit."

"Bulltruth. It was only a last minute screw-up that brought me back on duty. And when I was brought back, I was given an abrupt and unexpected promotion, put in charge of the fucking Community Outreach Centre. That's in the bow of the ship, in case you didn't know."

At the time, he had been dismayed by the assignment but not entirely surprised. He had known for a while that he didn't play the right games, perhaps shared his opinions a little too readily. So, it made sense for him

to be assigned to command the squad of lost souls. They were simply trying to keep him out of the way.

He just never could have guessed how out of the way they intended to
keep him.

"Why would they leave you behind?" Kinsella asked.

Hogg looked up at the mayor and cracked a half smile. "I'm curious
to know myself. Don't know if I'd like the answer." He lowered his head
and studied his own feet.

Kinsella considered that for a moment, then smiled himself. "Okay.
So, you're being left behind. But if you believe that, and you believe me,
then, why, *oh why*, the fuck would you come to arrest me?"

Hogg threw his arms around his legs and squeezed. "I honestly don't
know. It's a job. Gotta do your job, right? Though I guess that doesn't
make a lot of sense, does it?"

Kinsella looked at him appraisingly. "You security guys are a different
breed."

"I've heard that."

"Huh," Kinsella said. He chewed his lip, staring at Hogg in a way that
made him feel extremely uncomfortable. "Goddamn," Kinsella said and began pacing. "Now, that is an interesting possibility. Not that I'm sure I'd trust
you enough to try." He stopped. "But what the fuck. Everything's worth a
shot." He turned to Hogg. "Do you have handcuffs? Binders? Whatever?"

Hogg nodded.

"Good. Put them on yourself."

Hogg fumbled in his belt for the binders. Cuffing yourself was a pretty
clear sign that something hadn't gone according to plan. But then he remembered that he hadn't actually had a plan coming here. Just a lurchy sort of
instinct that he should go at Kinsella and see what happened. And now he
knew what happened—you got shot a few times and had to cuff yourself.

He held up his bound wrists, showing them to Kinsella, who gave one of
his all teeth smiles. "Amazing." He began nodding tightly, clearly plotting
something. "We've got that cart still, right?" he asked one of his men. "Okay,
cool. Go get that. We'll need to put him on it." He crouched down to talk to
Hogg. "I'm going to have to shoot you again."

Hogg's shoulders slumped. "Are you sure?"

Kinsella nodded.

So, they shot him again.

The trolley slid to a stop at 10th Avenue, which was as far south as it
still went; someone evidently had the sense to change the trolleys' programming so that they wouldn't start slamming into closed bulkhead

doors, although Bruce supposed it was perhaps more likely that the trolleys had simply changed their own programming in the absence of any signs of operator sense. He stepped out of the rear doors, Ellen and Griese in tow, and headed confidently towards the escalator beside the intersection.

"I think it's a stupid plan," Ellen said as they descended down to the first level.

"Obviously," Bruce replied. "The stupidity is key. We need a lot of stupid for this to work."

"Dammit, Bruce, it's dangerous."

"It's safer than what you were planning," Bruce said and looked over his shoulder at the couple. "With that little toy of yours."

Ellen snorted. Griese looked back and forth between his wife and Bruce. "It's not little," he eventually said.

Bruce laughed. He had found them in one of their old hideouts, where they had spent most of the previous day tinkering with their smart rifle. A bulky, ugly, and profoundly lethal weapon, it was also a grim reminder of the ill-fated Breeder raid on the security base they had participated in a decade earlier.

When they reached the bottom, Bruce moved away from Africa. He spotted a few people pointedly loitering, but not many, not yet. *Good.* "You know how that thing works?" he asked.

"I've read the manual a few times," Griese said. "Before bed. You know. Light reading."

"I don't want to know what you guys do in bed."

"He just reads it, Bruce," Ellen chimed in. "But he does read it aloud. Slowly. With a sexy lisp." She fanned her face, her eyes fluttering.

Bruce made a pained smile, wishing he hadn't brought up bed stuff at all. "Do you even know *if* it works?" he asked, shifting the subject.

"It messed up that old bed pretty bad," Ellen said. Bruce recalled seeing a shattered bed frame in the hideout, but hadn't asked, because again, he never could tell with these two. "At the very least, we know when we pull the trigger something interesting will happen," Ellen continued.

They reached Flint Street and turned south. This was a smaller street, a wide hallway really, and was thankfully completely deserted. They stopped at 9th Avenue, a half block from the closed bulkhead door. Bruce hoped it would be equally deserted on the other side.

"We should all go," Ellen said. "This is a bad idea."

Bruce shook his head and examined his terminal. Three minutes to go. "Could. But three people will be more noticeable. And you're not dressed right. Give me a hand with this."

Bruce began stripping off the plain coveralls he had been wearing, revealing a rough approximation of a security uniform underneath. Ellen helped him ball the coveralls into a bag and hoisted it over her shoulder before stepping back and examining him. "Well. Okay," she said, not conveying any sense of confidence in his disguise. "But I wouldn't get too close to anyone. Because you look not a little bit like a stripper."

"But an expensive one, right?"

"Sure, sweetie."

Bruce's terminal beeped. One minute to go. "Get ready," he told Griese, who opened up his bag, revealing a sea of red pills inside. "That cost much?" Bruce asked.

"Personally? No. Just cashed in one real big favor Ellen had with a guy in a fab plant," Griese replied. "She won't tell me how she got it, so I'm just going to assume it was something incredibly innocent."

Ellen blushed. "Least I could do for Laura."

"You could have done nothing at all," Griese said. "That probably would have been less."

Shouts and hollers came from up the street. "Okay, guys," Bruce said, punching his friends on the shoulder in an attempt to ward off any hugs. "Thanks. And if you really want to help out, when we're done here, get your little toy and sit tight. Somewhere where you can move quickly. I'll call if I need help."

Ellen sidestepped another shoulder punch and hugged Bruce before he could escape. He grimaced but didn't resist. Down the street, he could see the mob coming, right on schedule. "Come on, I gotta go," he said.

Ellen released him. "Be careful."

"Fuck no," Bruce said, smiled, then turned and jogged down the street towards the bulkhead door.

When he arrived, he popped the access panel for the bulkhead door's controls off and withdrew a probe from his tool webbing. Jamming it into the controls, he prodded it to override the lockdown. Behind him, he could hear the mob approach and cursed at the tool, begging it to work faster.

It had taken comically little effort to summon the mob, a few messages sent to the right people, who had spread the word with no extra encouragement. There were incentives of course, even aside from the promise of something to do. As the door finally started sliding open, Griese and Ellen began handing said incentives out.

"Come get your Brash!" Griese's voice carried over the growing roar. "Got an old fashioned Brash Mob here!"

"It's really happening people! We're really doing it!" Ellen promised.

Bruce smiled as the door started to slide open. Technically speaking, this wasn't a stupid plan; it was kind of a brilliant one. It just involved a whole lot of stupid moving parts.

The door out of the way, Bruce stepped over the threshold, an army of amped up madmen at his heel.

She had a plan. All that was left was to actually do it.

It was funny how she was willing to procrastinate when it came to her freedom. She had never really been the procrastinating type; when she saw a problem, she fixed it. That she was willing to delay winning back her own liberty suggested there was something else going on. Maybe it was just comfort, the comfort of not having to unravel a horrible conspiracy, the comfort of not being hunted by said conspiracy. The simple animal comfort of having a warm place to sleep and eat.

For two days she had sat on her robot, making excuses why her plan wouldn't work. The security sensor—that was the biggest one. They would see her escape. She wouldn't make it very far at all before someone noticed and forcefully subdued her. So she lay back and slept and ate.

As the news feeds cheerfully reported, something was different this morning, something that finally broke her out of her spell. This particular morning, she was pretty sure nobody would be watching her; they would be watching the three hundred maniacs who had broken through the 'anti-terrorism barricades' and were terrorizing, in their own way, everything south of 9th Avenue. If she was looking for a distraction to disguise her escape, she had it.

Stein stood up from the desk and returned to the bed, retrieving the robot from under the blankets. Opening the access panel on the back, she turned the machine on, then did the same with the terminal it had thoughtfully come with. The terminal flickered to life and informed her she had two hundred unread messages. She ignored those, instead activating the robot's control programming, allowing her to control it manually. She took a deep breath, then set it down on the floor in full view of the security sensors. *Let's get stupid.*

The robot beeped, then scuttled across the floor, following the instructions she had programmed into it. When it reached the wall, it scaled the vertical surface, reaching the ceiling and the membrane separating the cell from the hall outside. There it began cutting through the bars covering the membrane.

With its small plasma cutter, the robot sawed contentedly away at the first bar in the grate. It shredded the membrane as it worked, causing warning icons to splash across Stein's terminal screen, the smell of burnt metal and plastic filling the room. She hadn't considered that; anyone with a nose even remotely close to the detention cells would know about her escape before it even got started.

The cutting took an agonizingly long time as the little robot sawed through the grate. After each bar was cut through on both ends, it would extend a manipulator, yank the bar from its place, and then drop it down to Stein with a cheery 'beep.' It took almost ten minutes—thankfully, the maniacs currently running amuck were running *extremely* amuck—but finally all the bars were cut through. The robot sliced through the membrane next, leaving it attached on the upper edge so it hung down, semi-concealing the gap.

Then came the hard bit. After tucking the terminal into a pocket alongside a pair of meal bars, Stein backed up to the far wall of the room and took a deep breath. She charged at the door, leaping, kicking off of it, and extending her arms upwards. She frantically clawed for the gaping hole where the membrane had been, catching the ledge with one hand, then the other. At which point she immediately let go, the heat of scorched metal burning her right hand.

"Beep," said the maintenance robot.

"Go beep yourself," Stein said, shaking her hand. It was a mild burn, and she ran it under some cold water in the sink, cursing to herself. Tapping furiously at the terminal, she directed the robot to briefly spray the cavity with a cooling foam. "All right, let's try this again," she said, after watching the robot complete its work.

The second try worked better than the first, followed by some decidedly unladylike scratching, clawing, and hoisting to get herself up into the membrane hole. A barely controlled, and no more delicate, face-first fall on the other side was her reward. Fortunately—and by that point predictably—there was no one around to see her tumble but for the little maintenance robot. "Thanks, buddy," she said, rolling onto her back and waving at the robot through the torn membrane. She got up and examined the door. At eye-level there wasn't anything immediately obvious to suggest she had escaped, though the pungent odor of melted metal and plastic gave away that something unusual had just happened.

Not that she intended to be around to explain it. Turning away from her cell, she crept down the hall, out of the detention center.

Bruce sidestepped the pair of security officers running out of the security base, hoping his stripper-esque disguise wouldn't arouse any suspicion, or, for that matter, arousal. But the officers continued out of the base without even looking at him, which he decided, in this particular case only, not to take as an insult.

Once through the bulkhead door, he had stepped out of the way into an old storefront, allowing the mob to pass by him so it could spread out and set to work being distracting. Which it did, comprehensively. Bruce saw only a fraction of the chaos unfold, but what he did see suggested security would have their hands full for the next several hours dealing with angry, partially naked people.

With every available officer seemingly out dealing with his new friends, Bruce was able to move deeper into the security base without seeing another soul, quickly making his way to the detention cells. He paused at the guard station at the entrance to the detention center, where he examined the desk display. All the cells were empty, save for one labeled, 'Stein.' Reaching out, he tapped the unlock button beside the door, unsurprised when nothing happened. Unlocking doors would require some level of access that he didn't have. Drumming his fingers on the desk for a moment, he began tapping through the menus, looking for another way in. He had one specific subroutine in mind, one he almost certainly would have access to. Finding it, he triggered the fire-alarm test function and stepped back. Down the hall, all the doors unlocked, red lights mounted overhead flashing. He raised an eyebrow, just a little surprised that had been so easy. "Well, life's stupid." He sauntered down the hall.

Reaching the cell Stein was supposedly in, he looked inside, finding it empty. He smiled. So, she had found some way out. Curious how she had done it, he stepped inside and looked around, quickly spotting the severed metal bars heaped in the corner of the room. He looked up, examining the maintenance robot clinging to the ceiling and the tattered membrane hanging above the door. He shuddered at the athleticism required to get through there. He sniffed the air, smelling the burnt plastic. He couldn't be far behind her.

The red lights in the hall stopped flashing. He looked down, watching in dismay as the cell door closed. "Ohhhhhhhhhhhhhhhhh," he groaned. The fire alarm test apparently operated on a short timer. "I knew that," Bruce said, not lying. He banged on the door. "But locking these should really be a manual function only," he yelled. "For safety reasons, if nothing else."

Stein retraced the steps the security men had taken when they had led her to her cell. The base was fortunately, or perhaps predictably, deserted, all the security forces busy dealing with the riot. She didn't dare look up at the security sensors surely embedded in the ceiling, hoping that they weren't being monitored.

The detention cells were on the first level, and the route she had planned was to head for the nearest door, out to the streets, and not look back. She stopped, frozen, hearing voices around a corner. She looped back, and climbed up a flight of stairs, ducked into the hall, and entered the lobby, heading to the second floor exit.

The lobby was thankfully empty, the exit unguarded. But she stopped short when she reached the door, seeing the backs of nearly twenty officers standing outside. A muster point, evidently; she heard someone in charge yelling orders. She clenched her fists, fighting off panic. More voices, this time from the staircase she had just ascended. She darted across the lobby and away from the door, heading back into the center of the security base, still thankfully deserted. Quickly she walked past empty offices, empty briefing rooms, empty locker rooms. *That's a thought.* She stopped, then backtracked to the locker room.

She searched through the lockers until she found a security uniform that was roughly her size. Slipping it on over her own conspicuously orange clothes, she pulled the hat as low over her face as she dared. After checking herself out in the mirror to see how suspicious she looked—very—she swallowed, then left the room, continuing to the other side of the security base.

She reached the lobby on the far side of the base, two guards at the door, shifting anxiously as they looked out on the street. Stein hesitated, not daring to walk right through them, not wanting to spin suspiciously in place again. She came to a halt on the far side of the lobby, head down, looking at her terminal.

Face buried in her terminal, but not really looking at it, she reevaluated her options. Back the way she came? Or go up another level to the entrances there? But those would likely be just as guarded. While she was desperately trying to come up with a confrontation-free way out of her mess, a new message icon flashed. Although absolutely the worst possible time for engaging in correspondence, she couldn't think of anything else to do, so she opened the message and read it.

"No way."

Bruce kissed and licked his singed knuckles, victims of his zealous attempt to double-check the torch-proof thickness of the cell door. He had already sent a message to Stein, who was clearly better at getting in and out of here than he was, but knew she was probably offline. He considered sending a similar message to Ellen and Griese, but that would be of a similarly dubious value. They would have to get there first, and even if they somehow managed that, they would probably just laugh at him. Shooting out the security sensor to bait someone to come investigate was also out of the question, he had discovered when he had tried to do exactly that; it was incredibly well-armored. Besides which, the fact that he was there and Stein wasn't suggested they weren't even monitoring the damn sensor. Still, they would get around to him eventually. He would just have to shoot his way past whomever opened the door. He maneuvered the maintenance robot so that it could look down the hall, then leaned back on the bed, watching the robot's feed on his terminal.

Twenty minutes after he had first checked in, the door slid open. He immediately rolled out of bed, landing in a crouch, pistol drawn. Not hearing any sounds of movement in the hall, he cautiously approached the door. Red lights twirled on the ceiling above. Frowning, he slowly slid his head out and looked down the corridor.

"You've got to fucking be kidding me," Stein said, standing behind the security console, a huge grin on her face.

"I'm not, actually," Bruce said, stepping out of the cell.

"Why are you dressed as a stripper?"

"Shut up."

"Where did you even get pants that small?"

"Shut up."

"Oh, come on. Don't be mad."

"You could have let me know the robot worked," he said, pointing up at the robot clinging to the hall ceiling. He frowned, then deactivated it with his terminal. The robot plunged to the ground, Bruce catching it, then tucking it into the webbing on his left hip.

"Sorry. I didn't know you were going to be so hot on its heels."

"*Finally,* someone thinks I'm hot. You have no idea how long I've been waiting for someone to notice."

The control room was only slightly less chaotic than the streets below, as Thorias' command officers struggled to coordinate their officers' activities. The room was filled with clipped and terse orders, drowned out by the displays broadcasting chatter from officers in the thick of the action.

"Move around to Flint, and hold position there."

"Looters in the dress shop on 6th and Chalk."

"Need more help at the escalator. Africa and 5th. Now! Oh, craaaaa..."

"They're looting the manikins. Why? What are they...oh, no!"

"Shoot him! Shoot him in the head!"

"That's the worst thing I've ever seen."

"...urine everywhere!"

"Why is no one stopping him? Why are they laughing and clapping?"

"They're hugging us! They're hugging us!"

"That manikin is ruined! *Everything* is ruined!"

Helot stepped up quietly beside Thorias. "Well?"

Thorias' hands flexed white on the table display. "I think we're okay," he said softly. "Got 'em contained, finally." He pointed to the map, where the approximate location of the rioters was sketched in, a rough horseshoe around Africa-1. "They're not really armed. And they're not heading upstairs at all."

"Good," Helot said. He looked at the map, at Thorias' defenses, and at the red horseshoe which indeed did seem to be shrinking slowly. "Do you, uh, know why they're naked?" he asked.

Thorias didn't know, and the expression on his face told just how deeply he didn't know. "They're not all naked. Just some," he said quietly. "But..."

"Some is more than enough," Helot finished the thought. He closed his eyes and felt his hands ball into fists, fingernails digging into his palms. If he had needed a reason for leaving these people behind, he was getting one.

"Well, shit," Bruce said, looking across the lobby. "You were right."

They were on the fourth floor of the security base, as far away from the riot as they could be. Stein had guessed there would be fewer guards up here and had been proven correct—the lobby was empty.

"It seems your distraction is still fairly distracting."

"That's too bad," Bruce said. "I was kinda wanting to shoot my way out." Bruce had come armed, pistols for both himself and Stein, rounded out with a pair of stun grenades. Stein's hand touched the weapon on her hip, fingers flicking away as soon as she did.

"Still might get the chance, buddy." They didn't have to take the same way out of the aft that Bruce had taken in, and indeed would have had to fight their way through a semi-naked melee to do so. Bruce still had his tools with him and could open any of the bulkhead doors he wanted. They just had to get to one first.

Stein walked across the lobby towards the front door, Bruce trailing just behind her. The doors slid open, and she stuck her head out, looking north. No bulkhead doors there—just one of the security checkpoints a block away, a half-dozen officers set up behind plastic barricades.

"Think they'll notice us?" Bruce asked, just behind her.

"Well, I don't want to go back inside," she replied. "So, let's find out. Be cool."

"Got it. I *am* inconspicuous," Bruce declared. Stein did a double-take at the big man with the too small security uniform and a robot strapped to his hip. She took a deep breath, then set out across the street.

They hadn't even made it halfway before they heard shouts of recognition from the barricade. Breaking into a sprint, they crossed the rest of the street at a run, rounding the intersection out of sight.

"They were looking for us!" she shouted.

"No, you were too conspicuous!" Bruce shouted back. They reached the next block, a side street, Stein turning north to the closed bulkhead door there. Bruce grabbed her on the shoulder to stop her. "No way. We're not gonna have enough time." He jerked his head south. "Come on."

So, they ran south, footsteps and shouts behind them. Stein followed Bruce as he picked his way through the smaller streets and hallways, finally realizing he was taking them to one of their old haunts, a pressure boosting room, from where they could access a variety of mechanical areas. Stein ducked inside the room, dominated by the massive air plenum. Bruce locked the door behind her. "Think we lost 'em?" he asked.

"No. Not at all," she replied. It wouldn't take long to track them down here. She turned to face the plenum, where a fan boosted the pressure on one of the ship's main arterial ducts. Her eyes followed the ducting out of the room, trying to remember where it led, where there were better places to hide. She stifled a chuckle. "You know what we're close to?"

"Death?" he guessed. "Or were you being sentimental? *Each other?*"

Stein squinted. "M. Melson's studio."

"I'm pretty sure we've figured out everything there is to know about that guy, Stein."

"Yes, but that guy's studio is a better place to hide than here."

Bruce looked at the ducting and groaned. "You're right, but fuck you for it."

Stein opened a hatch on the plenum, exposing the filter chamber, making way for Bruce to step through before following him, closing the hatch behind her. This was a narrow space, a spinning fan blade behind a grate on their right, a screen of cellulose filters on their left. Stein selected a filter at waist level, and lifted it from its slot. She crawled through the gap, then got out of the way, allowing Bruce to enter somewhat less gracefully, before carefully replacing the filter behind him. A series of smaller ducts were arrayed in front of them, screened by a set of dampers. Selecting one of these ducts, she turned sideways and easily slipped through a pair of damper vanes. Bruce simply bent one of the vanes out of the way then back in place. Beyond them, the duct soon narrowed, forcing them to begin crawling and Bruce to begin moaning.

Ten minutes later, Stein was over the spot where she could look down into M. Melson's studio. "Oh, Bruce, you sprightly fucking gazelle," she said, seeing the evidence of her friend's previous visit to the room, a damper hanging open and the ceiling laying in splinters on the floor below.

SEVERANCE

166
"It worked, didn't it?" Bruce asked from behind her.

Lowering herself through a little more gently, Stein examined the room. There were the removed ceiling tiles and the gash in the ceiling that Bruce had found. Which meant there must be a disconnect directly above the room. The conspirators must have known that one was going to jam, and cut through it before they attempted to separate. Nearly blinding a wayward intruder as they did so.

Bruce entered the room behind her, easing himself down from the vent with his powerful arms, landing on both feet with surprising grace. "Nailed it," he said, adding a bow. Stein shook her head, then entered the closet in the back of the studio. She bent down to open the access hatch, interrupted by a groan from behind her. "No way that's going to happen," Bruce said. "I'm not going to fit in there. We'll hide here."

"I know. Just considering our options."

From the studio came the sound of a door opening. Bruce and Stein turned to see a surprised-looking naval engineer staring back at them, carrying a massive bulky object by its two handles. Dark goggles hung around his neck. "Hey, guys. Just here to cut the clamps."

Stein nearly choked in surprise that two ill-fitting security costumes had fooled someone at close range. "We know," Bruce said, thinking slightly quicker than her. "We were just clearing the room for you."

"Huh," the engineer said. "Okay. But you guys will probably want to clear out of here." He fingered the goggles hanging around his neck. "This thing gets pretty bright."

"Oh, we know," Bruce said with a smile.

The engineer looked at him curiously. "Hey, why are your pants so tight? Wait. Who are you guuuMPH..."

His question was cut short by a fist to the nose, sending him tumbling backwards, the massive tool falling down on top of him. "Careful!" Stein yelled at Bruce, still advancing on the engineer. Bruce realized the danger, leaping back just as a bright blue blade erupted out of the fusion torch. Stein was staring right at it, immediately blinded, stumbling backwards into the closet. Again the letters VLAD danced in the center of her vision. The hiss of the fuse torch filled the room until it was cut off by another thump and strangled cry.

Stein opened her eyes again, blinking rapidly. "Balls! That is bright," Bruce said, somewhere off to her left. Her vision slowly returned to normal, the ghostly, misshapen VLAD slowly fading from view. She looked over to see the engineer on the floor, fuse torch beside him, Bruce standing over him, doing his own blinking.

"What'd you do?" she asked.

"Kicked him in the face."

Stein got to her feet. "Good." She crossed the room to examine the fuse torch. "Hey, did you see anything...funny...when that thing came on?"

"What?" Bruce asked. He bent down to pick up the fuse torch. "I saw you falling backwards on your ass. That was kind of funny, in a very rudimentary slapstick way. Why? What'd you see?"

Stein shook her head. "It's nothing." She looked up at the ceiling, ignoring Bruce's suspicious gaze. Her eyes traced out the scar in the ceiling, where the fuse torch had first shown her VLAD. "He must have been here to hack away at the disconnect again. I guess one or more of them jammed."

Bruce turned the fuse torch over in his hands. "Think we can use this for anything?"

"I think we can use it for cutting things."

"Okay. But do we need to cut anything?"

"Ah. I can't think of anything we need to cut, no."

"Well, I don't want to lug it around." Bruce said, smashing it against the wall. Various pieces of the torch rained down at his feet.

"You ever wonder if maybe those things explode when you do that to them?" Stein asked. "I mean, it is a fusion torch, right?"

"Seems to be safe," Bruce said, dropping it on the floor. He then started feeling the engineer's pockets, patting him down. Finding something, he pulled out a terminal. Seeing Stein's expression, he said, "What? We are terrorists now."

"We already have terminals."

Bruce grabbed the unconscious engineer's hand and slid the terminal into its grip. The screen flashed to life with what the engineer had been looking at. Bruce examined the screen and smiled. "But now we have all his notes." With a couple of taps, he instructed it to begin copying files to his own terminal.

Stein pursed her lips. "How'd you know that'd work?" she asked, looking at the engineer's limp hand on the terminal. "Never mind. Not the first time you've punched someone in the face."

"Hopefully, not the last, either."

Stein looked down at the unconscious engineer on the floor. "Someone's going to notice him missing before long." She looked back to the closet and the hatch over the crawlway access.

"Don't say it," he said.

"It'll work," she said. "You'll fit. It will suck, but it'll work."

Bruce looked at the closet unhappily. "I am going to get stuck and die down there."

"I'd come back to feed you."

After an hour of scraping and crawling and bitching, Stein and Bruce emerged into the light. Stein pulled herself out into the open and turned around to watch the little maintenance robot get pushed out of the tube behind her. A few seconds later Bruce emerged, looking not unlike an overused pipe cleaner.

Following a minute of stretching, knee massaging, and complaint ignoring, Stein got to her feet. They were in another pressure booster room, a massive fan dominating half the room, connected to another arterial duct. She crossed the room and opened the filter chamber, peering inside. They would hopefully have lost the trail of any pursuers by that point, but the plenum would still be an excellent place to hide. Pulling strongly on the hatch to open it against the negative air pressure, she stepped inside the plenum and through another filter wall.

"Jesus, it's hot in here," Bruce said, dripping sweat as he stepped through the filter wall behind her. A damp man in many conditions, Stein knew he wouldn't react well to their new hiding spot. Thanks to a reheat coil on the other side of the fan, the air here was much hotter than in the other artery, which is why it was such an ideal place to hide. He dropped the little robot on the floor and sat down beside it.

"Good place to hide from IR scans," she said. "Though I now wonder if they'll simply be able to smell us in here."

Bruce nodded and stripped off the upper portion of his uniform, fanning air under his upstretched arms. "So, what's the plan?" he asked.

"Don't have one."

"Good, me neither. Wanna play cards?"

Stein smiled and nodded sleepily. Whether it was the temperature, or the adrenaline wearing off, she suddenly felt very tired. She sat down against the thin metal wall of the ducting and slumped back, letting her eyes close. "So, you think we're safe here?" he asked.

She tipped to one side, lying down on the floor, head resting on folded arms. She could hear him messing around with the little robot, distracting himself with his hands. "Are we safe anywhere?" she responded, before drifting off to sleep.

Previously

Sure you could, but why would you want to?

Harold turned off the display and rubbed his eyes. Another dead end. The message from the fabrication clerk cut right to the heart of the matter: there was no legitimate reason anyone would possibly want to print disposable bits of plastic on the Argos. Every bit of information that anyone could possibly want to see could be displayed or distributed far more readily on a terminal. Everyone had one of those; they were practicably disposable themselves.

Three months had passed since Allan Eichhorn, the Argos Extreme editor, had been found strangled. The second murder in a year had attracted surprisingly little attention in the press, most of that from Argos Extreme itself. The other feeds had been faintly dismissive of the story. Harold got the sense the dead editor wasn't widely liked amongst his peers. And with other, more pressing events rolling around—mandatory genetic screenings, wide-scale gene tinkering, the Turn—Eichhorn would have had to have died multiple times a week to stay on the feeds.

Harold didn't know how the young editor had been discovered by the conspirators, but he could guess. Security was monitoring the network, scanning it for copies of whatever information Kevin had stolen. That in itself was a gross abuse of their powers, but not a surprising one, at least when considered in light of the gross abuse of their duty to not murder people. The lesson to take from it was clear: anyone who put that information on an active terminal ended up dead. Which was strangely comforting; all of his paranoia and precautions had not been in vain.

"And that is why, Mr. Fabrication Helpline, I can't simply send out an e-vite," Harold said to his desk. He sat up in his chair and stretched, back arched, hands grasping at the air behind him. The pamphlet angle had seemed like an ideal solution. He couldn't tell one person at a time—that just seemed to result in one person getting brutally murdered at a time. He needed to tell a lot of people, all at once. Without using the network. Handing out pamphlets on a corner was a laughably inefficient solution, but that in itself might be an advantage. It meant security probably hadn't even considered it. Harold could get flyers into hundreds of people's hands before security found out; he'd even drummed up a couple of cloak and dagger schemes for distributing them semi-anonymously. But if he couldn't even make the flyers in the first place....

His terminal flashed, alerting him of an incoming appointment. Harold yawned and stood up, grabbed his lab coat, and left the office. The gene tinkering was going on around the clock and had been since the captain and mayor had agreed to make genetic screenings mandatory for every person on board the ship. It had taken a few months for Dr. Kinison to sign off on Harold's automation scheme for the gene-tinkerers, a delay which frustrated Harold no end. Although a bureaucracy of only two people, it was still, somehow, incredibly inefficient. But it was the law: gene tinkering was a fussy technology, prone to concurrency errors, overwriting problems, and a host of other spooky issues. However frustrating, the multiple layers of oversight were a necessary part of the work.

As he walked to the operating room, he examined his next patient's chart, refreshing his memory on the man's condition. Martin Stahl, 26 years old. 3.4×10^5 Denebs off baseline, across all major organs, higher variances in the liver and testicles. Not the worst he had seen. But not that great either. Mr. Stahl's life had been shortened by ten to twenty years without his permission. And he had no chance of procreating, at least not on this ship. Harold entered the operating room, "Hello, Martin. My name's Dr. Stein."

"Hey, Doc." Martin looked up from his spot in the comfy chair. The big padded chair which sat in the center of the operating room was a pleasant surprise for most new gene-tinkering patients. Whether the patient was relaxed or not turned out to have little effect on the tinkering process, but after the comfy chair had been tried once during an early trial, it had proven so popular that it soon became a tradition.

The only other furniture in the room was a desk set against the wall and a small, wheeled stool. Harold pulled the stool over to Martin and sat down. "So, I understand you've absorbed massive amounts of radiation," he said, smiling at his patient's suddenly enormous eyes. "Relax. It's entirely treatable."

Martin nodded, his throat clenching up and down. "The nurses said it was no big deal."

Harold smiled. If it had been no big deal, Martin wouldn't be sitting here. A simple system of screenings and pre-screenings had been set up to sort out the simple cases from the bad ones, and with a couple of decades of experience poking around in the genome, Harold didn't get tasked with the simple ones. "It's not." Harold said. "In fact, we're almost done."

"But I just got here. I mean you just got here. I got here about an hour ago."

"I'm sorry about the wait," Harold said, lying. "And the reason we're almost done is because I've been working on your course of treatment for the last three days." That was mostly true—he had started the process three days earlier. But most of the work was automated, the nanobot programming determined algorithmically, based on the statistical analysis of the patient's current genetic variance and the baseline genome kept on each patient's file. Harold only had to review the work. His main role was simply being human, a living mind to ride herd over the nanobots, a bit of technology that humanity still felt a bit uncomfortable around. Laws on Earth and the Argos ensured these machines were only let out of their cage under the close supervision of someone who possessed several degrees and was capable of passing regular sanity tests.

"Basically, we're just going to need you to ingest a couple pills, and then enter quarantine for about four weeks while the tinkering takes effect."

Martin looked at the clear plastic bottle Harold produced from a pocket and the large gray pills inside. "Are these nanobots?"

Harold smiled warmly. "They are. Don't worry. It's completely safe." Seeing Martin look unconvinced, he added, "They almost never drive anyone around like a puppet anymore." A pause. "I'm kidding, Martin."

A choked mockery of a laugh slipped from Martin's throat. "Thanks, Doc," he eventually wheezed out. "I guess I owe you one. If you ever need anything, just let me know."

Harold nodded absentmindedly. *A lot of people owe me favors these days.* He tapped a couple of notes onto his terminal. "The nurses told you about the quarantine, correct? Your family knows? Your work knows? Supervisors?"

"Yeah, they know. They made some jokes."

"I'll bet. That's what friends are for," Harold said. He checked Martin's chart one last time. "What do you do, Martin?" he asked as he did so, just to make conversation.

"I run a pair of lines at a fab plant."

Harold looked up. "Oh, yeah? Cool." He wondered what the odds of that were. A fabrication engineer who owed him a favor had just fallen into his lap. Harold felt his heart beat faster, his ever present paranoia squeezing his adrenal glands.

"Doc?"

"Yeah? Right. Okay, we're ready for your treatment." He opened the bottle and allowed the two robot pills to slide into his palm before retrieving a cup of water from a basin at the side of the room. Returning to Martin, he handed over the pills and water. "So. You take these and go through that door over there. That's our quarantine ward. There should be a bed set aside for you—there's a nurse who can show you around. It's pretty full right now, so apologies for the lack of privacy. Although I hear they throw some pretty good parties in there." He smiled, then watched Martin swallow the pills. Helping the young man up, he guided him to the door. "Good job, Martin. I'll see you when you get out."

Martin gone, Harold returned to the stool and sat down, rotating back and forth, thinking about his possible in at a fabrication plant. *If it isn't a trap. It probably isn't a trap. It hopefully, probably isn't a trap.* He spun around on the stool, considering the possibilities. It definitely sounded like it was worth pursuing. But his paranoia had served him well so far. What if it was a trap? Were there any precautions he should take?

He hadn't allowed himself to think about it, but couldn't afford the self-deception now: there was a good chance that if he kept pursuing this task he had taken on, it would end up poorly for him. He shuddered involuntarily but felt no rising wave of panic. *Good, Harold. Steady on.*

If he did die, if he failed to spread the word himself, he needed to find a way to pass this information on post-mortem. Kevin's trick, stashing a terminal in a closet, having that terminal not get found and deleted by a janitor, had been a massive stroke of luck. By all rights, the truth should be lost by now. If the knives came out for Harold, he would want a sturdier backup plan.

There were some snags with that. First, who to send the message to? He had no next of kin. Both parents long dead, no siblings. His closest friends were work friends—not that close, and certainly not people he wanted to drag into this mess. The way some of them talked, many of their sympathies might even lie with the conspirators. In truth, the only person he had fully trusted was his almost-son Kevin. And he didn't think he had any more sons left in him. He did have a reproduction credit that he had never cashed in, but it was a bit late in life for that now. And if he read the political winds right, they weren't going to let him build any more canned babies.

He looked at the big comfy chair that Martin had recently vacated and the empty pill bottle lying on it. *But they were letting him do that.* He swallowed. It was as unethical an idea as he had ever had. But it could work.

And fortunately for Harold, flexible ethics were rapidly becoming a specialty of his.

7

Worst Case Scenario

Kinsella poked at the heap of green and brown mush on his plate. Bletmann had assured him that there was nothing different about the food, but watching the way it clung and clutched at his spork, Kinsella wasn't so sure. It was possibly a psychological effect—in the good old days, people would have paid a tremendous amount of money per plate of mush for the opportunity to speak with him, even more to get their picture taken with him, post-mush. Now, in the bad new days, Kinsella was lucky he didn't have to pay for the mush himself.

"Come on, Stan," he said, pointing a mush-laden spork at Stan Reynolds, an old friend of the apparently fair-weather variety. "You know this will pay off." He directed his spork along the length of the table, threatening the others gathered at the Reynolds home with the trembling mush. "You all know I'm good for this."

Reynolds put down his own spork. The current chair of the Argos Club, a collection of some of the ship's most self-important assholes, Reynolds had supported Kinsella for years. He hadn't done this out of any special passion for public policy; it was more in the same manner in which an ancestor of his might have taken an interest in fast horses. Or really mean chickens. "Eric, you've been a good friend to us. And you're always welcome here." He smiled, obviously thinking of a joke. "No matter which door you use." A trill of laughter from the lesser weather vanes around the table. Security had been almost invisible in this half of the ship since the riot two days earlier, but Kinsella hadn't let his guard down, still entering and exiting from back doors and side entrances, often bewigged. "But this doesn't look good for you, does it?" An obvious spot for a wig joke, though thankfully Reynolds didn't see it. "It doesn't look good for us," he said instead.

"Things will look better with your support."

Reynolds tented his fingers and flexed them back and forth. "Maybe. Maybe not."

"Don't pull any punches, Stan," Lady Cathy said. Kinsella did everything he could not to roll his eyes. *Lady.* Not actually a title, barely even a description. "We liked you when you were in charge, Eric," she said. "And you aren't in charge of shit now."

I'll take charge of caving your head in with your own severed arms, Kinsella didn't say, his face a mask of serenity. "I'm in charge of a lot more than you think. And I haven't failed you guys yet," he said, unleashing his winningest grin. "Three elections in a row."

"That's what the last guy said," Lady Cathy observed. "He won three in a row as well. Would have kept winning too, until he didn't."

Kinsella pushed back his chair and stood up, a signal to Bletmann, lurking at the edge of the room. Time to take charge of the situation; he was losing them. And he really did need their help; all of the slush funds and caches attached to the mayor's office had been frozen. He had already started drawing on his own collection of physical loot, built up from a lifetime of public service. But he would need a lot more for what he had planned. "Okay," he said, "I get it. I'm down now. You like winners, and I don't look like much of one." A few of the less subtle weather vanes nodded. "But let's be frank. I'm cheaper to bribe than the other guy. Has he returned your calls yet?" He watched everyone's reactions, a mixture of confusion and annoyance.

From down the hall, the sound of a door opening, followed by sputtering protests from one of Reynolds' servers. Moments later, Hogg strode into the dining room in full security regalia, every metal and hard plastic surface on his uniform shined to a deep luster. Beneath his outward expression of mild shock, Kinsella bit his tongue.

"Mayor Eric Kinsella, I'm here to place you under arrest," Hogg said, his voice firm and not at all wooden.

Kinsella stood up straighter, shoulders rolling back, gut in a little. "I'm afraid I can't let you do that."

"And I'm afraid you don't have a choice in the matter," Hogg said, rushing, trampling Kinsella's show of defiance, diminishing its impact. *You idiot.* Kinsella glared at the security man, who was now looking decidedly more nervous than his position would imply.

It had been too much of a stroke of luck to not use him like this. Kinsella had always suspected there was something a bit funny about the way security officers behaved. Too deferential. Too eager to please. He knew he was accustomed to the snake pit of Argosian politics, where everyone's motives ran ten layers deep. Most people were surely more straightforward. But there was something about security officers that went way beyond 'straightforward,' and after some quiet research early in his first term, he eventually figured it out. They *had* to follow orders. It hurt them not to. Most of the navy geeks were the same way. It was something bred into them, something Helot and his predecessors must have been doing for generations.

A useful fact to know, though Kinsella had never found a way to take advantage of it; security officers didn't normally report to him. It required a damaged one, a chance encounter with a reject looking for a new home, for him to put his theory to the test. And damned if he didn't seem to be right. Hogg would do anything he said, conduct any act asked of him.

But no amount of asking could get him to act well.

"What you're doing is illegal," Kinsella said, knowing he would have to carry the show on his own. "This is an illegal attempt to silence this ship's legitimate civilian government."

"I don't know what you're talking about," Hogg said. He seemed to remember he was supposed to be physically menacing the mayor, took two steps forward, then stopped abruptly, remembering that by this point he was now supposed to be doubting his purpose.

Strictly speaking, Kinsella did have the less challenging role: defiant self-righteousness. Barely a role really, for him. "It's also wrong," he said, his voice strong. "You're destroying this ship. You know what Helot's doing," Kinsella said. "You know what's going to happen to us."

"I still have to arrest you."

"*Even* if it's true, you still have to arrest me?" Kinsella said, filling in Hogg's misspoken line. "So, you admit it?"

Hogg hesitated. "I didn't say that."

"But it is true, isn't it? Helot is planning to split the ship."

This was the tricky part; there was a certain salesmanship necessary to handle the next exchange. "So, what if it is?" Hogg finally said.

Kinsella shook his head. "So, what if it is?" he repeated, turning to survey the room. Dim faces stared back at him. Kinsella held his breath, waiting. *I think we got 'em.*

"Are you two rehearsing a play?" Lady Cathy asked.

"What?" Kinsella said. *Or not.*

"You are clearly rehearsing a play," Reynolds said, "though I don't know why. Nor why you didn't rehearse it before you got here." Chuckles down the length of the table. "Was this supposed to impress us, Eric? Having some fake security officer try to arrest you?"

Kinsella held up his hands. "Well, *obviously*. But he is a real security officer."

"I am a real security officer," Hogg acknowledged.

Reynolds looked Hogg up and down, and wagged his head back, seemingly unsure. "He does look like a security officer," Lady Cathy said, her voice a bit breathy.

"No, look," Kinsella began. "Yes and no. This isn't what it looks like, except it is a bit."

Reynolds interrupted him. "You were actually able to bribe a security officer?" he asked. "I'm impressed. I had no idea you had this kind of sway anymore." The weather vanes murmured and nodded. Kinsella blinked, completely stunned. "Look, Eric. You've got a good point about the other guy not really playing ball with us. So, yes. I'll help." Reynolds looked around the room. "*We'll* help. But you've got to cut it out with this crazy ship splitting stuff. It's completely insane. No one's buying it."

"Okay, sure," Kinsella said, not believing his luck. He directed a pointed glance at his costar, but could see Hogg didn't need to be told when to shut up.

"And this little skit is a great idea," Reynolds went on. "It's classic you. Just maybe, you know, get a real fake security officer next time? I think the fake ones might be more convincing."

Many people noticed the large, bulky object Griese and Ellen carried down the street. But they were all locals, unlikely to tattle on them. And by that point, almost all of the security sensors had been shot out on the third level, following a dedicated few days of work by a group of goons in Kinsella's growing militia. They would do the same on each level in turn, but had been told to make the third level a priority, presumably because it was the fastest level to move around on, and Kinsella was tired of his selection of wigs.

So, they were pretty sure they weren't noticed by anyone official when they entered the service entrance of an art gallery, the main floors of which extended up to the garden well. Once inside, they picked their way to the rear staircase of the building, hefting their load upstairs. When they reached the uppermost floor, they found an unmarked door, which opened to reveal the roof access staircase. Climbing this, they emerged on the roof of the gallery, facing the north, the bulk of the gallery's roofline blocking their line of sight to the south. Crouching, they picked their way across the roof to the spot they had observed from across the garden well, an odd architectural feature which created a fold in the roof permanently in the shade.

There they unrolled the garish carpet that concealed their load. Long, bulky, and matte black, any observer at any time in human history would immediately recognize it as something nasty. A boxy frame mounted on a low profile tripod, with a thinner rectangular block extending out the front, surrounded by a series of other protrusions sprouting out in a seemingly careless manner. This was a smart rifle, as ugly as it was rare.

Smart rifles were an Earth invention that had immigrated to the Argos about halfway through Argos War I. While a computer-assisted rifle was

useful on Earth, on the Argos it was absolutely necessary for anyone who
wanted to shoot something further away than they could yell. In a spinning cylinder, where the very concept of gravity was openly mocked, the
ballistics of a projectile weapon became incredibly complicated. Bullets
followed long, spiraling paths, making accurate shooting over distance an
impossible task. Several friendly fire incidents during that first conflict
provided grim illustrations of this. A smart rifle was capable of compen-
sating for all these insanely complicated ballistics with the help of a small
processor and some extremely accurate sensors. Because the ship hadn't
sailed with military hardware, the smart rifles on board the Argos were all
makeshift, designed from first principles and cobbled together using whatever components were available. Only three had survived the first war,
none of them fired in anger since.

They carefully positioned the rifle in the darkest part of the shadow,
Ellen setting up behind it. Griese lay on the other side, his terminal in
front of him with its sensor on maximum zoom. For ten minutes they lay
there, slowly scanning the aft wall of the garden well.

"I think I got one," Griese whispered.

"What?" Ellen asked, her voice tight.

"I think I got one," he whispered, somewhat louder.

Ellen rolled her eyes. "Darling, you are looking at something over a
kilometer away. You could scream 'SHOOT IT! SHOOT IT IN THE
HEAD!' and no one but me would know."

"The whispering felt appropriate."

"Where is it?"

"Eleven o'clock, maybe a third of the radius out from the center. Just
underneath the light panel."

A few tense seconds passed while Ellen maneuvered the rifle around,
searching. "Got it," she finally said. Through her scope she could see a
dark patch just underneath the blinding glare coming off the light panel.
The security sensors at street level were small, only practicably detectable
with special terminal programs. But the ones mounted in the garden well,
like the one she was looking at now, were much larger.

Ellen centered the crosshairs on the boxy shape. She tapped the target
lock button and watched as *CALCULATING*...appeared on the viewfinder.
After a couple of seconds, a blue arrow appeared on the right hand side of the
screen. Tilting the rifle to the right and up a bit, she chased the arrow a few
degrees until it disappeared and a blue reticule appeared on the scope, superimposed on an otherwise unremarkable piece of wall. She lined up the crosshairs
with the reticule. "I love this thing," she said, smiling. She rubbed the sweat off
the palm of her right hand. "Okay. 3...2...1...go." She pulled the trigger.

The rifle burped out a 'pwwwww-schwack' noise, followed by a sharp crack, as a series of magnets propelled a lump of ferrous metal out of the barrel at twice the speed of sound. Immediately after firing, she panned back to the security sensor, missing the impact, seeing a cloud of debris floating in the lowered gravity of the upper well.

"Nice shot," Griese said, watching the same scene beside her on his terminal.

She winked at him. "Damn right it was. You set 'em up, I knock 'em down."

"I've seen it happen many times in other contexts," Griese agreed. He looked back down at his terminal and began searching for their next target.

There was no real reason for blowing away security sensors other than to satisfy that particular type of boredom that people with really large guns often experience. A boredom possibly enhanced by frustration that they were unable to help their two friends, currently trapped in medium-to-high danger. A brief message from Bruce had let them know he and Stein were safe-ish, and that they needn't worry, but if they did want to worry, they might busy themselves by distracting Helot.

Three shattered sensors worth of distraction later, Griese looked up from his terminal. "Hey, they have more of these, right?" He patted the body of the smart rifle, its case warm to the touch.

Ellen looked up at him. "Yeah, probably. Why? Ohhhhhh," she said, getting it.

Quickly they scuttled back into the shadows, dragging the rifle with them, until they reached the cover of the roof access stairs. There they slumped against the wall, breathing heavily, adrenaline pumping.

"I mean, I don't know that they'd actually shoot back at us," Griese said.

"No. They would," Ellen said. She pounded her fist into her thigh. "Just give them an excuse. They would have no hesitation at turning me into a widow."

Griese gasped, mock shock on his face. "Why would they shoot me? You were the one with the gun."

Ellen smiled sweetly. "This time. It's your turn next." She patted his shoulder, then smiled. "I love you."

"That's a dirty trick, lady." He looked at her sternly, shaking his head at the coy expression she was trying to pull off. "Don't you pout. I mean it," he added, shifting over, propping his knee up over her leg. "I'm very upset with you."

"Mmhmm."

Stein woke up with a start, wondering why she was so uncomfortably warm, before remembering where she was. She groaned. A fugitive living in the ship's lungs. She sniffed. With a very smelly co-fugitive not far away.

She rolled over to look at Bruce, who was still messing around with the little maintenance robot. In his hands, he had a funny-looking tool he was apparently trying to bind to the robot's manipulator. "What is that?" she asked.

Bruce didn't look up from his work. "Lube-planer."

She nodded sleepily, watching him twist the robot's manipulator around violently. "Okay."

"Would you like to know what that is?"

"Thank you, I know..."

"It files down a surface and then applies a thin coat of..."

"I know what a planer does."

"It makes stuff smooth." He looked up. "You only had to ask."

Stein rolled over and closed her eyes, sincerely intending to go back to sleep. This sincere intent lasted about twenty seconds before it was interrupted by Bruce. "You're not going to be able to get back to sleep."

"And why is that?"

"You won't be able to sleep without knowing what I'm doing. It will eat you up."

She rolled back over to face him. He'd seemed to have gotten the planer attached to the robot, and was now poking something into his terminal. "What I'd really like to know is where you got a lube-planer," she asked.

"Outside," Bruce said with a half shrug. "There's a workbench on the other side of the plenum."

She sat up, wordlessly conceding the point that she would not likely fall asleep again. "And you decided to risk being seen for...?"

"To do something awesome."

"I am filled with immediate dread." She watched him fuss away on his terminal, deep in concentration, the tip of his tongue poking out of the corner of his mouth, silent but for the occasional cackle. She wondered how many times he had done this before.

"There." Bruce picked up the robot and popped a filter out of place, stepping through. Stein watched curiously as he opened the outer hatch and set the robot down on the floor of the fan room. With a flourish, he made a final tap on his terminal and stepped back. The robot aimed its new tool down at the floor and waited as the tool glowed faintly. A couple of seconds later the tool shut off, and the robot retreated a short distance. Bruce walked over to the spot on the floor and rubbed it with his finger. "Slippery!" he said, looking back at Stein triumphantly. He tapped one final command into his terminal and watched as the robot pivoted and trundled off, crossing the room and entering the maintenance crawlspace where they had emerged.

"What's it going to do, Bruce?" Stein asked again as Bruce closed the hatch and climbed back into the plenum.

"I told you. Something awesome." Seeing her bemused expression, he expanded his thought. "It will move around to a random spot at street level and make it ultra-slippery smooth. Repeat."

"To what end?"

Bruce stared back at her, mock shock on his face. "For people to slip on and fall over."

Stein sighed. "And you think that your lifelong commitment to physical comedy was worth lugging that thing with you all this way?"

"I do."

She shook her head and lay back down on the floor, feigning sleep again. This farce lasted about a minute before she gave up and rolled onto her back. "What are we going to do, Bruce?"

She heard Bruce tapping on his terminal. "Well, Sleeping Beauty, you'll be happy to know that Sweating Beauty has been putting some thought into just that question," he said. "And I've come up with a couple options."

"Sweaty options, I hope."

"Invariably. The first option: Escape to Freedom. This is a tricky one, seeing as we've moved several blocks away from where we wanted to go, namely, Freedom." Stein snorted, and rolled over to face him. "We could maybe make a run for it, or try going back the way we came and then making a run for it. I think we can get within about four blocks of one of the bulkhead doors before having to go outside. Might be able to cover that distance unseen."

"Lot of cops around those doors now, I bet."

"No bet, here," Bruce agreed. "According to the news, they've dug in quite a bit since my little distraction riot." He cocked his head to the side and tapped again on his terminal. "So, that's if we want to escape. Or..." he began, letting that hang in the air.

"Oh, shit," she said, shaking her head. "I hate it when you say *or*."

"*Orrrrrrrrrr,*" he said louder, drawing it out, his voice growing shriller. "Or we could try doing something else."

"That sounds promisingly vague."

Bruce looked back down at his terminal. "Remember how I punched that guy in the face and broke his shit?"

"That's happened a few times in my presence, but I'll assume you're talking about the most recent occasion with the guy and the fuse torch."

"Well, they can't have too many of those fuse torches, can they?"

She frowned. They would have had to fabricate the fuse torches from scratch. There was no telling how easy that was, but there was no reason they would have made a lot of them. "Maybe," she allowed.

"No maybe. Definitely. And his terminal had a map of all the disconnects. Including which ones were jammed and needed to be cut open. If I read it correctly—and I must reiterate, I was doing this while sweating extremely heavily—they only had three or four fuse torches."

"So, what?"

"Well, we broke one of them. That's got to slow them down. Delay them from doing Split Plot again."

"I never agreed to calling it that."

He ignored her objection and held up his terminal. "And we know where they're going. So option two: Escape to Destruction. We intercept the last cutting teams. And break their shit." He watched her carefully for a moment before shrugging. "Or we don't. We run. Or nap. You look like you want another nap."

Stein sighed, seeing what he was getting at. "I don't want to run."

Bruce directed a long, thoughtful gaze at her. "Are you sure? Because you didn't seem so sure before."

"Before," she echoed. "Before I got shot in the face. Before I got kicked in the face for resisting arrest." She rubbed one of her still fading bruises. "After? Yeah, maybe I've got my fur up a bit."

She crawled across the floor of the plenum to Bruce, taking the terminal from his hands and examining the map. She groaned. "There's like a hundred of them."

"You're not reading it right, sleepy." Bruce poked at the map, toggling another layer, showing more information on the various disconnects. "Some of them are flagged, see? These ones are functional. These ones jammed but have already been cut. And these ones still need to be cut through."

"That still leaves like thirty. You want to check all of them?"

"Of course not." He toggled another layer on the map. "They've got one team cutting this set in the upper-decks here. That's only twelve. And honestly? We're bound to get caught and killed long before we check all of those," he said with a grin. "Really, checking them all is the worst case scenario."

Kinsella stepped out to meet the public, this time thankfully to the sound of applause. He crossed the stage to the grinning idiot and warmly shook her hand before sitting down on the couch. He crossed his legs and looked important. "Thanks for coming, Mayor," the idiot said.

Kinsella wondered if she had any idea of the amount that Kinsella had paid to be there. "I can always make time for you...here...," Kinsella said, his voice trailing off as he tried to dredge up the idiot's name.

"Great, great." A big empty smile. "So, what's going on lately Mister Mayor? What's all this coup business we're hearing about?"

"Well, Captain Helot has staged a coup and stolen control of the ship."

"Now, hold on..." The idiot held up a finger and looked up at the lights, straining her brain mightily. "I thought it was you who was couping Helot?"

Kinsella laughed lightly. "It's a common misunderstanding. You see a coup is when the army takes over the government. And I certainly don't have an army." He held up his hands innocently, showing his lack of armies. "That's clearly what Helot is doing, not me." A massive round of applause burst out from the gathered audience. Kinsella had paid more for that, but even without seeing the post-interview polls, he could tell it was worth it.

"And that would explain why they're doing such bad things?" the idiot asked. "Those awful shootings outside the anti-terrorism zone. And those attacks on the businesses along Europe-2?"

"That's right. It was awful, wasn't it?" Kinsella shook his head compassionately.

One of the screens on the side of the studio began replaying footage of the incident. A half-dozen security officers, kicking in the stalls of a pornography vendor. That particular stretch of Europe-2 did a healthy trade catering to the kind of pervert who got a thrill from being seen in public being a pervert. "Why would they beat up a simple, honest freak like that, I wonder?" the idiot said, probably legitimately wondering.

On the screen, the security officers continued to demolish storefronts and rough up passersby. "This is a coup!" one of them shouted. "Give us all your belongings!"

"You'll have to ask Helot, I'm afraid," Kinsella replied. "Maybe his thugs need that material to boost morale? Maybe they need pornography to fuel their fevered dreams of a totalitarian, porno-centric state? It's all possible."

"I wonder," the idiot said, still doing just that. "Isn't that your body-guard there?" She pointed at the screen. Kinsella's toes clenched.

"I don't think so."

"No, it is. Can we get a zoom on that?" the idiot asked. Quickly—too quickly Kinsella realized—the footage paused, rewound and zoomed in on one of the security officers in the feed. The frame settled on a close up of Angry Gus, one of Kinsella's large men, who had not earned his name because of his great intelligence.

The feed quickly switched to Angry Gus looking confused and angry backstage. The idiot looked at Kinsella and smiled. A flicker in the corner of her mouth—Helot had bought her first. "Let's get a side by side," she said, the feed doing that a fraction of a second later. They had probably rehearsed it.

"Mayor, did you dress up your goons in security outfits and send them to tear up the skin-rag-district? Why? Is this part of your coup business?"

Kinsella swallowed. "The captain has clearly been sending security spies to pose as my bodyguards. This is a terrible violation of...the identity theft laws. We can add it to the list of the crimes he's carried out."

"Really? Because that man has worked for you for quite some time." The feed displayed a series of dated photos of Kinsella at various public events over the past decade, all of them featuring Angry Gus in the background, looking angry.

"This is appalling. The worst case of identity theft I've ever seen," Kinsella said, shaking his head. "I ask you...*as the host of this show*, have you ever seen such a violation of one man's rights?" Kinsella swallowed. *They don't have to believe you for the right reasons. Believing you for the wrong ones works just fine, too.*

"Hmmm," the idiot said. "Hmmmmmmmmmm," she added. Kinsella nodded at her encouragingly. Their trap was slipping. They had rehearsed everything up to this point, but they hadn't rehearsed him barreling through it so brazenly.

"I'm really impressed," Kinsella said, seeing the out, "at the level of journalism and...commitment to public truthbringingness that this show has displayed—and always displayed—in exposing the captain's plot like this. Identity theft is a very serious crime, and your ability to bring this to light is just...really, really good." Kinsella sat back in his chair and took a breath. "Nice work."

"Thank you!" the idiot said, beaming. She blinked, looking up at the floor director's frantic signals. "Thank you so much, Mayor Kinsella!"

"My pleasure." Kinsella smiled broadly, right at the floor director, whose face was buried in his hands. "If I could add one thing," he continued, "I'd say that if people are tired of all of these coups we seem to be having, and the identity theft, and even this case of security officers beating up innocent pornography users..." He paused for effect, enjoying the moment. He hadn't felt this excited about lying *in years.* "Then they should come on down to the public arena. We're getting a big old group of like-minded people together, and we're going to have a hell of a fun time kicking old Helot out on his ear." He stood up, wanting for all the world to dance back and forth from foot to foot like a prize fighter. "I cannot tell you people *how much fun* this is going to be. There's going to be guns, and justice, and guaranteed good times! And guns. Guns for all!" Big smile now, the biggest he had. "So, come on down folks. You won't regret it." He pointed his finger at the camera sensor in the shape of a gun. Then fired.

Hogg wrestled another manikin into place on a rolling chair. This was deeply, fundamentally, unhappy work, and repetition had not made it any more bearable. They had needed something to serve for target practice as part of Kinsella's scheme to turn an army of bakers into something that resembled a fighting force. This close to the arena, the epicenter of the ship's athletics district, there had been one obvious source for targets, however distasteful they might be. But as soon as Kinsella had heard the idea, he had flipped out, and now Hogg was tasked with moving a pile of training manikins from the ship's competitive lovemaking league up and into wheeled chairs.

From the far side of the stack of manikins, another beast with two backs approached, stumbling towards a chair. Hogg watched it separate, the half that looked like Linze dropping the half that looked like a manikin clumsily into the chair, where it slid off to the ground, coming to rest in what Hogg recognized as a dismount with a very high degree of difficulty. "Fuck this," Linze said.

With Kinsella's wary approval, Hogg had engaged some of his former unit to help with the training. Croutl and Linze had been the only takers, having deduced more or less the same thing about their former employer that Hogg had. Also, Hogg hadn't asked any of the others in his squad. Only the best of Team Reject for him.

Linze hoisted her manikin back up into its chair, made sure it was going to stay in place this time, then planted a boot in its crotch and sent it wheeling across the arena. "Why'd I agree to help with this again?"

"Because you think our mayor is an honest, trustworthy man, worthy of our respect and lives?" Hogg suggested. Linze snorted, and he allowed himself a small grin. Bizarrely, with every sex dummy he handled, he was growing more convinced he was doing the right thing. Whatever oily qualities the mayor had, he certainly sounded like he was making sense when Hogg talked to him face-to-face. And Thorias had stopped giving him orders entirely. Although without any terminal—the mayor still hadn't given that back—Hogg supposed he wouldn't know if there had been any orders. Linze and Croutl had had to give their terminals up to Kinsella's goons as well, but that hadn't taken much convincing.

Hogg looked up to see his new oily boss enter the arena. A crew of idiots flocked around him, making a farce of their attempts to protect him from imaginary dangers—Hogg hadn't seen a security officer north of the barricades since the riot.

Kinsella and his flock gathered around a large crate at the far end of the arena. It had been delivered a few hours earlier by a different selection of idiots, though they wouldn't tell Hogg what was in it. While two of his larger idiots fumbled with the crate's latches, Kinsella looked up and waved at Hogg.

"Think he wants us to go over there?" Linze asked. "Or to stay away?"

"I can't tell what his waves mean yet," Hogg said.

"Hogg!" Kinsella yelled across the empty floor. "Get over here."

"Well, now you do."

Hogg shook his head. "Yeah, but now I forgot what the wave looked like."

Together they crossed the floor, watching as the lid of the crate was finally pried off. Kinsella reached into the crate and withdrew a pistol, his mouth forming an O shape as he stroked the gun. "What do you think?" he asked flipping the gun recklessly at Hogg. Hogg's eyes widened, and he side-stepped it, letting the pistol sail past and clatter to the ground behind him. Silence from the idiots as they evaluated whether that was a smart or cowardly thing to do. Hogg ignored them, bending down to retrieve the weapon.

"They're not toys," he said, examining it. "Sir." He turned the pistol over in his hands, nose wrinkling at the hot pink plastic they had molded it in. "Are they?" He turned, aimed at one of the closer training dummies, and fired. A burst of particles sailed across the arena, impacting the dummy's left shoulder, knocking it off its chair.

"Works though, don't it?" Kinsella said. High-fives amongst the idiots, as they began collecting weapons for themselves.

"Spread's a bit wide," Linze said, coming up beside Hogg.

Hogg looked at the focusing ring at the end of the barrel. "Not too bad, though. It'll work." He cast a glance back at the idiots, then grabbed Linze by the shoulder, tugging her out of the line of fire of the impromptu target practice session that was starting to develop.

A furious cascade of shots erupted, sailing across the arena, leaving the training dummies almost completely unharmed. This didn't bother the goons at all, amused by the simple joy of trigger pulling. But Kinsella seemed to notice and directed a meaningful look at Hogg. Hogg stroked his chin thoughtfully, watching the incompetence unfolding around him.

"Or maybe the spread's not wide enough," Linze said quietly.

"I was just thinking the same thing."

Trespassing beneath the mayor's mammoth desk, Koller shifted his weight, shaking his forearm to try and regain some feeling in the tingling limb. For seven hours, he had been peering out of the open window in the back of the mayor's office, methodically scanning the rooftops and streets arrayed in front of him.

It was work that could be done better and faster by the myriad of sensors mounted in the garden well, but of late those had started exploding. It was because of those dwindling sensors that the sensor he was using himself was attached to a smart rifle, which had certain abilities inherent in its design that the regular surveillance monitors didn't. And if necessary, those features came with orders to use them.

When Thorias had approached Koller specifically for this chore, Koller hadn't had to ask to know the chief was stretching his authority. For the last couple of years, every time Thorias approached him personally with orders, they were of the kind that weren't supposed to be written down. Things that needed to disappear. People that needed to be scared. That poor, dumb technician in the Bridge mechanical room who needed a bit more.

This was a trickier job than any of that. How the Othersiders got their hands on a smart rifle wasn't a complete mystery. It was clearly the one stolen during the Breeder raid years earlier. Which evidently still worked, to judge by the steadily shrinking supply of high altitude surveillance sensors in the garden well. Whoever was shooting it was still a mystery, although solving that was easily done—shooting him, then reassembling his various pieces.

Koller just had to find him first. The hard way to do that was what he was trying now. Slow, tedious searching of every rooftop and window in the garden well, looking for someone that didn't hang out in one spot for very long.

The easier way was what Koller was really banking on, but it would require some patience. One of the smart rifle's features was the ability to recognize and pinpoint muzzle flash. If the enemy sniper fired again within his line of sight, his rifle would spot the flash, and calculate a return trajectory within fractions of a second. If the Othersider didn't know about the feature—and Koller wouldn't have known about it himself if he hadn't read the documentation—he would be in for a very small, very fast surprise.

But for that to work, the Othersider would have to shoot first, and for the last half-day, he had been stubbornly refusing to do just that. Koller gave up on the rooftops and began scanning the wall at the far end of the well. Left to right in broad sweeps, moving up or down after each sweep and heading back the other way, working a rough grid. Every nook and crevice on the wall was examined in both light amplification and IR. Maintenance corridor—clear. Ventilation shaft—covered, probably clear. Odd-looking panel—odd-looking, but completely solid. And so on.

He nearly jumped out of his skin when the gun chirped in his hand. "What the heck?" he said. He blinked and looked into the viewfinder. A bright red arrow on the left of the screen. "Ohhhhhhh." The counter-sniper sensor, telling him where the shot had come from. He rapidly panned the rifle to the left. The arrow moved to the right of the screen. Swears filled the spot under the mayor's desk as he corrected to the right, overshooting again. Taking a deep breath, he tracked back to the left at a more measured pace. Finally, the arrow turned to a dot, hovering over a dark room on the far end of the garden well.

The sensor automatically adjusted the gain on the light amplification, revealing an observation room overlooking the garden well, seats arrayed on a gentle slope like in a theatre. One of the many rooms on the ship that had seemed like a good idea to whoever had designed it, it hadn't been enjoyed much by the actual citizens of the ship and had fallen into disuse over the past centuries.

Not complete disuse, however, judging from the movement in the back of the room. There, a figure struggling in the low-gravity, trying to haul a bulky object up the stairs to the door. Koller moved the reticule onto the door the figure was moving towards and hit the targeting button. A blue arrow appeared on the side of the screen. He knew what that was and slowly began panning towards it, until a blue reticule appeared almost in the center of his viewfinder. He settled the crosshairs on the blue reticule, took a deep breath, and pulled the trigger. The rifle shuddered beside him, snapping the projectile out with a pleasing sound.

Panning back to the observation lounge he watched as the door shut behind the retreating figure. A split second later a fist shaped hole appeared in the door accompanied by an explosion of plastic and metal splinters. Koller watched the hole for another several seconds. The fragments of the door wafted around the room, plastic and metal and foam, taking a long time to settle in the low G. The splinters were not, sadly, accompanied by any noticeable amounts of blood or gore. "Fuck!" he yelled, swinging the gun back and forth across the room in hurried, jerky movements.

Stein held her breath as Bruce pulled the massive hatch open. It had already been slightly ajar when they had found it, and although there were no sounds coming from within, they had approached it carefully, nonetheless. Bruce's shoulder sagged slightly. "Empty," he said.

They were on the 20th level, getting close to the central axis of the ship. Gravity was present but was more of a suggestion than a law. Getting there without being seen or shot had taken a ridiculously circuitous route involving a great deal of crawling, skulking, stairs, and complaining about stairs.

Bruce stepped inside the disconnect cavity, Stein moving to the entrance to look inside. There were the two clamps, just like the others they'd examined, this set still grasped tightly together. Bruce's terminal light flickered around the cavity, casting odd shadows on its curved walls. To Stein's eyes, the disconnect didn't look obviously bent. But their stolen notes indicated that it had indeed jammed. Someone would be getting to it soon.

"There's a hatch on the other side," Bruce said.

Stein stepped into the cavity, bracing herself against one of the big clamps with one hand, stepping carefully in the awkward gravity. She turned on her light and moved around the disconnect. Sure enough, there was another hatch on the far side of the cavity, clearly connecting to the aft core of the ship, the part that would ultimately separate. "Is it open?" she asked.

Bruce nodded. "A crack, yeah." He froze, then flicked his light off.

From the far side of the hatch, the sound of voices as people approached. Stein froze as well, turning off her own light. The voices stopped, just outside the hatch. "We'll have a better angle at it from this side," one of them said. "I'm going to start it up out here. This thing's a bastard to maneuver in low G, and I don't want to cut my foot off."

Stein swore under her breath and started backpedaling away. Standing nearly in front of the hatch that was about to open, Bruce crouched under the threshold, grabbing for his pistol. Stein reached for her own weapon, but with the terminal still in hand, she fumbled it, sending both the terminal and gun spinning away in the darkness. The access hatch opened, casting a dim light on them. A loud buzzing noise, and then a flash of light, as a blue blade shot into the room.

Blinded, Stein realized she was taking cover behind the thing that was about to be sawed in half. She pushed off, sending herself to the side of the cavity, scrambled for a moment before bouncing again, this time coming to rest on a small ledge directly above the access hatch that had just opened. She blinked, rubbing her eyes with her free hand. The strange, malformed letters shimmered in the center of her vision. *Dammit Vlad, this is not the time.* She looked down, using her hand to shield the blade from her eyes. Below she could see Bruce prone on the floor, unable to reach his gun, the blade of the torch directly above him. The engineer, still having not seen them, planted the edge of the blade in the disconnect and began sawing through it. Sparks rained down over Bruce, who pressed himself against the floor, willing himself to be thinner.

Suddenly, the fuse torch shut off. "Who's that?" Stein heard the voice ask from the threshold, presumably confused as to why an idiot would be lying on the floor in front of a fuse torch. Beneath her, she watched as the torch was withdrawn from the entryway and was replaced with a head and pair of shoulders. Seeing her opportunity, Stein pushed herself downward off the ceiling, planting a foot against the back of the engineer's head. An anguished cry, the engineer fell forward, smacking his face on the threshold of the access hatch. As Stein completed her own only marginally less clumsy dismount, the engineer fell backwards out of the access hatch, swearing loudly. Outside, Stein could hear the other one, sounding exactly as bewildered as she would have been in his position. Scrambling in the low-gravity to regain her feet, she managed to get upright enough to see through the hatch as the uninjured one stared back at her, mouth hanging open. At his feet sat the engineer she had kicked, rubbing the back of his neck, goggles twisted around his face. He looked up and pulled off the goggles. Stein's mouth fell. Curts. *She had just kicked her boss in the head.*

The uninjured one reached for the fuse torch. On all fours, Stein planted and sprang upwards as the blade flared to life and swung murderously back into the cavity. Again, the light and mysterious words blinded her, but growing more comfortable in the cavity, she coolly bounded off the edge of the disconnect clamp and returned to her perch above the door. She blinked and shook her head, squinting downwards. She doubted she would get another chance to jump on anyone's head again.

Two shots thundered in the cavity, abusing her senses further. The fuse torch snapped off. Stein blinked, shifting her head around, trying to look around the dancing letters in her vision as Bruce lunged forward. Moving like a torpedo, he slid through the access hatch, pistol in front of him. She heard three more shots as her friend/projectile subdued Curts and his colleague a bit more.

Her vision finally returning to normal, she dropped down to the floor of the cavity and looked around. Spotting her pistol and terminal, she scooped them up, then looked outside.

"Do you know who I just shot?" Bruce asked.

"I do! How'd that feel?"

"Like nothing. Really disappointing." He shook his head. "If shooting your boss doesn't feel awesome, then what else is there to believe in?"

"A question for the philosophers, buddy." She poked her head out of the hatch and looked around. The far side of the cavity opened out onto a hallway, running uphill in both directions. They were now in the core, the part of the ship that would actually detach. It looked like the engineering deck, but she hadn't been up here in years.

Bruce picked up the fuse torch and smacked it against the wall a couple of times. "Yeah! Escape to Destruction! Let's go mess something else up." He spun around in a circle. "Where are we?"

"The engineering deck, but..."

"Great! The engineering deck! Let's go find the reactor and *kick it!*"

"Bruce," she said soothingly, not sure how much of this was an act. "I think our luck is sufficiently pushed."

A strangled gasp from down the hall punctuated that thought, Stein turning to watch a wide-eyed naval engineer staring back at her. A pair of shots from Bruce thudded into the wall beside him, which sent him scurrying down the cross-hall he had come from. "No!" she yelled, reaching out of the hatch to grab Bruce's arm as he set out to chase after him. "Let's go!"

He stopped, glaring at her. "I could have got him," he said, allowing her to pull him back inside the cavity. Once in, he reached back outside and slammed the hatch shut behind him.

"I know," she said. "Come on."

They bounced across the cavity and out the far side, shutting the hatch on that side as well, hand-tightening down a couple of the fasteners. "You are like my least favorite person right now, you know that?" Bruce said as they ran back the way they had come. "No, Bruce, don't shoot the guy. Don't kick the reactor. *Thanks a lot, mom.*"

They rounded a corner, Stein pulling to a halt in front of one of the elevators. "Well, because you've been such a good boy, I'll let you use the elevator on the way out," she said, jabbing the button. Bruce stopped, grabbed her by the wrist and yanked her away. "Hey!" she yelled.

"They'll be able to stop us in there," he said, dragging her towards the stairwell. "Trap us," he added, giving her a push down the first flight of stairs. She squawked in protest, but floated down the drop elegantly enough in the low-gravity. "Besides, this way is more fun," he said, leaping down the flight himself.

Hurling themselves down the stairs became progressively more reckless as they went, and they soon found themselves descending more or less normally, at which point Bruce's interest in the elevator rose again. There was another problem with that, she realized a few floors later. They were almost directly above the fortified barriers right now—any elevator down to street level would deposit them in the middle of a group of amused security officers.

They were forced to slow to a tip-toe when they reached the fourth floor. These stairs extended all the way to the four street levels, emptying out to locked doors, emergency exits normally inaccessible to the public. The doors were locked and closed when they had come up this way, but if alarm bells were ever going to ring, this would be the time. And indeed, by the time they reached the second floor and started prying off the loosely fastened grate covering the pressurization duct, voices could be heard not far above them.

They quickly moved inside the ductwork, Stein gently closing the grate behind her once inside. As quietly as they could, they set out through the substantially-sized ducts, necessary for pressurizing the stairwells in case of fire. More footsteps and shouting from behind them, though thankfully no one saying, "They're in the ducts!"

Stein let Bruce take the lead, as he led her downhill, taking an obviously different route than the one they had arrived from. To Stein's sense of direction, they were heading away from the barricaded doors they wanted to head to. "You did have an escape plan for this, right?" she asked his ass, bobbing and weaving in front of her as the big man crawled away.

"Oh, yeah," Bruce replied from somewhere ahead of his ass. "Actually, that reminds me." He stopped, provoking an unseemly collision and fumbled around in his webbing. "E?" he eventually said into his terminal. "It's Horatio Q. Pseudonym. We're on our way out, probably around the Africa-1 area. We could use some big distractions if you've got any handy."

"Ellen?" Stein asked when he shut the call off. "Aren't you resourceful?"

"One of my many traits," Bruce confirmed, setting into motion again. "Resourceful, irresponsible, gassy, reckless, recklessly gassy..."

Stein sniffed the air. "*Oh, come on.*"

"What?" Bruce stopped, this time Stein managing to halt herself in time. Bruce sniffed the air ahead of her. "I swear that wasn't me."

"*Oh, come on.*"

"I'm being totally serious. But I think it means we're close." Bruce set out again, Stein reluctantly following. The smell got stronger as they went, Stein finally realizing where Bruce was leading her: into the meat farms.

Bruce stopped again, fidgeting around with something in his webbing. He finally found what he was looking for and rolled onto his back. Shimmying forward a bit more, Stein could see a diffuser directly above him, a faint light trickling down into the ducting. Bruce pressed a tool against the edge of the diffuser and began cutting into the thin metal with the plasma blade. The diffuser itself was far too small for them to pass through, so he spent the next few minutes expanding it. Finished, he pounded his fist a couple of times into the middle of the diffuser, punching his way through the floor above. "Oops. That one was me," he said.

"What one was you?" she asked, smelling the answer a moment later. "*Oh, come on.*"

Bruce clambered up out of the hole he had made, then reached down to help Stein through. On her feet again, Stein looked at the meat trees around her, suddenly remembering that she hadn't seen Mr. Beefy in almost a week. He was just a cute little guy compared to these monsters, who generated the bulk of the ship's protein. Up close, an orchard full of meat trees was decidedly not very cute.

"What now?" she asked Bruce, who had wandered down another row of the orchard.

"Basically, we run for it," he said. "Hoping of course that they don't know where we are."

This did not turn out to be the case, as they discovered a moment later when the door on the far side of the farm opened up, three security officers streaming in, not asking questions. A flurry of shots just missed Stein as she hurled herself to the floor in a hail of exploding meat, shards of awful confetti raining to the floor around her. A tremendous thump on the far side of the room, Bruce presumably using his stockpile of grenades. Collecting herself, Stein crawled to the end of a row of planters and peeked around a corner. Looking at the door through a tangle of meat trees, she thrust her own pistol out in front of her and crept forward. A helmeted head appeared behind a bench of meat seedlings, and she shot at it, missing, but causing the head to duck back down. A grenade sailed through the air and landed on the far side of the bench, exploding with a thud.

On the far side of the room, a burst of gunfire. She saw a female security officer standing, pistol blazing, presumably firing at Bruce. As Stein raised her own pistol to fire, a roar from the far corner as an enormous wad of meat charged forward, Bruce taking cover behind it as he ran. The security officer fired wildly, charged particles thumping into the meat uselessly. A fraction of a second later, an awful collision, Bruce, officer, and meat crashing to the floor in a heap. Some more thuds. Stein ran over, her pistol ready, only to see Bruce straddling the now unconscious officer. He looked up at Stein and smiled. "Did you see that?"

"I did."

"Can you believe there's people out there who don't love this stuff?" He kissed the bruised meat fruit, then tossed it to the ground. He stood up. "So...I think they know where we are."

"So it would seem. Hiding's probably out," she agreed.

"Then let's do the opposite of that." Bruce stepped over the unconscious security officers to the door of the farm. Peering out cautiously, a huge smile spread across his face. "Oh, yes!" he shouted, stepping outside. Stein trailed him out the door to see a security van parked nearby, Bruce already climbing into the front seat. She joined him on the other side of the van.

"Do you know how to use one of these things?" she asked, getting in.

"No. Do you?"

"No."

"Well, I'm a faster learner." Bruce pushed and twisted the control stick, sending the van around in a clumsy circle. "Where are we, again?"

"Uh, that's Africa that way," Stein said, pointing at the street that they had just lurched past. As she was pointing, she caught a glimpse of a group of security officers scrambling down an escalator. Behind them, shots rang out. "We're also heading south, incidentally."

"Gotcha."

"We want to head north."

"All right, then," Bruce said, hurling the van into another sloppy turn. They rocketed down a side street, Bruce fumbling with his terminal as he drove. "E? It's Horatio again," he shouted into it. "Slight change of plans. We're now in a security van. It's awesome, so don't shoot it." He dropped the terminal in his lap, swerving slightly. A block ahead, another security van turned into the street and accelerated at them.

"Shoot," Bruce said, knuckles white on the steering wheel.

Stein nodded. "Dammit!"

"No, I meant you should shoot. Shoot at them." He gave her several encouraging nods. She swallowed, then leaned out the side of the van, steadying the pistol against the frame. Taking a deep breath, she began repeatedly pulling the trigger, sending a woefully inaccurate series of shots in a direction that could just barely be considered forward. Not in any actual danger from this, the other van nevertheless swerved violently, bashing into both sides of the street. Before she could line up to take another shot, she was hurled back into the van as Bruce pulled another hard right. "Going north now, boss," Bruce said.

"Superb," Stein replied. She leaned out the window and looked behind them. The other security van had entered into the street on their tail and adopted her strategy of spraying crazily inaccurate gunfire across the road. She squeezed back a few shots of her own, no more accurate.

"There's another van behind us, E," she heard Bruce say. "That one's okay to shoot." Another violent swerve pulled Stein back inside the van. Stein faced forward and watched Africa Street approaching. Getting the hang of Bruce's driving technique, she braced herself. They turned onto Africa, the blockade visible five blocks ahead. She looked back, watching the other security van careen into the street behind them.

"Got it," Ellen's voice, tinny over the terminal speaker. "Stay right."

"Your right or my right?" Bruce yelled.

"My right!"

"So, my left?"

"Rrr...correct!"

"Ahhh! You were going to say right!" Bruce cackled.

"ARE YOU FUCKING KIDDING ME?" Stein shouted. "NOW? NOW? OF ALL TIMES?"

The van swerved in a direction, although facing backwards, Stein had no way of telling if it was the right one, or, for that matter, the correct one. A sharp crack, and a gaping hole appeared in the front of the tailing security van. It lurched and drifted to the left—its left—smacking heavily into the wall, grinding to a halt.

"Get in here," Bruce yelled, yanking her back into the van. She turned around, seeing the blockade only a block ahead, muzzle flashes blazing. No longer just a plastic barrier, it had been built up and reinforced by a variety of pieces of furniture in the last day. Bruce accelerated with his head down, peeking over the dash with one eye. "Also, hang on." She dropped the pistol to the floor and braced herself against the dashboard.

A thousand hammer blows of pain, all over every part of her body. No, not spread evenly. More hammers on the right side. And not all hammers. At least one axe. Blood in her mouth, cotton in her ears. She opened her eyes. She didn't know they had been closed. Feet. Not her feet. Too big for that. Bruce's? Yes, but from a funny angle.

She realized she was on the floor of the van. She turned her head, which made the hammer blows a bit worse. There was Bruce, swinging the control stick around, blood on his forehead. His mouth was moving, but she couldn't hear what he was saying. It looked like "Whooo." No, wait. It sounded like "Whooo," too. So, she could still hear. That was nice. Someone needed to do something about those hammer blows, though.

"Oh, man," Bruce said, as he twisted the control stick. He had a big grin on his face. That made Stein happy. "They were right to not let just anyone drive these things," he said. He looked down at Stein. "Laura? Oh, shit. Laura? Oh, fuck. I'm sorry. Shit, shit, shit, shit, shit. Hang on."

Previously

Data modulo 2 insertion in sanctuary will cause base pairs to align with great forth-rightness. Success!

Harold's eyes ached, dry and itchy from lack of blinking, as if they didn't want to turn their backs on the insanity he was making them read. A cookbook on illegal genetic manipulation techniques was open on the screen in front of him, part of a big text file of forbidden knowledge he had stumbled upon in his school days. He wasn't the only one; getting your first copy of this nonsense was a rite of passage, something the science nerds passed around for fun.

Most of the material in it was pretty tame, vast tracts dedicated to recreational pharmaceuticals and surely exaggerated cautionary tales about their usage. Anything that wasn't harmless—such as the genetic engineering section—was completely impenetrable. The section on data genes was written in some kind of mongrel, bio-mystic version of Chinese, and the translator was having a hell of a time sorting it out. Thankfully, it was heavily footnoted, explanatory notes attached by past readers, explaining their missteps.

Harold knew he could probably manage what he was planning with just the footnotes alone, but still wanted to step through the original text to ensure nothing important had been omitted. He needed as full an understanding of the process as possible, because he was pretty sure he was about to break new ground in it. The location where the data would reside was critical, lest something important—perhaps the bit that stops people from growing beaks—was overwritten. This had always been done by hand, by experts—apparently strange bio-mystic Chinese experts. Harold's plan, to program these strange instructions and logic into the gene tinkerers, had never been tried before. It was the only way his plan would work, autonomously, long after he was gone.

The key to his plan was the tinkering engine, the device that stored the nanobots when they weren't in use, maintaining their population at a fixed level. It also contained the broadcast mechanisms which imprinted the desired programming into each set of nanobots as they were prepared for a specific patient. This engine had its own logic circuits and memory, independent of the ship's central network. The data from Kevin's terminal could live there secretly and indefinitely, to be scribbled into the DNA of every person who ever got tinkered. Repair jobs, fetal screenings, canned babies, every one of them would end up tagged with Harold's graffiti. This was profoundly unethical—if he got anything wrong, the amount of risk he was putting these people in was enormous. But as profoundly unethical behavior seemed to be the only way things got done on the ship, well, why not roll the dice on some beak-people?

There was still the question of how to get the data out of these unsuspecting genomes once it was in there. There would be no one to explain to his subjects what had happened to them, and, hopefully, no outward sign at all that there was anything unusual about them. A very low-level genetic analysis would spot it, which was something anyone with a medical terminal could do if they saw the need to. But Harold didn't know any diagnostic methodology that prescribed an analysis of that detail. Which meant he needed a way to provoke one of his unknowing subjects into an investigation of that depth.

A beep on his terminal from Martin. His treatment completely successful, Harold had almost immediately hit the fabrication man up for the favor he had offered before entering quarantine. Martin had seemed a little surprised, obviously not having made the offer with any expectation it would be accepted. But Harold played it delicately, asking Martin to knock together a little shelving unit for his office, which he did genuinely need. He had received the shelving unit—a pretty nice one made of wood—and thanked Martin with a couple of drinks. Martin seemed happy to talk to someone with so many questions about fabrication. He reminded Harold of Kevin in a few ways. Smart, kind, slightly awkward. It was a shame to use him so utterly, but it was a small thing compared to everything else Harold was up to. Harold tapped at his terminal, reading the message.

Sure, I could make flyers. But why would you want to?

"An extremely good question," Harold said, shaking his head, as he tapped a message back.

It's for a retro party thing I'm planning for a friend.

Plausible enough. He set the terminal down on his desk, covering the translated nonsense that he no longer wanted to look at. He leaned back, rubbed his beard, looked down at the terminal, and sighed. "Come on,

Harold," he said, steeling himself. "You can do this." He brushed the terminal to the side of the desk and leaned back in over the cookbook.

Ghosts are the retrotransposons—tread wisely with enormous canons best left unused?

"Oh, come on," he said, eyes widening. "Now you're just fucking with me."

8

Come Get Your Guns

Leroy fidgeted as the gun made its way down the line. He wanted it. Why didn't they have more to go around? He was pretty sure the guy had said something about that. He hadn't really been listening at the time, had probably been looking at the gun. No, scratch that. No probably about it. He had been looking *the fuck* out of that gun. He had no time for listening—even his ears were looking at that gun.

A moment of self doubt washed over Leroy. Could it be possible that by listening more, he would get the gun faster? Leroy thought about that for a bit, but it mostly turned into thinking about the gun again.

Ricky had gotten scared and run as soon as he saw the crowd in the arena. Leroy had known he would and had made only a token effort to mock him. *Let him fiddle with himself in his room. Let him miss out on the coolest thing to happen on the Argos in infinity years.*

The trainer guy who knew how the gun worked seemed pretty cool-looking. He had a hat and a holster to put the gun in. Everything about him screamed 'Serious Gun Business.' Leroy knew that impressing him was the key to getting his own gun. Would listening do the trick for that, or would just a lot of looking work? Leroy looked and thought about the gun some more.

Trainer guy stopped in front of the dude next to Leroy. Leroy watched how the training guy explained how the parts of the gun worked. From what Leroy could see, there were really only two parts, a front and a trigger, and you didn't want to be on the front side when the trigger was pulled. But trainer guy dragged it out, way more than was probably necessary. Like he was some kind of big shot or something. *A gun joke!* Leroy was getting so close, he could think of gun jokes without even trying.

Eventually, his neighbor got his chance to hold the gun himself. Leroy watched as he tried shooting at the dummy on the wheeled chair a short distance away. Shot after shot in rapid succession, all misses. *What an idiot.* Finally, the dummy shuddered. "Got it!" the moron shouted.

Trainer guy—Leroy could see now he had a name tag that read Croutl—took the gun back. "Did you?" He walked over to the target. "Your first eight shots," he said, pointing at the dummy, "did not land here. Your next four," he said, holding his arms up searchingly, "may not have landed in this room." Finally, he pointed at the chair beneath the dummy. "Here's your thirteenth."

Leroy laughed. The moron glared at him, but Leroy didn't care. *This guy sucked.*

"You think you can do better, kid?" trainer guy said. He ripped the gun out of the moron's hands and flipped it around, holding it tantalizingly out in front of Leroy. "Were you listening to what I said about how this works?"

This was a trick question, but Leroy was pretty sure he saw a way through. "Yes," he said. And swallowed. The gun waggled in front of him. *Holy shit, it's really happening.*

But before he could reach out and take it, a thump from the front of the arena. Everyone but Leroy turned to see the double doors slam open, a pair of men pushing a big crate on wheels into the arena. "Guns here!" one of them yelled. "Come get your guns!"

The gun that was rightfully Leroy's withdrew, the trainer guy quickly sliding it into his holster. "Everyone calm down," he shouted to the excited trainees. "No one's getting any guns yet." To the men who had just entered with the crate, he shouted, "Put those away. They're not done yet."

"You've had like an hour with them!" one of them said.

"You're not teaching them how to write with the fucking things are you?" the other asked. They kept pushing the wheeled crate over to the recruits, who broke ranks, rushing over to it.

"Hey!" trainer guy shouted. "This isn't a fucking game."

"Relax, pig," one of the men delivering the crate said. "Get your guns here, folks. Use 'em for shooting assholes!"

Leroy had stayed rooted in place throughout this exchange, eyes having not left his gun, now in trainer guy's holster. Within seconds, the other recruits reached the crate and began arming themselves. Only moments later, shots began echoing around the arena, impacting target dummies, chairs, walls, the floor, everything else.

"Shit," trainer guy said, backing up into Leroy. A pair of shots bracketed his feet. Someone laughed. Another two sailed overhead, and as he turned to run, one caught him square between the shoulders. He collapsed on top of Leroy, sending them both to the ground.

Leroy wriggled out from underneath the comatose trainer guy. *This is fucking bonkers!* Leroy could tell this wasn't a particularly cool situation to be in, and he definitely intended to run away as soon as he could. But there was one thing first, one thing staring up at him from the trainer guy's hip. *Take me, Leroy*, it whispered.

"All right, gun," Leroy whispered back. He took it.

And it was awesome.

Helot stopped a short distance from the barricade watching his security chief throw a fit about a couch. Two wide-eyed security officers shifted the offending piece of furniture into a less objectionable position, reinforcing whatever weakness in the barricade Thorias had perceived. Thorias directed his attention to something else worth yelling at, and the process repeated itself, this time with a pair of desks. Beyond the slowly growing barricade yawned the inviting glow of the garden well.

They were on the fourth level inspecting Thorias' lines and arrows. Even aside from correcting couch placement issues, it was useful doing this in person; the Sheeping effect worked best when orders were delivered face-to-face. And indeed, Thorias had made a point of speaking with every officer at every barricade, a painstaking process of learning and forgetting names as quickly as possible.

No longer seeing anything worth yelling about, Thorias left the officers and returned down the street. Helot fell in step beside him as they rounded the corner onto 8th, moving parallel to the new front lines. A block later, they stopped at one of the side streets.

Here, the bulkhead doors were still closed. Thorias walked up to the door to inspect it along its seams. Helot had already seen this up close and knew the welded spots Thorias was looking for. Thorias knelt on the ground, if not actually sniffing the welds, then coming awfully close.

Helot liked the idea of welding the doors shut. He liked it a lot. He still didn't fully understand the chief's logic for leaving the doors open on the main streets, even if they were now all protected by fortified barricades. Thorias had said something about "fields of fire" and "cones of control," and Helot had let it go. It had sounded convincing enough; since the riot, Helot hadn't wanted to second-guess his security chief anymore.

Thorias got up and returned to Helot at the intersection. "We're sure they can't be cut?" Helot asked.

"Curts assures me they don't have any fuse torches," Thorias replied. "Though who knows how reliable that ass is." He turned and began walking to the next side street. "Explosives? Probably not. They could fab those, but it's fussy work. Would take them at least a few weeks."

"And what happens if a van hits it?"

Thorias growled but didn't say anything, instead rounding the corner to go smell another door. Helot didn't push him on it, didn't like thinking about it much himself. That the two people they had falsely accused of terrorism had turned out to be pretty capable terrorists was a bothersome irony. Two of the fuse torches demolished, Curts' schedule set back at least a month. Not even the hilarious bruise on the back of Curts' head could make Helot feel better when he had found that out.

After Thorias' door-smelling process repeated a few more times, they came to the broad expanse of America. Turning north, they passed the locked entrance to the Bridge and approached the barricade and officers stationed out in the garden well. This barricade had been pushed much further north than the rest, a necessary step to protect the Bridge. Helot couldn't give a damn about what the civilian government did or didn't do while he tried to cut the ship apart again, but Thorias had pointed out that from many of the civilian government offices a "terrorist" could access the upper-levels of the ship. Having this space defended was a necessary element for several of his arrows to be...something. Fully self-actualized? That sounded right.

Most of the officers at the barricade had their backs turned, a ripple of laughter spreading through the group, which came to a sputtering halt when someone noticed their commanding officer bearing down on them. "Chief Thorias. Sir," one of the brave ones said.

Thorias walked right up to the group and stopped, standing with his hands behind his back. "Carry on. Don't let me interrupt you."

The officer who spoke swallowed. "It's nothing, sir."

Thorias fixed his gaze on the officer. "It wasn't nothing. You were telling a joke. I'm in one of my rare joke-hearing moods right now. So please, go on."

Thorias waited while the young man weighed the pros and cons of disobeying a direct order versus telling a poorly thought out joke to a superior officer. "What's the difference between a Chinese kid and an Othersider kid?" he finally said. Helot felt his jaw tighten. It wasn't the first time he had heard that term used to describe the people on the other side of these barricades, but he still didn't like it.

A moment passed before the involuntary comedian delivered the punch line. "The Chinese kid doesn't want to be a popsicle when he grows up." The sound of a dozen officers shifting uncomfortably. Thorias pursed his lips and nodded. "Because they're going to freeze to death," the comedian added. The color began to drain from his face.

"What's the other kid being Chinese have to do with anything?" one of the other officers asked.

"Nothing. I don't know. It's a new joke. I'm still working on it."

"It's good," Thorias said, still not laughing. "I think it's funny." To judge by his officers' reactions, this was somehow much more intimidating than yelling. Thorias continued, "Just popping by to tell you to keep up the good work. Carry on." He turned and began walking away, a thin smile on his face.

"That joke was awful," Helot said quietly as they left the barricade. "For a lot of reasons." Thorias didn't say anything. "You need me to list them?"

"Just a joke," Thorias said.

Helot began collecting his words, needing to correct his valuable subordinate as delicately as possible. "We can't..." he began saying, interrupted by the sight of Thorias flying into the air, arms, legs, and seemingly several other limbs all flailing uselessly. With a sickening thump, Thorias went down hard on his back.

"Sir!" someone yelled. A half-dozen officers from the barricade ran over as Thorias gasped in pain. Helot stood back, still not sure what had happened. A pair of officers crouched beside Thorias, helping him up to a sitting position.

"What the hell did I step on?" Thorias yelled. One hand clasped to his back, his head darted back and forth, looking at the patch of floor he had just trod over. Helot couldn't see anything out of the ordinary.

One of the officers, the involuntary comedian, prodded his foot on the ground behind Thorias. "Careful, Brint," another officer said, too late, as Brint's foot slid out from under him, sending him into an uncomfortable looking set of splits. A strangled gasp escaped Brint's lips as he rolled to his side, clutching himself.

"What is that?" Thorias said, getting to his feet. His hand reached behind him for a moment before recoiling, clearly desperate to rub his ass, but unable to lest he further damage team morale and discipline.

"It's that slippery shit," another officer said, his voice rising to be heard over Brint's moans. "There's patches of it all over the fourth level." He got down on his hands and knees and probed the ground carefully with his hands. He then reached into his pocket and pulled out an orange marker, drawing a big circle with an X through it over the slick part.

"Where'd it come from?" Thorias asked. "Where'd *they* come from? And why hasn't anyone told me about this?"

The officer looked up from his handiwork, indecision on his face. "Would you tell your boss that you just fell on the floor like an asshole?" He looked around. "We don't know where they came from."

"It was that fucking little robot, I bet," Brint said, who had managed to get to his knees, both hands still buried between his legs. "Remember?"

"No one saw it except for you, Brint. And how would a robot make things slippery?"

"Get back to your posts," Thorias ordered them softly. The officers hustled back to the barricade, Brint hustling a bit slower than the rest. "I've seen enough," he added, before blinking, seeming to remember who he was talking to. "How about you? Sir?"

Helot didn't smile, but it was a struggle. "I've seen enough, Chief."

But as they walked back to the nearest elevator, his mood darkened. If he had needed any further proof that he had less control over the situation than he should have, the sight of his security chief demolishing himself on a simple walk would have done it. Slippery shit? Tiny little robots? *What the hell was happening on his ship?*

As the light from the windows turned the hospital room from yellow to orange, there was a noticeable click as the lights on the ceiling turned on. Stein looked up at the ceiling in surprise, then down as another glass of Grape was set in front of her. Griese winked as he poured another for himself. On the other side of her bed sat Bruce and Ellen, also Graped up. Their vigil at Stein's bedside had gotten quite a bit rowdier in the hours since Stein had woken up, much to her doctor's dismay.

"The infamous flying quadruple cockpunch!" Ellen squealed, doubling over with laughter. "I had completely forgot about that!"

"The what?" Griese asked.

"The infamous flying quadruple cockpunch!" Ellen repeated, no less delighted the second time around.

"It was a lot more than four punches," Bruce corrected her. "More like eight."

Ellen frowned. "Octocockpunch!" she squealed again.

"Seriously, what are you guys talking about?" Stein asked. She had thought they were talking about something about the Breeders, Stein mostly just listening as her shady friends illuminated the shadier parts of their past.

"It was when we were fabbing some stun grenades," Ellen said, her eyes flicking down to her bag at the foot of the bed. Stein knew full well that she was the only one in the room not armed, although at least her friends were still making attempts to conceal their weapons. "We nearly got caught by a security officer," Ellen continued. "Bruce saved us."

"With the octopunch?"

"Octo*cock*punch," Bruce corrected her.

"I'm going to need a little more than that."

Ellen swirled the Grape around in her glass. "We were in one of the ratty fab plants we were using at the time over near America. I forget which one. Zimmer was there, Bruce, myself, and Vince." Ellen looked around, checking that she had everyone's attention, then continued. "So, one of the fab lines breaks down. Vince, Zimmer, and me are trying to start it up again when we hear a voice behind us: Put up your hands, you punks!"

"This would be the victim of the infamous octocockpunch, then?" Stein asked.

"Ahh, don't spoil it," Ellen scolded her. "Anyways, we turn around and there's this little doofus of a security goon, and he's got his little pop gun out. We freeze. Zimmer was carrying—he was supposed to be watching the street, but had come inside to help us with the machine. Bruce was..."

"In the upstairs office," Bruce filled in. "Standing guard."

Ellen snorted. "Guarding a fucking sandwich."

"And did you see any security officers eat that sandwich?"

Stein smiled. "So, you're standing there, hands up. What next?"

Bruce drained his glass and tossed it across to Griese, drips of Grape specking the bedspread over Stein's legs. Griese caught it and poured another refill. "Well, I hear all this commotion below, and after securing the sandwich," he said, patting his stomach, "poked my head out the office window to have a look-see. Sure enough, there's a security officer standing there with a pistol. Directly below me."

"So, you jumped?" Griese asked.

"I did."

A pregnant pause, as they waited for Bruce to continue. "And?" Stein finally asked.

"He missed," Ellen said with a smirk.

"I didn't miss. The ship moved."

Everyone but Bruce groaned. "The ship moved" was the standard excuse for every botched athletic feat on the Argos, something everyone learned as a child. In this particular case, there was a bit of truth to it, though only a bit; from that height, the Coriolis effect couldn't have shifted Bruce's descent more than half a meter.

"So, we're standing there, about to be shot or arrested, when the dumbest projectile that ever was falls out of the sky. Boom." Ellen illustrated an explosion with her hands. "Everyone freezes. We're staring at the cop, he's staring at us, and we're all staring at Bruce lying on the floor. Then the cop starts laughing. So, we start laughing." Ellen paused here to refill her drink. "So, we're laughing, right, enjoying the moment, when in a blur, fatty there spins his legs around and trips up the cop. Bruce pounces on top of him, knocks the gun away, and they start wrestling." Grape sloshed out of Ellen's cup as she pantomimed this. "Somehow, Bruce here gets the security guard into an advantageous position, and then WHAM WHAM WHAM WHAM."

"The octocockpunch," Stein said.

"Not yet," Bruce corrected her. "WHAM WHAM WHAM WHAM. That's eight."

"At which point Zimmer zapped the poor guy, preventing the possibility of a...whatever nine is cockpunch," Ellen concluded.

"Noctocockpunch," Bruce suggested. Ellen threw her mostly empty cup at him, which bounced off his forehead and clattered to the floor. The group broke out laughing.

Stein immediately regretted the laughter, as it sent jabs of pain up her right side. Something awful had happened to her upper arm in the crash, involving some pointy part of the van's drive system driving itself through the floor and into her arm, nearly amputating it. Now wrapped up in a healing wrap, the arm didn't hurt too badly anymore, so long as she didn't move it. Her leg actually felt worse, despite just being bruised. Years of obtaining similar injuries in similar circumstances had caused her to start classifying them as *Brucing*. Seeing Griese looking at her with an expression of concern, she forced a smile. "How's the play coming along?" she asked.

Griese held up his hands. "It's not. All my players disappeared. Something came up. Some sort of riot. Don't know if you heard—you were gone for a while."

"Ahh." She watched the quiet fellow for a moment. "But you've been keeping busy though?" No one had yet told her what exactly Griese and Ellen had been doing while she and Bruce were on the run, but from a couple of hints, she got the impression they had been busy with some kind of deadly new toy.

Griese shifted in his chair and looked away. "Yeah."

"I won't ask."

He smiled sadly, still looking away. "You just did." Ellen gave her a small shake of her head. Bruce burped.

The door opened, an interruption everyone was probably grateful for. Stein's doctor, a lanky man called Berg, entered smiling. "How's my famous patient?" he asked. He broke step for a moment, seemingly surprised by the number of people in the room.

She shrugged, one arm doing a better job of it than the other. "Okay. How are you?"

Berg seemed to seriously consider that question. "I'll live," he finally said, before laughing at his own joke. He poked something into his medical terminal. "You've been up for a few hours now, so I'd like to run a brief brain scan on you. If I may? Check for a concussion, cognitive damage, tau wave synchronization. It's easier if you're awake." He looked at Stein's friends, then down at the Grape stained bedspread, then to the bedside table and the three empty bottles standing vigil there. "Might be easier if we're alone, too."

"I think he wants us to go, guys," Bruce said, standing up abruptly, knocking his chair over backwards. "As a student of human behavior, that's my reading of the situation."

Ellen rolled her eyes, but got up as well, patting Stein's leg as she did so. "We'll be just outside."

Stein smiled and watched her friends leave. She looked at the bottles on her bedside table and then up at Dr. Berg. "They're just happy I'm alive."

Dr. Berg nodded. "Well, they can hardly be blamed for that." He wheeled the bedside table out of the way and sat down beside her, poking some instructions into his terminal. "Could you look into the yellow light, please?" he asked, holding the terminal up to Stein. "Have you had any dizziness? Blurred vision?"

"No," Stein said to the yellow light. "Not lately. Not since I woke up." She remembered the fuse torch and the flash of letters, and quickly weighed the pros and cons of keeping that secret to herself any longer. "I was seeing one weird thing though. These strange shapes in my eyes. Before the accident, actually."

He looked up from his terminal. "What did these shapes look like?"

Stein swallowed. "They were letters. I saw an extremely bright light that nearly blinded me, and when I closed my eyes, I could see letters."

Berg's eyebrows crept upwards. "What kind of light?"

"It was the blade from a fusion cutting torch."

"What's that?"

"A really bright blue light."

Berg shook his head. "And it made you see shapes? That looked like letters?"

"They were definitely letters. Is there any way you could, I don't know, scan my eyes?" She pointed at the medical terminal.

"For what? I still don't know what you saw." Berg tapped something into his terminal, eyes scanning the screen as he waggled his head back and forth. "Okay. I guess this couldn't hurt. Now, look into the sensor once again. Good. Now look up. Look down. Look left. Open your eyes wider, please. Thank you. Look right. Your eyes are fi...huh."

"What?"

The doctor scratched his forehead. "I honestly don't know. But the terminal's seen something." There simply weren't enough doctors on board the Argos for more than a handful to specialize in the various sub-fields of medicine. Almost all doctors were generalists, relying heavily on the semi-intelligent diagnostic and prescriptive recommendations of their instruments. "Hang on," he said. "Okay. Look into the sensor again. This could be bright."

Stein looked directly into the sensor. A nearly blinding light appeared, which she struggled not to close her eyes against. Forcing them open, she watched the light as it started vibrating, flickering, and changing colors. The letters appeared in her eyes, fainter than before.

"Wow. Do you see data?" Berg asked.

"What?"

He looked up from the terminal and squinted at her face. "The letters in your vision. Do they say 'data' in all caps? Like this?" He turned the terminal around and showed her a false color image of her retinas, the word "DATA" etched in badly misshapen letters.

"It's upside down and backwards."

Berg snorted. "I guess it would be from your side of the retina, yeah." He chuckled. "That's funny. Strange as hell, but funny."

"I was starting to think I was crazy. I mean, seriously, *who the fuck is Vlad?*" Stein rubbed her eyes, relieved. "Not that 'data' means a lot more to me."

Berg looked at the terminal again. "Looks like there's maybe more off to the right. Or the left. Or whatever. An 'O' maybe."

"And it's not like 'data O' means much to me, either," Stein said. "So, why am I seeing it?"

"Scanner says it's probably a retinal tattoo."

"What's that?" she asked, remembering her earlier reading. "Is that like a corneal tattoo?"

Dr. Berg frowned. "Probably not, I'd think. I mean they're different parts of the eye, aren't they?" She watched his eyes scan rapidly back and forth over the terminal. "Okay. It's a tattoo imprinted on the retina, visible only to the person who has it. They're always visible, all the time, often obstructing huge portions of their vision. I guess a few religious folk tried this back on Earth. To overlay their holiest images on every thing they saw. Sounds like a great way to go insane if you ask me."

"Well, I've never had anything like that. And I don't see this all the time."

"Says here it's possible to do them so that they fluoresce only under certain lighting."

Stein snorted. "Okay, fine, but I've still never had anyone tattoo my eyes."

"Terminal says you have."

"How?"

Berg set down the terminal and looked at her thoughtfully. "Implanted when you were asleep? Sedated? Do you like to party?" His eyes flicked down to the stained bedspread. "Sorry." He scratched his chin. "Maybe when you were a child? Were your parents kind of crazy?"

Stein rubbed her eyes. "My parents." She shook her head, an idea popping loose as she did so. "Hey, you've heard of genetic tattoos? Artificial birthmarks? Could this be something like that?"

Berg's eyes widened. "Huh. I don't see why not. But I also don't see why." He looked down at his terminal again. "Well. Maybe. The edges of the letters are a bit irregular. Blotchy. That's characteristic of a genetic tattoo, I think. But that would mean your parents did this to you when you were conceived."

Stein swallowed. "You have my medical history on that thing, Doc?"

"Of course."

"Who are my parents?"

"What?"

"Just look."

Berg paged through his terminal. "Oh. Huh. What?" He looked at Stein. "You're a canned baby? Sorry."

"Uh-huh."

"I really am." Berg put down his terminal and looked at the ground. "I didn't actually know there were any of you left." He smiled weakly.

Stein looked out the window, at the last glow of the sunset. "They keep trying to make one every few decades or so. To see if we're less crazy. I'm one of the success stories, apparently."

"The mental stability issues," Berg said. "Right. I'd heard about that."

"Yeah," she said, looking at her feet. "Thought I was good for that. So, you can see why I'd be a little concerned about visions only I can see."

Berg nodded solemnly. "I can see that. Well, you're not crazy."

Stein laughed. "Nope. Just got graffiti in my head."

"You really don't know your parents?"

She shook her head. "Genetic material donated anonymously. Supposedly no one knows. Easy enough to do a parental screening against the database, I imagine. I asked—many times—when I was a kid, but no one would do it." She looked away. "So, I stopped asking."

He tapped a bit more on his terminal. "Yeah. That'd have to go through the navy docs, I guess. They're the real geniuses on genetics. Hang on. Here. This is the highest end genetic screening tool this thing has." He waggled the terminal. "Might tell you something about all this.

About your parents, I mean." He brought his finger down on the screen in a flourish. "It should take...wow. Several days." He looked up at her sheepishly. "I guess I'll get back to you."

She shrugged again, growing frustrated at the dead weight hanging off her right shoulder. "Knock yourself out, Doc. But I stopped asking for a reason."

"I'm going to shoot a billion of them."

"No, you won't."

"Yes, I will."

"There aren't a billion of them."

"I'll shoot them multiple times."

"No, you won't."

"Yes, I will."

"You'll get bored after like, the first hundred thousand."

"Ahhhhh...you're probably right."

Simultaneously, each soldier spat on the ground, setting off a wave of similar expulsions from the soldiers gathered in the alley. Someone had done it unthinkingly a few minutes earlier, and because it looked like a cool soldier-looking thing to do, it sparked an instant fad. Leroy had tried several times himself but found his mouth too dry. Not that he wasn't confident in his ability to mess up a hundred thousand dudes himself. He was totally confident in that. He just kind of thought it would be another few weeks before he had to mess them up. Why the rush? Give them time to get their affairs settled.

The plan for the morning was to charge the security guys who had camped out in the garden well, near 10th and America. They were asking for it, Supreme Commander Kinsella said. And the 'Good Guys' were going to give it to them. Kinsella had tried getting everyone to call themselves the 'Loyalists,' but no one really liked the sound of it. 'Good Guys' was a lot more straightforward and had caught on much quicker.

Leroy leaned against the wall of the alley they were using as a staging area. He stuck his jaw out in the way that made him look grimmer and more serious. For the tenth time since they got there, he checked his terminal to make sure it was still on. He needn't have bothered—everyone else's terminal would receive the same message when it was time. And sure enough, a few seconds later a chorus of chirps emerged from every terminal in the street. From a dozen different directions, the sound of Bletmann, the mayor's assistant and organizer of the night's attack, clearing his throat, then asking, "Everyone ready?"

In response, every soldier individually responded that, yes, they were ready. It was all pretty noisy and confusing, and Leroy wondered whether Bletmann would actually be able to hear if anyone said, "No." Leroy recalled this kind of thing was usually handled differently in books and movies. They had other leaders, he thought. Smaller ones, in chains. Was that right? There certainly didn't seem to be any chained dudes bossing people around tonight.

Evidently enough people had said they were ready, because a second later, the mass of terminals all shouted, "Go!" So, they went.

Leroy didn't make any special effort to push to the front and just allowed himself to be swept along with the rest of the group. On the main street, his team merged with a dozen other similarly-sized teams, all coursing towards the escalator. A bottleneck formed there, good guys bumping into good guys, starting arguments, which considering how armed everyone was, were never going to end well. The two or three comatose bodies that resulted from these arguments did not improve the efficiency with which the rest of the group passed through the bottleneck, and not for the first time that day, Leroy wondered if there might have been a better way.

By the time Leroy made it up into the garden well, he could already hear the sounds of gunfire off to the south. By now completely separated from the group he was supposed to stick with—Attack Squad Jaguar Sword—Leroy stopped, confused about what to do next. Soldiers charged off in every direction, bravely shouting requests for covering fire, or promises to provide covering fire, or simply getting cut down by their own covering fire, all of this happening still several blocks away from the enemy. Leroy spotted a group of less crazy-looking good guys moving south and followed them as they took up a position just behind the corner of a building. Someone who looked like they knew what they were doing stuck his head around the corner, then waved the rest forward. Leroy tagged along at the rear, pleased he had found someone new to run behind.

The team turned the corner of the building and jogged down the street to the base of an apartment block, entering it by the front door. Here, they scattered, most heading up the stairs to the second and third floors, from there spreading out in the hallways on the south side of the building. Leroy did the same, slipping into an apartment on the second floor, where he found three of his squad mates arguing with an old woman who evidently didn't want her apartment to be the scene of today's war. Her side of the argument was notably outgunned, and before too long she lay unconscious on the floor while Leroy and his new friends took up position by the windows.

Outside they could see the intersection at 10th and America and the fortified semi-circle the security forces had set up there. Park benches, landscaping planters, and a tremendous variety of repurposed furniture had all been dragged into place to provide cover for the gathered goons. Already on the ground in front of these defenses were the sprawled forms of the good guys first out of the gate, who had charged directly into the security force's guns, apparently eager to get their war over with quickly.

Someone yelled something about messing up thousands of people's days. A spray of fire erupted from the window to Leroy's right. *Here we go.* Raising his pistol up and out the window, Leroy pointed it in the direction of the bad guys and started shooting. There was no way to tell if he was doing anything useful, so he opened his eyes, but even that didn't tell him much. But perhaps most importantly, nothing bad was happening, so he kept at it.

Eventually, some return fire thudded into the walls beside him, but it took Leroy at least a few seconds to realize what it was and almost as long to hit the ground in a panic. From the floor of the apartment, he looked around. He felt more than a little embarrassed to see he was the only one cowering; everyone else was still shooting, and clearly having quite a bit of fun. Getting carefully back to his knees, he peered out the window again. The amount of security guys shooting back seemed to be diminishing, whether they were hurt or simply hiding. *We're winning!* From the other side of the street, a wave of gunfire erupted from the upper-levels of another apartment building, charged particles crisscrossing the street, slamming into the security fortifications from the other side. That put an end to most of the return fire, and Leroy could see a couple of security officers sprinting back south.

"You two, come with me," one of his new friends said, pointing at Leroy and the guy beside him. This was the guy who seemed to know what he was doing—he had knocked out the old woman very quickly and efficiently—so Leroy followed him without hesitation. Smart army guy paused at the door and yelled, "Everyone else keep those guys pinned down. And don't shoot us!" before heading outside and downstairs, moving to the rear lobby of the building. From there they could see out the glass doors as the suppression fire thundered down on the now mostly empty defensive perimeter, a deadly sewing machine stitching patterns in the street. "See over there?" their new leader said, pointing across the grassy area to a set of planters halfway between the building and the security fortifications. "We're going to run over there and see how that goes."

"How'd you get so good at this?" Leroy asked.

"Video games," the guy replied. Leroy nodded, wishing he had played more of those. "Let's go!"

So, they went. Somehow Leroy found himself leading the charge, possibly because the other guys were better at war than he was. Halfway there, a helmeted head appeared behind the planter, ducking down again just as quickly as a volley of fire kicked up dirt in the planter. Too late to turn back, Leroy kept running, sliding to a halt feet first behind the planter. Thinking even less than normal, he jabbed his gun around the side of the planter and fired repeatedly. He couldn't hear anything, but again, nothing bad seemed to happen, so he didn't stop. By that point, his new teammates caught up to him, sliding into place behind the planter beside him. "Nice job!" the smart one said. "Though I think you got him by now." Leroy sheepishly withdrew his gun. He looked at the smart army guy and shrugged. *Looks like I'm pretty good at war, too.*

Then the sun went out.

For two hundred years, the daylights in the garden well had gone on every morning at 7 a.m. and turned off every evening at 8 p.m. No war, labor shortage, or billing dispute had ever interrupted this cycle. So, when the daylights went out that morning at 11 a.m., it was fair to say that most people in the well were profoundly unprepared for it.

Except for the security troops who had been explicitly told it would happen.

On the monitors, Thorias watched those officers creep forward now, terminals awkwardly held out in front of them, scanning in the infrared. It wasn't just the daylights out—power had been cut to every apartment, streetlight, and other source of illumination as well. It was as pitch dark as the garden well had ever been, and would be until the Othersiders remembered that their terminals all had flashlights. He watched in amusement as a few of those Othersiders did remember that, turned them on, and were immediately shot for their troubles, the only thing the lights actually illuminated being themselves.

This had been one of his better ideas, a way to not just fend off the Othersiders, but to humiliate them on their first outing. Helot had loved it and immediately ordered Curts to help with the technical side of things. It was exactly the kind of plan Helot would like—short, relatively tidy, and with a bit of luck, one that would take the fight out of Kinsella's army without anyone having to die.

Sergei crept forward, pistol held in front of him, a terminal awkwardly mounted to the top of the gun with tape. Through the terminal, he could see dozens of other security officers creeping forward doing the exact same thing. It had taken them a few minutes to muster once the attack began, and then a few minutes more waiting while the Othersiders overextended themselves.

Lights flickered in the darkness as Othersiders scrambled with their terminal lights. The terminal lights were badly unfocused and could only usefully illuminate things a couple of meters away. Just enough to navigate by or to act as a glowing beacon which screamed, "Shoot me!" Security officers behind Sergei somewhere gladly obliged those requests, picking off the lights as they flared up.

Not all of the gunfire in front of Sergei had stopped, but all of it was blind, the Othersiders probably hitting themselves more than anything else. Sergei's team skirted the main battlefield, moving around to pick the Othersiders apart from their flanks.

A red blur staggered out of a building in front of Sergei. It could have been a civilian, but he shot it anyways. The blur crumpled to the ground, and as Sergei drew closer, he could see it did in fact have a pistol with it. *Take that, armed blur.* He bent down and scooped up the pistol, tucking it into the bag he had slung over his shoulders. He then slid a plastic pair of binders around the blur's wrists, snapping them closed. The rest of his unit moved into the building, doing the same with their own blurs.

That basic, confused process repeated itself for what seemed like hours, Sergei and his team calmly moving from building to building, knocking out blurs, shooting at bobbing white lights in the middle distance, then cuffing their victims and taking their weapons. Thorias had been adamant they were to do nothing else, but the riot a week earlier had created more than a bit of bad blood in the security corps, and despite the fact that the subjects were completely limp at the time, Sergei saw at least a few cases of 'subjects resisting arrest.' He didn't partake in too much of that himself, but he didn't stop it either. *They Started It'* wasn't security's traditional credo, but it seemed to be catching on now.

Leroy froze, blind, panicked. It was completely, utterly black. Even the streetlights had gone out. Although maybe they weren't on in the first place—it was, after all, eleven in the morning. He blinked, again and again, willing himself to see something. The terminal on his thigh squealed with senseless shouting and cries.

A short distance away, a blinding bright light appeared, the brightest thing Leroy had ever seen. Blinking, he realized it was a terminal light held by one of his new friends. A salvo of charged particles thumped into it, knocking down the light's owner, shutting off the terminal.

"Shit," someone said beside Leroy. It sounded like the smart war guy. "I think they just shot the kid," he said.

"No, I'm still here," Leroy said.

"Cool. Other guy? You shot?" Silence. "Yeah, I think they got him."

"What do we do?" Leroy asked.

"Should probably stop turning on lights, I guess." More gunfire, this time coming from behind them. "That came from our guys!" smart war guy said. "Hey, morons! Stop shooting!" Another volley of shots stitched the ground, thumping into him. Leroy heard him moan and slump over.

Considering his options, Leroy felt his way around to the other side of the planter, taking cover from the good guys. All around him he could hear and see lights flickering on and off, shots snapping those lights off. Somewhere behind him, he could hear the sound of confused moans. It sounded like someone who had been knocked out in the first wave was waking up, complaining of unexpected blindness. Leroy heard him stagger to his feet, then cringed as a sudden glow from his terminal announced his position. More shots from the south sailed over Leroy's head, bringing the darkness back.

Eventually, the remaining good guys smartened up, and most of the gunfire stopped, aside from some concentrated spurts off to his left somewhere. Knowing he was in the worst possible place to be when and if the lights came back on, Leroy rounded the planter and began crawling in a direction that seemed like home.

It was slow and awkward going, bumping into benches and buildings and bodies as he went. And somewhat worryingly, the spurts of gunfire seemed to be getting louder. He changed direction, trying to crawl away from them. But to no effect. Whoever was shooting was crawling a lot faster than he was. Or perhaps not crawling at all.

"Where do you think you're going?" someone said behind him, someone probably not crawling. An impact in Leroy's ass, then a tingling sensation, then somehow, the darkness got darker.

Hogg approached the front of Kinsella's garden well apartment, weary to get this over with. It had literally been a very long night, and he wasn't in the mood for whatever nonsense was going to be hurled at him next.

Hogg hadn't known the attack was being planned—he would have begged Kinsella not to proceed if he had, explaining as forcefully as possible that a group of armed fools were still fools. As soon as he had heard what was happening, he had rushed to the opposite side of the garden well to watch the disaster unfold overhead. Watching their initial success and forward progress hadn't dulled his concern in the slightest, the whole time confident that it couldn't last.

He was right. He just couldn't have imaged how right he would be.

When the streetlights started to come on at their normal hour, they revealed the last of the security forces retreating back to their former defensive perimeter, leaving a couple hundred good guys trussed up on the surrounding streets. Hogg had spent the rest of the night helping untie his fallen comrades, the whole time under the guns—and within earshot—of the mocking security forces.

He had expected some kind of rebuke from the mayor, though imagined it would come accompanied by a group of armed thugs. Even though he'd had nothing to do with the planning of the disaster, he knew that wasn't going to matter—the mayor didn't seem like a man who concerned himself with fussy details like that. Kinsella might even think Hogg had tipped Helot off. Hogg would protest his innocence—that was at least worth a token effort—but mostly he just felt resigned. Unwanted in one end of the ship and unpopular in the other. He had nowhere left to go.

The guards at the door recognized him, one of them stepping out of the way and holding the door open for him. It was the same pair Hogg had duped when he went to 'arrest' the mayor at the arena. "Hogg, sir. You can go right up," he said with a smile. Hogg tried not to let the surprise register on his face. This was a friendly visit? Neither had even cast a glance at the pistol on his hip. Which meant he wasn't walking into an ambush. What was it then? As he rode up the elevator, he wondered if Helot would let him back on the cool side of the ship if he shot Kinsella.

The doors opened, revealing one of the mayor's many interchangeable lackeys, who greeted Hogg, directing him down the hall to the mayor's bedroom. With the security forces no longer actively hunting him, Kinsella had finally let his wig down and moved home. Entering the bedroom, Hogg found Kinsella's aide Bletmann seated in an overstuffed chair in the corner of the room, slouching over one of the armrests. To judge by his blotchy, red face, Hogg guessed that he had been crying. Stepping further in the room, he approached Kinsella, who was fully clothed and sitting upright in his plush bed, back against the headboard. He beckoned Hogg over, gesturing for him to take a seat at the foot of the bed.

"Sergeant Hogg," the mayor began—the first time anyone outside of his original team had mentioned his rank. "Henry here was the architect of last night's little...what are we calling it again? Let's say, 'Sloppy Business.'" Hogg nodded once; that fit quite well. "Based on the results of Henry's 'Sloppy Business'...," the mayor spared a tired glance for his right hand man, "...he seems to think that this war isn't winnable." Kinsella looked pointedly at Hogg. "Tell me what you think about that."

Hogg chose his words carefully. "He's not far off. We basically suck at this. But I don't think it's hopeless. The way they're digging in, there's good reason to think Helot is going to take a long time to try to detach again. I think we have time. And with time, we might be able to do something."

"That doesn't sound very hopeless. Bletmann?" Kinsella said.

"With what army?" Bletmann moaned.

"With the troops we've been recruiting and training," Hogg said. "You should know about them. I've seen you there."

Bletmann looked up, casting a woeful look at Hogg. "They're not going to stay. They won't risk their lives for us anymore. Not after last night."

"I don't know about that, Henry," Kinsella said, a thin smile on his face. "Something about having the lights turned out like that," Kinsella continued. "That might wake a few people up. *Is that irony?* Shit, I think that's irony, isn't it? We can use that." Kinsella pounded his fist into his open palm. "I would not be surprised if the news feeds get pretty upset about this. And if some agitators maybe spend the next few days riling people up, why, I bet our recruitment numbers will be just fine." Kinsella smiled; he clearly hadn't been completely idle. "Sergeant Hogg, you've been basically running the entire training program, correct?"

"I've had a lot of help from my officers." He swallowed. "And some help from some of your people of course. Which has been very...helpful."

"Yes, of course." Kinsella's eyes flicked over to Bletmann again. "I'm asking if you could continue doing that without Henry's assistance."

"Yes, sir, I think I could."

"Good. I'm telling you to do that." Kinsella looked at Hogg for some sign of acknowledgment, seeming to be satisfied with Hogg's single nod. "In addition, do you have any thoughts on how we should best proceed, strategically?"

"Strategically," Hogg repeated. He wondered for a moment what kind of strategy was appropriate for an army of angry morons and whether 'strategy' was even the right word to be working with. "That will depend on what your long-term goal is, I suppose," he said, playing it safe.

"Good. Very good!" Kinsella said. He clapped his hands together three times. "Exactly the kind of question Henry never asked." He glared once again at his assistant, now quietly sobbing in the corner. "Our long-term goal is either killing Helot or moving his ass out of that end of the ship. Simple enough?"

Hogg bit his tongue. "Yes, sir. In that case, yes, I do have a couple ideas how to proceed. I think we could..."

"I don't need to hear them," Kinsella interrupted him. "I just need to know you have them. Thoughts are good. Need more of them around here, I'm thinking." Kinsella rubbed his hands together. "Because you're in charge of this whole shitshow now. I hope you're up to it. The job's had some turnover issues."

"So I see."

The mayor clapped his hands together again. "Great! It's a deal." He licked his lips. "Henry? Thanks for your services. You are of course still welcome to serve in your former role. I could use some coffee in fact. Please take your time getting it." His gaze hardened. Bletmann meekly got up and left the bedroom.

Hogg watched him go, then turned back to face the mayor. "He meant well. Just a little out of his depth."

"One of his jobs is knowing what his depth is."

Kinsella flipped the covers off of him and got out of bed. He walked over to the window, beckoning Hogg to join him. From there he could see down to the southern end of the garden well. Hogg bit his lip. No wonder the mayor was pissed; he must have seen every part of the debacle.

Kinsella looked over his shoulder for a moment, checking that the room was still empty. "What do you know about Laura Stein and Bruce Redenbach?" he asked.

Hogg blinked, surprised by the sudden change in direction the conversation had taken. "I arrested the Stein woman. The other one shot almost everyone else in my squad. Nice people. Why?"

Kinsella nodded. "You remember that thing the other night with the van?"

Hogg nodded. A day after the riot, a couple of maniacs had plowed a van through the back of one of the barricades. "What about it?" he asked. Kinsella smiled. "It was *them?*" Hogg shook his head. "Of course it was them."

"It was," Kinsella confirmed. "The Stein woman's hurt, though."

Hogg opened his mouth, about to say *'Good'* before catching himself. Abrasive though she might have been, she had also apparently been right.

"I ask," Kinsella began, leaning against the window sill and peering down the well, "because Laura Stein is supposedly the one who said I was behind this whole plot. 'Under interrogation,' the feeds said."

Hogg swallowed. "That interrogation never happened. I think Thorias just made it up." Hogg related the story of his capture of Stein, her tale, and the phony report of an interrogation that Thorias released soon after. "I guess it's one of the reasons I didn't try to arrest you too hard."

A far-off look crossed the mayor's face. "She said she'd figured this out on her own?" he asked.

"She seemed to know more about it than anyone else. Knew about it before your, uh, speech."

"Hmmmmm," the mayor said. Hogg winced. First, he locked her up for something she didn't do, and now he might have accidentally sent the mayor after her. *That woman is going to hate me.*

Kinsella shifted gears again. Gesturing down the well, he asked "So, what's your plan?"

Hogg was getting better at reading the mayor's shifts. "Simple. We stop sending our guys to get blown away."

"But we'd gotten so good at that. Seems a shame to ignore our only strength."

"I don't think we can ignore it completely," Hogg said. He looked down to the fortified semi-circle of security officers jutting out into the garden well. From up here, Kinsella was still far enough away to avoid seeing the human costs. No one had been killed yet, but that was coming. And it was now Hogg's job to make it happen.

"We just have to wait until we have *a lot more* to throw away," he said.

Stein brought her fist down hard on the end of the spork, propelling a lump of broccoli upwards. The overcooked green spun lazily through the air, ricocheted off a light fixture, fell back down to the cafeteria table, bounced twice, then rolled off the table to the floor. "Five for twenty-three," she said quietly, setting up another. One more night in the hospital so her rattled skull could stay under observation. Her friends, evidently satisfied she wasn't imminently about to perish, had left her to her own devices. Devices which had led her to the cafeteria, where she had found a new way to entertain herself.

"You're not very good at that, are you?" someone said behind her. She turned to see a doctor, one she hadn't met before, though he did look familiar. And oily.

"Mr. Mayor," she said, recognizing him through his disguise, which on closer inspection, appeared to consist of little more than a lab coat and costume stethoscope. "Why are you dressed as a stripper?" she asked.

Kinsella walked around to the far side of the table and sat down without waiting for an invitation. "I can see why they wanted to lock you up," he said.

She looked down at the pile of broccoli sitting beside her spork and fidgeted with a piece. "Is there anything I can help you with?" she asked, not looking up from her work.

A tortured, raspy noise slipped from Kinsella's mouth. She wondered if he was getting used to his new, less-prestigious station in life. "Yes," he finally said. "Our captain called you a terrorist. Are you one?"

Stein fiddled with the spork some more before she shook her head. "I wasn't at the time, no."

"But maybe since? Van girl?" Kinsella asked, a thin smile on his face. "Okay. So, you're not a terrorist. Or maybe just a casual one. So why'd he call you one? What'd you do to piss him off so much?"

Everything about the man in front of her was disagreeable, which she longed to tell him about, in great detail. But, she reluctantly had to admit, they were on the same side. At least the side that Helot wasn't on. Whatever shenanigans she'd accomplished with Bruce, they paled beside what the mayor was surely planning. She had noticed the battle yesterday, couldn't help not to, when the *fucking sun went off*. And as spectacularly poorly as that had gone for the mayor's idiot brigade, it was only the first battle. If anyone was going to keep the ship in one piece, it was this oily, oily man. So, she told her story, explaining how she had blundered into Helot's plot, embellishing the good bits and fudging the parts which badly incriminated her.

Kinsella listened attentively. "That's incredible," he said when she finished. "And thank you for glossing over the parts where you clearly broke the law. That could have been awkward."

Stein smiled and shrugged, rewarding herself by setting up another piece of broccoli on the spork. "Why do you care?" she asked, launching the green into the air, this one landing neatly in the light fixture. "Six for twenty-four." She set up another piece. "It sounds like you knew all that already."

Kinsella's eyebrows did a funny kind of waggling motion. She realized he was trying to be coy. "Indeed, I did," he said. "The captain told me himself. Straight from the horse's mouth." He leaned back and grinned. Stein wondered what animal orifice Kinsella was in this analogy.

"He told you he was going to split the ship in half? Why? When?"

"Just before he tried. I think he was bragging. He seemed a little desperate to tell someone how clever he'd been," Kinsella said, chuckling. She returned her attention to the spork and launched another piece of broccoli into the air, watching it rise up, ricochet off the light, and come back down on Kinsella's head. He snatched the spork away from her. "Will you listen to me?"

"Never stopped."

Kinsella threw the spork over his shoulder. "Well, listen harder." He swallowed once and spread his hands flat on the table. "One thing our captain also mentioned was that if the ship were to split in two, our half could survive for hundreds of years. What do you think of that?"

One of the nice things about being wrongfully imprisoned was that she had had plenty of time to consider exactly that question. "We do have the auxiliary reactor," she said. "And lots of fuel. So, you know, on paper it could work."

"Paper," the mayor echoed.

"But I'm worried about the insulation," she said. Seeing the blank look on the mayor's face, she continued. "All around the outer hull of this thing is a whole bunch of something that looks like metallic diapers. That's what keeps us warm, more than anything else. Stops us from leaking energy." Kinsella nodded once, at least faking comprehension. "But if Helot pops the ass end of the ship off, that exposes a whole different chunk to space. An uninsulated chunk. Even if it is airtight, with no insulation along that surface, we'd start bleeding energy like crazy."

"How long would it take for us to run out?"

"One year? One hundred? Who knows?" Out of her pocket, she produced another spork and set it up in front of her. "Ask a math guy."

Kinsella glared at the new spork but let her keep it. "And we couldn't make more insulation?"

"Maybe. We can make most things. But we've never made that before. And we'd need a few square kilometers of it."

Kinsella rubbed his hands together. He reached out and turned the spork over in his hands, then set it back down, placing a piece of broccoli on it. Stein watched this all carefully, as he made the same mistakes she made her first time. Tentatively he raised his hand up in the air, looked at her for some sign of encouragement, saw none, frowned, then brought his hand down hard on the end of the spork, sending the piece of broccoli smashing into his face.

Kinsella rubbed his cheek, glaring at Stein, who, having seen it coming, didn't need to work too hard not to smile. His throat worked up and down, swallowing. "How much time do we have, do you think? To stop him?"

"Before he tries again?" She shrugged. That depended on how many fuse torches he had left and how long it would take to make another one. "No idea. A month? Maybe two?"

"So, if we want to stop him, we have to do it soon." Kinsella flipped the spork aside and rubbed his face again. "Can you help? I'm not going to demean you by asking you to do it for the sake of your fellow shipmates; I will make this worth your while."

"And if my while is incredibly expensive?" she said, gesturing at the pile of broccoli.

He raised an eyebrow, then shook his head, chuckling. "Look. I need someone with your knowledge." Kinsella pointed at the light fixture. "Remember how he turned off the fucking sun? Can you maybe stop him from doing that again? And can he do that with anything else? Stop our food mills? Shut off the life support?"

Stein bit her lip. "Yeah. He can." Seeing Kinsella swallow, she added, "I can probably stop that, though."

"Good." He pointed at her. "Do that, and you can have anything you want. All the broccoli on the ship? It's yours." He sat back in his chair, looking pleased with himself. "After that, well, we'll see if we can't find some other way to make use of your remarkable resourcefulness." Another unsettling smile. "Maybe you can come up with some poison or sleeping gases we could pump through their air. Knock them all out." Seeing her completely undisguised look of shock, he held up his hands defensively. "Just thinking aloud." He patted the table a couple of times, a gesture that looked like it was meant to conclude conversation, then stood up and stepped away from his chair.

As she watched him adjust the stethoscope around his neck, mumbling something about looking more doctor-y, she realized there was still a big piece of the puzzle missing, then wondered how much of that was deliberate. "Did he say why he was doing it?" she asked.

Kinsella stopped, turned back to face her. "Helot?" he asked. She nodded. *Who else?* Kinsella shrugged. "Nope. He didn't say. Because he's an asshole, I suspect."

Stein nodded, playing along. "He certainly acts the part."

Kinsella laughed again. She realized she hadn't see him laugh before and could see why he avoided doing it in public. "He certainly does," he agreed. With a wave, he turned and left the cafeteria.

Alone again, Stein fidgeted with the spork, spinning it around in front of her, not really looking as it danced between her fingers. *How do you tell when the mayor is lying?* It sounded like a trick question, the set up to a creaky old joke. The punch line—"When his mouth is open"— didn't feel helpful here. Not when so much of what he had said was obviously true.

"Helot? Nope, he didn't say." That was certainly plausible—she had a hard time understanding why Helot told anything to the mayor at all. But what if he had said? Why was Helot splitting the ship anyways? This was something else she had had time to think about alone in her jail cell, and *"Because he's an asshole,"* was about the best she could come up with herself.

But only after her surprise mayoral visit did she realize how dangerously lazy that reasoning was. Asshole though he might be, Helot clearly wasn't a dummy; he had a reason for splitting the ship. And Kinsella, oily though he might be, was also no dummy. He would have come to the same conclusion she had. Whatever reason Helot had for splitting the ship, it would almost certainly be good enough for Kinsella to do the same.

Helping Kinsella wasn't the answer. It was just trading one monster for another.

She took the final step in this line of reasoning and smashed the spork down in frustration, flinging a chunk of broccoli against the ceiling. *We might actually need a monster.* If they really did have to split the ship and leave thousands to die, it would certainly take a monster to do that. And if that was the case, it might be a useful thing to get on the good side of at least one of the monsters.

She just wished it didn't have to be the oily one.

Koller chewed methodically on his meal bar. Bite, chew, chew, chew, chew, chew. Swallow. On occasion, he breathed. He had heard somewhere that it was a bad sign being conscious of your own breathing. It meant you were dying, he thought. Or very, very bored. He breathed again, and wondered if it could be both.

He had been camped in the tiny duct for a day, sleeping and taking all his meals there. Thorias had been insistent on that; now that he had advertised his existence, no more setting up in a place where he could be shot first.

But no going home yet either; Thorias wanted the Othersider sniper taken out. The sensors he was picking off were becoming increasingly valuable. There were only a half-dozen left, and they had proved useful coordinating the defenses during the previous day's battle. And if the Othersider sniper wanted to get nastier, there were an awful lot of security officers in the well to get nasty on. Which meant that until he was stopped, Koller was doomed to be conscious of his own breathing.

He breathed and craned his neck over to look at the display on the smart rifle. Still on. He breathed. He wasn't doing any manual searching this time—he would stay still and rely on the counter-sniper software to react when the Othersider finally came out of hiding and took a shot. Which had been a long, long wait. He breathed.

The gun chirped. He spit a chunk of meal bar out and rolled behind the gun, spotting the bright red arrow on the edge of the screen and rapidly panning the gun to the right, chasing the arrow. No overshooting it this time, the arrow changing to a red reticule in the center of his screen. It was the roof of a building in the garden well, covered in rooftop shrubs, swaying in a slight breeze. *There.* The motion of the foliage highlighted the stillness of the long rectangular object concealed within.

He tagged the gun, then began tracking to the left, already anticipating the smart rifle's response. Only the second time around, but already much,

much faster. "I got you this time," he hissed and breathed once more. He settled the crosshairs on the blue reticule.

Griese laid on the ground, covered in an IR cloak, itself covered in a piece of gray felt roughly matching the shade of the roof surface he was lying on, part of a rather attractive rooftop garden. He breathed in, slowly, held it, then began to exhale, stopping half way through. Everything was still. He pulled the trigger, hearing the crack, feeling the gun smack his shoulder in response.

He immediately rolled out of the way, abandoning the gun, ducking behind the edge of the planter. Three seconds passed before he felt the planter shake beside him, accompanied by another sharp cracking sound and a cloud of dirt and gun parts raining down on him. *They were way quicker this time!* Three more seconds passed, the longest three seconds Griese had ever felt. Another sharp crack, much closer, coming from the other side of the roof.

"Got him!" Ellen shrieked. Not doubting his wife, but knowing he wouldn't get a 'told ya so' if she was wrong, Griese crawled behind the planters along the edge of the roof until he reached the safety of the penthouse. He sat up, back against the wall, and looked at the shrapnel littering the roof, the shrapnel that had very nearly been parts of him.

He had been using a dummy rifle, cobbled together with the help of a team of amused fabrication nerds over the past few days. It had turned out to be pretty straightforward, a combination of three of the linear motors used by the ship's elevator systems. Not quite the same as a real smart rifle; although it could still whip a projectile at a hell of a good speed, it wasn't going to hit anything it was aimed at, lacking the advanced optics and tracking software that made smart rifles actually useful.

It had taken another read through the manual to figure out what had happened their last time out. Helot had his own smart rifle and sent it hunting for them. The wise plan at that point would be to hang up their rifle and never speak of it again. The dumb plan, baiting their hunter into exposing himself and then shooting him back, was, well, *dumb*. But it was an interesting kind of dumb.

Griese would have probably gone for something less interesting if he was deciding for himself, but Ellen was in one of her not uncommon moods where she wasn't going to be talked out of things. So, it was going to happen. And if it was going to happen, then he wasn't going to let her fill the dangerous role.

"You okay?" Griese asked, still not seeing his wife return from the supposedly safe role. Finally, Ellen appeared around the corner, dragging the smart rifle carelessly behind her. She slumped to the ground beside him.

"I got him."

"I heard. Are you okay?"

She shook her head. "I got him." Her eyes were watering. He reached out and took her into his arms. "I shouldn't have looked," she said, starting to shake. "But I did. I got him."

"It's okay. He was going to do the same to us. They're all trying to do the same to us. That's what you said. They started it."

She nodded, now crying uncontrollably. "I know. I know. It's just..." Griese held her tight as she let go with another full body shiver. "I got him."

"They started it, they started it, they started it," Griese said. "Say it."

Ellen gasped, a choked intake of air. "They started it, they started it, they started it."

"Just keep saying it."

"They started it, they started it, they started it." More shaking, accompanied by a long, noisy sniffle. "They started it, they started it, they...."

It was the most spacious room on the ship that wasn't the garden well. Enormous ductwork hung overhead in the center of the room containing the primary air handlers. Inhaling air from the massive return vents mounted on the end of the garden well, the primary air handlers filtered, treated, and redistributed it throughout the ship via another braided set of massive, room-sized ducts.

Stein bounced across the floor of the room to the fan control center and examined the controls there. Kinsella's paranoia had been spot on; from his cozy little nest in the ship's asshole, Helot could shut off every other critical system aboard the ship. Heat pumps, circ fans, carbon dioxide scrubbers, everything. He had a gun pressed against their head, and the only reason no one had noticed it yet was because it was too big to see.

During the Sunset Surprise, as the feeds were now calling it, she had examined her own terminal to see how Helot had done it. It hadn't taken long to find the settings for the garden well lighting controls, nor to find out that their regular programming had been overridden by a custom schedule. A custom schedule she was prevented from changing, according to the error message identifying that access for that system was limited to Curts.

Overriding such a block from afar was impossible. But the very nature of the ship's systems meant that anyone physically at a piece of equipment could lock it out from the ship's central controls, useful for preventing a fan from turning itself on when a technician had his arm in it. Normally, this isolation functionality was used to isolate a unit in the off position, but there was no reason it couldn't be used to keep equipment permanently on, which Stein had spent most of the morning doing in each of the light towers. She did the same again on each of the main air handling fans. "My ship, now," she muttered.

She stepped away from the controls and floated down to the end of the massive room, where the return air was run through the carbon dioxide scrubbers. Cartridges packed with engineered life, which sucked up electricity and carbon dioxide, turning it into oxygen and some kind of smelly, sugary crap which got shunted to farms on the first level. She locked out these as well, even if she had a hard time imagining Curts being crazy enough to mess with the ship's supply of oxygen. That said, the company Curts was keeping these days seemed to be in no short supply of crazy.

She took the side door out of the air handlers into the auxiliary reactor room. It was deserted, just as she had expected—Max was a naval officer, and would have certainly been recalled to the aft before the detachment. Which stung a bit—she had liked Max.

She sat down in the chair behind the primary control panel for the reactor. She had never driven the thing before and spent a few minutes trying to familiarize herself with its controls. She was a little surprised to see that she had full access to the system—she had assumed she would be locked out of the naval equipment. Helot must have unlocked the system prior to the botched disconnect, so that the leftovers could tend their own power supply. But even with access, most of it was incomprehensible to her, all flux ratios and Planck whatsits. One screen was dominated by a graphic of an extremely important looking donut, pulsing with intent. The reactor was still obviously operating; Curts hadn't dared shut this off from afar, if he even could. And she could find no way to turn on any safety interlocks to stop him from doing so. She slumped back in the chair; she was way out of her depth here.

She looked at the reactor embedded in the floor, physically and functionally opaque to her. If Helot was successful, if her loser half of the ship was going to carry on drifting through space, they would have to find someone who knew how the reactor worked. *How often does the thing need to be repaired?* She remembered the last time she was here, with the school tour and the little wiener kid. There had been a couple of naval technicians here then, working on the thing. She wouldn't know where to begin with something like that. What kind of laser-genius did you need to be to spin wrenches on an antimatter reactor?

"What were they doing on this thing, anyways?" she asked aloud, pivoting in place. She recalled that they were mostly just standing there, not in itself an unusual thing for a technician to do and something that she hadn't paid much attention to at the time. Thinking back on it now, she guessed they were waiting for the tour group to leave before they got back to work.

Purely to satisfy her own sense of curiosity, Stein then tried to figure out what they had been working on. Pacing around the room, she tried to get her bearings, tracing out the general layout of the reactor. The auxiliary fuel pods were behind the far wall. Fuel lines would probably run beneath her feet. She bent down and started prying up the floor panels.

She found it under the third panel she tried. The part they had replaced was sitting in a cavity on the floor, humming slightly, fuel lines extending out either side to the fuel tank and the reactor. A pressure regulator or perhaps a throttle. It otherwise looked wholly unremarkable, just another object in the room that she only vaguely understood.

But even to her untrained eye, there was something about it that looked a bit odd. There wasn't any dust or grime on it, like the rest of the cavity, which made sense if it was a new part, just replaced. But the more that she looked at it, the less new it looked. It looked more like it had simply been wiped down recently. Out of curiosity, she withdrew her terminal and inspected the component under a variety of wavelengths. It was old. She could see corrosion spots along one of the fittings and stress marks along its entire length. Maybe they hadn't replaced it yet? But then why wipe it down? No, they had definitely been working on it recently. There were fresh tool marks on the fittings.

Stein sat back and folded her legs under herself. So, had they replaced the existing pressure regulator with a worn out one? Why? Given the sinister plots already in progress at that point, she didn't put a lot of faith in it simply being a coincidence. Those were naval technicians, acting under Helot's orders. Were they trying to sabotage this reactor? She couldn't see the point in Helot ordering that. She tilted her head and looked at the pressure regulator again. Maybe they needed the one that had been here. Stein ran a finger along the regulator as she tried to piece together her theory.

The navy guys hadn't been repairing anything—they had been *taking* spare parts from here and moving them to the aft. To replace theirs? That made sense—the bow and aft reactors must have been nearly identical. And they might not have had time to make their own replacement parts. Everything in this room must have been incredibly tricky to manufacture. The aft core would have some fabrication capacity, just maybe not enough to fab up another pressure regulator in time for the detachment.

Well, there's a thought. If the aft reactors were broken, Helot couldn't detach, not if he liked electricity, or propulsion, or all those other good things antimatter reactors did. Stein drummed her fingers on the floor, thinking through the details. Destroying the reactors completely was out of the question, assuming she didn't want to annihilate the entire ship. It would have to be some kind of carefully planned sabotage, enough to disable, but not destroy. *Kick them*, in Bruce's terms. Then, with the only source of spare parts a long way from where Helot could get his hands on them, Kinsella and his idiot brigade would have a tremendous amount of leverage. Certainly enough to bargain for a better seating plan. A seating plan which might have room for the girl who came up with the idea.

A beep from her terminal startled her. A call from Dr. Berg. An annoyed sound passed her lips before she slapped the terminal, taking the call.

"Hi, Laura. How's your arm doing?"

She blinked in surprise and looked down, realizing she was holding the terminal in her damaged right arm. "Still hurts, I guess. But I'd stopped even noticing." She flexed the arm in its healing wrap, testing its strength.

"Want to come down and have me check up on it? We can also, uh, talk about that other thing."

What other thing? Stein remembered their chat about her parents, and felt her shoulders slump.

"I've found something you might be interested in. But, uh, we should talk in person. It's kind of weird."

Now, I really don't want to know. She sighed and looked around the reactor room, deciding she had saved the ship enough for one day. "Fine. I'll be there in a bit."

The light towers faded out, legitimately this time, although it was a nervous sunset for much of the ship. Indeed, the streets were all but empty as Bruce approached the entrance of an apartment building in the mid-well. Far enough north that it should have avoided the fighting, the building still sported several broken windows and a shattered front door, the result of an impromptu session of target practice by Kinsella's idiots, or perhaps just some spectacularly inaccurate cover fire.

But with no one actively shooting at it now, Bruce crossed the street and stepped inside, carefully bypassing chunks of shattered glass. Making his way up the back staircase to the third floor, he found the suite he was looking for at the end of the hall. He rang the buzzer. A formality, as he was certain this particular apartment was empty. Not waiting for a response, he cast one quick look over his shoulder, then with a twist of his arm, allowed the plasma cutter concealed in his sleeve to drop into his hand. Pressing it against the side of the frame, he cut into the lock of the door—there was no subtle way into this particular apartment. With a pop, the lock gave way. He tugged the door out of the way and stepped inside.

Tidy and dull—just like the owner. He clipped his terminal to his jacket, the value-scanning application running, and began looking around. Curts would have had plenty of time to move all of his most valuable belongings long before the detachment process. But there was always the chance he had forgotten something—he had been living here right up until the day of the detachment. Besides which, there was nowhere else Bruce could burgle right now. Whatever ethical lapses he had, looting during a war wasn't one of them. But he felt pretty comfortable stealing Curts' stuff. "Assuming the prick has anything worth stealing," he said, looking at a crystal statue of a duck which the terminal was not impressed with.

He wondered how Curts was doing. How involved had he been in the detachment failure? Maybe his boss was in trouble with *his* boss. Having to scramble around now to find some new way to split the ship apart. Hunched over a desk, sweat dripping off his brow, furiously trying to invent a huge crowbar.

The thought of Curts' slick forehead made him remember the little maintenance robot he had left behind in the aft, running around with its micro-planer. He supposed it would have run out of lubricant by now, if it was still alive. He should check on it. He flopped down on the couch and called up the robot's controls on his terminal.

An image appeared of a sidewalk, shot from a sensor about ankle high. He was impressed; he had been certain someone would have caught the little guy and put a shot through its brain box by now. It was hard to tell where it was, but the robot was still moving, so he sat and watched for a while. There was a sign post. Blue. Still on the fourth level, then.

Amused, Bruce sat and watched the robot for the next hour or so, hoping it would see something interesting. He had given it a few targets—spots close but not too close to the barricades, the base of escalators, and so on—but had told it to self-navigate to those locations using its own judgment. The robot would be biased to do most of its traveling in the belowground passageways, to keep it out of traffic, but spent at least some of its time above ground. Bruce got a few distant looks at barricades and security troops but nothing else of interest.

There was no way to check the status of the anti-friction planer, but Bruce was certain it was out of lube. He didn't have any other bright ideas for the robot right now, but with it still alive, decided there was no point letting it run around above ground any more than it had to. After spending a couple seconds looking at a map, Bruce took over manual control of the robot and instructed it to drop the tool. He then directed it to turn at the next corner and go down the street, towards the nearest access point for the belowground crawlways.

On the screen, where a barricade should have been, there was nothing, just the last rays of sunlight setting in the garden well. He stopped the robot, confused, zooming in, finally seeing the dispersed fortifications staggered a block out into the well. It was America, the site of the hilariously one-sided battle from a few days earlier.

Now, why are they hanging their asses way out in the garden well? It seemed far more vulnerable than the other barricades, all well back from the garden well. He spun the robot around, looking back down America. As he did, it panned past the ornate doors of the Bridge. He stopped, getting it.

They were protecting the Bridge. And he knew why. The Bridge was one of the few places on the ship where you could walk into a room at street level and from there move up to the fifth floor and beyond. *You could even walk right up to one of the fucking disconnects.* Bruce groaned, recalling his earlier adventure.

Absentmindedly, he spun the robot around, moving it back into the safety of the crawlways. Done, he leaned back on the couch, quietly impressed with Helot's tactics. There were a half-dozen ways to infiltrate the aft from within the Bridge; it was no wonder they'd secured it. Which was also why they weren't moving into the garden well anywhere else. Other than the elevators and a handful of emergency staircases—all already behind the barricades—the Bridge was the only place in the aft you could move upstairs from the fourth level.

His body stiffened. *Except for the wall-punchers!*

Now, that was a hell of an interesting idea. Getting to it would be a little stupid. But stupid in a fun way. Stein wouldn't go for it, not at first. He would have to bring it up delicately. Seduce her with the stupidity. Tease her with it.

He got up from the couch, mind racing, devising ways to blow stupid little nothings into her ear.

Stein sat in the treatment room, watching as Dr. Berg methodically probed the healing wrap on her arm. He hadn't said anything other than pleasantries since she had arrived; either he hated multi-tasking or was still working up the nerve to say what he had found out about her parents. She had to admit that he did look tired. The hospital has gotten a lot busier in the past week. Stun weapons perhaps, but a lot of people had still taken some pretty nasty spills during the last round of fighting.

Apparently satisfied with her arm, or just done with the pretense of examining it, Berg sat down on the examination table, facing her. "So?" she asked.

"You've got a data gene."

She took that in stride, having lots of practice at absorbing the insane bullshit which seemed to be regularly hurled in her direction. "Okay."

"Do you know what that is?" Berg asked, surprised.

"I was waiting for you to tell me what it is, because I know you're very eager to do that."

Berg recoiled a bit. He pursed his lips, then continued, "A data gene is information artificially programmed into the non-coding sections of the DNA."

She tried to force the glazed look off her face. "Okay," she said, rotating her fingers in a circular motion, directing him to continue.

"You see DNA's full of information, but only a fraction of it appears to have any kind of useful effect on how an organism behaves. So, a data gene overwrites some of this hopefully useless DNA."

"Hopefully useless?"

"Well, that's the thing. Just because we don't know it's useful doesn't mean it isn't. There's still kind of a lot of things we don't know about that stuff. If you overwrite it, it's hard to say what the effect could be. It could be nothing or, it could be instant centaur. Real mad science stuff. Completely illegal."

"Like a genetic tattoo?"

"Oh, yeah. Your eye thing." Berg nodded, his back straightening. He seemed to be livening up from the conversation. "Yeah, you definitely have that, too. It showed up like a crater in your scan. But the data gene was more subtle."

She sat down in the chair opposite the table. She was suddenly tired of it all. Any other time in her life and it would have been a different story, but now? She was out of damns to give. If someone wanted to spray graffiti all over her DNA, *fucking let them*. "What does it say? A pep talk from my folks? 'You can be anything you want to be! Reach for the stars, kiddo!'"

Berg frowned. "Don't know yet. The scanner's only detected the presence of artificially coded information, not been able to pick it out yet. It tells me it has to find the table of contents first. Whatever that means."

"How long's that going to take?"

"Don't know. The progress meter on the terminal reads fourteen percent. So eighty-six percent more, I guess."

She rolled her eyes and looked away. She didn't care. Didn't want to care. She stood up and smiled wanly at the doctor. "Thanks, Doc. When that meter gets up into the triple digits, let me know if anything interesting pops out." She left the room abruptly, leaving the doctor before he could say something else useless.

She had barely left the room when her terminal buzzed, which she responded to with an incredible stream of obscenities. Frightened and dirty looks chased her down the hall as she reluctantly dug the terminal out of her webbing. Another, briefer set of obscenities when she saw the message was from Abdolo Poland.

I've just thought of something incredibly stupid. Where are you?

Previously

Harold tapped the door controls, his breath catching at the slight delay before the door slid open. It always took about half a second, right? Not a quarter of a second? It felt like it took a bit longer this time.

He had some right to be in the naval medical bay, just not a lot. Normally, he would only remotely send his programs to the tinkering engine, which would automatically handle fabricating and imprinting the nanobots. Delivering the completed capsules to the treatment annex could be accomplished by someone with far less education than Harold, which meant that normally, he would never have to come anywhere near here.

Which was why he had spent the last month laying the groundwork, a carefully balanced array of lies and excuses, to explain why he had to be there at that specific moment. Repeated conversations with Dr. Kinison about treatment efficiencies. Raising concerns about triage decisions. Very public musing about methods of increasing the treatment rates. This was all spectacularly rude of him, grossly overstepping his bounds into Dr. Kinison's domain. He was pretty sure if he kept it up for much longer he would provoke a fistfight. But it was at least plausible for him to be interested, and that was all he needed. A plausible excuse to visit the tinkering engine and examine its statistics packages. He would claim he was here investigating whether the engine was capable of handling a specific change in treatment methodology and what effect that would have on their treatment rates. He had even spent weeks coming up with this new, actually quite clever, change in treatment methodology, lest anyone ask to see it.

He turned on the lights, finding the room empty, as well it should be at this time of the morning. That had been the hardest part, actually, cultivating a reputation as an early riser after years of being the exact opposite.

He yawned fiercely and walked to the other side of the room, to the unmarked door there.

This door slid open in the same identically slow way the first door had, which meant that he was paranoid and that everything was fine, unless it meant the exact opposite. He stepped inside, allowing the door to close behind him, sealing him inside with the scariest machine on the ship.

In spite of its terrifying capabilities, the gene tinkerer itself was pretty harmless looking. A large transparent sphere comprised the business end of it, filled with the carefully controlled population of nanobots. At the base of the sphere, barely visible in the gray haze of the nanobot cultures, sat the programming apparatus. Collected and compiled nanobot populations were then packaged into capsules somewhere below there, before dropping out of a little slot in the base of the machine. Harold sidled up to the small terminal mounted on to the side of the unit and turned it on.

He covered his excuses first, instructing the unit to send a package of statistical data to his terminal. That done, he looked over his shoulder in what he would later decide was the most suspicious way possible, then turned back to the terminal. He flexed his fingers, took a deep breath, and triggered the engine into its low level command mode. Much harder to use but necessary for what he needed to do next. There were no excuses for this, and he began quickly tapping commands into the terminal, desperate to get it over with quickly.

```
GT-20298 COMMAND? ENTER HELP FOR HELP.
>upload -i
UPLOADING NEW COMMAND KERNEL. WARNING! THIS
MAY CAUSE YOUR GT-20298 TO CEASE FUNCTIONING.
ARE YOU SURE YOU WANT TO CONTINUE? (Y/N)
>y
SELECT .TINK FILE
>splitplot.tink
splitplot.tink NOT FOUND. SCANNING NEARBY DEVICES.....
splitplot.tink FOUND!
ANALYIZING..........INCOMPLETE KERNEL DETECTED.
CONTINUE IN PATCH ONLY MODE?
>y
BEGINNING PATCH PROCEDURE
PATCHING.....................COMPLETE!
>log
LOGGING SUBSYSTEM. ENTER HELP FOR HELP.
>ll -kernel
```

```
197836 U –p splitplot.tink 508 10/28/52 hstein
122465 U –p shp8patch.tink 1723 18/10/49 lkinison
103784 U –p shp7patch.tink 2128 4/2/48 lkinison
79844 U –p sheep6.tink 1343 1/3/46 lkinison
56733 U –n baseline-1-45-23.tink 1010 23/7/43 lkinison
30709 U –p s5.tink 1103 9/5/42 lkinison
^z ^z
>rl –l 197836
DELETED
>ll -kernel
122465 U –p shp8patch.tink 1723 18/10/49 lkinison
103784 U –p shp7patch.tink 2128 4/2/48 lkinison
79844 U –p sheep6.tink 1343 1/3/46 lkinison
56733 U –n baseline-1-45-23.tink 1010 23/7/43 lkinison
^z ^z
>exit
```

Harold smiled and allowed himself another suspicious look over the shoulder. Still no one there to ask what the heck he was doing. Back in the upper-level menus, he downloaded a final batch of statistical data, looked at it while making thoughtful noises, then pushed himself away from the terminal. He blinked, realizing he had almost forgotten something, and then deleted splitplot.tink from his terminal, lest he get intercepted while walking out.

Splitplot.tink did two things. The first was the hardest, at least technically, programming the logic necessary to safely insert a data gene into any given patient who got tinkered. This data gene contained all the text that Kevin had sent him, along with a brief note authored by Harold, explaining to any readers what the hell this information was doing inside them.

The second thing splitplot.tink did was substantially easier but took him a lot longer to figure out: how to prompt his subjects to actually find the data gene he had embedded. The solution to that came to him while flipping through his genetic cookbook one evening. Towards the back, he stumbled upon a section discussing genetic birthmarks, which immediately sparked his imagination. Planting a message or a clue as a genetic birthmark might work—a short hint that something funny was going on inside their DNA. Something simple, but enough to prompt a visit to the doctor and a deep genetic scan. It wouldn't even need a doctor; really, an interested hobbyist with a medical terminal could do it just as well.

But a birthmark would be incredibly and immediately visible. His message would be discovered within days of the first baby coming out of the womb. Too soon, too isolated. Too much chance the message would be read by the wrong person. And too easy to trace back to him. Ideally, he wanted to set a time delay so his message could be planted within more people before it was found. What he needed was an information time bomb, something that wouldn't go off for years, but when it did, by the hundreds.

His eureka moment came when he read about the retinas. The same genetic birthmarking procedure could be performed on retinas, where a message would only be seen by the subject. It was even possible to make them nearly invisible, to only fluoresce under certain lighting conditions, an occasionally necessary step to prevent the mild insanity which seemed to accompany retinal tattoos.

He spent a long while debating what message to write, strongly considering 'README' and 'LOOK OUT BEHIND YOU,' before finally settling on 'DATA GENE.' That would be enough to prompt someone to do a bit of research—a simple search for 'data gene'" would be enough—which would lead to a scanned genome and, finally, the data gene itself. And with a rare, but not too rare, lighting condition to serve as the trigger, that would take years to happen.

Leaving the naval medical bay, he couldn't help but marvel at how easy it had been. This elation almost immediately triggered a wave of self-doubt, and panic, convinced he had forgotten something. As he walked back to his office through the still slumbering Argos, he replayed everything that had happened, trying to figure out what he had overlooked.

But there was nothing.

It was done.

9

Breakthrough

The security van fishtailed around the corner, its rear-end sliding lazily into the wall on the far side of the street. The van regained traction, slammed into the opposite wall, bounced off of that, and continued in this way for another half block before it finally straightened out and bore down on the Africa-1 barricade.

The officers at the barricade, having had some experience with reckless van attacks, reacted smoothly. The commanding officer ordered his men to back away from the center of the street, out of the van's path. This was only a precaution—the van would certainly bounce off this time, the barricade in its path having been immensely reinforced since its last time through.

Five seconds later, the van did not bounce off the barricade, instead opting to violently explode. Barricade and van parts rained down on the street. Moving away from the impact area ended up saving the security team's lives, though it was safe to say that their day was completely ruined.

"Go!" Linze shouted, leading her team out of its hiding spot two blocks shy of the barricade. Down the sides of Africa, running towards the smoking crater, clatter and shouts behind them as the bulk of the Loyalist army set into motion. They reached the remnants of the barricade without encountering any return fire and picked their way through the wreckage. The barricade was completely gone, replaced by an enormous hole with the smoking hulk of a van in it. Stepping carefully around the van, Linze snap-fired at anything that moved, picking off the blinking and helpless security officers writhing on the streets. "Hey, co-workers. Remember me?"

Leaving the smoking hulk of the barricade, her team continued down Africa. At 8th, a security officer blundered around the corner at a run, only to be picked off in a scattered flurry of shots. Linze stepped into a hairdresser's studio on the corner of the intersection and methodically blew out each window, before ducking down behind the counter inside. From here, she could see down streets to the south and west and began shooting at the disorganized security officers unlucky enough to approach from those directions. Outside, the rest of her unit took up similar positions around the intersection, while the second wave of Loyalists leapfrogged them. This group didn't do as well, many of them seeming to slip and fall on something on the ground. Most of the rest were knocked down by fire as they crossed the intersection, the security forces having regrouped a bit by that point. The attack stalled, as the still conscious members of the second wave sought cover in not terribly useful locations, the middle of the street being one popular choice.

"Keep moving!" Linze yelled out of the window. Their beachhead had to get a lot bigger, down to 6th, at least. And that had to happen soon, before the bulk of the security reinforcements showed up. Frustrated, she squeezed off a pair of useless shots at silhouettes well out of range. More gunfire, this time from the north, as the braver and dumber third and fourth waves began to arrive, taking a ridiculous amount of abuse, but overwhelming the remaining security forces with numbers alone. At that point, the trickle became a flood, a wave of hooting and hollering Loyalist soldiers surging past Linze's position and spreading out into the neighboring streets. Linze left her perch, moving out to the street, where she began serving as a traffic cop, directing the arriving help to where it would do the most good.

Ten minutes later, when the security forces eventually attempted a counterattack, they were easily beaten back by the overwhelming, if slightly uncoordinated, mass of Loyalist guns that had recently arrived. The lines on the map had been redrawn.

Stein hurried to keep pace behind the assault team as they picked their way through the crowded streets, filled with bored Loyalist troops who couldn't figure out where the fight was. The assault team was a little more organized than that, the best that Kinsella supposedly had, though Stein hadn't asked what qualifications earned them that praise. *Capable of dressing themselves? Not currently doing needle-drugs?*

"Ahh man, my van!" Bruce said as they crossed the wreckage of the former barricade.

"We'll get you another one," she said.

"But I liked *that* one."

They were playing the most critical part in the night's exercise and had been held in reserve, waiting for Kinsella's maniacs to establish a beachhead. It had taken surprisingly little effort to convince Kinsella to attempt her plan; the look on his face when she had told him suggested he had been expecting her to come up with something like this anyways. The other surprise had been her introduction to the commanding officer of Kinsella's maniacs, her old friend Sergeant Hogg.

"Don't say I told you so," he had said.

"Fine," she had replied. "So long as we're both thinking it."

As they pushed deeper into the aft, Stein stopped at one of the elevators, trying its controls, an unfriendly squelching sound its only response. Helot had already locked it out to prevent any maniacs from accessing the upper-decks. *That would have been too easy.* She hurried to catch up with the rest of the team. They weren't really banking on using the elevators anyways, having another route in mind.

They were forced to slow down as they pushed further south, the crowd of morons growing denser. Hogg's mob outnumbered the security forces five to one now, but he had labored to explain why that was less impressive than it sounded at every opportunity he had had over the past month. Because his soldiers "were idiots" who "sucked" seemed to be the general problem.

"Why are we stopped here?" Croutl shouted, somewhere ahead of her. He was the leader of the assault team and part of Hogg's original security unit. During their introductions, Bruce had pantomimed shooting him in the crotch. Relations had been strained ever since.

Stein finally caught up to Croutl and the rest of the team, who had piled into the back of crowd that was unwilling to move any further into the intersection. "Why'd everyone stop?" Croutl yelled again.

"They keep shooting at us!" someone complained.

"Well, shoot back!"

"It's really hard!"

Croutl backed away from the mob and gathered the team together a short distance away. "This place? You're sure it's just over there?" he asked Bruce, pointing over the crowd's head, across the intersection to a corner apartment.

"Yeah, that's it," Bruce said.

"Well, it looks like the dipshits stopped short of where they were supposed to. And if the dozen dumb bastards napping in the middle of the street are any indication, there's a lot of angry security that way who are shooting anyone who steps out of cover."

"That sounds bad!" Bruce said, his mouth hanging open. Stein gritted her teeth. This wasn't the right time to mock their help.

Croutl glared at Bruce. "I don't suppose you have any bright ideas for getting across there without getting shot?"

"Human shields?"

Croutl seemed to consider that. "You say it takes three seconds to blow through the lock once you're there?"

Bruce nodded. "That's right. Not that I'm admitting I've done it before."

Croutl ignored him and stepped away from the group, taking a couple of his soldiers with him. They pushed their way through the crowd of Loyalist troops to the building's corner, to peek at the security forces down the street.

"Think he bought it?" Bruce asked.

"Definitely," Stein replied. Her terminal vibrated, a message from Ellen, wishing them luck. When they had heard about what Bruce and Stein were doing, Griese and Ellen had immediately offered to come along. Stein hadn't even mentioned it to Hogg—neither had any skills that could justify a place on the team—and told them their moral support was more than enough. Bruce also appreciated their moral support, but indicated the financial type would be appreciated, as well.

Croutl returned from his scouting and started whispering orders to his team, which soon dispersed into the crowd. "Okay," he said, turning to Stein and Bruce. "We're going to try that human shield thing..."

"Yes!" Bruce was excited.

"What?" Stein was not.

"It's fine," Croutl said. "But, you know. We're not going to tell them. They think we have a secret weapon that will protect them."

Bruce nodded emphatically. "Is the secret weapon *treachery*?"

Croutl was getting good at ignoring Bruce, and continued explaining his plan. "Us three charge out there with some...help. You blow the lock." He pointed at Bruce. "We run inside. Everyone else joins us."

"And the human shields?" Stein asked.

"What the fuck do you think?" Croutl snapped. "Shit, they'll be fine." With a jerk of his head, he summoned them over to the corner of the building, and slowly edged towards the intersection. Standing on his tiptoes, he looked over the crowd to his soldiers dispersed within, looking for some sign they were ready.

"Now!" Croutl yelled. With a roar, a surge of maniacs dashed into the street, shooting wildly. Croutl waited a beat before dragging Stein and Bruce out of cover, trailing slightly behind the mob. They made it across the intersection easily, Stein and Croutl sliding to a halt beside the door, Bruce thumping right into it, a plasma torch already in his right hand. He pressed the tool against the threshold of the door, sending a tongue of flame into the doorframe.

Down the street, flashing muzzles lined the doorways and windows of the street, marking the locations of security officers. It was a unique sight,

Stein thought, seeing so many guns shooting in her direction. Really, it was impossible that she wasn't getting shot. But the security officers seemed to mainly be shooting at whoever was shooting back at them, a group that for the moment consisted entirely of duped Loyalist troops, scattered across the street in front of Stein. One of the dupes closest to Croutl groaned, catching a shot in the chest. His legs folded under him, Croutl rushing up to catch him under the arms and drag him back to the door, now literally using him as a shield.

A soft clank from the doorframe as the locking mechanism gave way. Bruce placed a meaty paw on the door and shoved it out of the way before stepping through. Stein following close behind, shouting for Croutl as she did. A second later, the security officer appeared, backing in through the door, stumbling on the threshold. He collapsed, his poor stupid shield falling on top of him, the pair falling backwards, crashing into Stein's legs.

A massive increase in the volume of fire caught their attention. Four slumped bodies in the middle of the road were new, belonging to members of the assault team. The rest of the team remained behind cover on the other side, out of sight of the security reinforcements that had obviously just arrived. Croutl got up and stepped to the threshold of the door. He took a peek down the street and immediately ducked back inside, another volley of fire stitching the street around him. He waved the rest of the team back, then tugged at the edge of the door, sliding it back into place. He turned back to face them. "Just the three of us now."

"Can we do this with just us three?" she asked.

Croutl checked his tool webbing, where five small explosive charges were securely fastened. "Five bangers. You tell me?"

She did some math in her head. "To cripple the pressure regulator, any spares they have, and a big chunk of the fuel lines...yeah, five charges will probably do. Worth a try, I guess."

"Then, let's go." Croutl turned to Bruce. "Lead the way, Magellan." Bruce grinned and beckoned them deeper into the apartment that he had been so insistent they get to.

The place was big, and although not obviously dusty, it had the feeling of being underused. A space that someone had stopped caring about. Odd, mismatched furniture in the main room, a stack of broken sporting equipment by the wall, a single sex swing hanging lamely in the corner. It was also, as expected, completely empty, the owner having obviously not been spared the same eviction that every other aft dweller had received.

In the back, Bruce led Stein and Croutl up a set of compact stairs, winding their way up the second level, and then the third. It was these stairs that made the apartment so unique, a destination worth a few bruises on some human shields. Knocking holes in walls had always been a popular and greyly-legal way to expand one's living space on board the Argos. This was normally seen in the form of double-wide suites on the lower decks, but in a few cases there were people who had done the same with vertically contiguous rooms, making taller suites.

"Who owns this place?" Croutl asked, voicing the same question that Stein was thinking.

"Some government guy. From a long family of government guys," Bruce said. He opened another door, revealing another set of stairs up to the fourth level. "From a long family of stair fetishists, also maybe." He led them upstairs.

The fourth level was obviously the most lived-in floor, but even here, Stein wasn't impressed with what she saw. It was the wastefulness of it all that irritated her. Someone hoarding space and not using it. And she knew there was still more space to come.

There had always been rumors of extremely well-connected people with suites that extended above the fourth level into the normally off-limits floors above. Stein had never cared enough about the rumors to wonder whether they were true or not. Even Bruce, with his healthy passion for prowling around secret places, never gave the stories of these illegal suites much credence.

An opinion he was forced to change when he was bribed to fix the heating in one. As Bruce explained the story—and Stein knew to never completely believe these—an extremely nervous-looking man had pulled up to Bruce at the bar a few years ago and asked him if he wanted some work under the table. Bruce, with a lukewarm attitude to work independent of its position relevant to tables, had humored the man only out of a sense of curiosity.

His curiosity did not go unrewarded. The man explained that the suite, which had been passed down in his family for generations, both contained and stood testament to his family's greatest secret: that they were fucking morons. At one point they had turned their beautiful, palatial, entirely legal nest into a beautiful, palatial, wildly illegal nest by expanding it into the fifth floor above. So illegal that it actually limited the amount of usable space they had, guests restricted from the upper-levels of their home, lest the secret attic be uncovered. Cocktail parties became tense and uncomfortable affairs, velvet ropes guarded with unusual diligence. The family gained a reputation.

Eventually, the suite passed into the hands of the current owner, who had managed to shed his family's reputation of being weird and was now simply unpopular. With no guests wanting to spend any length of time around him, the illegal suite no longer posed him any trouble, at least until something went wrong with the heat. Something happened upstairs, something which turned the entire apartment, top to bottom, into a sauna. Months of sweaty, sleepless nights passed for the sticky, unpopular owner before he had heard about a fellow who might be capable of both fixing such a problem and keeping his mouth shut about it.

"I was that fellow," Bruce had explained.

"Yeah, I got that, Stein had replied.

Bruce arrived with his tools the next evening, where the man, stripped to the waist, quickly hustled him through the front door. The hidden space above, originally a hydroponics farm, had been converted into a wholly unremarkable fifth bedroom, furnished quite haphazardly in comparison with the main floors below. Bruce deduced that they had been reluctant to be seen carrying too much furniture in and out of the space. Amongst the haphazard decorations was a dingy wall hanging, which Bruce decided probably concealed a door connected to the rest of the fifth level. Bruce finished the job at a leisurely pace, checking carefully for anything worth stealing via the great back door he had found. But not finding anything immediately interesting, he had finished the job and filed the information away to be used at a later date.

"It is now a later date," Bruce said, opening the door of a suspiciously large wardrobe. "Welcome to the future, everyone."

Inside the wardrobe, a cramped set of ladder stairs led up to the secret level above. The three of them climbed the stairs, Bruce fumbling for the lights on the floor above. The ugliest floor yet, dingy and haphazard, just as described. "He hasn't changed a thing in three years," Bruce said.

Croutl looked around, a distasteful look on his face. "The fucking thing is so illegal, he was afraid to even use it."

"Nice temperature, though," Stein observed, finger extended at her friend.

"*Thank you* for noticing," Bruce said, beaming at her.

Bruce walked to the side of the room, where the aforementioned deeply unattractive wall hanging lay. With a swipe of his hand, Bruce tugged it to the ground, revealing a door. He pressed his ear against it, then shook his head—no sounds from the other side. "Well, I got you this far," he said. "Which is the point where I'm officially out of ideas."

Stein opened the map on her terminal, double-checking the route they had already planned. "It's all supposed to be mothballed hydroponics past there," she said. "Shouldn't be anyone around for blocks. Or halls. Whatever. And the staircase heading up is just down the hall."

Croutl moved to the door, readying his pistol. "All right. You guys ready?"

"Wait. Moving stairs or the bad type?" Bruce asked.

"The bad type."

"This plan sucks."

"They're pretty dug in along here," Hogg said, pointing at an intersection on the map. "They recovered really quickly." He straightened up as Linze crouched over the display set into the coffee table. They were in the living room of a largish apartment, just south of the shattered barricade. A double-wide unit, one of the nicer apartments in this part of the ship, it had been repurposed as the forward command center for the Loyalist army.

"Yeah, well, we knew that would happen. Okay, let's not bang our head against a wall. So, we tell everyone to go the other way," Linze said.

When Hogg arrived, he had seen them carting away the injured officers who had been by the barricade when it exploded. They were pretty messed up. And he had known every one of them. The explosion was way larger than what he had imagined. Way larger than what he had asked Kinsella for. "I don't know," he said, hearing his voice tremble, feeling ashamed. "We could stop here. Regroup. We were lucky to get this far. If our guys are attacked with any kind of intensity, they'll crumble."

Linze's eyes widened. "Come on, Hogg. Our only advantage is numbers. We throw as many of us at as few of them as possible. Just keep moving and shooting. Don't give them time to set up. Look here...we tell squads...Tiger, Monkey, Laser, and Potato to push south, then west around here."

Hogg's face twitched. Too much, too fast. Intellectually, he knew Linze was right: their only advantage was numbers, and the longer this went on, the more likely his side was to get scared and run away. *Or bored and walk away.* But the intellectual part of him was drowned out by the part that had seen three of his former colleagues with blood streaming out of their ears, a part of him that was screaming, *Slow Down.* "Let me think about it." Linze balled her hands into fists, but retreated to the dining room, where a group of volunteers were coordinating the communications.

Hogg sat down heavily on the couch of the apartment. The last four weeks had taught him that he liked following orders more than giving them. He had a modest talent for leadership—he had had to, to make it as far as he had in his career. But that was small scale stuff. Stuff that didn't result in blood streaming from ears. He closed his eyes and rubbed his knuckles into them, trying to see anything else.

He took a deep breath and opened his eyes, examining the map on his terminal. He tapped around a bit, watching the battle unfold, the good guys marked by red dots. The red dots had simple orders: if they see a bad guy, take cover and start shooting. If they don't see a bad guy, move around until they do. The plan was messy by design—his soldiers couldn't handle anything more complicated. And once they had breached Helot's static defenses, numbers and messiness should work for them. That was what he had told Kinsella, and what he had told himself.

His terminal beeped. He examined it, an incoming call from Kinsella.

"Have we won yet?" the mayor asked.

"Uh, not yet, sir. Might take awhile," Hogg said. Linze returned to the room, looking at him impatiently. He turned away from her. "We're actually thinking of slowing down for a bit and consolidating our gains."

"Yeah? Okay. Why?"

Hogg licked his lips. "Just so...we can...have them consolidated."

A long pause while Kinsella considered that. "Yeah, I don't know what that means. You keep going, Hogg. You win this war immediately."

"Yes, sir," he said into a blank screen, Kinsella having already ended the call. Hogg looked up to see Linze staring back at him, a faint hint of mockery in her eyes. "Okay, do it," he said. "We keep going."

Helot slumped forward in his chair, chin resting on the tactical table. He watched from this low angle at the dots and blips moving around. There were an awful lot of red dots. Thorias manipulated the table controls like a dervish, shouting orders into his commlink, ordering his units to stop getting shot. Two other officers assisted with the display, drawing lines and moving icons around, indicating tactical items of interest, places where people weren't getting shot fast enough, presumably. An enormous chunk had been carved out of the lines they had held for the past month. *It had been so easy for them.*

They had known an attack was coming—couldn't not see the mass of armed morons slowly gathering all day. But Thorias' careful schemes of staggered retreats and fall back positions had been shattered by the explosion on Africa Street. There had been some feint attacks prior to that, which Thorias had overcommitted to, rushing support away from where it was actually needed. By the time they knew what was happening, thousands of Othersiders had poured through the gap.

The fighting was dying down a bit now, the Othersiders stopping and consolidating their gains. No tactical expert, that still seemed like a mistake to Helot. *They had us on the ropes.* They just had to keep spreading out, and it would be over.

"Captain?" Thorias asked from across the table. It was the most deferential Helot had ever heard the chief. "I think it's time to stop playing nice." The room didn't go quiet—too many people doing too much work for that to happen—but it seemed quieter to Helot. Without needing to be told, Helot knew what Thorias was referring to—the small cache of lethal weapons they had. To his credit, Thorias hadn't discussed these at all during his defensive preparations. There probably were secret plans, with larger, angrier arrows on his terminal that took the bigger guns into account. But Thorias hadn't even hinted at them until now.

Helot looked down at a corner of the tactical table, where a loop of footage from the feed on Africa-1 was playing. He watched in slow motion as the stolen van accelerated at the barricade, the officers there scrambling out of the way of the driverless vehicle. Then the explosion—a sure sign the Othersiders had gotten around the safeguards preventing the manufacture of volatiles. *Kinsella tried to kill them.* If those officers survived, it was by luck, not design. That was real blood on the streets, real screams of pain.

"Yeah. I think so, too," he said, looking up at Thorias. *Just be careful,* he thought, but didn't say, while Thorias turned away to make a quick call. *I really should offer some words of restraint.* He watched Thorias hurriedly leave the room, finally off the leash.

"Go get 'em, Chief," he said softly instead.

From the fifth floor, they went straight up, using one of the emergency staircases. At this latitude, they were still outside the core, though paralleling its border as they rose up to the 20th floor, where a connecting passage would allow them to pass through.

The climbing got easier as they rose, but they nevertheless paced themselves, taking breaks at regular intervals. "I guess they're not chasing us," Stein noted during one of these stops, sitting on the landing of the 17th floor.

"Seems that way," Croutl said. He stretched up, bent his knees slightly, and sprang upward, bouncing off the ceiling before coming back to rest.

"You coming, Bruce?" Stein asked down the stairs. Heavy, labored cursing answered her. A few seconds later, Bruce appeared, wheezing. He sat down heavily—no easy trick in low-gravity—and leaned against the wall.

"No taking off this time. You guys keep taking off as soon as I catch up." A hoarse, lispy wheeze. "It's bullshit is what it is."

Croutl looked like he was about to say something, but thought better of it. "Wait here," he said instead, getting to his feet. "I'll scout ahead." He continued his climb, rapidly moving out of sight.

"Bruuuuuuce," Stein whined, "you're making us look bad in front of the army guy."

"Sorry, Stein. I didn't know this was a dating opportunity for you."
Stein patted Bruce on his hand. "Ha."

"I should have guessed when I saw you'd shaved your mustache," he
added, earning a punch in the neck in response.

They sat quietly for a few minutes, Stein looking at the map on her
terminal, Bruce breathing. Eventually, the sound of footsteps approaching
from above, both of them readying their pistols. A landing above, then
Croutl's face appeared, staring down.

"We've got a problem," he said.

"Yeah, that's definitely not a regular gun," Griese said, looking at the mag-
nified image on the terminal he had pressed against the window. "Muzzle
flash is too blue."

"Sure sounds different," Ellen agreed. Lying one window over, she
shifted behind the rifle, panning it slightly to her right. "What do you
think?"

Griese watched the blue flash a few more times, thinking. They had
set up in the upper floor of an apartment on the corner of Africa and 7th.
Kinsella's army had stalled; all of the fools who enjoyed getting shot had
gone down in the first few waves, leaving the slow and gun shy to carry on
with the advance. Those still interested in the fight were taking cheap
shots at the security forces from range, but that was a diminishing number; most were milling about somewhat aimlessly. A few had started looting. The security forces seemed content with that state of affairs, simply
holding their new defensive perimeter, not trying to push the mob back.

That was the case until the past few minutes, when new, bluer muzzle
flashes started appearing on the security lines. "I dunno," Griese finally
said. "Though I've got a guess."

"Yeah, so do I." A moment later, "Ahhh, hell."

"What?" Griese asked.

"He's bleeding. Shit, he's really hurt. They're really doing it, those
fuckers. They brought out the bolt throwers."

"What is it?" Griese looked up at Ellen, who had shifted her rifle to
look down at the streets closer to them.

"Some dumb kid's bleeding on the ground. Screaming his head off.
They shot him, Griese. They shot him."

Griese tilted his terminal around until he could see what she was looking at. A young man on the ground, blood pouring from his leg. Too far
away to hear him, but he looked to be screaming in agony. Eventually,
some brave soul dashed out into the street and dragged him behind the lee
of a building. "Was that what we were waiting for?" he asked.

Ellen seemed to have more or less recovered from her previous experience with the security counter-sniper, or at least claimed she had. Griese had his doubts, but he carried them quietly. And with Stein and Bruce doing something dangerous, there was no way his wife wouldn't want to help, or at least do something equally dangerous herself. And with only the one obvious tool at their disposal for 'helping,' they had marched into the aft to do just that. What their 'help' would entail wasn't explicitly discussed; they had yet to decide what rules of engagement they were going to use. Griese hoped it would be obvious when they saw it.

"It might be, yeah," Ellen said quietly. "Where was he shooting from again? I lost him."

Griese began panning the terminal back to where he had first seen the blue muzzle flashes. But he couldn't find them—all fire from the security officers seemed to have stopped. "Maybe it was a warning?" he said.

"Yeah, well, maybe we should warn them, too."

Griese swallowed and began panning the terminal around some more, looking for the guns. "Whoa."

"What?"

"It couldn't be him."

"Who? What? Where?"

"Back. Back. Like to 2nd Ave. Standing in front of the van on the right. Who's that?"

He waited for Ellen to find what he was looking at. "The chief of security?"

"That's where, what, and who I'm looking at." On the screen, Griese watched Chief Thorias gesturing down the street, at this magnification, almost seeming to point right at Griese. A couple of the officers gathered around him were clearly holding long guns.

So faint he could barely hear her, Ellen said. "I'm going to do it."

Griese licked his lips. "Are you sure? I could..."

"No." He looked up from the terminal. Her back rose as she took in a breath. A click from the rifle. She shifted slightly to the side. Her back fell. A familiar crack filled the room. Griese didn't even bother to look.

"Hey...," he said softly, crawling over to her.

"I'm fine," she said. She rolled away from the window. "We should reposition."

"Ellen..."

"I'm fine, Griese!" She glared at him. "He brought it on himself. They all did." She grabbed the rifle and stood up, moving to the back of the apartment. Griese felt incredibly cold and looked down at the goose bumps on his forearms. He got to his feet, rubbing his arms, and followed her downstairs.

Outside, they stayed on the edges of the street as they moved to their next spot. They headed back to 8th Avenue, a block closer to safety, a prudent move should this suddenly lethal war get any worse. Ellen stood out of Griese's way as he blew the lock on the door of an almost identical apartment. Across the street, Loyalist soldiers streamed in and out of another apartment, the Loyalist's makeshift headquarters.

The lock popped, and Griese shoved the door out of the way, stepping inside. "Oh, goddammit," Ellen said behind him, stopping just inside the entrance of the apartment.

"What is it?" he asked, turning around.

She looked back at him, hands on her hips. "You didn't happen to bring the charging cable, did you?"

"Are you serious?"

"Don't be mad at me."

"I'm not mad at you. I'm mad at us."

"You sounded mad at me," she said. A small grin. "I guess we forgot, after the last time."

He bent down to look at the gun. "So, it's done?"

"One shot left. Maybe two."

Griese looked at the orangish glow from the charge indicator. "Well. Let's go get the cable, then."

Ellen looked up at him. "Both of us? You're the one who forgot it."

"I'm pretty sure we both forgot it."

"That's not how I remember it. Go on. I'll be fine here."

"I'm not going to leave you here in the middle of a war, lady."

"I'll be fine."

"I don't doubt it. But I'm pretty sure this is one of those things that was in our vows. Sickness. Health. Peace. War zones."

"I don't remember you saying that."

"Well, it was maybe between the lines." Griese grabbed her hand. "Come on, let's go."

She twisted her hand out of his grasp. "I'll be fine," she said.

Years of experience had taught Griese it wasn't wise to push her when her fur was on end. Years of experience worth ignoring in this particular circumstance. "Ellen..."

"Griese!" She snapped at him. "If those assholes try anything, I will shoot them."

"You've got one shot, Ellen."

"Then you'd better fucking hurry back with that charging cable!" Her nostrils flared. An uneasy moment passed between them. Finally, her expression softened. "Look. If anything goes wrong, I'm out of here in a second. I won't do anything dumb. Now, please. Go. Hurry back. I'll be fine." She smiled and squeezed his hand.

"I'm not going to..."

"I want you to go." Griese felt his face sink. "It's..." she tried to explain. "I just don't want you around for this."

If I can't be around for it, then you shouldn't be doing it. That was a wise thing to say. *I'm getting you out of here right now, you bloodthirsty bitch.* Less wise, but certainly to the point. There were, in truth, many things he could have and should have said, other than "Okay," which is what he did.

She bent in to give him a kiss, a good one. She stepped away. "I'll be fine."

He nodded dumbly, and backpedaled awkwardly to the door. He stopped. "If our guys start running away..."

"I'll run, too. In front of them. Let them be the dead heroes."

"Good."

Ellen smiled, then crept upstairs. Still not sure how it was happening, or why he was letting it, Griese backed out the door.

When they finally reached the 20th floor, Croutl showed them the problem. "That's not supposed to be there, is it?" he said, pointing at the closed bulkhead door.

Stein examined the door. It looked similar to the bulkhead doors currently in place along the street levels of the ship, but much less dirty. Trails of fresh lubricant along the edges told her someone had been maintaining it recently. "I'd say it looks like it's meant to be here."

"Kind of a shame that it's closed, though, isn't it?" Bruce said.

"Can you open it?" Croutl asked. Stein tried the controls, found them locked off, and shook her head. Beside her, Bruce tried pushing on the door. "So, now what?" Croutl asked.

Stein looked at Bruce, who nodded, jerking his head down the hall. "We probably have another way," she said.

They began making their way along the steeply curving hallways, Croutl a short distance in front of them, moving in a crouch so that he could see further ahead. A minute or so later, Croutl held up his hand, signaling for them to stop. Stein and Bruce nervously waited, watching Croutl frozen in place in the middle of the hall. A few seconds passed before he moved, waving them forward again.

"I recognize that," Bruce said, seeing the disconnect hatch that had caught Croutl's attention.

It was the same hatch they had ambushed Curts in. The fasteners on the hatch were still loose, Stein and Bruce easily undoing them while Croutl prowled up and down the hall. The hatch open, Stein stepped inside, turning on her terminal light, illuminating the massive set of interlocked C-clamps, now cut completely through. "Looks like they got another fuse torch," she said. Bruce nodded and stepped past her to the other side of the cavity. "How's the hatch?" she asked. "Can you see a way to open it?"

"I think pushing on it will work."

"What?"

"It's already open." Silence for a moment, then a squeaking sound. "Yeah, it's open."

"Where's that take us?" Croutl asked, peering suspiciously into the cavity.

"Closer."

"Good enough." Croutl stepped into the cavity to join them.

Stein joined Bruce on the far side, crouched down with his head close to the hatch. He shook his head when she approached, then pushed the hatch a little further. She could see down the core hall, no one in sight. "I'll go first," Croutl said. He pushed the hatch a little further open, then stepped quickly through, gun drawn. "Come on," he said after a moment.

Bruce followed through the hatch behind him, Stein following a second later, stepping into the core hallway. A noise behind her, Stein turning to see a startled naval engineer gaping at them. A shot, *a loud one*, from beside her head. Charged particles smashed into the engineer's neck, sending him to the ground. "Yeah!" Bruce hissed beside her, jogging over to inspect his handiwork. "I think it's the same guy as before!" he said, looking up with a big grin on his face.

"He's going to develop a real fucking complex about walking down this hall," she said, rubbing her ear. She turned around, not seeing Croutl anywhere. "Uh...," she said.

"He went the other way," Bruce said. He bent down to pick up his quarry, and dumped him back into the disconnect cavity, shutting the hatch behind him. "We should probably catch up."

They heard him before they saw him. Together they ran up the curve of the ship to see Croutl firing rapidly around a corner. "Two of 'em right in front of the reactor," Croutl said, ducking back out of their return fire. "They were fucking waiting for us." He pulled a grenade from his webbing and heaved it down the hallway. Screams of recognition echoed down the halls before a massive thump. Croutl looked around the corner and was again turned back by a flurry of return fire. "How the fuck are there *more of them now*?" he shouted. He looked at Stein and shook his head. "This isn't going to work," he said. Stein felt Bruce's hand on her shoulder and allowed herself to be tugged back the way they had come. She watched Croutl deliver one last salvo, screaming obscenities before he turned to follow them.

Bruce had just reopened the access hatch to the cavity when a second group of security officers appeared in front of them. Stein cried out in warning, cut short by Bruce shoving her through the hatch. Gunfire erupted behind her. In the cavity, Stein rolled off the naval engineer's still unconscious body and regained her feet. She looked back into the hall at Bruce, who was clambering into the hatch himself. "Croutl?" she shouted.

"Go, go," Bruce hissed, pushing her to the other side of the cavity. She opened her mouth to protest, before he said, "He's down." Another ungallant shove sent her through the hatch on the other side.

Bruce rejoined her outside the cavity and slammed the door shut. He slotted in one of the fasteners, spinning it partially tight, then added a second one. Before he could finish, an enormous thump from the other side of the door, the vibrations kicking up clouds of dust from the floor. "That wasn't a grenade," Stein said. "Shit," she added a moment later, getting it.

"The charges," Bruce said. Stein's shoulders slumped. The explosive charges Croutl was carrying must have been hit. Her mouth went dry and she started to slump to the ground. "Come on," Bruce said, grabbing her under the armpits and spinning her in the direction they had come from. "We'll be unhappy later." Another shove, and they were off.

She would remember very little about their retreat down the stairs. The gravity kept getting stronger, that much stuck out. Unless it was her legs getting weaker.

Half an hour. That's how long it took someone to tell him that Thorias was dead. Incompetence by design; the only people who knew were security officers, and the only person they knew to report to was Thorias. There was no second-in-command. Thorias had five or six third-in-commands, but none of them had anywhere near the authority to speak directly to Helot.

It had been up to Helot to notice that his security chief wasn't answering his terminal. It had been up to Helot to ask someone directly. It had been up to Helot to ask again when that someone froze solid. "He's dead, sir," the officer manning the tactical table eventually said. He pointed at something on the map, a squiggly line which evidently meant something to him. "See? Dead."

"What." Not a question, just a statement. The only thing Helot could think to say. The officer squirmed some more before confirming what he had just said and explaining what had happened. Someone had apparently shot Thorias in the head, that's what happened.

Helot didn't really recall what happened for the next few minutes, although by the way people treated him afterwards, it may have involved a

little bit of going completely berserk. He definitely recalled some screaming. He also may have tried to flip over the tactical table, the seven ton
behemoth that wasn't just fixed to the floor as much as it was an essential
part of the floor. And he definitely recalled ordering everyone to go kill
everyone else, an order which thankfully wasn't acted on. Even once the
scope was clarified—*"Kill them, you fools!"*—someone probably pointed out
that that was impossible. There were too many of them.

Whether he calmed down, or simply ran out of gas, Helot eventually
found himself on the floor, leaning against the unflipped tactical table,
Curts gently reminding him that they only had another few days left to
finish cutting the disconnects. They could dig in. Hold off the Othersiders. This didn't sound berserk enough to Helot, but it had a certain appeal,
in that it was the only plan they had.

And then someone informed him that the Othersiders had almost
snuck into the core. They had actually been two decks *above* Helot. Where
they were setting off bombs and killing more people.

Another short spell of berserking, more calls for everyone to kill everyone, now accompanied by a strange, deafening static noise, which he later
realized was probably the sound of his brain failing. Again, Helot woke up to
find himself staring at Curts' uselessly flapping jaw. *Why wasn't he out killing
everyone? What was so important to say that he had to stop killing everybody?*

"Sir?" Curts said, his voice trembling.

Helot jabbed a finger into the engineer's chest. "What? What is it?
We're about to be overrun by bomb-throwing morons, and you're standing there burbling like an idiot."

Curts flinched, looking away. Not meeting Helot's hate-filled gaze, he
said, "I've got an idea. How to stop them, I mean." He fidgeted with
something on his terminal. "It's a little crazy, though."

"Good. Make it crazier," Helot said. "All the way crazy."

"Sir?" Curts blurted, looking confused. Helot felt a pain shoot up the
right side of his face, then realized he was clenching his teeth too hard. He
waved his hand in a circle, beckoning the engineer to continue.

"Okay." Curts moved forward to the tactical table, bending over
the map. He zoomed the screen out until it displayed the entirety of
Level 1. "Here's where th-th-the Othersider forces are," he said pointing at the shaded semicircle that was the source of Helot's troubles.
"Okay, here's my idea. We still have c-c-control over the bulkhead
doors. All of them—across the ship." He tapped on the map to indicate
a bulkhead door on Africa Street just past the barricade the Othersiders
had blown through. "They could have disabled our controls, but I don't
think they'd have done that. Can anyone else think why they might?"

He looked around the room as a sea of blank faces looked back. "Anyways, I don't think they have yet."

"Hurry the fuck up, Curts."

"Right. So, my plan is, we close the bulkhead doors here, here, here..." He drew lines on the map, drawing in bulkhead doors, tracing out an enclosure that encompassed the Othersiders' main force. "Now, look at..." he said, his finger tracing over the map, searching for something. "This room here." His finger stopped over a room near the Othersiders' perimeter. "We c-c-can get people in here without them seeing. So, we send in a team of engineers with a fuse torch, and," he swallowed, hesitating. "And we c-c-cut a hole in the floor."

That got Helot's attention. He stood up straighter, waiting for Curts to continue.

"If we cut a big hole—say a meter or two, in this room here, and then blow open this door somehow..."

"You'll suck all the air out of that section of the ship," Helot finished his thought. "Just that section, right?" Maybe he didn't want to go all the way crazy. That was a good sign.

"Uh, just that section, sir. Once the pressure starts to drop, there's no way they'll be able to open these bulkhead doors. The vacuum would be c-c-contained."

"How long would it take for the air to evacuate?"

"From the streets? A few minutes. There would be air pockets in all of the rooms and buildings, of course, once the membranes shut. There'd be enough air in there for a few hours—maybe a day—of breathing."

"So, they die quickly, or they die slowly," Helot said, nodding slowly. "But they'd die."

"If they like breathing air, yes." Curts stared at the map. "If we wanted to, with some c-c-careful control of the bulkhead doors, we could reintroduce air to this section small bits at a time. Enough for security to rush in and overwhelm anyone t-t-trapped in the rooms. To capture them."

"How long would it take you to do this?"

Curts took a deep breath. "Maybe a c-couple hours?"

"Then you should have started a couple hours ago." The static seemed to fade from his hearing. Helot felt a shudder as the adrenaline started to leave his system. "Good work, Curts. It's refreshing hearing something positive from you for once."

"Thank you, sir."

Helot nodded. "*Now, don't fuck it up.*"

Curts maneuvered the fuse torch slowly and deliberately in the envirosuit, not wanting to take any chances. He hadn't worn an e-suit in years.

Move slow, that was the rule of thumb. Leavened in this particular case by the urgent need for haste the captain had impressed upon him. *Don't fuck up, indeed.*

Curts shut off the blade and moved to his right a bit, grabbing at the heavy cord secured to his waist and dragging it with him. The tethers necessitated even slower movement than normal, although he wouldn't have done the job without them. From his waist, the thumb-thick cord snaked across the floor and out the door to a neighboring room, where it had been fastened to the floor with massive bolts. He had watched the installation of those very carefully.

There were other people more qualified for this, more capable with the fuse torch, more experienced working in e-suits. But the job was risky, and it was his idea. And, not long ago, he had been kicked in the head. That angered up the blood a bit.

Truthfully, he had been looking for an opportunity to do something like this. He had weaseled his way into this plot, betrayed everyone around him for the chance to touch real dirt. And everyone knew it. He was tired of the looks he got, from Helot, from the security officers, from everyone else around him. They knew he didn't belong and let him know with every sneer. A miserable life awaited him on the surface of Tau Prius living with these people. He needed a chance to prove he had earned his ticket.

Another wedge of rock loosened, he turned off the torch while two naval engineers crawled into the hole. They were almost two full meters below floor level now, just past the sandwiched insulation layers. Anywhere from one to five meters to go. The navy guys wrestled the rock out of the hole, fighting with their own tethers. Hopefully, those would just be safety measures. Hopefully. The plan wasn't all the way crazy, just very close.

The chunk of rock removed, he climbed down into the hole, slightly deeper this time, and aimed his fuse torch at the lowest spot. He hit the trigger, and a bright blue blade shot out the end, the facemask of his suit immediately darkening to obscure it. He twisted the blade around, slicing into the rock. He waited a few seconds for it to penetrate to its full depth, then slowly dragged the blade around, chopping another wedge of rock out of the ground.

A tremendous hissing noise filled the room. Curts let the fuse torch blade snap shut and scrambled back out of the hole as fast as he could. Everyone watched the hole anxiously. There was nothing to see, but the sound told them volumes. A tiny sliver had been chopped clean through the hull of the ship. Above them another sound, as the membrane above the door snapped shut, sealing the room off from the street outside. Curts sat back, and took several deep breaths. This was good news. It meant the two rooms would depressurize slowly. Beside him, he watched one of the other engineers monitoring the air pressure on his terminal. He gave a thumbs up and went into the neighboring room to examine the emergency airlock they had sealed around the door there.

After five minutes, the two rooms had almost completely emptied of air. Curts tested the tether again, then set back to work with the fuse torch. He could afford to move a little more quickly now and started sawing away at the hole. Working in the deepest part, he cautiously sawed out another small chunk of the floor. He felt rather than heard the crunching sound as a little piece broke loose and fell away, rocketing through the floor and out into space. He looked down; there were stars in the floor.

Now that they didn't have to pull the chunks out of the floor by hand, he began slicing off larger pieces from the perimeter, letting them drop through the floor on their own. In short order, he had quickly expanded the perimeter of the hole until it was almost a meter in diameter. He stepped back, admiring his work. Good, but probably not good enough yet—he had calculated that they needed a hole almost twice as big to drain the air fast enough for their purposes. Confident in the work now, he began making even larger slices. The hole grew progressively wider.

While bending down to make a cut at an awkward angle, the worst feeling: movement. The ground was sliding out from under him. Leaning back, Curts screamed, as one foot completely gave way. He fell backwards, spinning around, hand flapping, desperate to gain a solid purchase on something. The blade of the fuse torch was still glowing, his hand on the trigger, refusing to let go of anything solid.

He watched in slow motion as the blade sliced through a loop of thumb-thick cable.

Everything after that was just math, as the chief engineer of the Argos suddenly found himself in a new frame of reference, one heading quite rapidly away from his last one.

Hogg lingered at the edge of the room, watching Kinsella vibrate in rage. "Can you try again? Find another way?" the mayor shouted into his terminal.

"No, we can't try another way!" Stein shrieked back, her voice audible even to Hogg. "Weren't you listening? They were ready for us! They will remain ready for us. Fuck you, you f..." She presumably went on like that, but with a tap of the finger, Kinsella ended the call.

"Bad news?" Hogg asked. Judging by the expression Kinsella directed at him, Hogg decided that he had better stop speaking for a while. Kinsella had finally felt it safe enough to come visit the forward command post and arrived a half hour earlier wearing an extremely tight, vaguely military-looking uniform. Chevrons everywhere, multiple layers of epaulets, that kind of thing. He had expected to be told that he was now the undisputed ruler of the ship. Which he wasn't. What he was—overdressed—didn't satisfy him, and he had spent the last half hour making the command post a very unpleasant place to be.

Kinsella whipped his terminal across the room, smashing it against the wall. "Yes, Hogg. It was bad news. All the way bad," he said, his voice remarkably even. "They're fucked. Those two tits managed to escape, but the rest of your team's captured. Or dead. Or whatever." Hogg's hands clenched—those were some of his friends that were now 'whatever.' Kinsella pointed a finger at him. "This is your fault somehow. You fucked me. You waited until I turned my back, and you fucked me."

"I've done nothing but try and win this fight for you."

"*Then why do you keep losing?*"

"Because you gave me an army of losers!" Hogg winced when he said it. A large number of those losers were within earshot.

Kinsella pointed at one of the losers and snapped his fingers. "Your terminal." While the young soldier fished his terminal out of his webbing, Kinsella turned back to Hogg. "Yeah, well, I gave you a lot of them." He snatched the terminal out of the hands of the young soldier and poked something into it.

"What are you doing now?" Hogg asked.

Kinsella looked up at him. "You'll see the same time everyone else sees. Because the hell I'm telling you any more of my plans in advance, *officer.*"

What an idiot. Helot felt his face flush, watching the white-faced security officer who told him about Curts. "What an idiot," Helot said, deciding to not keep the thought to himself. "Why in hell would he do that? Doesn't he know how to delegate? I mean, holy shit, Curts."

"Everything else is done, though," the security officer reported. "The charge is in place. Everything's ready to go on your order."

"On my order...," Helot repeated. He took a deep breath. It was a hell of an order to give.

His original plan had been perfect. No one had to die! The ship would have been in two before anyone even noticed. Everyone gets to live. His new plan was not perfect. People had to die. They already were dying. He really shouldn't be speeding that up, should he?

His terminal vibrated. He looked down at it, curious. Only a handful of people on the ship could contact him directly, most of whom were in this room, or recently deceased, or...

"Mayor," he said, taking the call on speaker.

"Ahh hello, Captain," Kinsella's voice slithered out of the terminal. "I'm doing quite well, thanks," he said, answering a question Helot hadn't asked. "And yourself? Awfully, I hope."

"I admit, I've had better days, Eric."

"That's a shame. Whatever's the matter?"

"You, killing people," Helot said. "That's kind of ruining my day. Is it not ruining yours?"

"This isn't going over the feeds Helot, so I'd like to take a moment to ask you to *eat my shit*. You started this, remember? Don't complain to me." A long pause. Helot gritted his teeth. *Get to the point, you asshole.* "Now then," Kinsella said, ending the foreplay. "You are open to negotiations. Correct?"

"What sort of negotiations?"

"Well, I'd suggest we start with a ceasefire. No further hostilities."

"Wasn't that how we started today? How did this begin, again?"

"Eat my shit," Kinsella suggested again, apparently running low on even token insults. "Along with the ceasefire, you will surrender, unconditionally. All further efforts to damage or separate this ship will halt immediately. In return, I promise that you, all naval and security personnel, and every civilian currently located in the aft will be left unharmed."

"That's not really negotiating, is it?"

"It is what it is. Because if you don't surrender, we will run you down. We outnumber you twenty to one. It's taking everything I have to hold them back. They hate you, Helot. I've told them some awful things about you. They'll pull your throat out and drop it at my feet as a gift."

Helot felt sad. *This was going to happen.* He hit the mute button on the terminal. "Can he do that?" he asked the security guy who seemed least afraid to speak. "Do they outnumber us twenty to one?" Seeing the slow nod, Helot closed his eyes. "Dammit." He took a deep breath and stood up straighter. He unmuted the terminal. "Kinsella, I'm going to need some time to think about this."

A lengthy pause from the other end. "Well, then I suggest you think quickly. You've got ten minutes."

The terminal went dead. A sea of faces in the control room, all watching their captain paint himself into a corner. He had become everything Kinsella said he was.

"Blow the charge."

Leroy shook himself, struggling to stay alert. For two hours he had sat, watching the back of a guy who was watching another guy fifty meters away watch him. Commander Hogg had told them to stop and watch, so that's what they were doing.

Leroy didn't know why they had stopped shooting but wasn't happy. Having a gun had actually gotten kind of boring. He hadn't even fired his yet, not this time. He had been near the back when the attack started. By the time he had gotten close enough to the front to see where bad guys might be, everyone was telling him to stop. The bad guys were shooting too much. So, he had stopped.

Moore ducked behind the counter again. Leroy could hear him there, rummaging around in the mass of tattered and dusty plastic plants that filled the florist's shop they had taken cover in. Eventually, Moore reappeared beside the counter, sitting on the floor. He extracted a meal bar from one of his pockets—the third meal bar he had eaten since they had arrived. "We're not here to eat, genius," Leroy said. Moore sneered at him but got back to his feet, leaning on the counter, mouth working on the meal bar.

"Oph scphit," he said, spraying food across the counter.

"What?" Leroy asked. Moore swallowed, and Leroy crawled over beside him, peeking over the edge of the counter. There was no one across the street anymore. "Where is he?"

"He disappeared," Moore said. "Oh, well."

Shithead. Leroy scanned the neighboring windows, looking for movement. Nothing. He raised his pistol and moved out from behind the counter. Walking closer to the window, he peered down the street to the south, just barely catching sight of a figure running around a corner. He stepped out the front door and scanned up and down the street. There were a couple of good guys in the front door of a massage parlor. But no bad guys.

Stepping back inside, he tapped his terminal. "Command, this is Leroy at Slate and 6th. I can't see any more bad guys. They ran away."

"Okay. Sit tight."

Leroy stared at the terminal for a moment, trying to decide what the most soldiery way to sit tight was. He really wanted to shoot some guys and go home. He took up a position by the doorway, practicing soldiery ways to look down the street. Nothing to see, nothing to shoot. The only sound was Moore grazing behind the counter.

A sudden rumbling to the south caused Leroy to leap back inside, falling on his ass. He lay still for a while, until his embarrassment coaxed him into action, eventually getting up and returning to the doorframe. The bulkhead doors a block south were closing. Still no sign of the enemy. More rumbling, closer by. He took a deep breath and broke cover, jogging to the corner, where he could see down the street to the west. Another bulkhead door closing. He ran back inside. "Command,

Leroy again. I've got bulkhead doors closing to my...." He was interrupted by an explosion to the south.

Again, he threw himself backwards into the store, landing ass first,
less embarrassed this time. He sat there for a moment, hearing no other
explosions or gunfire or really anything at all, until Moore started eating
again. Leroy clambered to his knees and returned to the door, looking
outside carefully. *There.* Down the street, the door of an apartment was
bulging out, just this side of the bulkhead door that had closed. Leroy
held his breath and listened. A strange noise could be heard coming
from that direction.

"Command, we just had an explosion down here. Still no sign of bad
guys. Orders?"

"Hold position for now, Leroy."

For thirty seconds, then a minute, he stood in the doorway, listening
to the sound. It didn't get louder, but he definitely wasn't imagining it.
Beyond that, nothing seemed to be happening at all. It had suddenly become, of all fucking things, boring again. He made a decision. "Hey, food-
bag. Cover me. I'm going to go have a look."

Moore swallowed and nodded, moving over to the door himself. Leroy
set out walking as quietly as possible, swinging his pistol left and right as he
crossed the intersection, imagining how much like a soldier he looked. Still
no one to be seen on the streets. He slowed down as he approached the broken door. It was bulging out from the center, like it had been punched by an
angry giant. One of the corners had come loose. The wall on one entire side
of the doorframe was run through with cracks, and he could see chunks of
the wall lying on the floor. The sound grew louder as he got closer, some
kind of whistling. He stopped, directly across the street from the door and
tried to decide what to do next.

He felt a breeze.

Light breezes and gusts could be felt in the garden well, for reasons
Leroy had never cared to learn, but they weren't common in the lower
decks. There was something important about that, he decided. *I should definitely tell someone about this.* Having made that decision, Leroy turned away
from the twisted door.

Before he could move more than a couple steps, the door frame im-
ploded, taking the door and half the wall with it. Leroy was yanked off his
feet, tumbling backwards towards the opening, twisting around as he fell,
barely catching a glimpse of the room beyond. The entire floor of the
room was gone, replaced with a huge gaping hole the size of the whole
universe. Leroy screamed, but the sound didn't travel far. He was spared
the indignity of being the second involuntary astronaut in Argosian history

when he cracked his head on the edge of the hole, dying instantly. The void vacuumed up the mess without complaint.

Hogg gaped helplessly as the bulkhead doors crept across the street. They had heard the rumbling as well, the entire command center running into the street. It was a wide street, and the door was taking its time, many of them dashing across the threshold to the presumed safety of the north, others dashing across the threshold to the presumed safety of the south.

Kinsella didn't hesitate; he went north. "Not you," he said, stopping, pointing at Hogg. "You win me this war."

"Sir, I think something really nasty is about to..."

"Hogg," Kinsella said calmly. "I order you to win me this war. You take your little soldiers, and you shoot Helot until he stops being nasty."

Hogg stared helplessly as both sides of the door rumbled closer together. "Sir, this is bad. You can't."

"Hogg, I order you to win this war."

"Ohhhhh kaaaaaay," Hogg said, not really sure why. The doors met in front of him with a thundering sound.

Linze had stuck with him and looked skeptically at him. "Now what?" she asked.

Hogg wasn't sure what the answer to that was or if he would have much of a say in it. He returned to the command post to find one of the communications officers waiting for him. "We're getting reports from all over. Bulkhead doors are closing on all sides. In the escalators, too. All visible security troops have retreated." Hogg tried to visualize this. Helot was boxing them in. Containing them. That wasn't so bad. They would get to sit this out for a bit.

"He's cutting off our ways of escape," Linze said behind him. Hogg hadn't considered that interpretation. He didn't like it as much as his own.

"Okay, order everyone to hold positions for now," Hogg said. The communications officer nodded and ran back to the dining room.

Hogg's peace didn't last long. "Sir, there's been an explosion near 6th and Slate!" the communications officer shouted a moment later. "Still no signs of enemy movement." Hogg crossed the room to lean over the map. That was in the southeast corner of their perimeter. Far from where the main bulk of the security troops were. "Who saw the explosion? Put it on the speakers," Hogg asked.

A panicked voice shrieked out over the desk speakers. "Holy crap! He's gone! Leroy is gone! He got sucked through the hole! He got fucking sucked through the hole! Command? This is Moore! Leroy just got sucked through the hole! Oh, shit."

Hogg mashed his hand down on the transmit button. "What hole? Soldier! What are you talking about?"

"The air is moving! The air is moving! It's wind!" came the confused response.

Hogg stared at the screen for a few seconds, the gears spinning. His heart stopped. *Oh, no, they wouldn't. Oh, holy shit.* He strained to think of something to say, an order to give, but he couldn't. He felt like he was choking.

"They trapped us in here and are sucking out all the air," the communications officer said slowly, vocalizing the problem Hogg couldn't.

Hogg's brain snapped back into motion. "Order all troops to fall back to the 9th and Africa blast doors. We've got to open them now!" He ran outside to the bulkhead door, furiously pounding on the control panel. Soldiers streamed into the street behind him, masses of them. They stopped at the door, leaving space for him as he beat on the workshy controls. *Where was Stein? She'd know how to open these things.* He gave up and turned around, looking at the expectant faces staring back at him.

His heart sank as he realized what he had done. *They were all going to be trapped out in the street.*

Somewhere in the crowd, Linze's voice, shouting orders. "They're sucking the air out of the streets! Everyone get inside! Take cover indoors right now! Get inside! Now dammit!"

Mayhem. Not prone to good behavior at the best of times, the Loyalist forces stampeded away from the doors, trampling over the ones too far away to hear Linze's advice. Linze fought her way to Hogg's side, grabbed him by the arm, and led him back into the command post. Hogg let himself get placed in a chair, and watched as his second in command took over, doing what he couldn't.

The image on the screen shifted and moved. It was a face. Yes. She could tell it was a face. But whose face? Whoever it belonged to, they were saying something. But there was no sound. There was something wrong with the terminal. Where had the sound gone?

Ellen had known something was up before almost everyone else, having watched the security officers retreat from her vantage point. When the bulkhead doors closed, she was already on her way out, taking the stairs of the apartment two at a time, banging the heavy smart rifle against the walls as she descended, finally dashing out into the street. She wasn't the only one with that idea, finding herself surrounded by panicked soldiers outside, making their way to the Africa Street bulkhead door, too late. There they watched Hogg and his saucer-eyes pound on it helplessly.

"Get inside." Ellen had been close enough to hear Hogg's lieutenant and managed to avoid being trampled in the resulting stampede, though she did drop the smart rifle in the crush, not caring. She returned to the apartment she had been shooting from, two soldiers on her heels, thinking she looked like she knew what she was doing. Inside, she had sprinted upstairs, bypassing the sitting room with its shattered windows, and slammed face first into the bedroom door. It was locked. She pounded at the door controls hopelessly. The door had locked automatically when the outside air pressure dropped past a certain point. She was too late.

The other soldiers had fled, leaving her alone, sitting on the floor. A short and awful terminal conversation with her husband had followed. Panic in his voice, calmness in hers.

That's who the face belonged to! It was Griese. She knew him. He was her husband. He was shouting something at her, but she couldn't hear what. Something wrong with the sound. She closed her eyes and tried to focus on her breathing. In through the nose. Hold. Hold. Hoooooooooold. Out through the nose. Hold. Hold.

It was exhausting work, and she soon fell asleep from the effort.

Outside the bulkhead door, the mayor was a shrieking mess, stamping his feet like a child. "What do you mean you can't open it?" he shouted.

Stein hauled back and slapped him. It was the fourth time he had asked it, and a hand upside the face was the only response she hadn't tried yet. "There is a vacuum on the other side!" she said, repeating responses one through three again to see if they would sink in this time. She pointed at the flashing red light on the control panel that read, 'Vacuum.' She tapped at it just to be sure he was looking at it. "The safety interlocks won't let us open the door."

Kinsella's voice rose several octaves. "Well, then disable them! Or blast through it somehow!"

"And what, then? Do you know what a vacuum is? We open that door, and all the air in the rest of the ship gets sucked out through that hole in there. It will kill us all."

"Well, then figure something out! I'm the only one here coming up with solutions!"

A closed hand slap was the only solution she could immediately think of, but Stein exhaled slowly, controlling herself. No need to push her luck too far; it was already a small miracle that she and Bruce had slipped the trap themselves. At some point during their escape from the upper-decks she had reopened the wound on her shoulder, and after making it back to the first floor and sprinting across the street to safety,

Bruce had taken her to the field hospital that had been set up a few blocks north of the initial attack. It was here, while getting a fresh healing wrap set around her arm that they'd heard the rumbling noise of the closing bulkhead door.

"We're working on something. Just give us some time," she told Kinsella, stepping away from the horrible man before he could say something else. She crossed the street to where Bruce and Griese were standing. "So?" she asked. "We are working on something, right?"

Bruce stared at her blankly. "I've sort of roughed out an idea for a makeshift airlock. But we'd need a bunch of tools we don't have. And it would probably kill whoever went through. And everyone else on the other side. And over here." He glanced at Griese, whose eyes were red and raw. "So, no."

A crowd of soldiers gathered around the bulkhead door, no less helpless and dumbstruck. One of the medics—a conscripted doctor—had been fending off questions from the mayor, asking how long people could survive in those rooms before the air became too stale to breathe. The doctor could only guess. Anywhere between four and forty-eight hours. Depended on the size of the room, how many people were in it, how much they were breathing. Outside one of the rooms? The doctor looked like he was about to laugh, before he caught himself.

"Even if we could get on the other side, getting—what, 4000 people—all out through an airlock would take days," Stein said.

"We don't need to get them all out." Griese said.

Stein looked at her shoes. "Yeah. No, you're right. Good point." She chose not to say what she was actually thinking. *If Ellen wasn't inside...*

Bruce's face lit up. "Where was the hole, again?" He looked at the map that they had pieced together from Hogg, who was safe inside for the time being, busy sending them information. "What if we close these two doors here?" Bruce asked. "Isolate the area where the hole is. Then we could open this door," he waved at the bulkhead door beside them, "and re-pressurize the whole area."

Stein was careful to keep an even expression on her face, not wanting to shoot his idea down. "Okay. But we can't do that remotely. We'd still need to get in there somehow."

"No, we wouldn't."

The maintenance robot trundled down the vents and stopped just in front of the closed duct membrane. It extended a manipulator arm against the duct wall to brace itself, then used its plasma cutter to carefully poke a hole in the membrane. A hiss announced the loss of atmosphere, and air rushed past the robot and out through the incision. Somewhere upstream, another membrane closed shut, limiting the total loss of air. After a couple of minutes, the sound of the rushing gas had quieted down to a small hiss, and the robot resumed its work, cutting a hole large enough for it to pass through.

A few minutes later, the robot dropped through the ceiling above Africa, landing in the center of the street. The robot turned and scurried south, making its way to the area where they had figured the hole in the hull was. Atypically, it chose to travel in the center of the street, its collision detection system noticing several obstructions piled up on the edges of the street, around the sealed entrances to rooms.

"Are those bodies?"

"Yeah." Bruce said. "Jesus."

After a few minutes, the robot reached its destination. A non-descript stretch of street that happened to contain a set of bulkhead doors—the first of two sets that needed to be closed to isolate the hole in the hull. The robot climbed up the wall to the control panel. Reaching out, it activated the panel, paused, and then pressed the button that would close the door. Its sensor pivoted to watch the door slowly slide shut.

"That was easy," Bruce said, watching the door on his terminal.

"Yeah. Huh," Stein said.

"Why did that door just close?" Helot asked. He had been watching the area in vacuum ever since the attack. Othersiders trapped in the streets, banging on doors, clutching their throats. He had made himself watch. He was trying not to think about how little he felt. He was pretty confident he should feel a lot worse than he did.

Manipulating the controls on his display, he zoomed in on the door and scanned around the nearby street, eventually spotting the answer to his question.

The maintenance robot traveled the short distance to the second bulkhead door. Lying across the plane where the door would slide shut was a body. After a few seconds of consideration, the robot cautiously moved forward, grabbing the dead soldier by the collar. Slowly the robot reversed, trying to drag the body out of the way. But as the corpse started to move, the collar gave way, torn apart by the manipulator. Another few seconds passed while the robot reevaluated the obstacle. Eventually, it backed up a short distance, reversing in a curved line until it faced the body squarely. It then charged forward, slamming into the corpse. The friction holding the body in place gave way, and the robot and body slowly slid past the door.

Helot fumed at Curts' idiocy. He would probably know how to disable the robot remotely, if he wasn't off in fucking space somewhere.

He watched the robot and its pallbearing learning curve. Beside him, one of the security officers said, "I've got an idea." Helot looked at him, vowing to learn his name the next time someone casually mentioned it. The officer moved over to a different panel and found the right set of controls. "Now, this will require some timing."

The robot had mounted the wall beneath the control panel and slowly reached out to press the button. The bulkhead door slowly started to close. The robot retreated to the floor and backed up to watch the door slip into place. Its sensor rotated around to view the first door it had activated, just visible behind the edge of a building corner. The door had opened again.

"What?" Bruce and Stein said in unison.

The robot returned to the original door, climbed up, and shut it again, watching it close carefully. The door slid into place, and the robot climbed down, taking a minute to inspect the door's perimeter to ensure it stayed shut. It did. The robot turned to look at the second door.

"Oh, son of a bitch!"

"They're fucking with us," Stein said, looking at the second door, now opened again. "We should have done this the right way from the start."

"Hehehehehehehe," Helot said. "Dummies." He looked at the other people in the room, who stared back, blankly. It occurred to Helot that he was laughing at a desperate attempt to save people's lives. His smile evaporated. Turning back to the screen, he said, "They're going to figure it out soon. How long until your guy is ready?"

"He's ready now."

The robot pried off the access panel underneath the controls and delicately extended its plasma cutter. With a short, sharp burst, it severed the link between the door mechanism and the controls, locking the door in the closed position. It descended the wall and made its way over to the second door for the final time. There, it climbed the wall, pried off the access panel, and exploded.

An e-suit-clad figure, rifle held somewhat awkwardly at its hip, walked over and kicked the remnants of the robot. Another shot into its guts. Satisfied, the figure retreated around the corner, entering the room with the puncture. He carefully sidestepped the hole into the rest of the universe, and made his way to the temporary airlock installed in the neighboring room.

Bruce smashed the terminal on the ground. "Why is nothing easy? Why does everything have to be so fucking hard?"

Stein stared at the largest piece of the terminal, which had come to rest on her foot. They had lost contact with the maintenance robot and had spent the past five minutes trying to reconnect. "I don't get it," she said.

"They blew it up," Bruce said, balling his hands into fists.

"How?"

"I don't know. Wizard magic? But robots don't just drop offline like that. I've never seen that happen."

Stein pulled out her own terminal. "So, it's not worth sending in another robot to try again?"

"What's the point? They'd just break that, too. Besides, it'd take hours to get one into position."

Stein cocked her head at him. "Well, what else are we doing?" She stared at Bruce desperately, mainly so she didn't have to look at Griese, whose gaze she could feel on the back of her head. A chirp from her terminal, from everyone's terminal. She looked down to see an incoming message from Helot. A fraction of a second later, Helot's voice erupted through the ship's PA system.

"Attention, Argos. This is Captain James Edward Helot. Recently, a large group of armed men and women attacked and killed several security officers stationed on the anti-terrorism perimeter. These attacks, these *murders*, are appalling. They cannot go unpunished."

The captain paused, his last words echoing slightly in the streets. "Our remaining security forces moved quickly to apprehend the villains responsible for these crimes. In an attempt to escape, these attackers caused an explosive decompression to occur in the aft of the ship. This accident has left many of them trapped, in imminent danger of suffocation and death. I'm inclined to think it's a fitting end.

"However, these men and women can be saved. But not by the man behind this attack: Eric Kinsella. If it was up to him, these men and women would die. Only I can save them."

"Crap," Stein said, seeing where this was going.

"And I will save them. But before I do, Kinsella must put a stop to all hostilities. No more attacks on security officers will be tolerated. Any and all weapons must be surrendered.

"To the citizens of the Argos: the reason I am showing you such mercy following these unprovoked assaults is because I know that these men and women have been lied to and misled. The true criminals are the ones who organized this attack, the ones who tricked you and sent hundreds of people to their deaths. As I have said many times before, the stories told to you have been lies. And these lies have gotten your husbands and wives, sons and daughters, trapped, and about to die.

"To Eric Kinsella: if you surrender immediately, your people will be rescued. They will be held in detention until order is restored but will not be harmed or prosecuted. They will live." Helot waited a beat before delivering the kicker. "Or you can ignore me, and leave your people to die."

The PA system clicked off. Stein, as well as everyone else present, turned to look at the mayor. Kinsella stared straight ahead, wide-eyed, face covered in sweat. Beside him, one of his bodyguards was speaking urgently into his terminal. He abruptly grabbed the mayor around the shoulders, and hurried him off to the north.

"Wait, what?" Griese said, watching the mayor's retreat. "Is he going to surrender or not?"

"I would probably say so," Stein said. "He's a dead man if he doesn't."

"He might be a dead man either way," Bruce said.

"So, Ellen will be okay?" Griese asked aloud.

Stein looked at Griese. She held his gaze for a moment, still unable to say it. A moment passed, and then she didn't have to; Griese collapsed to the ground, his body wracked with sobs. She looked away, numb.

Hogg felt sticky. It was too sweaty in there. *This is no way to die. Gross and sticky.* He levered himself up to a sitting position, with his back to the wall. Too much sweat, too many people: there were twenty-seven soldiers in the apartment. That made sense: it was one of the closest rooms to the bulkhead door. Of course it was going to fill up with people, sucking up all the air, dooming each other. Linze should have known better. She should have picked somewhere else to hide. But Hogg knew that was being unfair. Linze had acted, he hadn't. Someone, hopefully, somewhere, will have survived thanks to Linze's quick thinking. Just not here.

He supposed there was still a chance they would be rescued. Kinsella had surrendered. That had gotten everyone excited, again using too much of their precious oxygen. And Helot had said rescuers were coming. But

Hogg knew it would be a slow process reclaiming the ship from vacuum. And he doubted Helot's rescuers were going to work that fast.

He thought back on his time as Supreme Commander. How had he gotten here? He had done everything he had been told, as well as he could, better than most others. There was something deeply, profoundly unfair about how this had played out. It bothered him, like an itch he couldn't quite reach. He had done everything he had been told. Why wasn't that enough? It was frustrating and infuriating and exhausting to think about. So exhausting.

He closed his eyes and went to sleep.

Previously

The fabrication engine rumbled and hummed, making the floor vibrate, a thin layer of dust dancing in time. The pitch of the hum grew higher and fainter, past the limit of Harold's hearing. Then it changed, slowing, winding down, as the engine slowed to a stop. The light on the display panel flickered yellow, then green. On the far side of the machine, a mechanical noise, and a thin plastic sheet slid out into a bin. Harold picked it up and examined it.

Andy's Retro 40th Birthday Party
Everyone wear your wackiest, Earthiest clothes.
Ice Cream!

"Is that as fast as it goes?" he asked.

Martin walked over to the machine and entered something on the control panel. "Yeah. About thirty seconds per iteration for this template. Hard part's done now—the machine will keep spitting 'em out. You said you wanted fifty?"

Harold nodded. "Can we use the other machines?" Fourteen other identical fabrication engines sat idle, scattered across the floor of the fabrication plant.

Martin looked around. "Could. What's the hurry?" He activated the program, starting the machine up again.

Harold didn't want to push the point. "So, about half an hour, then?"

"Your math's better than mine, Doc." Martin looked over Harold's shoulder to the office on the upper-level of the fabrication shop. "Come on. We'll take a load off." He walked up the staircase set on one side of the room. Harold took one last lingering look at the fabrication engines, then followed Martin upstairs.

Inside the cramped office, they sat down on a pair of bruised and battered chairs, Martin putting his feet up on the desk. It looked like a familiar position for him. "Thanks again for helping with this," Harold said.

"No problem. I've never made anything like this. It's a real crazy idea."

Harold snorted. "Yeah. You're a regular Gutenberg."

"Thanks." A pause. "A what?"

Harold didn't answer, looking around, examining the office. "Hey, what's that?" he asked, pointing over Martin's shoulder.

Martin turned to look at the uninteresting chunk of wall Harold was pointing at, then recoiled, clutching his neck where Harold had just slapped it. "What the heeehhhhh..." he said, before falling to the floor, unconscious.

"Sorry, Martin," Harold said, bending down to check the anaesthetizing patch he had slapped on Martin's neck. He checked his pulse—still there. Finally, he straightened out his friend's limbs and stood up. "But it turns out I'm kind of a maniac."

Harold left the office and descended back to the main floor, where he shut off production of the party fliers. Repeating the steps Martin had just showed him, he created a nearly identical template with a different, far more politically explosive message printed on it. There was a lot of material to cover, and he had had to size the text quite small to get all of his points across. He hoped it didn't come out too crazy. He turned on the fabrication engine and waited anxiously for the first one to emerge. It looked pretty good—not that crazy at all. Setting the machine to repeat the process, Harold then made a lap of the fabrication plant, programming the rest of the engines to do the same. The room hummed and throbbed as his screeds streamed into the hoppers.

Harold did some quick math. The patch on Martin's neck was good for about an hour, which meant he could get over a thousand of these done before he woke up. He looked at the bag he had with him, wondering if a thousand leaflets would fit in the thing. He had no idea how much room they would take up or how much they would weigh. He was sure it would be fine. He felt really sure, in fact, surer and calmer than he had in a while. He guessed it was because, one way or another, it was all coming to an end. The story would get out. It was the end of a work week—the bars and garden well parks would be crowded with people, all of them certainly eager to read something as novel as a flyer. And once they knew, well, security couldn't kill them all, could they?

Even if that was, ultimately, their plan.

His backup plan was also, for now, completely undetected; no one had said a peep to him about his work on the tinkering engine. If everything went right, if his flyers exposed the plot and he emerged a hero, no one would ever even know about it. He would quietly remove the patch from the tinkerers, leaving no one the wiser. He felt a little annoyed by that; it was amongst the most brilliant things he had ever done. But still, *morals*.

He was about halfway through the print run when the doors of the fabrication shop opened, three security officers sliding into the room, pistols drawn.

"Hands up, asshole!"

"Put your hands up, asshole!"

"Hey! Hey! Asshole! Asshole! Hey! Asshole!"

Harold watched all this happen without moving. His stomach sank; he knew there was no point in resisting. He was shoved to the ground, a knee pressed into his back, binders slammed around his wrists. He wheezed and sputtered, struggling to breathe with the officer's weight on him.

A familiar voice. "Let him up." Harold was grabbed roughly by the arms and pulled to his feet, to see Chief Hatchens standing in front of him. "Hello, Doc. What *are* you doing here?"

Harold resisted the urge to look at the drifts of incriminating evidence scattered around the room. "Friend's having a birthday party," he offered, nodding at the small pile of flyers that wouldn't get him killed.

"Uh-huh." Hatchens inspected one of the birthday leaflets. "Sounds like fun. Although," he added, looking thoughtful, "I wonder if people will be in the mood for a party with all these horrible murderous conspiracies that have been going around lately." He set down the birthday flyer and picked up one of the others, fresh from the machine. "You're going to tell me these were here when you got here, right?"

Harold ignored him. "You were monitoring the fabrication engines."

"That's right." Hatchens smiled. "Not for this of course—this was actually quite creative of you. No, just for regular old fashioned contraband." The smile left his face. "So, let me see if I can piece this together. Somehow your boy Kevin passed you a message. Is that right? You don't have to answer; that part's obvious. We found a copy of it on that poor reporter. He said he found it in a men's room. That was you who did that? Also pretty creative of you—though maybe a bit cowardly. Wouldn't you say?"

Before Harold could reply, he was interrupted by a noise from above. He looked up to see two of the officers dragging Martin's still unconscious body out of the upstairs office. "Who's that?" Hatchens asked.

"He didn't have anything to do with this," Harold said, voice tight. "I knocked him out before I started."

"Did you?" Hatchens asked. He watched the officers deposit Martin on the floor, then bent down to inspect the patch on his neck. "Yes, I suspect you did." He stood up, turning back to face Harold. "The problem with that though, Doctor, is that if I'm wrong, if you're lying to me, then this nonsense will keep going on. He'll tell his friend, who'll tell his friend, and they'll all have to die. It's an awful big risk. You can see my problem." He looked away from Harold and tilted his head back and forth, deciding something. Finally, Hatchens bent down, rolled Martin over on to his front, withdrew a knife from his boot, and thrust it into Martin's back.

An unearthly moan slipped from Harold's lips as he sank to the floor. He wanted to cry, knew he had to cry, felt the misery course through him. But the tears weren't there. He could only stare and shake.

"You see what's happening here, don't you, Doctor? Everyone who finds out about this has to die. *Has to.* We can't have it any other way." Hatchens peeled the patch off Martin's neck and pocketed it, then stood up and pulled his pistol from his holster. "See this, Doctor? Looks just like all the other pistols we have, doesn't it? Works just like them, too." He smiled. "Essentially. Sometimes it hits a bit harder, I guess. Doesn't stun very effectively. Or is it too effectively?" Another smile. "You get me? Now, tell me about this evidence you have. How many copies are there? Where have you put them? Because if someone else stumbles upon it, they will die. And don't start squawking to me about that not being right. *I know it's not right.* It's not fair, and it's not just, either. But it will happen. And only you can stop it. *If you tell me what I need to know.*"

Harold moaned. He had been sure he was ready to die for this. He had told himself he could do it, that it was important enough to die for. That he had nothing left to live for with Kevin gone. But he had been wrong. Here on the floor, snot running out of his nose, he knew how brave he actually was. "Please don't kill me," he whispered, his voice barely audible.

Hatchens strained to hear him, or at least pretended to. But he seemed to get the message. He swallowed. "Because of your particular skills, we might be able to do something about that. Your recent work has done you much credit. But you have to tell me everything. Okay?"

Harold nodded eagerly, gasping, snot everywhere. "Of course."

"Where is the evidence? Every copy of it."

Harold sniffed. "A dummy terminal in my office. Hollow shelf in the cabinet." He snorted, more snot pouring from his face. "That's it. That's the only copy."

"That's it?"

Harold nodded. The tears were coming now.

"Could be lying," one of the other officers said.

Hatchens tilted his head, looking at Harold on an angle. "Could be. I don't think so, though. And don't look at me like that. We're not going to torture the man."

Harold looked up, face soaked. "Thank you. I swear it's the only copy. I swear."

Hatchens smiled. "Okay. I believe you." He pointed his pistol at Harold. "Still going to have to do this, though."

"But you..."

"Of course I said that. But we've got kind of a thing going here— need to frame you for stabbing that poor guy. Sorry, Doc." Hatchens smiled weakly, genuine sympathy on his face. The muzzle of the pistol flashed.

10

Outside the Box

Millions of stars drifted past the window, Stein hating every one in turn. She slumped forward on the bench, elbows on knees, chin resting in hands. Beside her, Bruce listed a bit to the right, insulting a number of different objects and persons, aided in this task by the large amount of purple liquor he had just consumed. On her other side, Griese, sober, quieter than normal, his arm resting on a small can in his lap.

It had been a week since the disaster in the aft. Kinsella hadn't taken long to fold, surrendering completely within minutes of the ultimatum, presumably right after he had found a place to hide. True to his word, Helot had immediately sent his rescuers in to save Kinsella's trapped soldiers. He had even been kind enough to provide footage of this to the news feeds. The images were humiliating, stern and competent security officers caring for the gasping amateurs. It was enough to make Stein ashamed, which was clearly the point. Everyone watching would come to the same conclusion—fighting Helot was hopeless. When they played the footage of the security forces retrieving Hogg's body—the feeds stressing his rank as "Supreme Commander"—she had flipped off her terminal, eyes choked with tears.

Ellen's body had been turned over a few days after that. That was lucky—Stein imagined security would have been reluctant to hand over anyone found near the smart rifle. Griese had gone to the hospital alone, firmly turning down Stein and Bruce's offers of support, returning a few hours later with the small can in his possession. In the days since, he hadn't said more than a dozen words.

An extremely conspicuous man walked in front of them, eclipsing the stars with his passage. His eyes were fixed firmly forward, almost deliberately not looking at them. Which didn't seem very likely; Bruce alone was in fine form, as worthy of attention as anything on the ship. Stein was immediately suspicious of the man and only grew more so when he sat down a couple of benches over, again pointedly not looking at them. Other than him, the lounge was completely empty. Most Argosians seemed a bit shy of the big windows since the vacuum disaster; the picture of the kid who had gone missing had been on the feeds more or less permanently the past few days. Stein looked out the window and shuddered.

A few seconds later, Stein heard more people arriving behind her. She turned to see two more figures entering the bow lounge, the larger of them a near twin of the conspicuous man who had first arrived. The smaller one was a woman with an awful haircut, ragged brown locks hanging over her face. The odd couple dropped down to the same tier of benches Stein and her friends were on, then turned, coming directly at them. A tense moment before Stein recognized the woman.

"Ms. Stein," the mayor said from behind another one of his disguises. He parted the hair of his wig so he could see them. Stein realized he had it on backwards.

"Mayor. I thought you'd be torn to small pieces by now." She watched him for a moment, not getting any reaction, then for the sake of politeness added, "Glad to see I was wrong."

Kinsella let half of his hair drop over his face and held up a hand in a gesture of resignation. "That's politics for you. Always ups and downs."

"Uh-huh. Like messing up a reverse-coup? How are you not in prison right now, anyways?"

The mayor swept the hair back out of his face. "Oh, I really should be. I think it was part of the deal. I guess I'm reneging on that bit."

"That sounds about right," she said. Beside her, Bruce made noises that indicated he was having trouble figuring out who she was talking to. Griese, still mute, tensed beside her. He may have guessed the same thing as Stein. "You're going to do it again, aren't you," she stated.

"Wouldn't you?"

"How many people did you get killed the last time?"

"I didn't count. And I also didn't kill them, don't forget. That was the other guy." He turned around to face the window, hands clenched behind his back. "It was a good idea, really. I just didn't go far enough. Not like what you did."

"What did I do?"

"It took me awhile to figure out. It was brash wasn't it?"

"What?"

"The brash. You goosed up those rioters with brash."

"I don't know what you're talking about."

"He's talking about the time when I rescued you," Bruce said. He hiccoughed, which seemed to startle to him.

"When I rescued you, you mean."

"That, too. There was a riot going on at the time. That I made." Another hiccough.

A lot of that escape was a blur to Stein, her time spent lying around in the hospital afterwards having eclipsed the finer points of her flight. "And you drugged them up. Of course you did."

Kinsella nodded. "I can't believe I never considered it myself. Clean living, I guess." He smiled. "Maybe I just assumed people would love their mayor enough to go get shot up for me."

"You weren't completely wrong," Stein pointed out. "That was a pretty big mob you formed at one point. Though I guess that's over now, wigboy." Kinsella's smile spread wider, and he waggled his head back and forth, looking coy. "No," Stein said. "There's no way you've got volunteers willing to help you anymore. Brash or not, there's no way anyone's going to take a pill from you."

"The way to their hearts...," he said, smiling broadly, waiting for her to finish the sentence. She stared back at him, her face blank, not wanting to give him the satisfaction. His face sank. "It's through their stomachs. You haven't heard that before?"

Bruce patted his belly earnestly. On her other side, Griese let out a disgusted sound. "You're going to taint their food?" she asked. Not needing him to confirm any more than his twinkling eyes already did, she turned away, looking back out the window. "You know how pointless that is? Because security's going to *blow away* anyone that comes near them, brashed up or not."

"Ehh," Kinsella said. "I'll get a few close. There will be a lot of them. And they only have to get close." Kinsella fished inside a fold of his dress and pulled out a small, flattish lump, which he tossed to Stein.

"What's this?" Stein said, recognizing it a second later. "Explosives?"

"Keep it. I've got like four hundred of them."

"You're going to send suicide bombers at Helot? That's insane."

"It sounds all right to me," Griese said. The conversation slid to a stop, everyone turning to stare at him.

"What's his problem?" Kinsella finally asked.

"What?" Stein said. "He's agreeing with your plan."

"Yeah. But my plan is obviously messed up. Why's he so keen on it?"

"His wife's dead."

"Oh." Kinsella bit his lip, looking abashed. "Man, what do you say to that?"

Stein just stared at the cretin. "Anything but that," she finally said. Griese looked down at the ground, removing himself from the conversation again.

"And they're not suicide bombers. I'm going to tell them to throw the things," Kinsella explained. "I'm not crazy."

"You're touting your plan to give four hundred explosive charges to people you've drugged as proof of your sanity?" Stein's eyes widened. "*Of course you are.* Why wouldn't you? What the fuck does anyone on this ship know about sanity?"

Kinsella pursed his lips, waiting for her to calm down. "Would you like to know why..."

"*Why you've come to tell me all this?* Yes. Obviously. Fuck. Of course I want to know."

"I could use your help."

"*Fuck no.*"

"You haven't heard me..."

"*Fuck no.*"

"...out." Kinsella rubbed his face. "You understand what's at stake here better than anyone. You said it yourself: if we don't stop Helot, we all freeze to death."

Stein glared at him. "And how many people freeze to death if we do stop him?" He blinked, seemed ready to protest, then stopped, looking at Stein appraisingly. "The same number?" she said. "Just a different selection?"

"Very observant, Ms. Stein."

She slumped forward onto her elbows. "You don't want to stop Helot. You want to replace him."

Kinsella took a deep breath and turned away, looking out the window. She got the impression he didn't even like admitting it to himself. "Helot's right, you know," he said. "We can't stop the whole ship. Not enough fuel, apparently. Not everyone gets to go." He looked at Stein and shrugged. "So, on the one hand, good for him! Taking the initiative like this, making the tough choices. But why does he get to pick? Why not me? So yeah, I'm going to do the same myself. Put my people in the core. Be stupid not to. And if you help..."

"I become 'your people.'"

"That's right." He gestured at the window, waving his arm. "Whichever one of those is Tau Prius. You help me, and then you, Mopey, and Surly here get to go."

"We're grateful," Stein said. Surprisingly, it sounded more sincere than she intended. "How about your army? Do they get to go?"

Kinsella's gaze narrowed. "Don't pretend you're that stupid." Perhaps sensing he was about to be struck—correctly—he frowned and changed the subject. "You'd have to do even less this time," he said. "Just show my people the easiest way into the core. They'll do all the work."

"There is no way. The way we used was exposed to space, may still be in space, and if not, is crawling with security officers. Who, if they catch us, *will throw us in space.*"

"Well, find another way. You know the ship better than anyone. Get my people to the core with a minimum of bomb-throwing."

"To do what exactly?" She knew exactly what was going to happen, but wanted to hear him say it, or see just how good he was at lying to himself.

Kinsella stared her down. "To kill Helot. And anyone standing near Helot. What did you think this was about?" His expression softened a bit. "We can do it with or without you. But I think we've got a better chance with you. And, seeing as you're so fucking concerned about these morons, consider this: a small, targeted attack will be a lot less costly than a pitched battle. You don't want those maniacs' lives on your conscience, surely."

"Like you do?"

Kinsella tilted his head to the side. "Don't worry about me. My conscience is incredibly robust."

She shivered and turned away. "And if I say no? Will one of your maniacs run up, hug me, and explode?"

Kinsella blinked. "I hadn't even thought of threatening you. Hell, I thought you'd want to help out just to save your own shitty fucking lives. But shit, if that works, *yeah.*" He held up his hands. "Boomhugs all around if you say no."

He let that hang in the air for a moment. "You say you're going to kill Helot?" Griese said, latching on to his new favorite conversational topic.

"Absolutely, I will," Kinsella said.

"When do you need us ready?" Griese said, speaking two consecutive sentences for the first time in days.

Kinsella looked at Griese appraisingly. "Tomorrow. Let's say high noon, like a cowboy fight." He glanced back and forth between Stein and Griese, not needing Griese's help at all and not completely convinced he had the pull to commit Stein to anything.

And Stein definitely wasn't going to commit to anything. But she also had no problem lying, if only to buy some time. "Okay," she said. "We'll help."

"Great!" Kinsella said. He stepped back and reset his wig over his face. His bodyguards moved closer, bracketing him. "I've got a lot of things to get organized, so I'll leave you to it." Another oily smile, one last adjustment of the wig. "We'll be in touch." Then he turned and left.

"Who was that?" Bruce asked, head turned to watch him leave, body pitching dangerously forward. "Was that...was that Stein?"

"Right here, Bruce," Stein said.

"Oh." Bruce said, looking at her in surprise. "I knew it was you the whole time."

"Kay." She turned to her other friend. "Kinsella had a point there, Griese. What *is* your problem? You're not committing suicide on us, buddy."

"I know," Griese replied, convincing no one. "I don't want to die. I just want to kill a guy is all."

She wrapped her arms around him, forehead pressed to his cheek. "I know, buddy. Me, too. But not if a bunch of drugged-up patsies also have to die in the process."

Still hugging Griese, she turned to look out the window, watching the loathsome stars, tracing their paths as they rotated past the window, oblivious to her and her perfectly rational hatred of them. She frowned, just noticing something. The sun was missing. Whatever axis the ship was rotating around now, it wasn't aligned with their sun. The escape of air out the aft must have knocked the ship off axis; it was probably flipping around end to end, just slow enough for there to be no detectable difference in the gravity. Only someone looking for the pole star would notice, when they saw it wasn't there anymore.

"I just don't see a way to do it," she said.

A belch from Stein's right. She turned to berate her friend for ruining her moment of despair, but before she could, Bruce said, "We could try the plan again. Sneak in to the reactor. Cripple it. Blackmail a guy." He made a complicated gesture which was evidently supposed to communicate the idea of blackmailing. "Etcetera..." Stein looked at him suspiciously, wondering how much of his drunkenness was feigned. "Kinsella won't need to send any maniacs to die then," he pointed out.

Griese shifted away from Stein. "That plan doesn't sound like it lets us kill a guy." Stein watched him fidget with the can in his lap. It was good to see Griese so lively again, even if the only thing he had expressed any interest in was murder-suicide.

Bruce put a finger to his mouth, lips pursed. "We could get Helot to stand on the reactor first, then blow it up."

Stein enjoyed visualizing that for a moment. "Okay. But the impossible bit still remains impossible. They know about every way we've found to sneak back there. And they're apparently shooting to kill now. We can't get anywhere close to the reactor."

Bruce burped again, then looked extremely satisfied with himself. "What's the stupidest idea I ever had?" he asked. Stein stared back at him, not sure if it was a rhetorical question. "Come on. What's the stupidest idea I ever had?" he repeated.

"Honestly, buddy, I've known you for a long time. You've had a few, but I haven't been keeping track of all of them."

Bruce shook his head. "You know. You just don't know you know. It was the really stupid one. The stupidest of them all."

Stein took a deep breath. "Bruce, I want you to listen to me very carefully. *Fuck. You. You. Fucking. Drunken. Sphinx. Motherfucker.*"

Bruce snorted. "Why don't we go outside the ship?"

Stein just stared at him, shaking her head softly. Then something clicked. "Oh, lord," she said, remembering. "That was a stupid idea." She turned to stare out the window again.

"What are you guys talking about?" Griese asked.

Stein looked at Bruce. "Do you want to explain?" she asked. Bruce burped and waved his hand, offering her the floor. "Okay," she said, collecting her thoughts. "Bruce's idea is beyond stupid. It is the most powerfully insane thing that has ever been thought. The air curdles when it is spoken."

"Get on with it," Bruce said. He burped again.

"Fine." She took a deep breath. "It involves going out the bow airlock, circumnavigating the outer hull of the ship, and re-entering the airlock in the aft."

Griese nodded. "And what's wrong with that?"

"*Everything is wrong with that.* One, I've seen some spacesuits up there, but there's no chance there will be any extra vehicular equipment. The naval guys kept all that stuff in the aft. So, we can get outside, but we can't do anything out there except float around and die."

"Stupider," Bruce said. "Go stupider."

Stein elbowed him. "Bruce is of course referring to the second draft of his idea. Which involved clinging to the outer surface of the ship like monkeys, and climbing around to the other side. I think he was originally suggesting using climbing gear, but he may now just be considering holding on really tight." She studied Griese's face, looking for some sign that he concurred with how stupid the plan was. "I told you it was stupid."

"Yeah, it is!" Bruce yelled triumphantly.

Griese licked his lips. "Why won't it work?"

Stein stared at him. "Because the ship is spinning. It would be the equivalent of climbing hand over hand for three kilometers. The deadliest set of monkey bars ever conceived. One slip, and you fall away." With her fingers, she walked across the back of her hand, then pantomimed her fingers flying off into space.

Griese nodded, digesting that. "It sounds doable."

"It's not." She stood up, turned to face them, grew infuriated by their eager expressions, and turned away. "I think we can come up with something better than amusing methods of committing suicide." She turned around again and glared at Bruce.

"Well, while you're doing that, I'm going to go find some climbing equipment," Bruce said, standing up. He listed to the right again. Stein still wasn't sure whether he was feigning soberness or drunkenness. "Climbing equipment for one. Or two...?"

"Two," Griese said standing up, tucking the small can up on one hip like a ball. He patted the big man on the shoulder. They shook hands.

Stein stared back and forth between the two men, incredulous. "You guys are insane. I absolutely forbid you from doing this."

Griese tilted his neck to look at her. He adjusted his grip on the small can, looked down at it, ran his fingers along the seam of the cap. "You're not allowed to tell me what I can't do." Stein's face fell. He walked away.

"And you," Bruce said, pointing his finger somewhere to the left of her. He frowned, then adjusted his aim, eventually aligning his finger more or less with her chest. He finished his thought, "You are not my real mom. I don't have to listen to you." He left in the opposite direction, kicking over a pile of empty bottles as he left.

"Dammit, guys," she said after they had left. She slumped back down on to the bench and turned to the window. For a while, she just sat there, trying to find where the sun had gone. Her terminal could probably figure it out, assuming it was still in their field of vision. But to the naked eye, it was gone.

She would let them sober up a bit first and come to their senses. That was the smart play. But Griese was already sober, wasn't he? And as for Bruce's senses...even sober he would still think this was a good idea. Spotting one of Bruce's empty bottles, she kicked it, watching it sail across the lounge and bounce into the window. If the pair of them did actually go, there was no doubt in her mind that she would go along with them. Not after what happened to Ellen. They were all she had now, no more splitting up.

But she didn't have to be happy about it.

"Man, I don't want to die in space." She looked back out the window. "Fuck you, space."

Sergei took a few playful bounces down the hall, still amused by the joys of low-gravity movement, even after a couple days on duty in it. He stopped, turned around, and bounced back. In the hall ahead of him, blue light flickered over the walls. He stopped just short of the hatch the blue light was emitting from, held his hand up to shield his face, and bounced past the hatch. He wouldn't make that mistake again.

Since the whole mess began, this was far and away the most relaxing chore Sergei had been assigned. Low-gravity babysitting. Even better, it meant he wouldn't have to help with the cleanup on street level. After de-pressurizing the ship, the Othersiders had left a real mess behind, many of the Othersiders part of the mess themselves. Thankfully, Sergei had seen just scraps of that, really only whatever the feeds thought fit to air. Not that he was supposed to be reading the feeds, but this was a seriously easy task he had, and the first assignment in weeks that gave him time to kill.

The buzzing sound from the hatch faded out, and he turned to see the blue flickering had also stopped. He waited a few seconds, having nearly rushed back into the path of the torch once already. A couple of long bounds and he reached the hatch, a massive, ugly thing normally con-cealed behind the soft plastic panels which lined the walls. Cautiously, he peered into the cavity beyond the hatch. The two naval techs, clambering over the massive mechanical whatever. They seemed pleased with them-selves; one of them gave Sergei a thumbs-up.

After examining their work, the pair of techs casually leapt off of the mechanism to the floor of the cavity. One of them picked up the massive cutting tool and moved to the edge of the hatch. Sergei stood back as they climbed out, not offering to help; he had tried once, but they wouldn't let him anywhere near their fancy tool. It was apparently pretty valuable. "And growing increasingly rare," one of the techs had said, whatever that meant.

He had at least managed to convince them he should know where they were going next, and once they were all outside the cavity, led them down the halls to their next destination, doing his best to act the escort and not the mascot.

It was still a bit of a mystery to Sergei what exactly they were doing. The techs wouldn't tell him and had in fact gotten kind of weird about it when he had asked. It seemed pretty clear to him that they were repairing some sort of damage caused by Othersider saboteurs, so he couldn't imagine why they were being so secretive. But navy guys were famously weird, and he didn't want to do anything to offend, lest he lose his new, bouncy gig.

Stein stroked one of the nearly-ripe fruits hanging off Mr. Beefy, hefting its weight in her palm. The little meat plant had being doing well lately; he was almost ready to be harvested. She wondered if she would be around to do that and whether she should drop him off on a neighbor's doorstep just in case.

Her terminal beeped, and she looked down, expecting to see another horrible climbing pun from Bruce. She had told the two of them that if they were going to insist on being so crazy, she would be forced to at least try and keep them out of trouble. They had protested, but not seriously, and agreed to meet in the upper-decks of the bow that night.

She sighed when she read the *From:* line; a message from Bruce would have been preferable to this.

Hope you're still okay. I didn't see you pass through here in all that mess, so I guess you probably are. Here's the stuff I found in regards to that matter. I tried not to read too much. It's your business, not mine.—Berg.

She'd forgotten about Dr. Berg and his trek through the shadier bits of her DNA. Attached to the message was a single file, a large archive. She opened it, revealing a bunch of documents represented with unfamiliar icons. After a moment, she realized they indicated the files were damaged and that she was looking at the best interpolation of what they might be. They must have gotten banged up a bit on their long journey—she had never even thought to be careful handling her own DNA. She crossed the room to her couch, sat down, and began to read the first file, helpfully labeled Readme.

Hello.

Sorry for troubling you like this. If everything's gone according to plan, you're reading this after seeing the words DATA GENE glow in your eyes. I hope that's not too troublesome. If I set it up right, it should only bother you when you look directly at a light tower. And it was the only way to point you in the right direction, to find this file you're reading.

I'm afraid I had little choice. This was the only place I could hide this message where I knew someone would read it. I'm being hunted down because of this information and can carry it alone no longer. It pertains to a grave threat to the Argos. See the attached files.

I pray you do something more useful with it than I have.

Dr. Harold Stein, October 28th, 52 A.L.

A sharp intake of breath. She had heard that name before, owed her own name to him. But she had never thought twice about the man, and now that she was forced to, decided that she didn't like him very much. Planting junk in people's cells like some kind of asshole. An incompetent asshole too—he wrote his damned sign upside down, cut half of it off, and got the trigger wrong. "Thanks, Grandpa," she muttered.

She stared at the list of files, almost tempted to toss the rest of them away, sick to death of ship-threatening conspiracies, only hours away from probable death thanks to one. But it was too tempting. However annoyed she was with her figurative father, she was holding a message buried in her own DNA. *How do you not read that?*

The next file was a note from a young naval officer called Kevin Delise, apparently written to a reporter. He explained that he had knowledge of a plot to split the ship in two. "Well, golly," Stein said, rolling her eyes. She was mildly intrigued to see that the plan was far older than Helot, but everything mentioned in the note was all old news to her.

Kevin had also attached evidence to prove what was happening. Most of the evidence was a mass of information on navigational calculations, stellar drift, all of it impenetrably dense to her. But the logs and transcripts were more accessible, detailing conversations the captain and his senior officers had when discussing various operational issues. The section on their fuel problems also caught her eye. One log contained a discussion about how the matter/antimatter reaction wasn't as efficient as they had first anticipated—some problem with the containment. This was potentially an enormous problem, as there was no way for them to generate more antimatter on board the ship. They had needed to run the M/AM mixture 2.3% rich to ensure complete reaction of the antimatter, leaving big wafts of un-reacted matter blowing out the exhaust. This caused their supply of deuterium to be used up faster than anticipated, forcing them to start mixing it with 'powdered amorphous carbon.' It took her a few seconds before she realized that meant chunks of the actual ship.

Which sure made it sound like the ship had the fuel problems that Kinsella had described. And a few pages later, she found confirmation in a transcript of a conversation between the ship's senior officers. Huge chunks of the dialog was missing, but one of the surviving sections jumped out at her.

———

Medical Officer Kinison: "...doesn't have to be us that decides?"

Captain Higgins: "Right. If we go with a Modified-B, we just set it up so that the captain at the time has the ability to make the call. He can evaluate the situation better than we can now."

Security Chief Hatchens: "And the fuel?"

Medical Officer Kinison: "It'd be the same deal! We don't have to decide. Just kick the can down the road. If they need to tell people about the fuel, let them."

Captain Higgins: "Okay. But these calculations have been public for a long time. Burn rates, the delta-v budget, all of it. We've

got to start quietly reeling that in off the network. If we need 1.38 million tons of AM to stop this bastard, that's a number only the captain can know about."

Security Chief Hatchens: "I've already got someone working on that problem."

———

But you didn't think to look in my fucking DNA, did you?

Stein sighed and scratched her head. She was intrigued and at the same time annoyed with herself for being intrigued. She didn't have time for this. Another beep from the terminal saved her from considering it further.

Wait till you see what I've rigged up. It will give you an incredible climax. I am being totally serious here. I have already made a huge mess of my pants. —Bruce

Fucking Bruce. *And fucking Bruce's plan.* She suddenly went rigid, thinking about what they were going to do.

"Come on, Laura," she said. "Positive thinking." She entered her bedroom, stripped out of her street clothes, and put on her spare orange jumpsuit. It was early yet to head to the bow, but she was done hanging around. Back in the living room, she picked up Mr. Beefy, took a step towards the door, then stopped. Setting him down on a neighbor's porch was just as likely to result in him getting caught up with the local morons in a rousing game of *Kick The Plant.* "I'd never let that happen to you, Mr. Beefy," she cooed. She turned and set him back down on his shelf. "You sit tight. I'll be back."

Stein looked down, the headlamp on her e-suit playing across the craggy features of the outer hull of the ship as it curved away beneath her. A long way down. Or a long way left. Bearings were a little hard to come by up here. She was looking towards her feet, that much was certain, and reason enough to call it down.

Below—or to the left of her—the outer surface of the ship's bow stretched away out of sight. She was standing on the edge of an airlock mounted just below the axis of the ship's rotation and not feeling good about it. Along with the weakened gravity, there was a more alien feeling dancing around her inner ear. The ship now had a distinct yawing motion, caused by the sudden explosion of air from the aft, and was now slowly flipping around front to back. The normal rolling rotation of the ship wasn't affected by this, so the pseudo-gravitational effects weren't readily apparent to those on the first four decks. But near the ship's axis, it was causing a very noticeable tilt of gravity away from the vertical.

Beside her, Bruce stood in his enviro-suit, decked out identically to her, each with a small arsenal of weapons strapped to their bodies. Three piton guns, all fastened to a harness securely strapped around their suits. In the back of the room, Griese finished tightening his straps, identically equipped as the other two, with the minor addition of a small can strapped to his leg with some tool webbing.

The three of them had spent the last hour familiarizing themselves with how the piton guns worked, swinging around in the floatarium. The only preparation they would get before attempting the most ridiculous stunt in the ship's history. "Feels like there should be cameras here to record this," Bruce said via the commlink wired into his suit.

"I think that'd defeat the purpose of this, Bruce," Stein observed.

"Amusing suicide?"

"No, not the primary purpose. Our tertiary purpose: shooting Helot in the face," Griese said, his voice growing more cheerful with every minute. "Well, no time like the present." After attaching himself to a tether secured inside the airlock, he jumped out into the void and swung around to Stein's left, following the ship's rotation.

"That was the dumbest thing I've ever seen," Stein said, eyes wide. "*Fuck*." She took a deep breath and followed him.

Vertigo. The stars pitched and wheeled around her, as she fell into the bottomless expanse of space. A yank on her harness and she spun around, facing the bulk of the ship, moving rapidly beneath her feet. She impacted the side of the ship, bracing the fall only partially with one hand and foot. "Oof."

Beside her, Griese had landed on his feet and already fired one of his piton guns into the rock face. He gave it a sharp tug. Stein clumsily clambered around into the same position, then grabbed a hold of one of the piton guns tethered to her waist. According to Bruce, these pitons could hold "some amount of weight" in standard gravity. At no point did they intend to rely solely on that needlessly broad claim, which is why they each had two other identical piton guns. By using them in concert, they planned to have multiple pitons secure in the side of the ship at all times.

Beside her, Bruce thumped into place, landing gracefully on his feet. She glared at him, annoyed at his unlikely agility. "Tell me you've done this before?" she asked.

"Come on. It's not too hard," he said. She could practically hear him grinning through the commlink. She raised her gun and fired its piton into the rock at his feet, watching it bury itself. She gave it a sharp tug. It seemed to hold, and with a glance at the controls, she saw it flash green. She did the same with the second gun, then sat back, taking a deep breath.

She looked around. Bruce had already disconnected from the airlock tether, and had started descending. Griese was himself already several meters away, dangling beneath her.

"Hey, wait up, guys," she said to herself, not triggering the e-suit's communications. After another deep breath, she disconnected herself from the tether. She fell down, tumbling backwards, onto her ass, then her side. Her legs swung around until they pointed down. The pitons held tight.

"Careful," Griese said. She looked down to watch him, her headlamp casting long shadows of him down the length of the ship. He had all three pitons in place now. He shifted down, putting all his weight on his pair of lower pitons, slackening the uppermost, then detaching it.

Stein grimaced and climbed back on to her feet. Best not to put these suits under too much abuse, she decided, looking at the rock, glad it wasn't as jagged as they had worried. She pointed the third piton gun at the rock face, and fired it. Then, moving between the three guns, she allowed all three cables to unwind. She swung downwards in a semi-controlled fashion.

The first few transitions were slow, with much double and triple-checking of the pitons before proceeding. But within a few minutes, she had gotten the hang of it and was soon making fairly rapid progress. The bow of the ship curved substantially, so within a few minutes of their descent, they had to begin firing their climbing guns upwards at the wall rather than straight ahead. There had been no way to practice this inside, the ship's interior lacking massively tall, curving walls. Bruce claimed that he had heard of someone doing this on a habitat orbiting Earth, small comfort, when he announced that he couldn't remember whether the fellow had survived the experience or not.

Passing the observation lounge was a little tricky, involving a gap to clear the window larger than they had been working with. But it was otherwise uneventful, and incredibly, unwitnessed. "I can't believe no one's here to see this!" Bruce said. Stein watched as he aimed a kick at the observation lounge window, only just missing.

The transition from descent to horizontal travel was gradual, due to the ship's rounded cigar shape. But about a half hour after they started, Stein decided that they were definitely traveling in an entirely horizontal direction. From the perspective of an outside observer, they would look like three lumps, swinging around in an orbit of the ship, balls twirling on a string. Crazy balls, the outside observer would probably think, balls with little instinct for self-preservation. From their perspective, it was only marginally less crazy and now resembled little more than a three kilometer-long exercise in vine swinging, like something a monkey would do if he was trying to prove something. If the pitons weren't secured directly to their harnesses, this would be completely impossible, their arms would have given out meters from the door. With the harnesses, it was merely improbable.

The process they established beforehand worked well. From a point hanging from two pitons, they would fire the third piton upwards and forwards, securing it into the hull. They would then adjust the lengths of all three guns, until they had swung forward and their weight was held entirely by the forward two pitons. From this point, they could release the rearmost piton and start the process again. This upside down caterpillar movement would ensure that they would always be supported by at least two pitons at any time and would hopefully minimize any swinging back and forth.

An hour into their journey, Stein marveled at how astoundingly smooth things were proceeding. By that point, they had managed to get their transition time down to about twenty seconds per step. Stein ran some calculations in her head. At the rate they were going, the whole three kilometers would take about six hours—a figure that sounded reassuringly achievable. Their biggest risk seemed to be a slip in concentration. The piton release buttons had warnings and fail-safes, but she knew it would still be possible to screw that up if they weren't paying close attention.

They took breaks every twenty minutes or so, hanging, letting their arms rest. Although the harness held her entire weight, Stein found it exhausting work, requiring her to hold her arms over her head for extended periods.

"Try shooting from the hip," Bruce suggested. "It looks way cooler."

She ignored him, spinning around a bit to look at Griese, who had been lagging behind. "How you doing, Griese?" she called out.

"Not bad, all things considered," Griese replied. Stein could hear him breathing harder than normal.

"This isn't nearly as stupid as I'd hoped," Bruce said.

"I think you're selling yourself short, buddy," Stein said. "This is cretinous." She looked past Griese. "How far do you think we've come?"

"Maybe a third of the way?" Griese suggested. "Ship looks a lot bigger from out here."

"Well, hang in there," Bruce said.

Stein laughed. "Ass."

It was Stein who had the first mishap. As she was reeling in her foremost piton, it slipped out of the ship's hull, taking a chunk of rock with it. "Oh, balls," she called out, a lump forming in her throat. Her other two pitons held tight, and she swung backwards, arms and legs flailing.

Griese, who was in front of her at the time, turned to watch. "What happened?"

"Piton slipped. Scared the fuck out of me."

Stein waited for the swinging to die down. She reeled in her misfired piton gun, and fired again, aiming at a different part of the ship's hull. The piton smacked into the rock and held.

After a short, unscheduled break for Stein to "change her pants" as Bruce put it, they continued on their way. They traveled a bit slower from that point, everyone a little more wary with each step. The section of the hull they were passing through seemed to be less stable, and slips of that nature began happening more and more frequently.

They were about two-thirds of the way through the trip when Griese fell. They had changed tactics and were now traveling one in front of the other, swinging in each other's footsteps, minimizing their exposure to any unstable rock. Stein was behind Griese at the time and saw the whole thing happen.

After releasing his rear piton, Griese swung forward too quickly, having not adjusted his other pitons to split the load evenly, putting almost all his weight on to his frontmost anchor. The rock gave way, and he fell hard on his sole remaining piton. Stein's heart caught in her throat as she watched him bounce once, hang motionless for a second, then fall away, the jolt having loosened the piton from the ship's hull.

"Ohhhhh, crap!" Griese screamed out over the commlink. "Crap, crap, crap, crap, crap! Fuuuuuuuuuuuck!" Stein watched in horror as he fell, curving to the left rapidly out of her view.

"Griese!" Stein called out, but her cry was drowned out by Griese's continuing wave of exclamations.

"Fuck, fuck, fuck, fuck, fuck, fuck, fuck, fuck, fuck, fuck..."

"What happened?" Bruce asked. In the front of the group, he twisted around to get a better look.

"Griese fell," Stein replied, raising her voice to be heard over the stream of cusses.

"Oh, no..."

"...fuck, fuck, fuck, fuck, fuck, fuck, fuck." The sounds grew fainter and fainter.

"Griese?" Stein called out nervously after a few seconds. Nothing. "Griese?" she tried again.

"Is he out of range?" Bruce asked.

"I don't think so," Stein said. "Maybe he's behind the bulk of the ship." She waited, calling his name every few seconds, hearing the panic in her voice.

"Fuck, fuck, fuck, fuck, fuck. Fuck." Griese's voice poured through the commlink again a minute later. She looked around frantically, trying to pick him out, not knowing how far he had traveled. He stopped swearing. "Ahhhhh, crap."

Despite having some time to think about it, Stein realized she didn't have anything to say. "I'm so sorry, man. I'm so, so sorry."

"It's not your fault." A pause. "It's not your fault, is it?"

"Uhhh. I don't think so."

"Okay, then."

"Dammit, Griese," Bruce said. "I'm sorry, too." Silence. "Griese?" More silence, Griese having swung over the horizon again. Stein hung from the bottom of the ship, her eyes closed, listening to Bruce call out their friend's name.

"Ship doesn't look so big from here," Griese said his next time around. Some more soggy apologies from Stein and Bruce, which he cut through simply, saying, "Shut up, guys. Just go on. There's nothing you can do. Don't worry about me. I'll keep myself busy."

"Griese..." Stein said, the word coming out more as a moan.

"How will you keep yourself busy?" Bruce asked, a banterer to the bitter end.

"You'll see."

Stein watched Bruce hanging in front of her. He seemed to shake his head. Just as she was about to say something, the sound of Griese's voice jumped into her ears: "Fuck, fuck, fuck, fuck, fuck, fuck, fuck, fuck, fuck..."

Stein choked. Tears welled into her eyes, at least some of them from laughter.

"What if we made it to the aft and got one of the landing crafts?" Bruce asked.

"Yeah. We could try." Stein had already considered it and found too many problems with the plan to count. Didn't know how to fly a landing craft. Didn't know if they actually worked. Didn't know where Griese was. Didn't know where he was heading. He could survive out there for another few hours in the suit, but at the speed he was traveling, she didn't know how they would ever find him. But she didn't want to shoot the idea down. "Yeah, could work," she said.

"Don't waste your time," Griese said, evidently having heard Bruce's suggestion. "Just," he said, then stopped, making a choking sound. "Just don't. I'm gonna turn this thing off in a second. That will be it."

"Griese!" Stein shouted.

"What?" he shouted back. "You'd do the fucking same," he said. "Dammit. You'd do the same. I'm sorry, guys. Goodbye, Laura. Goodbye, Bruce."

"Griese," she began, not knowing what else to say.

"Goddammit," Bruce said. They hung together in silence, watching the universe pass beneath their feet.

"I just realized something," Stein said. They had reached the aft edge of the ship and were resting there before the climb back up.

"What's that?" Bruce replied. He was using his best feigning interest voice.

"That big bright star there..."

"Which one?"

"The bright one. By your feet." Stein waved her hand in the general direction she was looking at.

"What about it?"

"That must be Tau Prius."

"It's so small! How were we ever going to all fit on that?"

"I think it gets bigger as you get closer."

"Oh," he said. "Like everything."

"Yes, Bruce. Like everything." There was a grim deliberateness to their banter now, but by some unspoken agreement, they kept at it.

Their plan for turning the corner of the ship was a little fussy. The aft surface curved up rapidly from the plane they had been traveling on, quickly receding out of sight, preventing them from getting a good angle to shoot a piton into it. Eventually, Bruce came up with a plan, where by manipulating the length of his two anchored pitons, he would swing out past the rear plane of the ship, from where he could plant a piton into its flank. Stein watched, feeling a mixture of awe and annoyance as the big doofus got it on his first try. It took her three increasingly desperate attempts before she was able to duplicate the feat, but she eventually managed to get a hold in the rear surface of the ship, and slowly reeled herself up. For the first time in hours, her legs were in contact with the wall. Astoundingly, they felt tired. "Stupid lazy legs," she said, reaching down and thumping them with her fist, trying to get the blood flowing.

Secure in her new climbing position, Stein looked up. The massive cylinder of the engine exhaust protruded from the ship's core, almost a hundred meters above her head. Essentially an inverted tumbler glass, extending almost fifty meters from the rear surface. Playing her headlamp across the surface of it, she could just make out some white lettering emblazoned on the side, upside down.

"We're on the wrong side," Bruce said.

"Yeah." There were two airlocks on the aft surface of the ship, one of them a massive hangar bay from which the ship's mothballed landing craft would one day dispatch from. The other airlock was beside that, human-sized, a twin of the one they had departed from. But both of those were on the opposite side of the engine from where they were.

"Go over it?" Bruce asked eagerly.

"I think around," Stein said. "Looks much, much easier."

"You just don't want to crawl on the ship's anus."

"Wow. I hadn't considered that, but yeah, I really don't want to now."

They began their ascent. Within a few meters, they had run out of rock and were now firing the pitons into the metal structure of the ship itself. The pitons could grab the metallic surface easily enough, but Stein wondered what kind of noise it was making on the inside. *CLANG, CLANG, CLANG,* she presumed, like a pair of attacking gong-pirates.

The climb got easier as they rose, although their curving route around the engine core and the ship's yawing motion complicated their wayfinding. No longer a simple vertical ascent, it slowly transitioned to a horizontal traverse and then a short descent as they rounded the corner of the engine exhaust.

They had checked beforehand that the airlocks could be cycled from the outside—"That would be hilarious," Bruce had observed when Stein brought the issue up. Opening an airlock from the outside would probably be detectable in the ship's control center, but they were hopeful that no one inside was monitoring that particular blinking light. Given the amount of abuse the ship had taken recently, there were probably a lot of flashing warning lights right now. Stein maneuvered her way to the entrance of the airlock and found the cavity that contained the control panel. Reaching inside, she smacked the only control there, a big, red button. Despite probably not having been used in a couple hundred years, after a few seconds the outer doors slowly slid out of the way, revealing the brightest room Stein had ever seen. After a few seconds of blinking, she realized it was probably very dimly lit, and it was just her brain dazzled by the sight of any lit, confined space. She grabbed the handle on the perimeter of the door and swung herself inside, Bruce doing the same on the other side. The pair disconnected their pitons and reeled the cables inside the airlock. Finally, Stein smacked the big red button on the inside and watched the doors slide shut.

Stein propelled herself across the airlock and hit another big red button, this one labeled with a pictogram that was apparently supposed to mean 'Air.' A faint hissing sound as atmosphere was slowly readmitted to the room. The treated air heated the room noticeably, as well, Stein feeling uncomfortably warm for a moment before her suit could compensate. A few seconds later, the inner door slid open. Bruce lunged through into the airlock control room, Stein floating behind him a little more languidly. She closed the airlock door and watched it seal before taking her helmet off.

A huge deep, gasping, beautiful breath. "Oh, wow." Bruce had already removed his helmet and was moving around the room, kissing the floor and every other surface he could see. She allowed herself to come to rest on the floor, the odd gravity slowly dragging her into a corner of the room.

"I can't believe that worked," Bruce said, sitting down beside her.

"Only two-thirds worked."

"Oh," Bruce said. "Yeah." She rested her head on his shoulder. They sat in the corner of the room for quite some time.

Eventually, Stein got up and examined their surroundings. A big bay window dominated one wall of the room, displaying the cavernous vehicle airlock below. A dozen oddly shaped objects were visible on the floor of the airlock covered in plastic sheeting, the landing craft presumably. Beside her, Bruce stood up and stripped his enviro-suit off, revealing a matted and sticky-looking maintenance jumpsuit underneath, along with some webbing that contained a variety of hand tools, firearms, and explosives. Stein did the same, finding her jumpsuit and equipment in a similar state, albeit a bit less smelly.

"What do you think Griese would do if he were here now?" Bruce asked.

"Go kill a dude?"

"Yeah," Bruce agreed. He made a show of looking around. "He doesn't seem to be here, though. Wanna do it for him?"

Stein rubbed her tongue over the back of her teeth, thinking. "I didn't think we'd get this far, to be honest."

"Me neither."

Stein watched her discarded suit slide back into the corner of the room. "I'm not really feeling in the killing mood."

"Me neither," Bruce said. "So...back to Plan...A? I guess? Nuclear blackmail?"

Stein took a deep breath before nodding. "I guess so. Though I'm having a hard time remembering how we decided that putting bombs on an antimatter reactor was our *best* plan."

Bruce shrugged. "They're little bombs."

They bounced down the hall to the nearest elevator, finding the place deserted. All hands on deck, just not this one, apparently. Stein guessed most of the security and naval personnel were busy tidying up various messes downstairs.

They reached the elevator. Bruce leaned against a wall, looking very deliberately casual. Lips pursed, he blew and sputtered, flecks of spit flying down the hall.

"What was that?" she asked.

"Whistling."

"You don't know how to whistle?"

"It's harder in this gravity." He tried again, this time producing a wobbly sour note and a still not-inconsiderable measure of spit.

"You're actually making us look more suspicious, you know that, right?"

"Suspicious people don't whistle, Stein. Fact."

With a chime, the elevator arrived, the doors sliding open. Inside was an elderly naval engineer, one Stein recognized.

"You!" Max rasped.

"Hi, Max," Stein said.

"You!" Max said again, apparently struggling with the very idea of them.

"What are *we* doing here?" Bruce said, finishing his thought. Max's jaw flapped around uselessly, now at least two steps behind in the conversation. "You know this guy?" Bruce asked Stein, his pistol leveled at the elderly engineer.

"Yeah. He used to run the reactor in the bow."

"Uh-huh. And would you be upset if I shot him?"

"What?" Max shrieked.

"Oh," Stein said. "I guess not."

"What?" Max shrieked again, a little harder and a little shorter, his wailing cut short by a shot to the chest. He fell awkwardly to the floor.

Stein bent down to look at him. "Did you see the way he fell? I hope you didn't break his neck."

Bruce prodded the engineer's body with his foot. "He'll be fine."

"You can tell that with your foot, can you?"

They entered the elevator and took it up to the engineering level. There, they stepped outside, leaving Max on the floor of the car, and continued run-floating their way to the reactor. The halls were less deserted up here, their passage alarming a few naval officers despite Bruce's whistling. Stein had never felt more conspicuous; security would certainly be after them within minutes.

But they reached the reactor without any confrontations, ducking inside to find two naval engineers who had barely had a chance to protest before Bruce forcefully introduced himself. Making cowboy noises, Bruce proceeded to hogtie the pair with plastic straps before dragging them into the corner.

The room was laid out quite similarly to the bow's auxiliary reactor room, just on a larger scale. Long and narrow, with the much larger reactor partially buried in the floor in the center of the room. Another door on the far side of the room, across from where they entered, that led to the aft's life support section. Assuming their maps of the aft were accurate, that would be a dead-end with no other entrances or exits.

"So, what now?" Bruce asked.

Stein pointed at the floor panels where the fuel supply lines would be running, connecting the engines to the fuel pods. "Start there," she said, crossing the room to the reactor control desk. Now somewhat experienced at moving around the reactor's controls, she confirmed the location of the pressure regulators and the fuel lines, then found the lockouts that would isolate them. That was the only part of the plan that was the slightest bit sane, emptying the fuel lines before destroying them. While an explosion on an empty fuel line would be good fun, the same explosion on a line full of antimatter would be considerably less memorable for anyone nearby.

She crossed back across the room to watch the door as Bruce leapt down into the cavity to set the charges. "Are we the bad guys now, do you think?" Bruce asked.

"Depends on the perspective, probably. Do you feel bad?"

"A little," Bruce said, slapping a charge into place. "And I don't want to be a bad guy. I don't know if I've told you, but I have a very high opinion of myself."

"I think I heard someone saying that about you." Stein helped pry up another panel to make more room for him. "And I don't want to be a bad guy either, buddy."

"You're not that bad," Bruce said, shaking his head. They had uncovered the pressure regulator, which was, as Stein suspected, an exact twin of the one in the bow. "You're not planting the bombs. Hell, you haven't even shot anyone yet."

Stein's jaw dropped. "I must have." She frowned. "Haven't I? In the van I shot..."

"Nope."

"Well, I've shot...at people, certainly."

"You haven't shot anyone. Your hands are clean, ma'am. That's why you keep me around, I think. To keep a clear conscience."

"I'll shoot someone if I have to," she said. She pulled the pistol out of her webbing and pointed it at the wall, squinting down the barrel. "You just keep shooting them first! I think that's the real issue here. My badness is simply being overwhelmed by yours."

"Uh-huh." Bruce finished mining the pressure regulator and stood up. She turned to look at his work. It looked good. Or bad, she supposed.

Behind her, the sound of the door opening. Bruce's expression changed, hands fumbling for a pistol he had set down too far away. Stein turned, saw the gun and the security uniform behind it. She kept turning, rolling, falling to the ground, firing.

"Laura!" Sergei hissed, the shot thumping the air from his chest. His eyes went up as the rest of him went down, face first onto the floor. The door slid shut behind him.

"Ahahhahahahhahhahha!" Bruce laughed. He leapt out of the cavity. Three quick strides and he was over Sergei, quickly rolling him onto his back. "You got him. Ahhahahhahahhahhahaha."

"Fuck you, Bruce. I really liked him."

"Yeah? *I wonder how he feels about you!*" Bruce rolled Sergei onto his side and retrieved his binders, sliding them around his wrists. "Seriously though, this will make a funny story to tell your kids one day."

"Fuck you, Bruce." She covered her eyes with her hand.

Done restraining her now-probably-ex-lover, Bruce dragged him into the corner with the naval engineers, cackling the entire time. "Better move quick now," he said, returning to the floor cavity.

"Yeah." Stein returned to the reactor console, careful to keep her pistol handy again, lest she need to protect Bruce from any more lovers. Splitting her attention between the controls and the door, she maneuvered through the menus again until she found the controls for the fuel supply. "You ready yet?" she called over the reactor. "Come on, man."

"What are you gonna do? Shoot me?" Bruce yelled back. "'Cause you're so bad?" She whipped a shot into the ceiling above him. "Ahahahahhahhahha."

Frustrated, she turned back to the console, double-checking the steps she would have to take to isolate the fuel lines. Then something caught her eye. She blinked and double-checked the figure, not completely sure of what she was seeing. "Hey, Bruce, is 1.54 bigger than 1.38?"

"Depends on the font, I guess," Bruce called back over the reactor. "Why?"

On the edge of the console, the current status of each fuel pod in a neat column. All operational, all about half full. At the bottom, a summary. *1.54 MT Anti-Deuterium remaining.*

"What is it?" Bruce asked.

She grabbed her terminal, completely forgetting about the pistol or covering the door. She frantically tapped through to the files Dr. Berg had sent her, the data gene. Quickly, she zeroed in on the transcript she had read before, the two-hundred-year-old conversation between the captain and his officers. *"If we need 1.38 million tons of AM to stop this bastard, that's a number only the captain can know about."*

"Oh, shit," she said. "That fucker. Oh, shit. He's..."

"What?"

"He's a fucking monster."

"What are you talking about?" Bruce asked. He hopped out of the cavity and rounded the reactor to see what Stein was looking at.

"Why do we think Helot is splitting the ship in two?"

Bruce frowned. "You very recently were mocking me for speaking in riddles."

She rolled her eyes. "Because there's not enough fuel to stop the whole ship."

"Okay, sure."

"What if there is enough fuel?" She pointed at the reactor console, at the figure he couldn't possibly understand.

"How do you know?" he asked. "Are you sure?"

Even if she had the time, she would have been reluctant to tell the story. Thankfully, she didn't have the time. "I just know. And no, I'm not sure." She licked her lips. "But I think it's *really* possible. Like it's the kind of thing we should look into."

A moan from the corner as one of the naval engineers started to wake up. Bruce shot him in the neck and turned back to Stein. "Look into. What are you thinking?"

"Okay," she said, then stopped, her brain moving faster than her mouth. "Let's say there is enough fuel to stop the whole ship. No one dies, everyone goes to the planet. Like we've been taught our whole lives, happily ever after, like a fucking fairy tale. What if we could find a way to do that?"

"I love happy endings." He gave her an enormous wink, and then just in case that wasn't clear, made an obscene gesture. "So, how do we do that?"

"I don't know," Stein said, not lying. "I mean Helot's obviously cutting the ship in half for *some* reason."

"Maybe because he's a dick?" Bruce suggested.

"Maybe. I don't know. Regardless, he's not going to stop being a dick if we just ask."

"So, we do what we're doing anyways. We blow the fuel lines and get Kinsella to blackmail him into stopping the whole ship in exchange for the spare parts."

"I guess." She looked at the time on her terminal, trying to remember how long it would be until the mayor sent his near-suicide bombers into action. "But Kinsella's kind of a dick too, hey?"

"He has many dick-shaped qualities," Bruce allowed.

"Right. And he sure as fuck doesn't seem too interested in saving the whole ship, either. He wants to split it as much as Helot. Hell, probably more. And I'm not sure he'd change his mind if we told him we didn't have to."

Bruce nodded. "*Such a dick.*"

Stein began pacing back and forth. "We need to stop either of them from splitting the ship. We need to stop *anyone* from splitting it."

"You're thinking a lot of glue?"

She shook her head. "Too late for that. Too impermanent." She pounded the console in frustration.

Another moan from the corner as the other naval engineer came to. Bruce knocked him out again. "Okay," he said. "So, we don't stop them from separating. But can we make it so they don't want to separate?"

Stein's hands were shaking, sure she was close to the answer. "What, like make them feel guilty about killing fifty thousand people? Because no one but us seems to give a flying damn about that."

Bruce shook his head. "No, you don't get it. What does the aft of the ship *need?*" he asked. "This has to be a separate spaceship, right? So, what can't it live without? Like, can we eat all their food or something?"

"That's it!" Stein hissed. "Wait! No, it isn't! They have farms all over the fifth and six decks. No. *Craaaaap!*" She kicked the edge of the reactor, hard. "They've got plenty of food, and fuel, and air..." she trailed off.

Bruce turned around and looked at the door on the far side of the reactor room. "Oh, yeah. The scrubbers."

"The scrubbers!" Stein yelled. "They'll need those."

"They'll need *the fuck* out of those."

She laughed. If the core detached, it would need its own carbon dioxide scrubbers if it didn't want to suffocate everyone within a few hours. She nodded, working through the details. "If the core's attached to the rest of the ship, it doesn't need its own scrubbers; it can stay hooked into the main circ system for as long as it wants. One spaceship."

"Blow the scrubbers?" Bruce said.

"Yeah." She began pacing again, piecing together Plan B. "Fuck, demolish the entire room. Everything in there. Something that would take years to repair. Years they don't have."

"Gonna take a lot of boom." Bruce patted himself down for show. "Out of boom."

Stein pulled off her own webbing and the explosives it contained. "Take these. And take the ones you set here. All but one," she said, running around the reactor. She pointed at a single charge, on the pressure regulator.

"Why leave one?" Bruce asked, leaping into the cavity to remove the other charges.

She looked at the door. "Plan A. In case I'm wrong." She looked around the room again, sizing it up for a different purpose.

"How will you know you're right?"

Behind the reactor. She would have a lot of cover behind the reactor. She swallowed. "How do you feel about death threats?"

Bruce paused for a moment, thinking about that. He looked up at her. "Pro."

"Pro-death threat. Good to know." She looked from the reactor, to her unconscious boyfriend in the corner, to the door. "Well, while you're planting those charges, I'm going to be death-threatening."

Bruce pulled himself out of the cavity again, laden with explosive devices. He jerked his head at Sergei. "And it's just a coincidence that you're asking me to leave you alone with your special hug buddy over there?"

Stein sighed. "Probably not much chance of special hugs. I don't think he's pro-death threat at all."

Two ensigns exited the elevator just as Helot arrived, immediately springing out of his way, backs pressed against the wall. Helot entered the elevator and jabbed at the controls violently. *A bomb on an antimatter reactor.* Laura Stein, the dupe he had tried to pin the failed detachment on, had evidently taken his slander really, *really,* personally. Apparently, just to spite him, she had actually become a terrorist. Or were his powers of suggestion so great that claiming she was a terrorist actually made her one? As the elevator rode up to the engineering deck, he wondered if a public announcement declaring Ms. Stein was a perfectly sane pacifist would help.

The elevator stopped, and he lunged out, loping down the hall as fast as he could, taking only a few seconds to reach the hallway outside the main reactor. A squad of heavily armed security officers stretched out down the hall in front of him, bracketing the door on both sides. Their chatter stopped as Helot pulled to a halt in front of the officer in charge.

"She's inside," Lieutenant Jensson said. After Thorias' death, it had taken a bit of sorting out within the security corps to figure out who was in charge of what, a process which was immeasurably simplified when Helot had pointed at Jensson and told him he was in charge of talking to him. "There's at least one other with her, we think," Jensson continued. "They have three hostages, including a security officer. Only stun weapons we think, but, also, obviously a bomb on the reactor."

"Are we sure she has a bomb?" Helot asked.

"We didn't go in to find out. But in general, yeah, the Othersiders have explosives. So, we didn't want to take the chance. Don't know what it'd do to the reactor."

Helot stared at his new deputy, forcing a blank look on his face. "It would destroy a small part of the universe. A small, but to us, very important part." He looked at the door and licked his lips. "Okay. You have any plans how to get them out of there?"

"This is the only way in. We could try a stun grenade with an extremely short delay. But that's still pretty risky."

"Stupid risky," Helot agreed. "Any demands? Aside from me?"

Jensson shook his head. "She just wanted to talk to you. Didn't say why."

Helot could think of a few reasons. To beg for him not to split the ship. Or to beg for a ride on his part of the ship. Or either of those, with blackmailing swapped for begging. *Or maybe just to kill me.* "Okay," Helot said. "Everyone back up out of sight. When I open it, don't say anything or do anything. I'm going to see what she wants."

"She might just want to kill you."

Helot dug his fingers into his palms. "I had considered that, thanks." Good to look tough in front of the troops. But as he reached out to the door control panel, he knew it was less bravery and more resignation. He didn't have a choice.

And maybe it was about time he risked his own life for this scheme.

The door slid open. He stepped inside.

"Ms. Stein?" someone called out from the doorway. She had never met him but recognized the voice immediately.

Stein swallowed. *Here we go.* On the far side of the room, her back pressed to the bulk of the reactor, she turned, pistol pointed in the direction of the door. "Captain," she called out. "I've got a bomb."

"Okay." A pause. "Please don't blow it up." She heard an inaudible discussion on the other side of the door. "I'm unarmed."

She didn't think he was lying but saw no reason to trust him, either. "If you try anything..." she said, trailing off. "Boom." She looked over her shoulder to the corner of the room at Sergei, who was just starting to come to.

"Ms. Stein, just keep yourself together for one second, please. Okay?" Helot said. He was trying to sound annoyed, but there was a distinct tremble in his voice. It seemed she was believable as a lunatic. The sound of the door sliding shut. "I'm inside now," Helot said. "Alone."

Helot's hands appeared on the far side of the reactor, moving slowly, eventually revealed to be attached to his arms, which were in turn, as expected, attached to the rest of Helot. The captain stepped out from behind the reactor, moving across the room. He stopped and looked at the pile of bodies in the corner. "Are they hurt?"

"I'm...urk," Sergei said. He looked it.

Stein fired a shot into the floor in front of Sergei's feet. "Please just be quiet for a minute," she said. "Please?"

"What?" Sergei asked. He blinked several times, seeming to have a hard time focusing on Stein. "What the...urk...Laura?"

"Just be quiet, please." She smiled as warmly as the circumstances dictated.

"Ms. Stein, you need to calm down," Helot said, moving towards her. A shot at his feet stopped him in his tracks.

She waggled the gun at him. "I'm plenty calm. Now, sit down. Back to the wall."

Helot watched her carefully for a moment before backing up to the wall and lowering himself to the ground. "All right, Ms. Stein. Or do you prefer Laura?" Seeing her not immediately disagree, he continued by asking, "Do you really think you can blow up the ship?"

She fished her terminal out of a pocket and set it down in front of her, a big button marked *Boom* glowing on it. "There's a charge on the main antimatter fuel line. You tell me."

Helot's throat contracted. "That'd do it. Okay. Second question. Do you really *want* to blow up the ship?"

Her hand hovered over the terminal. She tried putting a cruel smile on but could only hold it for a couple seconds before it slipped. "No," she said, setting her hand down on the floor beside the trigger.

"Well, that's a relief." Helot turned his head, craning his neck a bit to look at the missing floor panels. "So, what exactly are you doing then?"

"Dunno." Her shoulders sagged. She worried for a moment that she was overplaying her role and looked down, not meeting Helot's gaze.

"Want to give up, then?" Helot asked.

"Sure."

A relieved sound from Sergei's direction. "Hey!" she shouted. "I'm serious, *pig*. Keep your mouth shut." It might have been less painful just to knock him out again. But she really needed him quiet for the next bit. She pleaded at him with her eyes.

The message didn't get through. Perhaps because he was stung by the pig comment, or possibly because his vision still hadn't cleared up, Sergei instead shouted, "Or what!?"

"Or I'll shoot you again," she said, shooting him again. Her shoulders sank. And that was probably that; the second shot would be *really* hard to explain. Her mouth felt dry.

After a moment, she looked up at Helot, at the relaxed expression he was trying and failing to shape his face into. He was terrified. *It was working.* "I'm not as crazy as I look," she said. "But maybe that's not saying much." She took a deep breath. "I don't want to blow up the ship. And I won't. If you answer some questions for me, first."

The captain swallowed, but slumped back against the wall, seeming to relax. "All right."

"First, I want to hear you say it. You're trying to split the ship in two."

Helot looked her in the eyes. He looked sad. Deeply, fundamentally, irreparably sad. "It's true," he said. "I'm trying to split the ship." She shivered, not having ever doubted it, but still a little frightened to hear him actually say it. "Do you want to come with us?" he asked. "We could make room for you."

Stein snorted. It was essentially the same deal as Kinsella's, though perhaps from a source more capable of delivering. She mentally weighed the offer and felt her resolve waver a moment when she realized *it weighed pretty good.* But she set it aside and took a deep breath. "Why are you doing it, Helot?"

Helot looked away, shaking his head. "Honestly? We don't have enough fuel to stop the whole ship. We messed up. Burned too much during course corrections, during the acceleration. We messed up," he repeated. He looked back at her and shrugged.

"That thing right there," Stein said, pointing over her shoulder to the reactor console, "says we have 1.54 million tons of antimatter. That's not enough?"

A tremor from Helot's hand. Was that a sign? Was he hiding something? *Or was he just shit-scared of the crazy bomb lady?* "No, it's not enough," he said.

"Because I have it on good authority we need only 1.38 million tons to stop this ship." She watched his eyes widen. "The whole ship." His throat contracted. *He is definitely hiding something.*

"Where did you hear that?"

She grinned. She had him. She fired a shot into the wall beside him. "I'm asking the questions here," she said, starting to enjoy her role. She wondered if this was how Bruce felt all the time. "And I'm right, aren't I?"

The shot seemed to startle him. He worked his jaw around, almost visibly assembling his next sentence piece by piece. "It's not that simple, Laura."

Another shot into the wall on the other side of him. "Make it simple for me."

Helot held his hands up defensively. "Okay! Okay. That figure is accurate. I don't know how you heard about it. You are a remarkably, infuriatingly resourceful young lady." He rubbed his hands against his pants leg. "Yes, on paper, we only need about 1.4 megatons of antimatter to stop. But it's not that simple; we have to account for all sorts of contingencies. Burn efficiency, equipment failure, that sort of thing. In simple terms, there is a *chance* we have enough fuel to stop the whole ship. But it's not a great chance."

Stein felt her pistol sag. "What kind of chance?"

Helot looked away from her. "Not a great one."

"What chance, Helot?" she shouted. Her gun snapped up to point directly at him. "What exact odds? You've calculated it out, I'm sure."

He rubbed his face. "About eighty-seven percent."

A strange mixture of emotions surged through Stein. She was right and felt suitably elated about that. *Who doesn't like being right?* She was also talking to a monster, which tempered her self-satisfaction somewhat. *"There's an eighty-fucking-seven percent chance you could save the whole ship?"* she hissed.

"It sounds bad when you...hiss it...like that," Helot said. "But there's a ninety-five percent chance if we just decelerate the core. And when you do the math, with the right weightings, that is the better choice."

The flux of emotions slowly settled into a steady state of deep, primal revulsion. For the first time, she saw the simple truth and beauty behind the idea of 'just killing a guy.' But a better plan was on its way. "You're an abomination," she said, both stalling for time and meaning it sincerely.

"Maybe," Helot agreed. "Although I accounted for that, as well. If you get the weightings right, even a monster can make the right decision."

"The weightings," Stein said, again nearly hissing. "You're murdering fifty thousand people. For what? To save a few hundred? Your chosen few hundred? I notice you've stacked the invitation list pretty heavily with your buddies. Can you trust a monster to pick who lives and dies?"

Helot looked away, obviously uncomfortable. "I guess not. But I did it. And compared to the hard decision that preceded it, that part was actually pretty easy." He looked at the stack of unconscious people in the corner. "If you can only take a few, then yeah, you'll take the competent people who can follow orders."

"And leave the rest of us ornery folk behind."

Helot chuckled. "Ornery is one thing. I could deal with that. But you people..." He paused, then shook his head. "Not you. You are actually different, aren't you?" He smiled. "I read your file. The mostly sane canned baby. You're okay, I think. Must have been something to do with the process." Another chuckle. "Because you're obviously not Sheeped."

"I'm not what?"

"Very long story. Not relevant here. My point was, most of the people on the ship are..." he said, trailing off. "Did you know there are people out there who go around peeing on things? Just for the hell of it? Because of the interesting smells? I wonder how useful they'll be on the ground. I wonder how long it will take for them to freeze to death. *I wonder if they'll make a fucking game out of it.*" He shook his head. "No, picking the guest list was the easiest part."

"And what gives you the right? You're not even elected, you fuck."

Helot tilted his head back, his mouth open, laughing silently. "Have you met our mayor? Would you want him to make this call?" Helot saw something on Stein's face that he took for a sign of agreement. "Exactly!" He sat back triumphantly for a few seconds before his eyes flicked down to her hand hovering over the terminal and its glowing bomb trigger. Remembering where he was, his voice softened. "Look," he said. "I understand why you're upset. No one should ever be given the right to make the decision I made. But someone gave it to me. And once I had that right, that responsibility, I couldn't pass it off."

"It should have gone to a vote. Or a lottery."

"I looked into that. There would have been a riot. A larger riot. Way more people dead that way."

"*You looked into it?* You wrote a little report on it, did you? Looked up democracy in the dictionary maybe? Decided it didn't fit here?"

"Listen, *you little shit,*" Helot said, a single finger thrust out at her. "I've been making this decision for the last twenty years. Looking at it from every angle. This is the best way." He looked her in the eye. "You'd have done the same, I bet."

"The hell I would."

"I felt the same way at first. You'll come around." Helot looked at his hands, turning them over in front of him. "Look, Laura. You don't fully understand what we're up against." His hands clenched up for a moment, balled into fists, before he allowed them to relax. "Do you know what happened a hundred and ninety years ago? Well, it probably happened a millennia or so before that, but it didn't really make a difference to us until we smacked into the light cone."

She couldn't think of what he was referring to. 190 years was right around when they'd discovered they were off course.

"The ship passed through a pulse of very high energy radiation. Our shielding wasn't entirely effective. A lot of people became sick. Really, awfully sick. Does that ring a bell?" He waited for some sign of agreement, which she didn't offer. But it did sound familiar. "It was, I'm told, worse than you've heard," he continued. "Cancer rates through the roof. Birth defects—really bad ones. We almost didn't make it." He swallowed. "But a few years passed, and the anti-cancer meds seemed to work, and the gene-tinkerers stopped the worst of the damage. On the surface, it looked like we'd gotten through it okay."

Stein stood up, no longer comfortable on her knees, taking the terminal with her. Gun still carefully leveled at Helot, she took a couple of steps back and leaned on the reactor control console. "On the surface?"

"There was a problem." Helot looked away. He seemed uncomfortable. "Did you know that within a generation, the average IQ on board the Argos probably dropped about 45 points?" Helot wrung his hands together. "We're the descendants of scientists and engineers, Laura. Some of the smartest people on Earth. Now, how many people out there," he waved his hand to the north, "do you think have shit their pants today?"

"What?"

"We got dumb," Helot summarized. "All of us, in differing degrees, some not as bad as others, got dumb. You can believe that, I'm sure." Years of handling public complaints gave her little cause to disagree. "We noticed it happening," he continued, "but couldn't figure out why. Too dumb, I guess. It wasn't until maybe twenty years ago that the navy docs finally pieced it together. It was the gene tinkering. There was a problem with the software. A concurrency issue they called it. Two programs interfering with each other."

"We've been made dumb?"

Helot nodded. "Accidentally, yes. It's so..." He chuckled. "*It's so stupid.*" He watched her carefully for a reaction which wasn't forthcoming. "We—my predecessors I mean—were just trying to make everyone docile. Sheeping they called it." He looked over at Sergei's slumped form. "So, that one was on us. But there was some even weirder stuff going on in those tinkerers, real mad-scientist shit that we're still trying to piece together. Whatever it was, we can see the impact it had when those two programs started interfering with each other: stupidity." He looked her in the eyes. "Do you get it now? Every person born in the past two hundred years has been put through those stupid tinkerers."

"That's the dumbest thing I've ever heard."

"Amen," Helot said. He leaned back against the wall and stretched his legs out. He looked like he was enjoying getting this off his chest. "Here's the thing, though. Although this specific problem was *insane*, and completely unexpected, the ship has long had contingency plans for something like this. That's the reason it even can split in two. Plan A was always to stop the whole ship with the whole population. But the ship's designers anticipated the possibility of the population decreasing, due to disease or famine or some other reason..."

"Space wasps?"

Helot looked at her blankly. "Sure. So, they made the ship capable of Plan B: the engine core could separate and arrive at Tau Prius as a smaller, more efficient ship." Helot patted the deck beneath him. "This ship."

Stein felt physically ill as she thought of a question and the probable answer at the same time. "In Plan B, the rest of the ship is left to drift away. Empty."

"That was the original intent, yes," Helot said, now avoiding eye contact.

"But that's not what you're doing."

Helot's face paled. "Not long after the cosmic bombardment, when the extent of the genetic damage became apparent, my predecessors began weighing their options. 'Modified Plan B' was what they came up with. A pretty antiseptic term for what they were proposing." Helot rubbed his pant leg again and licked his lips. "In this plan, we keep the ship's population relatively high. The genetic repair work continues, attempting to repair any damage caused by the external radiation. Then when we reached Tau Prius, if the symptoms had waned, we would stop the whole ship as normal."

Stein finished the story. "And if that didn't work, you would arrive, take the best and healthiest of the population with you, and discard the rest."

"Yeah." Helot blinked and poked at the corner of his eye again. "They left the decision to me. Imagine reading that memo your first day on the job."

Stein felt her face flush. "Don't you dare feel sorry for yourself."

Helot smiled sadly. "I don't. But honestly, what would you have done, Laura? Save the whole ship?"

"Obviously! They're healthy! You're throwing lives away because they're too stupid? Because they messed up your goddamned weightings?" she spat the last word out. "You decided that fifty thousand people were dumb enough to be shed off. To save fuel."

"Laura, please..." Helot began, almost whispering.

"No! You're murdering thousands of people. To save fucking fuel!"

"Laura!" Helot hissed. "Want to guess what my job is here? It's to start a colony on Tau Prius III. It's not to protect every person on this ship. It's to start that fucking colony. Out there are fifty thousand people who would be *useless* on the ground. Tau Prius III is a frozen shithole. Have you seen the brochures? Half these people would be dead within a year. I know it." He looked away, shaking his head. "You know it." He turned back to her and pounded the floor, ignoring Stein's hand as it wavered over the terminal. "Those people out there, they're not healthy. They're dumb as rocks. Really, it was no choice at all. The best chance of starting this colony is without the morons. I've run the calculations."

"You've run the calculations?" Stein's eyes widened. "You keep saying that. Holding your spreadsheet up like it's a security blanket. You think you can figure out whether or not to murder people because a computer told you?"

"You have no idea what you're talking about, Laura. I was groomed to make this decision. All modesty aside, there is *literally no one better suited to make this call.* So, when I say that I've run the calculations, that means something!" Helot's nostrils flared. "If you spent the last two decades in my shoes you'd do the same thing."

"Then maybe it's your shoes that are the problem," she spat. "*Asshole,*" she added, because that too needed to be said. "I've at least met the people you're talking about killing. When was the last time you left your little calculation-nest?"

Helot laughed. "Laura Stein, speaker for the people? Did you know I talked to Curts about you? I know who you are. You *fucking hate* the people."

Stein smiled through clenched teeth. "Yeah, I maybe do. But you don't even know them." Her terminal flickered. On the screen there were now two buttons, *Boom 1* and *Boom 2*. She frowned. The sound of a door opening, her heart skipping, hand fluttering over the terminal. She ducked down behind the reactor again. "Stay back!" she yelled. "I will blow the crap out of this fucking ship if you come in here!"

"Please don't," Bruce said. He rounded the reactor behind her and stopped, looking down on her. "We need that to live." He waved at Helot. "Hey, Captain. Nice work with all the treachery."

"Who the hell are you?" Helot asked, eyes wide.

Bruce walked over to Helot and extended his hand. "I'm Bruce. We haven't met yet, but I've been quietly foiling you for some time now." He waggled his hand in front of Helot's face. "Well, sometimes not that quietly."

Some moans from the corner of the room. The two naval technicians were awake again, and to judge by their somewhat alert expressions, may have been for some time. Sergei was coming around again, as well. *Time to get this show on the road.* "Bruce," Stein said, "I've got two buttons here, marked *Boom 1* and *Boom 2.*"

Bruce turned around to look at her. "Are you actually going to do it?"

She smiled. "Yeah. He said I was right."

"Well, okay then. Still, you've got some serious lady-balls, Stein."

"Thanks." She tilted her head in the direction of her terminal. "So?"

"Ahh, yeah." He looked to the other side of the room, his brow furrowed. "I would have made that *Boom 1,* I think," he said, pointing at the base of the reactor.

"Are you sure?"

He looked past the reactor, to the door to the life-support section. "I am totally sure. The others are definitely linked to *Boom 2.*"

"What others?" Helot asked. "Other whats?"

"Because if you're not sure," Stein said, "...and if this is our last conversation ever, I'm going to be very upset with you."

"This is a pretty bad last conversation ever," Bruce agreed. "Maybe some more puns?"

"Boom 2?" she asked again.

"It would *blow* if I was wrong, wouldn't it?"

"Fuck you."

"Helot, do you know how hot antimatter annihilation is?" Bruce asked, turning his head to the captain. "Because if it's going to get *balmy* in here, I'm going to take my shirt off first."

"I'm serious. Fuck you," Stein said. Her finger hovered over *Boom 2.*

"Laura! Urk. Don't!" Sergei urked.

"Relax, kid," Bruce said, stripping the upper half of his coveralls off. "She's not an *abomination*," he added, his mouth hanging open in delight.

"This has to stop," she said.

She pressed *Boom 2.*

Epilogue

The broken thermostat popped out with a simple twist. Stein tucked it in her webbing and popped the new one into place. She checked it was sending signals to the heating coil upstream, then slid the access panel back into place. "That should do it," she said, climbing down off the ladder.

The office manager offered a thin-lipped remark about how long it had taken, which Stein simply took as the 'thank you' it was probably meant to be. He did seem less put-out then he had been when she arrived, and she left the office with the slightly satisfied feeling of having fixed another problem.

She walked down the halls back to the maintenance office, carefully maneuvering her ladder through the afternoon crowds. Almost quitting time for her, well past quitting time for everyone else it seemed. Though it was a Friday, she supposed. She reached the maintenance office and stowed her ladder before stepping into the locker room to change, running into two of her team members finishing their shifts, as well. Tools stowed and pleasantries exchanged, she soon left the maintenance office, finding Bruce waiting for her outside. He wordlessly fell into step beside her as they rounded the corner and boarded the escalator up.

"Should have left early," he said behind her. "It's going to be busy."

She turned around to face him, one step higher, temporarily taller. "No one was stopping you, big guy," she replied. "Or did you need me to hold your hand?"

"Brave talk," Bruce said, shaking his head. "And you know how much I hate boasting."

Upstairs, they had to pick their way through a group of government workers enjoying a post-work game of freeze tag. "Morons," Bruce said, sidestepping a statue frozen in a vaguely obscene position.

Stein didn't say anything, only allowing herself a faint smile. She hadn't told Bruce that part of the story, for fear he might take it the wrong way. Not that she thought any less of him; he was still one of the smartest people she knew. But she didn't want to imagine what he would do if he was told he had a genetic predisposition to idiocy. A lot of moping around in a cap and gown, probably. Calculus-themed tattoos. Months of spite-fueled study and self-improvement. He would be happier not knowing.

They stopped outside her apartment, Bruce waiting while Stein checked Mr. Beefy quickly, before grabbing her umbrella from the hook beside the door. "I'll let you borrow it later if you ask nice," she said once back outside, ignoring his rolled eyes.

They continued down the street, passing crowded stalls of vendors hawking recreational beverages to the crowds, warming them up for the weekend. Before long, they were forced to slow, the crowd thickening as it pushed through the bottleneck formed by the bulkhead doors just ahead. She let Bruce move ahead of her, trailing behind in the lee of his shoulders as they approached the first set of doors. Brightness ahead as they approached the second set, passing through those to the outside.

The sky was very, very big. Too big, really. Regardless of the weather, umbrellas were always a popular accessory for people outside the colony. Stein opened hers now, pulling it low over her head so that she could only see the ground. Bruce made amused noises beside her, only his lower body visible as they walked the well-worn path to the Prairie. *Such a tough guy.* Although if she could see his head, she was sure she would see his eyes carefully focused on the ground in front of him.

Helot had almost been right. The contingencies had contingencied, leaving the Argos—all of it—just barely enough reaction mass to slide into orbit around Tau Prius III. A success, but not a complete one. There was essentially no fuel to transfer to the surface for the colonization efforts. The first year was marked by a few very necessary, very unironic bonfires; a few people had indeed frozen to death. Helot had been polite enough not to crow about this.

But only a few died. And when one of the landing crafts found a vein of uranium a few months later, and the ship's fabricators cobbled together an enrichment apparatus and simple nuclear reactor, things got a lot better. With a source of power, some of the fabrication equipment was moved to the surface, allowing construction of the colony to begin in earnest.

Not unexpectedly, the colony that developed ended up looking a lot like the Argos. Mostly underground, almost entirely enclosed. This wasn't just to protect against the cold, although it certainly did that. Argosians, it seemed, just liked being indoors.

Stein tripped over a rock, stumbling forward a few steps before catching herself. She still had to concentrate on picking up her feet with each step, especially on uneven ground, even after being down here longer than almost everyone. Of all the people who had wanted to—and a lot had—she had one of the most legitimate claims to stay on the Argos, in that she had something actually useful to do up there. But she hadn't hesitated when volunteers were sought out, and was on one of the first crafts down to the surface.

There were still a few thousand on the Argos. Naval personnel mainly, along with a sizable amount of the ship's security corps, who had felt more than a little unpopular after 'all that business,' as the incidents just prior to D-Day were now called. The full story never came out; few knew there was a story in the first place.

Perhaps unsurprisingly, Bruce had a knack for demolitions—nearly every component of the aft's life support was ruined. A partial evacuation of the core had actually been necessary; security, naval officers, and their families hustled back down to street level for their own safety. It hadn't taken long to explain to Helot what they had done and what it meant. He didn't put up much of an argument; Stein thought he seemed almost relieved that someone had forced his hand. One last bit of blackmail followed, when Stein explained that only she could stop Kinsella from unleashing his suicide bombers. It had barely counted as blackmail, really; all the fight had gone out of Helot by that point. Unlikely as it might have seemed at the start of the day, Stein and Bruce ended up walking out of the core under their own power.

A year later, the Argos finally arrived at its destination. Although still quite isolated, they were at least out of deep space and now moving at a much more sedate speed. In a small way, it felt like they had rejoined the rest of the universe.

How the rest of the universe felt about that was still unknown.

Stein flicked the edge of her umbrella up a bit, catching a glimpse of the summer sky and the metallic roofs of the Prairie just over the next rise. The New Prairie really, although no one called it that. One of the few outlying buildings in the colony, the proprietors had felt it thematically necessary to build the thing outdoors, however much it might hurt business.

Bruce tipped the edge of her umbrella up and looked down at her. "Wanna go see a play tonight?" he asked.

Stein's eyes widened. "Why? Am I in trouble?"

"You need to spend more time around people that aren't at work. Or in a bar."

"I like bar folk. I think you need to spend less time around people that aren't in a bar."

When her feet hit the tiled terrace of the bar, Stein folded her umbrella and ducked inside, away from the dreaded sky. She settled in to a table at the back, Bruce plopping down beside her. "Four beers, please," Bruce said when the waiter approached. They sat in silence for a while, looking at anything but each other, watching the bar get progressively noisier as the after work crowd streamed in. Stein could see the grassy area outside filling up with braver sorts, daredevils who could look at the sky without throwing up, along with a handful who just enjoyed recreational vomiting.

When the waiter returned with their drinks, Bruce seized one and drained half of it. Stein took a slightly more ladylike approach with hers. "So, what's up with this play?" she asked. "You hate that kind of thing."

Bruce evaded her look for a moment, then seemed to think better of it. Returning her gaze, he shrugged. "I do. Just heard a guy talking about it today. Thought you might like it. Thought you might like him." A long, loathing gaze from Stein. "Just trying to get you out there," he said defensively.

This had traditionally been Ellen's job, and Stein felt a momentary wave of sadness wash over her. "I'm out there," she finally said, speaking more into her beer than to her friend.

"Who was the last person you talked to outside of work?"

Stein spun the glass around in her hands, not looking up. "So, I'm out there at work. That's legitimate. I've got work friends is all."

Bruce snorted. "No, you don't. You're their boss, Stein. Don't try to be that friendly boss who's always up in everyone's business. People hate that. Imagine Kinsella hanging out with you all the time, just being friendly all over you," he said. "That's what you look like to work people."

Nominally, Kinsella was now Stein's direct boss, but he mostly left her alone. He was pretty busy now, governing the colony and being generally appalling. Of all the lessons to be learned during 'all that business,' the only one the mayor took away was the observation that no one seemed to mind or even notice that democracy had been suspended during Helot's coup. And when the colony had been established enough for people to stop dying, he had inserted himself into the position of Colony Administrator, a position with some curiously unspecific term limits. Admittedly, he wasn't doing that bad a job of it yet, aside from the half-dozen violent tantrums he threw each day.

"I'm sure he's not that bad. I bet he'd be a pretty cool friend," Stein said.

"Oh, sure. You and Kinsella just hanging out. Braiding each other's wigs. Bathing with each other."

"What do you think friends do, exactly?"

In a single motion, Bruce drained the rest of his beer, flagged the waiter, and ordered another one. Some more silence, Stein ignoring Bruce's gaze. "Look, I get it. You like being distant. And it totally works for you. You're kind of prickly up close."

"Thanks."

"Especially your mustache."

Sergei had stayed on the Argos, their post-face-shooting reunion being predictably awkward and relationship ending. He had missed the important parts of her conversation with Helot, the parts that exonerated her, at least to the elements of her crime that didn't involve shooting him in the face. Those elements had proven too big a hurdle to get over.

The waiter arrived with Bruce's second beer, which hadn't hit the table before half of it disappeared as well. "But," Bruce continued, slapping his palm on the table, "Jagged, spiky mustache or no, you can't keep this up forever." He swept his arm, gesturing outside the window. "Remember, we have to populate this planet."

"Oh gross, Bruce."

"Not 'we' as in 'you and I.' That would be gross. You're like a little brother to me. Besides, I've already got a very full waiting list."

"That's great," she said, rolling her eyes. She knew he was just trying to help. But being prickly and distant had worked out well for her so far in life. Gotten her to where she was. She had done fairly well for herself. Certainly not much to complain about.

On the other hand, you did shoot your last boyfriend in the face. Justifiable as that may have been, it is possible you might be able to dial the prickliness back a whisker.

"Maybe," she said.

Bruce raised an eyebrow. "Maybe what?"

"I am maybe agreeing with you." She stared him down. "I will maybe go to a play. *Maybe.*" She took another sip of her drink. "But can we not talk about it right now?"

"Okay, boss." Bruce finished his second drink with another healthy pull. Stein took her time with hers, nursing it while Bruce distracted himself leering at a young woman two tables over.

The bar was almost full now, and Stein could see more than a few people eyeballing the two extra chairs at their table. Stein drained her glass, setting it down firmly to attract Bruce's attention. She looked at the two remaining beers on the table, in front of the two empty chairs. "So."

"So," Bruce agreed.

"I guess, same time next year, then," she said. Bruce nodded. They stood up and walked out of the bar, leaving the table with the pair of untouched drinks behind.

Outside, she realized she had left the umbrella behind, hesitated, then decided she could fake toughness as well as Bruce. Bruce noticed but didn't offer any comment. Together, they walked back to the main compound, heads carefully bowed in terror.

"So, if you're now maybe cool with meeting people," Bruce said, breaking the silence as they crossed a low rise, the bulk of the colony suddenly visible ahead of them, "are you also maybe cool with helping me with something?"

"This sounds like it will be entirely legitimate." She had done little but work over the past year and been pretty happy about it. But she knew Bruce had started getting itchy.

"Most definitely not. You see, I was fixing this guy's heating coil today, and I saw that he had a really incredible hat, and now I want it."

"You could probably just have one made."

"That'd reduce its value. *Inflationary haberdashery.* Come on, Stein, you're not new at this." He leaned over and whispered, "I've already got a plan."

She sighed. "And if you need my help that means it involves going somewhere cramped and smelly."

Bruce laughed, a big, showy stage laugh. "The old team, together again!"

"I didn't say yes."

"Stein and Bruce! Crawling through sewers, kicking ass, and taking names!"

"I didn't say yes."

"Sometimes not even kicking the ass! *Sometimes just watching!*"

They continued back to the colony, Bruce laying out his plan as they went. Stein, as always, protested each step, each protest, as always, somehow binding her tighter to the scheme.

ABOUT THE AUTHOR

Chris Bucholz is a professional video game and humor writer. His weekly column at *Cracked.com* offers his readers a mix of historical curiosities, short fiction, and spectacularly bad advice. During the day he works as a writer for the video game developer *Stardock* on various game related projects, including the latest entries in the *Galactic Civilizations* and *Star Control* franchises. He lives in Vancouver, B.C. with his wife and son.

APEX PUBLICATIONS NEWSLETTER

Why sign up?

Newsletter-only promotions. Book release announcements. Event invitations. And much, much more!

Subscribe and receive a 15% discount code for your next order!

If you choose to sign up for the Apex Publications newsletter, we will send you an email confirmation to ensure that you in fact requested the newsletter and to avoid unwanted emails. Your email address is always kept confidential, and we will only use it to send you newsletters or special announcements. You may unsubscribe at any time, and details on how to unsubscribe are included in every newsletter email.

Visit

http://www.apexbookcompany.com/pages/newsletter

APEX MAGAZINE

ISSUE 63   AUGUST 2014

EDITED BY SIGRID ELLIS
COVER ART BY CYRIL ROLANDO

2014 HUGO AWARD-NOMINEE FOR BEST SEMIPROZINE!
APEX-MAGAZINE.COM

A MONTHLY EZINE OF SCIENCE FICTION, FANTASY, AND HORROR

Hugo Award nominee for Best Semiprozine

New issue released the first Tuesday of each month

Visit at http://www.apex-magazine.com

42378071R00202

Made in the USA
Lexington, KY
18 June 2015